W9-CFH-152

Storeys from the Old Hotel

Tor books by Gene Wolfe

Storeys from the Old Hotel

Gene Wolfe

A Tom Doherty Associates Book

New York

STOREYS FROM THE OLD HOTEL

Copyright © 1988 by Gene Wolfe

A Tor Book
Published by Tom Doherty Associates, Inc.
175 Fifth Avenue
New York, N.Y. 10010

Tor ® is a registered trademark of Tom Doherty Associates, Inc.

Library of Congress Cataloging-in-Publication Data

Wolfe, Gene.
    Storeys from the old hotel / Gene Wolfe.
        p.   cm.
        ISBN 0-312-85208-8
1. Fantastic fiction, American.   I. Title.
    PS3573.052S76   1992
813'.54—dc20   91-38908
                                                                          CIP

First U.S. edition: April 1992

Printed in the United States of America

0 9 8 7 6 5 4 3 2 1

Acknowledgments

"The Green Rabbit from S'Rian" copyright © 1985 by Gene Wolfe; first appeared in *Liavek*, edited by Will Shetterly and Emma Bull.

"Beech Hill" copyright © 1972 by Gene Wolfe; first appeared in *Infinity Three*, edited by Robert Hoskins.

"Sightings at Twin Mounds" copyright © 1988 by Gene Wolfe.

"Continuing Westward" copyright © 1973 by Gene Wolfe; first appeared in *Orbit 12*, edited by Damon Knight.

"Slaves of Silver" copyright © 1971 by Gene Wolfe; first appeared in *Galaxy*.

"The Rubber Bend" copyright © 1974 by Gene Wolfe; first appeared in *Universe 5*, edited by Terry Carr.

"Westwind" copyright © 1973 by Gene Wolfe; first appeared in *Worlds of IF*.

"Sonya, Crane Wessleman, and Kittee" copyright © 1970, 1978 by Gene Wolfe; first appeared in *Orbit 8*, edited by Damon Knight.

"The Packerhaus Method" copyright © 1970 by Gene Wolfe; first appeared in *Infinity One*, edited by Robert Hoskins.

"Straw" copyright © 1974 by Gene Wolfe; first appeared in *Galaxy*.

"The Marvelous Brass Chessplaying Automaton" copyright © 1977 by Gene Wolfe; first appeared in *Universe 7*, edited by Terry Carr.

peared in *Speculations*, edited by Isaac Asimov and Alice Laurence.

"Death of the Island Doctor" copyright © 1983 by Gene Wolfe; first appeared in *The Wolfe Archipelago* by Gene Wolfe.

"On the Train" copyright © 1983 by Gene Wolfe; first appeared in *The New Yorker*.

"In the Mountains" copyright © 1983 by Gene Wolfe; first appeared in *Amazing Science Fiction Stories*.

"At the Volcano's Lip" copyright © 1983 by Gene Wolfe; first appeared in *Amazing Science Fiction Stories*.

"In the Old Hotel" copyright © 1988 by Gene Wolfe.

"Choice of the Black Goddess" copyright © 1986 by Gene Wolfe; first appeared in *Liavek: The Players of Luck,* edited by Will Shetterly and Emma Bull.

Contents

An Introduction

W hat you are holding is, quite unabashedly, a collection of some of my most obscure work. Jim Goddard and I shook hands on the deal at Conspiracy, the 1987 world science-fiction convention in Brighton. It has taken us over a year to surmount the obstacles and produce this book for you, but here it is at last. I think we both knew from the beginning the sort it was to be.

Perhaps the best way to explain it is to tell you something about "In the Old Hotel," a short piece you'll read not far from the end. At about the time the winter of 1980-81 was fading, my wife Rosemary and I rode a crack train called the Empire Builder from Chicago (where we live) to Seattle and back. Sitting in the observation car with a notebook on my lap, I wrote six very brief stories. When we got home, I typed them up and sent them off to *The New Yorker*.

With no great hope. One tends to gamble with short pieces—if they are accepted, their acceptance will bring a noticeable gain in prestige; if they are not, little has been lost. All in all, I suppose I've submitted at least twenty stories to *The New Yorker*.

This time I got a surprise—one of the six, "On the Train," had found a home; it's still the only success I've ever had with that notoriously picky publication. Furthermore, the letter of acceptance revealed that the junior editor who had real all six had wanted to accept another, "In the Old Hotel," but had been overruled. Needless to say, "In the Old Hotel" at once became a great favorite of mine. My agent submitted the remaining five to *Amazing,* where George Scithers, its editor in those halcyon days, bought four—bought all of them, in fact, except "In the Old Hotel," which appears in this collection for the first time anywhere.

The stories you find here are, in short, more or less like that: they're mostly stories that I feel are good, but that have received little or no praise.

"The Green Rabbit from S'Rian" was written for the Liavek series edited by Will Shetterly and Emma Bull. The idea was to make up a fictional city-state (Liavek) with its surrounding geography, technology, religions, laws of magic, and so on and so forth, and to persuade a variety of authors to submit stories laid there; compilations of this rather freakish kind are called shared-world anthologies. "The Green Rabbit from S'Rian" was my first contribution and appeared in the first book in the series.

It was not well received. A great part of the fun of these anthologies lies in shared jokes; in this one, for example, a vicious camel was featured in one story, shot in another, cooked and eaten in a third, appeared as a ghost in a fourth, and so on. I was told about this serial camel and urged to include it somehow in my own story, but I couldn't see how it could be made to fit. I hope that you will enjoy my story anyway—a magical jade rabbit should be fun enough, I think, without a resurrected camel for company.

"Beech Hill" is a rather early piece, written after I had attended my first Milford Writers' Conference. (I had no idea when I wrote it that a Sycamore Hill Writers' Conference lurked in the future, life being an imitation of art.) Milford died away as Damon Knight, who had conducted it, grew more and more interested in teaching and less involved in writing; but for ten years or so it was a wonderful sort of fair at which serious SF writers of varying talents mingled with mountebanks frequently more gifted still. From it I conceived the notion of a convention of fictitious persons, of extraordinary poseurs who were themselves their own fiction. After all these years, it is still one of my favorites.

"Sightings at Twin Mounds" was written last year as a sort of experiment—when you turn from "Beech Hill" to this story you will be passing across ninety-five percent of my career. From time to time, no reading gives me more pleasure than supposedly factual accounts of UFOs, black dogs, vanishing hitchhikers, and similar apparitions, although all such accounts are ultimately unsatisfactory. (I recommend *Sasquatch: the Apes Among Us,* by John Green, should you ever come upon a copy.) It seems to me that a good, and indeed entirely satisfactory, story could be written in that style. It is a framed story, if you like, in which the frame is the whole story; and if you like it, that makes two of us.

"Continuing Westward" reflects my first hobby, many years ago buried beneath the press of schoolwork—building models of First World War aircraft. I've done another one, "Against the Lafayette Escadrille," but it's not in here. Both are rather Kiplingesque, like my earliest published story, "The Dead Man," which isn't here either; a few months ago Sandra Miesel asked for some Kipling-influenced pieces for two anthologies she was editing, and I sent her "Continuing Westward" and "Love, Among the Corridors."

"Slaves of Silver" is the Sherlock Holmes pastiche all of us seem compelled to do. Its sequel brings in—as a robot—my favorite private eye, Nero Wolfe. At one time I dreamt of a whole series of these; little does the world realize just how narrow its escapes have been.

"Westwind," written in 1972 during a time of considerable stress, remains one of my favorites to this day. According to Hollywood legend, a certain poor screenwriter was summoned to the vast estate of the head of one of the great studios of the '30s. Asked afterwards how he had liked its acres of manicured grounds, the writer said, "Wonderful! It just goes to show what God could have done if He'd had the money." When I wrote this particular story, I was speculating upon what God might do if only He had the technology. Or at least, that's what I believe *now.* Others have found a great many other things in there, and sixteen years is a long time. Anyway,

I had a CB radio back when everybody in America had a CB radio, and my handle was *Westwind*.

"Sonya, Crane Wessleman, and Kittee," an even older tale, is a magazine story in a special sense. In those days I was crazy about dogs, and I used to subscribe to *Dog World,* devoted to purebreds. When I had read twenty issues or more, it struck me that models were never employed to sell the dogs advertised in its pages, as they are to peddle cars, perfume, and virtually every other product. Or rather, that the models were the dogs pictured in the ads, the champion fox terriers, rottweilers, or whatever. For a long time I'd realized that the most attractive thing in most ads was the model.

"The Packerhaus Method" embodies one of the few story ideas (perhaps the sole story idea) I've ever generated by one of the standard methods taught in such books as *Creating Short Fiction.* This is not because those methods don't work, I hasten to add—they do. One is to choose some branch of science or technology and speculate on the result if it attains perfection. I picked embalming, in which the object is to render the late lamented more lifelike.

"Straw" is fundamentally a hot-air ballooning story. Every so often I like to think of things that could have been invented a long time before they actually were—or that might easily have been invented but weren't. For example, for hundreds of years, wars among the Greeks (possibly the most brilliantly creative people in history) were fought by heavy infantrymen armed with long spears and circular shields. Most of them were won by the Spartans, the acknowledged masters of hoplite warfare. Then, around 379 BC, Thebes produced a general of real genius named Epaminondas. And Epaminondas came up with the simplest *great* military innovation I know of: he cut a notch out of each round shield. That was all it was. Instead of looking like a whole cracker, the shield looked like a cracker from which a tiny bite had been taken. But that bite permitted the solder to use his left hand to assist his right in managing his long spear, and the Thebans crushed the Spartans at Leuctra.

The point is that Epaminondas' notch could have been cut a thousand years sooner—in Homer's day, for example. In the same way, it seems obvious that the hot-air balloon could have been invented well before the end of the ancient world. You need a little rope (it's been around for a long time), a lot of silk (which by then was coming steadily along the spice routes), some straw, and an iron basket to burn it in. There are no moving parts, and the design is simplicity itself—a bag held over a fire. But if the hot-air balloon had been invented in 500 AD, what would have been done with it?

"The Marvelous Brass Chessplaying Automaton" turns the idea we've just been talking about on its head, asking, "What if an invention that did not in fact survive the fall of civilization (the chess-playing computer, in this case) were believed to have survived?"

Once in a rare while, I have a dream so vivid and organized that it can be written with a minimum of polishing; these dreams are always nightmares, like "To the Dark Tower Came." I can't imagine why anyone would want to psychoanalyze me, but if anybody does, that's the place to start.

"Parkroads," a short story in the form of a movie review, is as good a piece as I've ever turned out. After half a dozen rejections, it appeared in *Fiction International,* a literary magazine published by San Diego State University. I'm happy to say that several people wrote to Larry McCaffery, the editor, asking where they could rent the film.

In 1982, Ed Bryant, Michael Bishop, and I taught a three-week course in science fiction and fantasy writing at Portland State University's Haystack Summer Program in the Arts. We had a grand total of four students, but I'm happy to say that one of the four, David Zindell, is rapidly becoming a very well-known author. During my week, I did the exercises I assigned to the doughty four. One was to write a science-fiction story about a blocked writer; "Alphabet" was my own homework.

"A Criminal Proceeding" is just my impression of real-life courtroom drama as it's presented in the popular press. When

I read one of these things, usually while buttering yet another slice of toast, I never know who anyone is or what the person on trial is supposed to have done. Do you?

"In Looking-Glass Castle" harks back to one of the earliest science-fiction ideas: the human society modeled on that of bees or ants. It got me an unasked-for grant from the Illinois Arts Council, the only grant I've ever received.

"Cherry Jubilee" is a science-fiction mystery story, among other things. Alex Schomburg gave it a marvelous illustration showing dinner aboard the spacecraft; if you're going to try to solve the mystery, you'd be wise to draw a picture—or at least a chart—of the same sort.

"Redbeard" is a horror story based upon a house I used to drive past every so often. It has since burned to the ground, which may be a good thing. Maybe I should write a story about John Gacy, the killer clown; he lived a few miles from here, and my friend Jerry Bauer used to take pictures for him.

"A Solar Labyrinth" is another favorite. Labyrinths seem to fascinate just about everybody, and for a while I was almost equally interested in what used to be called dialing. I tried to keep the sinister element well in the background, and it seems I kept it so far back that few readers notice it at all; but I like it that way.

"Love, Among the Corridors" is a homage to Kipling's lovely "The Children of the Zodiac." Like "Alphabet," it originated in a Haystack assignment: write a fantasy in which a woman's touch brings a statue to life.

"Checking Out" was written for Pamela Sargent's *Afterlives,* an anthology of life-after-death stories. Similarly, "Morning Glory" was written for Anne McCaffrey, who was editing a book of stories with university backgrounds. "Trip, Trap" was the first story I ever sold Damon Knight for his *Orbit* series; it marks the real beginning of my writing career.

"From the Desk of Gilmer C. Merton" is the story my agent (Virginia Kidd) dislikes the most; she thinks Georgia Morgan's modeled on her. Nah. I should point out that Velo's a village near here. I don't think there's really a North Velo

City, but in a few years there might be—this is Barrington, and there's also North Barrington, South Barrington, Lake Barrington Shores, and Barrington Hills. So you see.

"Civis Laputus Sum" is one of my periodic semiserious hits at academics, who often seem to feel that the only good writer is a dead writer. I do it mostly to show that I'm not good yet, and because it's such fun to see tenured professors who've built whole careers on criticizing some poor bastard who had to hustle to make the rent bluster and huff when they're criticized a bit themselves.

"The Recording" drew the comment, "At last! Calling it like it is!" from Isaac Asimov. If that isn't enough to make you want to read it, what would be?

The next story, "Last Day," was written on request for an editor who had asked for a religious science-fiction story. I don't think it can have been quite what he had in mind, because he rejected it without comment. Since I've already talked about writing stories for Pam Sargent and Anne McCaffrey, perhaps I should warn you that editors who ask specifically for stories rarely buy them. What usually happens it that the editor has some earlier piece in mind and rejects what you write for him when it doesn't resemble that.

When we were discussing "Civis Laputus Sum," I implied that I dislike all academics, at least in the humanities. "Death of the Island Doctor" proves I don't. There are still a few left who got into their fields because they actually *love* them. Not many, but a few. Needless to say, they are scorned by their colleagues, though frequently worshipped by their students. It seems to me that there used to be a lot more of them than there are now.

"In the Mountains" and "At the Volcano's Lip" are two of the stories I wrote on the train; I've already told you about "On the Train" itself and "In the Old Hotel," from which this book takes its name. The closing story, "Choice of the Black Goddess" presents the further adventures of Captain Tev Noen, Ler Oeuni, and their meery crew, whom you will meet first in "The Green Rabbit from S'Rian."

And now it's time to check in. Please don't forget to sign the register—our porter isn't available at the moment, but I'll be happy to carry your bags upstairs myself. I do hope you have a pleasant stay. Perhaps someday you'll want to return.

Gene Wolfe
Barrington
Illinois

The Green Rabbit from S'Rian

CAPTAIN TEV NOEN TOOK OFF HIS GILDED DRESS HELMET and scratched his shaven head—not because he was puzzled by the sight of two of his best hands nailing up a placard at the mouth of Rat's Alley, but because it had occurred to him that the placards might be ineffective, and he had not yet decided what to do if they were. He had composed them himself that afternoon, and Ler Oeuni, his first mate, had lettered them with sweeping strokes of the brush.

> JOIN THE LEVAR'S NAVY!
> THE GALLEASS *WINDSONG*
> IS NOW ACCEPTING RECRUITS!
> THREE COPPERS A DAY
> PROMPTLY PAID AT EVERY PORT!
> AMPLE FOOD, DRINK, AND CLOTHING, AND
> GOOD TREATMENT!
> SIGN TONIGHT AT THE BIG TREE!
> FIVE COPPERS WHEN YOU SIGN!!
> PRIZE MONEY COULD MAKE YOU RICH!!!

It was a simple appeal to self-interest, and Noen wondered whether sounding the trumpets of Liavek and Her Magnificence, as most captains did, would not have been better. He thought not. In his experience, recruits did not care about such things.

The hands drove home their final nails with resounding

whacks and turned to face their captain, touching their foreheads with all fingers. Automatically, Noen replaced his helmet and returned their salutes. "Good work. Now we'll rejoin
Lieutenant Dinnile and see if these have brought anyone yet."
Recklessly he added, "I'll buy you each a tankard, if there's a
good hand already."

The sailors grinned and took their positions like proper
bodyguards, the woman ahead of him and the man behind
him. Noen tried to recall their names; they pulled the first
(that was, the rearmost) starboard oar—Syb and Su, of course.
Each wore a sharply curved cutlass in a canvas sheath now,
although the hammers they carried would be nearly as effec-
tive.

He himself was far better armed, with his sword and double-barreled pistol. Not that swords or "villainous saltpetre"
should be needed for the drunken sailors of Rat Alley, or its
cutthroats either—Naval officers were notoriously savage
fighters and just as notoriously broke.

If they were attacked, it might even be possible to carry the
fellow—undamaged, Noen hoped—aboard *Windsong*. There
he would sign on or chase a sack of ballast to the bottom.

"Why, if we were attacked by fifty or so . . ."

"Sir?" Su looked over her shoulder at him.

"Talking to myself," Noen told her brusquely. "Stupid
habit."

There were always the judges. A judge could pardon an
offender willing to enlist. And judges *did* pardon such offend-
ers—for well-connected captains, and for captains who could
offer rich gifts in return. Not for Tev Noen, to be sure.

A rat scampered across Noen's boots, and he kicked it. It
sailed past Su's head, and in the darkness of Rat's Alley someone swore and spat.

"Good 'un, sir," Syb whispered diplomatically.

Noen had recognized the voice. "Is that you, Dinnile?"

"Yes, sir, Some filthy devil just flung a rat at me, sir."

Inwardly, Noen damned his luck. The story would be all
over the ship by morning, and such stories were bad for

discipline. Aloud he said, "Officers who leave their posts have to expect such luck, Lieutenant." Or perhaps they were good for discipline after all, or could be made to be. Syb and Su would be the cynosures of the main deck, and he himself shouldn't come off too badly.

"I didn't leave my post, sir." Dinnile's brass breastplate gleamed now in the faint light. He spat again and wiped his mouth on his sleeve. "I got 'em."

"Got what?"

"Fifty-two rowers, sir. You said not to take no more, remember? No use payin' more than's authorized."

Noen squinted at the dim column that trailed after Dinnile in the dark. "You got fifty-two in a couple of watches?"

"Yes, sir! They come together, sir. They're nomads from the Great Waste." Dinnile halted before his captain and touched his forehead. "There's been a drought there, they say, so it's worse than usual—cattle dyin', and all that. They come to Liavek to keep from starvin', and somebody that saw one of Oeuni's placards sent 'em to us."

Noen nodded. It seemed best to nod in the face of Dinnile's enthusiasm. "That's a piece of luck."

"For us and them—that's what I told 'em. We'll sail tomorrow with full complement, sir."

Noen nodded again. "They're strong enough to pull an oar, you think?" Dinnile was not the most brilliant officer in the fleet, but as a judge of what could be extorted with a rope end, he had no peer.

"Give 'em a little food and they'll do fine, sir. They spent their five coppers on ale and apples and such at the Big Tree, sir. And I promised 'em, too, a good feed when we get to the ship."

"Right," Noen told him. Anything to keep them from deserting on the way. "We'll go with you."

Away from the beetling structures of Rat Alley, there was more light, and Noen counted the recruits as they filed past. Forty-nine, fifty . . . he held his breath . . . fifty-one, fifty-two. Then the pair of crewmen he had assigned to help Dinnile. All present and accounted for. It was beyond belief, too good to be true. For a dizzy moment he wondered if it were his birthday—could he have forgotten? No. Dinnile's perhaps. No. Or—of course—one of the nomads'. What better luck could the poor devil have than seeing himself and all his friends fed and safe aboard the *Windsong*?

Or what worse?

Noen asked one of Dinnile's sailors if there had been fifty-two exactly.

"Oh, no, sir. More like to a hundred, sir. The Lieutenant picked out the best, and let them sign."

Let them sign! It was a night to remember.

Ler Oeuni touched her forehead as he came aboard. Noen touched his own and said, "We'll put off for Minnow Island as soon as Dinnile has the new hands at the oars."

"There's a bit of night breeze, sir."

"Under oar, Lieutenant, not under sail." Oeuni was sailing officer (and gunnery officer); Dinnile rowing officer. Ordinarily it would be best to spare the rowers as much as possible, but the new hands had to be taught their job, and the sooner the teaching began, the better—tomorrow they might have to ram a pirate.

Noen mounted to *Windsong*'s long, lightly built quarterdeck and watched Dinnile shoving the new hands to their places, most to forward oars from which they would be able to watch the trained rowers at the aft oars and would be caught up in the rowing rhythm that was almost like a spell. "See that there's at least one experienced hand at each oar, Dinnile."

"Aye, aye, sir." The tone of Dinnile's response managed to imply that the instruction had been unnecessary.

"Do they speak Liavekan?" Noen cursed himself for not having found out sooner.

"Some do, sir. Some don't."

"Then *talk* to them. They've got to learn, and quickly."

"Aye, aye, sir."

"Foreigners?" Oeuni ventured to ask.

"Nomads from the Great Waste," Noen told her. She would have to deal with them, after all, as they all would. Eventually, she would have to train them to reef and steer.

"They're subjects of the Empire, then."

Noen shook his head. "They're not Tichenese, if that's what you mean. And whatever they were, they became subjects of Her Magnificence when they signed with us."

Dinnile had pushed the last of the nomads into place. Noen cleared his throat. "Listen to me, you new hands! I'm Tev Noen, your captain. Call me Captain Noen. This is Ler Oeuni, our first mate. Call her Lieutenant Oeuni. Lieutenant Beddil Dinnile signed you—you should know him already, and the petty officers you'll learn soon enough. You'll be treated firmly on this ship, but you'll be treated fairly. Do your best, and you'll have no cause to worry.

"You've been promised a good dinner tonight, and you're going to get it. There are navy kitchens at the base on Minnow Island, and they'll have hot food for you." It was probably better not to tell them they would not be permitted to leave the ship, that the food would be carried on board. "When I give the order 'out oars,' watch the trained hands and do as they do."

Noen glanced at Oeuni. "You may cast off, Lieutenant."

"Stand by to cast off!" she shouted at the sailors stationed fore and aft. They leaped onto the wharf. "Cast off!"

A few moments more and *Windsong* was under way, her oars rising and falling awkwardly, but more or less together, in a beat as slow as the timesman at the kettledrums could make it.

A fresh wind touched Noen's cheek as the dark wharves and warehouses of the waterfront vanished in the night. Little cat's-tongue waves, the hesitant ambassadors of the lions in the Sea of Luck, rocked *Windsong* as a mother rocks her child.

"Not so bad," Oeuni said.

Noen answered with a guarded nod. How hard were a nomad's hands? Not as hard as a sailor's, certainly. These men would have blisters tomorrow, if the wind failed, and—

On the main deck, Dinnile's rope end rose and fell. There was a shout that sounded like a curse, and the flash of steel. Dinnile's big fist sent someone reeling over the next oar. Something—a knife, surely—clattered to the deck. Noen called, "Tivlo! Bring that to me." Tivlo was the petty officer in charge of the mainmast. "Dinnile! If he's conscious, put him back to work." Attacking an officer was punishable by death, but Noen had no intention of losing a hand this early.

Tivlo handed up the knife, hilt first. Its blade was curved and wickedly double-edged.

"We'll have a shakedown as soon as we tie up," Oeuni said.

Noen nodded. The cresset burning atop the highest tower of Fin Castle was already in plain view. The nomads would need their knives to cut rope and do a thousand other tasks. But they would need nothing more, and there was no telling what else they might have.

Oeuni had lined the new hands up and hoisted lanterns at the ends of the main yard when Syb came to the quarterdeck, touching his forehead. "What is it?" Noen asked.

"About Su and me, sir."

"Yes?"

"You promised us a tankard each, sir, if there was a hand signed."

"So I did." Noen bent over the quarterdeck rail. "Would you as soon have the money?"

"No, sir. Perhaps, sir . . ." The words trailed away. Hands were forbidden the quarterdeck, except upon order. Noen said, "Come up."

"Thank you, sir!" Syb mounted the steps. "I thought it might be better to speak more private-like, sir. Su and me—well, her folks and mine live here on the island."

Noen shook his head. "I can't let you go ashore. We'll be sailing at dawn, and perhaps before dawn."

"Sir . . ."

Noen knew he should cut the man off, but there was something in his face that forbade it. "Yes?" he asked.

"Let us go just for this watch, sir. If we're not back when

it's over, you can put us both in the irons. It's not to drink or nothing like that, sir."

"What *is* it for?"

"They're fisherfolk, sir. It's not no easy life, sir, and now we've got our pay, and . . ."

"I see," Noen said.

"A prosperous fishing village, sir. That's what they call it, those that don't live there. It means they've generally got enough to eat, if they fancy fish, and maybe enough to mend the boat or buy the twine to make a new net. But it's a terrible hard life, sir."

Noen began, "If I gave you leave, I'd have to give it to others who have just as good a—"

He was interrupted by a touch at his elbow. It was Dinnile, now officer of the watch. "A sojer, sir. Got a letter for you."

When Noen had carried the note to the binnacle light, he announced, "I'm going ashore, and I'll want bodyguards. Syb, you and Su did well enough last time, Dinnile, see that they're issued cutlasses."

"For goin' ashore on Minnow Island, sir?" Dinnile was utterly bewildered.

"You're right," Noen told him. "Their sheath knives should be enough, and there's no time to waste."

Fin Castle rose from a rocky headland at the easternmost tip of the island, where its great guns commanded the principal entrance to the harbor. Noen dismissed his "bodyguards" at the castle. "I'm going in to see Admiral Tinthe. I don't know how long I'll be, but when I come out, I expect to find you waiting here for me. Understand?"

They muttered their aye-ayes, touched their foreheads, and hurried away.

Noen needed no guide to direct him to the admiral's chambers. High in the keep and facing south, they permitted Uean Tinthe to scan the Sea of Luck. As Noen climbed stair after weary stair, he wondered how often the old man did so, and when he would decide the price of his view was too high.

Noen's knock brought a gruff invitation. He ducked from

habit as he entered, conditioned by *Windsong*'s low cabin. Admiral Tinthe was in his favorite spot by the window; beside him sat a distinguished-looking woman of middle age.

"Captain Noen, Serkosh," the admiral said, returning Noen's salute. "Noen, Serkosh the Younger."

Noen bowed. "A great pleasure, Lady."

She nodded stiffly.

"Told you to be ready at sunup," Tinthe continued.

"Yes, sir."

"You're undermanned like the rest. I can send you a scant half dozen."

"*Windsong* has a full complement now, sir," Noen said.

For an instant, the admiral studied him. "Sailors?"

"Landsmen, sir."

Admiral Tinthe turned to the woman beside him and winked. She smiled; he had been a handsome man once, and traces of it still remained in his scarred old face. "Recruiting practices," he told her. "Best left to the young ones. Best not to know too much."

"All signed in due form, sir," Noen told him. Inwardly, he blessed his foresight in inspecting Dinnile's roster book.

"Good. Sail you will. Course south and a point east. That's the best of them, and your crew's earned it for you."

Noen forbore asking what made it the best. "Pirates, sir?"

The admiral shook his head. "You'd better hear the story. Know what you're up against. Tell him about the green rabbit, Serkosh."

The woman said, "Perhaps you might ask him to sit, first."

When Noen was settled in a chair, she continued, "I am a jeweler, Captain. I own the Crystal Gull—possibly you've seen us? We're situated near the Levar's Park. The next time you've need of a gaud for some young woman, perhaps you'll stop in."

"I'd like to," Noen told her, "if I had the money."

Serkosh nodded. "And if your mission is successful, you will. I've promised to pay twenty thousand levars to the captain who returns the green rabbit to me."

Noen said nothing. It was a fortune, a prize so great it stunned the imagination.

"You're aware, I'm sure, that there was once a city called S'Rian on the hill overlooking our bay."

Noen nodded.

"Occasionally—very occasionally—something is discovered there. I do not say something of value, because they're very seldom of value; but something of interest to collectors and antiquarians. Perhaps once a year. Perhaps less. Do you understand?"

Noen nodded again.

"Such things are invariably brought to me. My reputation for honesty is second to none, and I pay the highest prices—often a good deal more than the item is worth."

Noen said, "I'm certain you do," trying his best to keep any note of sarcasm from his voice.

"Such a find was made last winter by men digging a well. It was—it is—a crouching rabbit carved in jade." Serkosh used her hands to indicate the length of the rabbit, then its height. "About half the size of a living rabbit. The size of a very young rabbit, if you wish to think of it so."

"I understand."

"We often have to hold such things for years. In this case several noble collectors were interested, but we had not come to an agreement about terms." Her face hardened. "Three days ago, the rabbit was stolen from my vault."

Noen asked, "Someone broke in?"

Serkosh shook her head. "It seems the thief was an employee. My assistants are allowed to enter the vault. My apprentices are permitted to enter when accompanied by an assistant. Nothing else was taken. That suggests, to me at least, that the thief supposed that the absence of the rabbit would not be noticed, as the absence of a diamond—"

Tinthe cleared his throat.

Serkosh glanced at him, then back to Noen. "Your admiral and I differ in our interpretation of the crime, though we are both determined that the thieves be brought to justice. He will give you his own view, I feel sure."

Noen said, "A jade rabbit the size of a rat isn't worth twenty thousand levars."

Serkosh shook her head. "Of course not. But the security of the Crystal Gull is worth much, much more. If we are robbed successfully just once, there will be a hundred more thieves eager to try. But if you, Captain, can intercept the ship carrying the rabbit, it will be seen that the thieves were *not* successful."

A massive brass telescope stood on the admiral's work table. He picked it up, sliding its jointed sections in and out. "There's something more, I'm afraid, Noen."

Serkosh exclaimed, "That absurd story!"

Tinthe closed the telescope with an audible click. "Absurdity doesn't matter if people believe it. And they do—maybe I do myself. Know what a magic artifact is, Noen? A magician puts his luck into something. The thing's magic then, and it doesn't matter if the magician lives or dies."

"And this rabbit—" Noen began.

Serkosh cut him off. "Nonsense! I had it tested by a competent professional. He conjured it, instructed it, burned incense, sacrificed, did everything! It's no more magical than your shoe."

Tinthe smiled and opened his telescope again. "But there's a rumor it is."

Noen asked, "What is its function supposed to be, sir?"

"Nobody knows. Or anyway, nobody agrees. Brings you women. Brings women children. It's a rabbit after all. Should be something like that, eh? But there are S'Rians living in the city. You probably know that. And they say it's magic. Serkosh's magician said he found nothing. Suppose he did, returned it, stole it himself by magic?"

"I see, sir."

"Or suppose it brings women. Would he tell? Or would he think it his own doing? Suppose it's wealth. He got a good big fee. And you'll get twenty thousand if you bring it back here, Noen. That's wealth, wouldn't you say?"

"Do you know it left the city on a ship, sir?"

Tinthe nodded. "We thought it might. That's why I had every ship here make ready. Report reached the Guard to-night. There's a lip in Old Town. Always is. *Zhironni,* big carrack, sailed yesterday. Probably making for Ka Zhir, though we can't be sure." Tinthe leaned forward. "Noen, maybe the rabbit's a magic artifact. If it is, and the Zhir get it . . ."

"I understand, sir."

"Wish I had a magician to send with you. I don't. We've got them looking for the rabbit, but no one available to go to sea." The old admiral hesitated. "Serkosh's professional may be on board—the Guard can't find him. All this under seal, Noen. Very much so."

Day had dawned with a weak breeze that soon died, leaving *Windsong*'s triangular sails flapping against their masts. Noen had ordered them furled and put the oars out. A few moments ago Oeuni had cast the log, and now her face was grim. "A scant two knots, Captain."

"They'll get better," Noen told her.

"They'd better, sir."

Though the air was dead calm, there was a nasty chop; the galleass, long-bodied, narrow-waisted, and shallow-keeled, rolled in it like a belaying pin. The new hands were sick at their oars. Dinnile had four sailors filling buckets and swinging swabs, and *Windsong* left a trail of filth behind her that would have done credit to a garbage scow.

Noen squinted at the horizon, then at the sun. "Oeuni, how much do you know about magic?"

"Not enough to make sailors of Dinnile's recruits."

"We'll do that. How long would you say it would take a good magician to raise a wind?"

"You're serious, aren't you, sir? I have no idea. I suppose

it would depend on the size of the wind he wanted—longer for a storm to wreck a ship than for a zephyr to cool a garden."

Noen nodded to himself. The wind had been gentle yesterday when the *Zhironni* sailed—a big ship wouldn't have gone far on those light airs; and now *Zhironni* was probably as becalmed as they were. Worse in fact, because they were at least making two knots. A carrack would be drifting with the current. Perhaps *Zhironni* had no magician after all.

"Look at that! You served on one once, didn't you, Captain?" Oeuni was pointing aft. Barely visible, the triple-banked oars of a trireme rose and fell like the wings of some enchanted bird.

"Yes," Noen said. "They must have got under way a good deal later than we did." That was a little consolation at least. He turned away to look at his own ship once more. Like most galleasses *Windsong* had only a single oar bank; but five rowers pulled each of her oars. Four rowers, or three, Noen reminded himself, when the crew was understrength.

With his telescope trained on the trireme, he tried to guess how many of its oar ports were empty. How beautiful she was! They had put up the mast, and it pointed to the heavens like a single white arrow.

But why? A trireme under oar normally shipped its mast, laying it flat in two cradles on the narrow storming deck that ran all the way from the quarterdeck to the gun deck on the forecastle. And why did it look so white? Could the captain of the trireme, still far behind him, see something he could not?

He turned to Oeuni. "You're supposed to be keeping a weather eye out, Lieutenant."

"Yes, sir." Her face puzzled, she scanned the horizon.

"Try northward," he advised her.

She squinted, shading her eyes with one hand.

"We're in for a blow, Lieutenant. A carrack's wind."

And a soldier's, as it proved, a wind that blew from dead astern and sent *Windsong* flying under reefed sails, pitching as if to shatter her flimsy hull each time her great bronze ram smashed into a wave.

"Pass the lard bucket, Lieutenant Dennile! The new hands will need it."

"Tev Noen," Oeuni asked at his ear, "what are we after?" Surprised, he stared at her.

"I know, the *Zhironni,* and the rest is secret instructions. But what if you're killed? I'll be in command, and I won't know what our objective is." Her hand touched his, as if to remind him of how desirable she was.

He knew what she was offering him, and he knew he must refuse. The price of love bought with secrets would be his self-respect. He said, "I'll try to tell you before I die, Lieutenant," and she turned away.

Another watch, and stinging hail pelted the ship. Noen pulled the hood of his sea-cloak over his head, wondering if he should have his steward bring his helmet. They would be fighting soon anyway; he could feel it. Armor might save an officer's life, but it endangered it as well. Many a captain, many a lieutenant, had gone to the bottom weighted with armor. Noen found that he was thinking of Oeuni drowned, helmetless, the green sealight shining on her shaven head, arms and long legs tossed in death's parody of swimming. Oeuni whom he would never possess, drawn down to the dark by her cuirass. Ler Oeuni lost.

The lookout in the maintop shouted something that was blown away by the gale. Noen went to the quarterdeck railing. "Lookout! I can't hear you!"

"Sail! Point to starboard!"

"Point to starboard," Noen told the woman at the wheel, and vaulted the railing. Dinnile was still supervising the distribution of lard, seeing that each rower who needed it used it and that none took too much. Hands with infected blisters could not row; heavily greased fingers could not hold an oar, if rowing should be necessary again.

"Can they fight, Dinnile?" Noen asked as softly as the wind allowed. "Will they?"

Dinnile shrugged. "I dunno, sir."

One of the nomads appeared at Noen's shoulder, still rubbing his palms together. "Yes, we fight. Give us swords."

Dinnile roared, "Stand to attention there!"

The nomad had better sea legs than most of them, and he stood as he must have seen the sailors stand, his brown rags flapping about him.

It was the first time, Noen realized, that he had looked at one of the new hands as an individual. Like all of them, this one was small and wiry—dark, though not so dark as a true Tichenese. Every line of his skull showed in his face, and Noen might have thought a candle lit there from the fire that burned in the bony sockets of those yellow eyes.

"Sir, we will fight. With our knives if we must. With our hands."

"I think you will. Dinnile, break out the arms. Everything we've got." Noen turned back to the nomad. "What's your name?"

"Sir, Myllikesh."

Oeuni was on the gun deck, checking *Windsong*'s main battery. When Noen put his telescope to his eye, she told him. *"Zhironni."*

"Thank you," Noen said, his voice expressionless. He forced himself to add, "Lieutenant."

"You must have seen her at the docks. Fifty guns at least."

"Mostly rail pieces." On the pitching gun deck, it was hard to keep his telescope trained on *Zhironni,* but Noen glimpsed figures on her quarterdeck with their own lenses trained on him.

"And what have we got, aside from Poltergeist here?" Oeuni patted the big culverin affectionately on the muzzle. "Four basilisks and a couple of sakers. If those aren't rail pieces, what are they?"

"And the ram," Noen told her, shutting his telescope.

"Ram that? It will damage us more than it will them."

To himself, Noen admitted she was probably right. Aloud he said, "Have the crew stand to quarters, Lieutenant."

She shouted the order to the timesman aft. "Are we going to attack her straight out, sir? Shouldn't we give them a warning shot—"

A smudge of black appeared at the carrack's taffrail, instantly whisked away by the howling wind. The boom of the gun—a long basilisk much like the two on his own quarterdeck, Noen thought—was nearly lost.

"Waste your powder," Oeuni told the Zhir. "You couldn't hit Kil Island at this range."

Noen wondered. *Zhironni* was a far more stable gun platform than *Windsong*.

Aft, the timesman had begun the long, fast roll that called every sailor and officer to fighting stations. The gun crews boiled out of the forecastle below the gun deck, some carrying baskets of the premeasured charges Oeuni liked, others shot and slow match. Just one of Poltergeist's big iron balls was a load for any sailor—in so rough a sea, almost too much of a load.

The tompions were jerked from the muzzles of Poltergeist and the two swivel-mounted basilisks, powder and shot rammed home. (Privately Noen regretted the loss of the old system, in which the powder was poured down the gun bores from a scoop; then at least a captain could note its condition.)

The gun captains had kindled their slow matches at the galley firebox; they spun their glowing tips to keep them alight in the wind-blown spray.

Zhironni's sternchaser spoke again, a bit more loudly this time. An instant later the port forestay parted with a snap. The bosun and his mate hurried forward to repair it.

"They're rigging boarding nets, sir," Oeuni reported.

"So I see," Noen told her. "We won't be going over the side anyway. Bosun! You've seen a xebec?"

Surprised, the bosun turned, touching his forehead. "Aye, sir."

"You know how they slope the foremast forward to give the foresail more room? I want *Windsong*'s foremast to look like that. Tighten those forestays and slack off the backstays until the masthead's raked as far forward as our ram. And I want ratlines from the deck to the masthead."

Dinnile was at the aft gundeck railing, touching his forehead. "Oars, sir?"

"No. Just have them ready to board—old hands first." It was not necessary to tell Dinnile to lead them. He would anyway—probably would, Noen reflected, even if he were ordered not to. "Oeuni, see how that gallery overhangs at her stern? I'm going to bring us in under it. Disable the rudder as we're coming in."

As Noen spoke, one of the many-paned windows of the carrack's stern cabin swung wide. The black muzzle of a gun emerged from it like the head of a snake as the other window opened.

"You can fire when ready."

As Noen reached the lower deck, the port basilisk went off with a crash. The foremast was lurching toward the beakhead, and Dinnile had his boarding party mustered forward of the mainmast. Looking at him, Noen realized the burly mate must be as frightened as he was, but like himself would rather die than show it. "Good luck, Beddil," he called. Then, "A place ashore!" It was something one said; the "place" was the grave, which could never be mentioned directly.

"A place ashore," Dinnile responded cheerfully.

The port corner of the quarterdeck exploded in a cloud of splinters. "Steersman!" Noen yelled. "Port a point. We're coming in the back door."

The steersman's "aye, aye" was strangely muted; when Noen reached the quarterdeck, he saw that a splinter had laid her cheek open, baring white molars in a misplaced grin. One of the starboard sternchaser crew was ripping up her shirt to staunch the bleeding.

The sternchasers would be no use in this fight. He sent the rest of their crews to join the boarding party.

The two sakers had already been shifted to the port rail. They would not be able to fire without damaging *Windsong*'s rigging until they were very close, he thought, but they might get a chance then.

Oeuni's hail came faintly from the gun deck. "She's luff-ing!"

Noen nodded to himself. *Zhironni* would try to turn in order to present her broadside to her attacker. But imposing though they were, carracks were notoriously unhandy, and now the wind made every plank in her towering freeboard work against her.

Dead ahead, a leviathan rose from the sea, golden-scaled, with eyes like pale moons and teeth like the blades of cutlasses. Poltergeist fired with a roar that shook the ship, and the giant fell backwards in a welter of blood. Noen braced himself for the shock when the ram struck its body, but there was none; it had sunk too quickly, or perhaps disappeared.

Somehow the culverin's roar had reminded him that he had not yet wound the wheellock of his pistol. He got out the key and did so. A pistol with a tight lock was always dangerous, and if the lock were wound too soon, the spring might break or lose its strength. But shapes like horned Kil were clawing at *Windsong*'s racing sides with crimson hands, and it seemed to him that the time to wind it had come.

"Magic," a crewman at one of the sakers wailed.

"Illusions," Noen told him, shouting against the whistling wind. "He hasn't had time for something new."

Poltergeist and the gun-deck basilisks went off together; *Zhironni*'s rudder flew to bits, and ragged holes gaped in her transom. An unlucky roundshot cut through the boarding party, leaving a dozen hands writhing on the reeling deck. They were close now, so close Noen could see the dark faces of the gun crews through the sterncastle windows. He fired at one, not with much hope of hitting him, but because it was bad tactics to permit your enemy to fire without being fired upon.

Zhironni's stern loomed above them. Noen felt they were hurtling toward a cliff, and it was no magical illusion, but the effect of the carrack's sheer size. The sakers banged like hammer blows, scouring *Zhironni*'s sterncastle windows with harquebus balls and scrap metal. Noen shoved his pistol back into his belt and grabbed the quarterdeck railing.

The ram struck with a shock that nearly knocked him off his feet. Only weakly braced by its angled backstays, the foremast snapped, fell against the carrack's stern, slipped, miraculously caught on the gilded moulding. As Dinnile's boarding party swarmed up the ratlines, a Zhir with a petronel appeared at the taffrail. Noen fired the remaining barrel of his pistol at him, shouted for the sakers' crews to follow, and leaped to the maindeck.

The ratlines were slack and thus hard to climb, lying almost against *Zhironni*'s stern gilding. Shattered window casements hung in shreds of iron, glass, and lead. A dead man slumped over the breech of one of the sternchasers. Noen hesitated, hardly daring to believe his eyes, put one foot on the gun muzzle, then the other. Half falling, he caught the window frame and swung into *Zhironni*'s stern cabin.

Outside, it had seemed impossible; but it was there. A circular, inlaid table was bolted to the floor in the center of the cabin; on it a small jade rabbit slid restlessly with the rolling of the ship, confined by the table rim. Only when he reached for it did Noen see the delicate girl who sat in shadow beside the cabin door.

"It is mine," she said. "But it could be ours."

The rabbit felt as cool as any river-washed stone.

"There are many isles—" She had risen and was coming toward him; her fingers toyed with a white rose. "—even in this little Sea of Luck. And there is the ocean beyond. We might master an isle and rule there together." Her face had a delicate beauty that made Oeuni and every other woman Noen had ever seen seem like a man. No, a beast.

The cabin door flew open, kicked by a nomad with a knife in one hand and a cutlass in the other. Noen said, "This woman is a prisoner, Myllikesh. Take her to our ship and put her in the wardroom. See that's she's well treated."

The nomad pointed to the rabbit with his cutlass. "Sir, move away your hand."

Noen picked up the rabbit.

"Sir, I do not desire that I kill you. But you must give that to me."

"You knew what it was," Noen said. "That was why so many of you signed on. You heard it had left Liavek by ship, and you knew our ships would be sent after it."

Myllikesh took a step nearer. "We told your stupid Guards of this ship, so your ships would be sent. Sir, I can kill you most easily before your sword is out. Put the rabbit down."

Noen did.

The girl said softly, "Do you know its secret, brave man of the wastes? Tell me."

Myllikesh turned to her, eyes flashing. "Yes, we know! Long ago our fathers were driven from S'Rian, but we remembered. Friends told us it was found, and we came!"

"Tell me. Now you will be a king." Her great eyes were fixed on Myllikesh; Noen was surprised at the pain that gave him.

"I am a king! Now I shall rule a rich land." The nomad laughed. "Rushing streams for us. Fruiting trees and fields of wheat! A great mage made this so S'Rians might have such a land, though the city was lost. But it was left behind, lost too. You must throw it down. That only! Then even rocks and sand will blossom."

The white rose flashed forward and vanished in the nomad's chest, then reappeared a red rose. He gasped and dropped his cutlass.

Noen hit the girl in the face with the twin barrels of his empty pistol. She staggered backwards; when she struck the canting cabin wall, she was an old man who grasped a scarlet dagger.

Myllikesh was half out the cabin window, one hand pressed to his wound, the other clutching the rabbit. Noen caught him by the neck and wrist, and the rabbit fell from his hand, tumbled down *Zhironni*'s towering stern, dropped between *Zhironni* and *Windsong*'s bow, and splashed into the sea.

When it touched the water, it seemed to bounce—the upward bound of a hunted hare who tried to sight its pursuers. It struck the water again running, jumping and skipping from wave to wave, racing across the restless sea as if the sea were an upland meadow.

Behind it, seals lifted sleek heads and a thousand dolphins bowed. The sea itself grew dark with the tiny creatures on which the smallest fish graze, and the great whales; fish surged in silver shoals, swirling and leaping everywhere after the rabbit for as far as Noen's eyes could follow it, until the sound of their swimming entered *Zhironni*'s timbers and filled the cabin like the humming of bees.

"Wasted," Myllikesh whispered.

Noen thought of Syb and Su, of the unpainted fishing cottages on Minnow Island and the wretched shacks on Eel Island. "No," he said. "Not wasted."

But the rattle of the last breath was in the nomad's throat.

From *Windsong*'s taffrail, *Zhironni* seemed a seaworthy ship. Her mainsail, maintop, and mizzen were all drawing, and though she listed a bit and the twin streams of water spurting from the lee side showed where Dinnile had prisoners at work on the pumps, Noen decided *Zhironni* might well limp back to Liavek even if they met with squalls. A captain's share of prize money was a full quarter. That would not come to twenty thousand levars, he thought, but it might come close. Even damaged as she was, the big carrack should be worth sixty thousand at least.

"Rekkue!" he called to the midshipman of the watch. "Make signal: 'reduce sail for night.' "

"Aye, aye, sir."

"Tivlo! Reef the mainsail. We don't want to lose her in the dark."

"Aye, aye, sir!"

The big triangular mainsail dripped. It was a great advantage of the lateen rig, Noen reflected, that the crew did not have to go aloft to take in sail or let it out. Some of the hands Tivlo was directing had been Myllikesh's nomads; some were former slaves from *Zhironni*.

Rekkue told him, *"Zhironni* acknowledges, sir."

Noen nodded. "I'm going below to write my report. In my absence, you're officer of the watch. You're to call me if anything happens. *Anything,* understand? Call me at the end of the watch and I'll relieve you so you can get some sleep."

"Aye, aye, sir." Rekkue touched her forehead.

She would be an officer soon, Noen thought. She was fit for one already. As he went down the steps to the lower deck, he decided to announce her acting promotion to third mate in the morning, if everything went well that night. He ducked automatically as he entered his cabin, pulled out his chair and seated himself before his little writing desk.

Ler Oeuni said softly, "I hope you don't mind, sir."

He spun around. She was in his bunk, her face, her bandaged arm, and one bare shoulder visible above the blanket.

"It was lonesome in the wardroom with Dinnile gone," she whispered, "and I wanted to tell somebody how brave I was."

When he had kissed her, she added, "I'll bet you were brave too, Noen."

Beech Hill

"**B**UBBA GOES OFF BY HIMSELF LIKE THIS EVERY YEAR—don't you, Bubba?" So Maryanne had said, and looked venomously at Bobs. He recalled it as he sat in Beech Hill pretending to read, his legs primly together, his back (because, no longer young, it hurt if he sat on his spine) straight.

"I suppose he needs it. Uh . . . needs the rest." Thus Mrs. Hilliard, a friend of Maryanne's friend Mrs. Main.

"That's what I always say. I say: 'Bubba, God knows you work hard all year. We don't have much money, but you go off by yourself like you always do and spend it. I can get around in my chair perfectly well, and anyway Martha Main will come over to look after me. Nobody ought to have to take care of a cripple forever, but if it wasn't for Martha I don't know what I'd do.' "

Mrs. Hilliard had asked, "Where do you go, Mr. Roberts?"

Someone came in, and Bobs looked up and saw the Countess, black hair stretched tight around her after-midnight face. His watch said seven and he wondered if she had been up all night.

At seven, fifty-one weeks of the year, he was at work. He looked at the watch again. Twelve hours later he and Maryanne had dinner, again at seven. Afterwards he read while she watched TV. At six he would get up, and at seven relieve the night man.

Bishop came in, followed by a young man Bobs had not seen before. The young man was pale and nervous, Bishop portly and assured behind mustache, beard, eyebrows, and tumbling iron-gray forelock. "You're among us early this morning, Countess."

"I could not sleep. It is often so."

Bishop nodded sympathetically, then gestured toward the young man beside him. "Countess, may I present Dr. Preston Potts. Dr. Potts is a physicist and mathematician—the man who developed the lunar forcing vectors. You may have heard of him . . ."

More formally he said to Potts, "Dr. Potts, the Countess Esterhazy."

"I *have* heard of Dr. Potts, and I am charmed." The Countess held out a limp hand glittering with rhinestones. "I at first thought you were a doctor who might give me something for my not sleeping, but I am even so charmed."

Potts stammered: "Our a-a-astronauts have trouble sleeping too. If you imagine you're in space it might help you f-f-feel better about it."

The Countess answered, "We are all in space always, are we not?" and smiled her sleepy smile.

For a moment Potts stood transfixed, then managed to smile weakly in return. "You are something of a mathematician yourself. Yes, we are all in space or we would not exist—perhaps that's why we sometimes have trouble sleeping."

"You are so clever."

"And this is Mr. Roberts," Bishop continued, drawing Potts away from the Countess. "I cannot tell you a great deal about Mr. Roberts's activities, but he is one of the men who protect the things you discover."

Bobs stood to shake hands and added: "And who occasionally arrange that you discover what someone else has just discovered on the other side. Please to meet you, Dr. Potts. I know your work."

"Looks a lot like Bond, doesn't he?" he overheard Bishop say as the two of them left him. "But he's different in one respect. Our Mr. Roberts is the real thing."

Bobs sat down again. There was a Walther PPK under his

left arm, but it was no help and he felt unsettled and a little afraid. Behind him, at the far end of the big room, Bishop was introducing Potts to someone else—Claude Brain, the wild animal trainer, from the sound of the voice—and he caught the words, "Welcome to Beech Hill."

Each year he came to Beech Hill by bus, with an overnight stop. The stop had, itself, become a ritual. In fact the entire trip from the moment he carried his bag out of the apartment was marked with golden milestones, events that were—so strong was the anticipation of pleasure—pleasures themselves.

To enter the terminal and buy his ticket; to sit on the long wooden bench with the travel-worn, with the servicemen on leave, with the young, worried, cheaply clothed women with babies, and the silent, shabby men (like himself) he always hoped were going to their own Beech Hills, but who, in their misery, could not have been.

To sit with his bag between his feet, then carry it to be stowed in the compartment under the bus's floor. To zoom the air-conditioned roads and watch the city slip behind. The hum of the tires was song, and if he were to fall asleep on the bus (he never did) he would know even sleeping where he was.

And the stop. The hotel. A small, old, threadbare hotel; they never put him in the same room twice, but he could walk the corridors and recall them all: *Here's where, coming, in '62. There in '63. The fourth floor in '64.* He stayed at the hotel on the return trip as well, but the rooms, even last year's room, faded.

Checking in; he always asked if they had his reservation, and they always did. A card to sign—*R. Roberts, address, no car.*

And the room: a small room on an airshaft, bright papered walls with big flowers, a ceiling fixture with a string. And the door, a solid door with a chain and deadbolt. *Snick! Rattle!* His bag on the bed. Secret papers on the bed. *Not NOW, Maryanne, I'm not decent.* His hand on the Luger. If Maryanne should see those—It would be his duty, and the Organization would cover for him as it always did . . . Suppose she hadn't heard him? *Come in—Snickback!—Maryanne, Rattle!* His own sister, they say. There's devotion for you!

He always changed at the hotel the day he arrived, not waiting until morning. This time too, he had removed his old workaday clothes, showered, and, glowing, gone to the open bag for new, clean underwear bought for the occasion—and executive length hose. His shirt of artificial fabrics that looked like silk stayed new from year to year; he wore it only at Beech Hill. His slacks were inexpensive, but never before worn.

He was proud of his jacket, though it had been very cheap; an old Norfolk jacket, much abused (by someone else) but London made. The elbows had been patched with leather; the tweed smelled faintly of shotgun smoke, and the pockets were rubber lined for carrying game. *Handy in my line of business.* Just the sort of coat the right sort of man would continue to wear though it was worn out, or nearly. Also just the sort to effectively conceal his HSc Mauser in his shoulder holster—at Beech Hill.

But not at the stop. Regretfully he left the Mauser in his bag; but this too was part of the ritual. The empty holster beneath his arm, the strange clothes, told him where he was. Even if he had fallen asleep . . . (but he never did.)

There were restaurants near the hotel, and he ate quietly a meal made sumptuous by custom. There was a newsstand where he stopped for a few paperbacks, and, next door, a barbershop.

A haircut was not part of the ritual, but it might well be. He might, in years to come, remember this as the year when he had first had his hair cut on the way to Beech Hill. The shop was clean, busy, but not too busy, smelling of powder and alcoholic tonics. He stepped inside, and as he did a customer was stripped of his striped robe and dusted with the whisk. "You're next," the barber said.

Bobs looked at another (waiting) customer, but the man gestured wordlessly toward the first chair.

"Chin up, please. Medium on the sides?"

"Fine."

There was a television, not offensively loud, in a corner. The news. He watched.

"Don't move your head, sir."

The man on the screen was portly, expensively dressed, intelligent looking. A newsman, microphone in hand, spoke deferentially:—*a strike . . . , pollution . . . , Washington? . . .*

"I know that man." Bobs twisted in the chair. "He's a billionaire."

"Damn near. He sure enough owns a lot around here."

When Bobs paid him the barber said, "You feel okay, sir?"

The next day he dropped the black Beretta into its holder. On the bus the weight of it made him feel for a moment (he had closed his eyes) that the woman next to him was leaning against him. The woman next to him became Wally Wallace, a salesman he had once known, the man who had introduced him to Beech Hill; but that seemed perfectly natural. Opposite, so that the four of them were face to face as passengers had once sat in trains, were Bishop and his wife, pretending not to know them. This was courtesy—the Bishops never spoke to anyone until it had been definitely decided what they were going to be. He knew that without being told.

"You," Wally began. Bobs suddenly realized that he (Bobs) was ten years younger, and the wistful thought came that he would not remain so. ". . . can't beat this place. There's nothing like it." Bobs had wondered if Wally were not getting a commission—or at least a reduction in his own rate—for each new guest he brought. Wally had returned the second year, but never after that. Lost in the jungle he loved.

When Bishop and Potts and Claude Brain were gone (they had said something about a morning swim) he remarked to the Countess, "I saw a friend of ours on television. On my way up." He mentioned the billionaire's name.

"Ah," said the Countess. "Such a nice man. But," (she smiled brilliantly) "married."

"He was here when I first came."

At first he thought the Countess was no longer listening to him, then he realized that he had not spoken aloud. The billionaire *had* been there when he had first come. Very young, as everyone had said, to have made so much money. Great drive.

And yet perhaps—he tried to push the thought back, but it came bursting in anyway, invading his consciousness like the wind entering a pauper's shack: *perhaps he had made it.*

He had wanted to badly. You could see it in his eyes. And then—

What fun! What sport to return, posing with the others year after year.

The bastard.

The bastard. Was he here yet?

He could not sit still. The fear was on him, and he stalked out of the immense house that was Beech Hill, hardly caring where he was going. The ground sloped down, and ahead the clear water of the lake gleamed. Half a dozen guests were swimming there already: drama critic, heart surgeon, the madame of New York's most exclusive brothel. Fashion designer, big game hunter, test pilot. He stood and watched them until Claude Brain, coming up behind him, said, "No dip today, Roberts?"

"I don't usually," Bobs replied, turning. Brain was in trunks. His arms were horribly scarred, and there were more scars on his chest and belly.

His eyes followed Bobs'. "Tiger," he said. "I was lucky."

"I guess it's hard to become a wild animal man? Hard to get started?"

Brain nodded. "There aren't many spots. A few places around Hollywood, and a few shows. You try and try, but most of them have already had so much trouble with greenhorns they won't touch you."

"I'll bet," Bobs said sympathetically.

"Hell, I did everything. For years. Sold shoes, worked in a factory. Bought my own animals. First one was a mountain lion. Cost me three hundred and fifty, and I've still got him."

"I know how you must feel," Bobs said. He watched Brain go down into the water. His back was scarred too.

There was a path along the water's edge. He walked slowly, head down, until he saw the girl; then she looked at him and smiled, and he said, "Sorry. Hope I'm not intruding."

"Not at all," the girl said. "I should be over with the others, but I'm afraid I'm shy." She was beautiful, in the blond-cheerleader girl-next-door way.

"Your first season?"

She nodded.

"You're the actress then. Bishop said something about you when I checked in last night."

"Thanks for not saying *starlet*." She smiled again.

"The star. That's what Bishop called you. Have you made many pictures?"

"Just one—*Bikini Bash*. You didn't—"

Bobs shook his head. "But I will, the next chance I get."

"They say a lot of important people come here."

Bobs nodded. "To look at the nuts."

The girl laughed. "I get it. Beechnuts."

"Yeah, Beechnuts. Listen, I want you to do me a favor." He drew his pistol and handed it to her. "What's this?"

Puzzled, she looked at it for a moment, then laughed again. "A toy pistol?"

"You're sure?"

"Of course. It says right here on it: *British Imperial Manufacture,* and then: MADE IN HONG KONG."

He took the gun and threw it as far as he could out into the lake. She stared at him, so he said: "Remember that. You may be called to testify later," before he walked away.

Sightings at Twin Mounds

T HIS PUZZLING CASE PRESENTS SEVERAL
UNIQUE FEATURES; because it is of more than ordinary interest, I shall quote several of the documents in full; my
attention was originally attracted by the United Press Wire-
Service story below.

UFOs Spotted Over Park

Residents of upstate Duke County report brilliant blue and white
lights circling over Indian River State Park after midnight. On
several occasions hundreds of persons from nearby Colbyville are
said to have assembled outside the park to watch. According to a
State Police report, a patrol car was dispatched to the scene Wednes-
day night. No lights were observed, but the officers who entered the
park, which closes at six, discovered an incoherent man. The man
has been hospitalized.

The *Guide to American Parks* supplied the following:

Indian River. Site of moderately extensive mounds *c.* A.D. 1300.
Picnic and camping facilities (no showers). Boat trips on the Indian
River. Apparently a cult site, there are several mounds of interest—
Eagle Mound, Twin Mounds, Snake Mounds—surrounded by an
earthen wall which remains nearly complete. An Algonquin legend
has it that the site commemorates a raid on an Algonquin village by
Iroquois, in which all the Algonquins perished with the exception of
the chief's daughter, who fled into the forest pursued by the Iroquois
warparty. Encountering the wendigo, she begged it to defend her.
It killed many Iroquois braves before both were slain. When

avenging Algonquins drove off the raiding Iroquois, the chief's daughter and the wendigo were buried under the Twin Mounds. This legend may arise from the similarity of the hemispherical mounds to a woman's breasts.

That sent me to the public library, where the *Encyclopedia of Amerind Folklore* told what the wendigo was—or at least, what one was supposed to be.

wendigo, wiendigo, or *windigo* A giant ogre in the mythology of certain northeastern tribes. Hunters lost in the forest without food are thought to turn cannibal and, through the effects of eating human flesh, become wendigo, fearsome enemies of human beings possessing great strength and appearing and vanishing at will.

While I was at the library, I requested a week's copies of the *Colbyville Courier;* they arrived a few days later. Several carried half-jocular stories concerning moving lights and "giant spaceships" hovering over Indian River State Park. I quote only that which appears to me most significant.

STANLEY J. ROBAKOWSKI FOUND UNCONSCIOUS
Stanley J. Robakowski of Colbyville, an employee of the Brewster Paper Company, was discovered in Indian River Park last night by troops investigating lights observed on park property. Police state that Mr. Robakowski was unable to account for his presence inside the park and allegedly appeared disoriented. After being administered a Breathometer test he was admitted to St. Joseph's Hospital. Asked whether Mr. Robakowski was thought responsible for lights observed at the park, a NYSP spokesperson stated that the police had no evidence to suggest that. Several witnesses stated emphatically that they had observed moving lights above the trees after police departed with Mr. Robakowski in custody.

After getting Stanley J. Robakowski's telephone number from Directory Assistance, I rang his apartment in Colbyville; no one answered. Saint Joseph's Hospital confirmed that he was still a patient but refused to put my call through to his room.

By this time I felt fairly sure that Stanley Robakowski was

a contactee, and I was very anxious to interview him; I drove to Colbyville the following day. Saint Joseph's informed me that Robakowski had been discharged nearly twenty-four hours before. I checked into a hotel and telephoned his apartment again. He answered and, though reticent, gave me his address and agreed to speak to me in person.

Here I must confess my own shortcoming—one I regret more than any other involving UFO studies: I was unable to locate Robakowski's apartment that night. I was in an unfamiliar city, it was raining (which kept those who might have provided me with directions indoors, besides reducing visibility) and the streets of Colbyville are dark and poorly marked. After two fruitless hours, I returned to my hotel room, telephoned Robakowski again, explained my difficulty, and asked whether it would be possible for him to meet me there.

He refused, saying that he had to return to work at seven the following day and intended to go to bed. I then requested an interview next evening, to which he agreed.

With a day to kill in Colbyville, I drove to Indian River State Park, where I saw the mounds and spoke to several persons who had seen lights over the park. All agreed that no lights had been present for the past two nights. They were described as very bright, usually white or blue-white, but occasionally yellow. One informant stated that they proceeded from what she termed a "wingless airplane"—that is to say, a torpedo-shaped flying object. She drew the object for me, her sketch showing a row of lights, much like the portholes of a ship, along one side of the object (Plate VI).

At seven I drove to Robakowski's apartment, having provided myself in the meantime with a four-cell flashlight with which to read building numbers. A fresh reason for my earlier confusion was soon apparent: I had been looking for an apartment building, while Robakowski's apartment was in fact the upper story of an old house, now provided with its own entrance. I had parked in front of the house and gotten out of my car before I noticed the shadow of what appeared to be an embracing couple thrown on the curtains. Thinking it better to leave them in solitude for a time, I drove to a nearby cafe, drank a leisurely cup of coffee, then telephoned the apartment, intending to ask whether it would be convenient for Robakowski to see me. There was no response.

I drove back to the apartment. Save for the absence of the amorous silhouette, everything appeared to be as I had left it; lights were still on in the front room and the curtains remained drawn. Admission was through a ground-level door leading to a steep, straight stairway. As I rang the bell, I could not help observing that this door was ajar.

No doubt I should not have done what I did. I can only say that I was extremely eager to speak with Robakowski, and at that point I was already afraid some danger had overtaken him. After ringing and knocking several times, I entered the apartment and discovered extensive bloodstains in the kitchen, bedroom, and hall. I called the police at once; Robakowski's body has never been found, and I am told that no arrest has ever been made.

Dr. Ernest Schwartz, who treated Robakowski during the time he was a patient at Saint Joseph's Hospital, has contributed an account to *The Journal of the American Psychiatric Society*. The brief section that I quote here is used with Dr. Schwartz's kind permission.

Stan Roland [the pseudonym by which Dr. Schwartz refers to Robakowski—Author] was a white male twenty-three years of age. He had been employed as a maintenance technician at a paper mill since leaving school. He appeared alert but confused, and at no time exhibited either hostility or aggression. There was no history of psychopathic or psychoneurotic disturbance.

Asked about the episode which brought him to the attention of the police, Roland said that he had gone to Indian River Park with friends in the hope of seeing lights that were occasionally sighted in the park at that time. After a wait of approximately an hour, during which the members of his party chatted and drank beer, Roland and another saw, briefly, a dim blue light moving in the area of the Twin Mounds; this was challenged by those who had not seen it. Armed with a wrench, Roland then climbed the fence surrounding the park (which is closed after dark) in order to investigate. He said that he had visited the park frequently in his boyhood and sporadically thereafter, and was intimately familiar with its geography.

Nevertheless, by his own account he would seem to have lost his way almost at once. He insisted that trails with which he was familiar had been "taken away," but that the heavily wooded area was, paradoxically, almost free of underbush, which is not in fact the case. He stated that he saw moving blue and white lights on several occasions but was never able to approach them closely.

At this point, Roland invariably became agitated, and the order of subjective events is unclear. "She ran into me in the dark." "I thought I heard somebody screaming off to my right—there was a lot of yelling, and all of a sudden this girl was holding onto me." "I was just walking along, trying to go fast, you know? And all of a sudden my arms were around her." There is no objective evidence for the existence of this mysterious young woman, who Roland said could not speak English and seemed terrified.

They ran though the park together, Roland said, until they were assaulted by invisible beings. Asked how he could know, in darkness, that the beings were invisible, Roland stated that it was not wholly dark and that he could dimly see the young woman beside him, but could at no time catch sight of their attackers, who were thus tactile and auditory hallucinations only.

Questioned regarding the outcome of this struggle with these invisible beings, Roland said that he had become separated from them and the young woman when he was detained by the police; but that he felt certain they and she were still searching for him. He described his attackers as making "little real quiet sounds," while the young woman called softly, something that sounded like "Where'd he go?" Reminded that he had said the young woman did not speak English, he declared that he did not think her words were in fact English, although they sounded something like the English phrase he repeated. He said that neither she nor those who had attacked them could see him now; nor could he see them.

And there the case of the sightings at Twin Mounds remains. UFO contactees have often reported being shadowed or threatened after their experiences were made public, most frequently by *men in black* (MIBs). Although I personally do not believe that Robakowski's attackers were MIBs, it cannot be denied that MIBs encountered in the woods at night might seem "invisible beings" to a frightened man. Reports of physical harm at the hands of MIBs are extremely rare, and murder almost unheard-of; and yet murder would appear to have taken place in the mysterious case of Stanley J. Robakowski.

Additional sightings in the vicinity of Indian River Park have been difficult to verify. Two years ago, an archeological excavation of the Twin Mounds was begun by a team from SUNY Brockport, although no report has been issued. All activity was suspended indefinitely when it was discovered that the site had been contaminated by "modern materials."

Continuing Westward

C ONTINUING WESTWARD UNTIL NEARLY
SUNDOWN we came to a village of stone huts. Earlier
it had been very hot, even with the wind from the airscrew in
our faces. The upper wing had provided a certain amount of
shade for me, but Sanderson, my observer, had nothing but his
leather flying helmet between his head and the sun, and I
believe that by the time we halted he was near delirium. Every
few miles he would lean forward, tap me on the shoulder, and
ask, "Suppose the landing gear goes too, eh? What then? What
shall we do then?" and I would try to shout something reassur-
ing over my shoulder as we jolted along, or swear at him.

Both the upper and lower wings had broken about midway
on the left. The ends of them and what remained of the
bamboo struts and silk trailed on the ground, the focal point
of the long plume of dust we raised. I was afraid the dust might
be seen by Turkish horse and wanted to get out and cut the
wreckage away; but Sanderson argued against it, saying that
when we halted it might be possible to effect some repairs.
Every few miles one or the other of us would get out and try
to tie it up onto the good sections, but it always worked loose
again. By the time we reached the village there wasn't much
left but rags and wires.

The sound of our engine had frightened the people away.
We stopped in front of the largest of the huts and I drew my
Webley and went up and down the village street looking into
doors while Sanderson covered me with the swivel-mounted
Lewis gun, but no one was there. A hundred yards off, camels

tethered in the scrub watched us with haughty eyes while we found the village well and drank from big, unglazed jars. It was wonderful and we slopped it, letting the water run down our faces and soak our tunics. Then we sat on the coping and smoked until the people, in timorous twos and threes, began to come back.

The children came first, dirty, very unappealing children with sad faces and thin or bow-bellied bodies; the smaller children naked, the larger in garments like short nightshirts, grey with perspiration and dust.

Then the women. They wore black camel's-hair gowns that reached their ankles, yashmaks, and black head shawls. Between shawl and veil their eyes looked huge and very dark, but I noticed that many were blind, or blind in one eye. They didn't touch us as the children had, or try to talk to us. They pulled the children back, whispering; and when they spoke among themselves, standing in small groups twenty yards away and gesticulating with flashing brown arms, the sound was precisely that of sparrows quarreling in the street, heard from a window several storeys high.

The men came last, all of them bearded, wearing grey or white or blue-dyed robes. They had daggers in their sashes, and although they never touched them we kept our hands on our revolvers. These men said nothing to us or to each other or the women, but stood around us in a half circle watching and, I thought, waiting. Only the children seemed really interested by our aircraft, and they were too much in awe to do more than stroke the hot cowling with the tips of their fingers. It came to me then that the scene was Old Testament biblical, and I suppose it was; people like this not changing much.

Eventually a man older than the rest came forward and began to talk to us. His beard was almost white, and he had a deep solemn voice like an ambassador on a state occasion. I looked at Sanderson, who claims to parley-voo wog, but he was as out of it as I. We waited until the old boy had finished, then pointed to our mouths and rubbed our bellies to show that we wanted something to eat.

It was mutton stew in rice when we got it, everything flavored strongly with saffron and herbs. Not a dish that would have appealed under normal circumstances, but these were far from that, and for a time I dug in as heartily as Sanderson, sitting crosslegged and dipping the stuff up with my fingers.

The chief and two of his men sat across from us, trying to pretend that this was a normal social dinner. More of the men had tried to crowd in at the beginning, but Sanderson and I had discouraged that, cocking our revolvers and shouting at them until all but these had left. It had resulted, as they say, in a strained atmosphere; but there had been no help for it. At close quarters in the hut we couldn't have managed more than the three of them if they had decided to rush us with their knives.

When we had eaten all we could, a sweet was brought out, a sticky pink paste neither of us wanted. Then strong unsweetened coffee in brass cups, and the chief's daughter.

Or perhaps his granddaughter or the daughter of one of the other men. We had no way of really knowing; at any rate a young girl in linen trousers and vest, with her fingers and toes hennaed red-pink and her eyes heavily outlined by some black cosmetic. Her hair was braided and coiled high on her head, bound and twined with copper wire and little black discs like coins, and she wore more tinkling junk, hundreds of glass things like jelly beans, around her neck and wrists and on her fingers. She danced for us, jingling and swaying, while an older woman played the flute.

In cafes I'd seen that sort of thing done so often, and often so much better, that it was absurd that it should affect me as it did. Perhaps I can make it clear: think of a chap who's learned to swim, and done it often, in tiled natatoriums, seeing the sort of pool a clear brook makes under a willow. Better: a dog raised on butcher's meat feels his jaws snap the first time on his own rabbit. I glanced at Sanderson and saw that, stuffed as he was with rice and mutton (the man has eaten like a pig ever since I've known him and is a joke in our mess), he felt the same way. Once she bent backwards and put her head in my lap the way they do, which gave me a really good look at her; she was a choice piece right enough, but there was one thing I must say gave me a bit of a turn. The little black thingummies I'd thought were coins were really electric do-hickies of some sort, though you could see the wires had been twisted together and nothing worked anymore. Even the glass jelly beans had wires in them. I suppose these wogs must have stolen radios or some such from the Turks and torn them up to make jewelry. Then she laid her head in Sanderson's lap, and looking at him I knew he'd go along.

They had pitched a tent for us near the plane, and after we had taken her out there the two of us discussed in a friendly way what was to be done. In the end we matched out for her. Sanderson won and I lay down with my Webley in my hand to watch the door of the tent.

In a way I was glad to be second—happy, you know, for a bit of a rest first. It had been bloody early in the morning when we'd landed to dynamite the Turkish power line, and I kept recalling how the whole great thing had flashed up in our faces while we were still setting the charge. It seemed such a devil of a long time ago, and after that taxiing across the desert dragging the smashed wings while mirages flitted about—a good half million years of that, if the time inside one's head means anything . . .

Mustn't sleep, though. Sit up. Now her.

She had taken off her veil when we had brought her in. I kept remembering that, knowing that no act however rash or lewd performed by an Englishwoman could have quite the same meaning that that did for her. She had reached up with a kind of last-gasp panache and unfastened one side of it like a man before a firing squad throwing aside his blindfold—a girl of perhaps fifteen with a high-bridged nose and high cheek-bones.

I had thought then that she would merely submit unless (or until) something broke through that hawk-face reserve. Sitting there listening to her with Sanderson, I knew I had been wrong. They were whispering endearments though neither could understand the other, and there was a sensuous sound to the jingle of the glass beans and little disks that made it easy to imagine her hands stroking an accompaniment to words she scarcely breathed. It seemed incredible that Sanderson had not removed the rubbish when he undressed her but he had not. After a time I felt I could distinguish the locations from which those tiny chimings came: the fingers and wrists, the ankles, the belt over the hips loudest of all.

It reached a crescendo, a steady ringing urgent as a cry for help, and over it I could hear Sanderson's harsh breathing. Then it was over and I waited for her to come to me, but she did not.

Just as I was about to call out or go over and take hold of her they began again. I couldn't make out what Sanderson was saying—something about loving forever—but I could hear his voice and hers, and I heard the ringing begin again. Outside, the moon rose and sent cold white light through the door.

They were longer this time; and the pause, too, was longer; but at last they began the third. I tried to stare through the blackness in the tent, but I could see nothing except when a wire or one of the glass beans flashed in the inky shadow. Then there was the insistent jingling again, louder and louder. At last Sanderson gave a sort of gasp, and I heard a rustle as he rolled away from her.

Half a minute and the jingling began again as she stood up; her feet made soft noises on the matting walking over to where I lay. She spoke, and although I could not understand the words the meaning was clear enough: "Now you." I holstered my revolver and pulled her down to me. She came willingly enough, sinking to a sitting posture and then, gradually it seemed to me, though I could not see her, lying at full length.

I ran my hands over her. In the half minute between Sanderson's gasp and the present I had come to understand what had happened; the only question that remained was the hiding place of her weapon. I stroked her, pretending to make love to her. Under the arms—no. Strapped to the calf—no. She hissed with pleasure, a soft exhalation.

Then it came to me. There is almost no place where a man will not put his hands when he takes a woman; but there is one, and thus this girl had been able to kill Sanderson after lying with him half the night.

A man will touch a woman's legs and arms everywhere, caress her body, kiss her lips and eyes and cheeks and ears. But he will not, if she is elaborately coifed, put his hands in her hair. And if he attempts to, she may stop him without arousing his suspicions.

She cried out, then bit my hands, as I tore away the disk-threaded wires, but I found it—a knife not much larger than a penknife yet big enough to open the jugular. I knew what I was going to do.

I threw the knife aside and used the wires to tie her, first stuffing my handkerchief in her mouth as a gag. Then with my revolver in my hand I stepped out into the village street, looking around in the moonlight. I could see no one, but I knew they were there, watching and waiting for her signal. They would be too late.

Back in the tent I picked her up in my arms, drew a deep breath, then burst out sprinting for the aircraft. Even with her arms and legs bound she fought as best she could, but I stuffed her into Sanderson's place. They would be after us in moments, but I squandered a few seconds on the compass, striking a lucifer to look at it though it was hopelessly dotty as usual, having crawled thirty degrees at least away from the north star. The engine coughed, then caught, as I spun the airscrew; and before the aircraft could build up speed I had jumped onto the wing and vaulted into the cockpit. The roar of the exhaust shook the little village now. We rolled forward faster and faster and I felt the tail come up.

I knew she couldn't understand me, but I turned back to the girl shouting, "We'll do it! We'll find something tomorrow, bamboo or something, and repair the wing! We'll get back!"

Sanderson was running after us in his underclothes, so I had been wrong, but I didn't care. I had her and the aircraft, racing across the desert while meteors miles ahead shot upwards into the sky. "We'll do it," I called back. "We'll fly!" Her eyes said she understood.

Slaves of Silver

THE DAY I FORMED MY CONNECTION WITH MARCH B. STREET has remained extraordinarily well fixed in my memory. This shows, of course, that my unconscious—my monitor, I should say; you must pardon me if I sometimes slip into these anthropomorphic terms; it's the influence of my profession—What was I saying? Oh, yes. My monitor, which of course sorts through my stored data during maintenance periods and wipes the obsolete material out of core, regards the connection as quite important. A tenuous connection, you will say. Yes, but it has endured.

The hour was late. I had finished the last of my house calls and it was raining. I may be more careful of my physical well-being than I should be, but my profession makes me so and, after all, quite a number of people depend on me. At any rate, instead of walking to my quarters as was my custom I bought a paper and seated myself in a kiosk to read and await the eventual arrival of the monorail.

In twenty minutes I had read everything of interest and laid the paper on the bench beside my bag. After some five minutes spent watching the gray rain and thinking about some of my more troublesome patients I picked it up again and began (my room being, in several respects, less than satisfactory) to leaf through the real estate ads. I believe I can still remember the exact wording:

Single Professional wishes to share apt. (exp. clst.) Quiet hbts, no entrtnng. Cr8/mo.

The cost was below what I was paying for my room and the idea of an apartment—even if it were only an expanded closet and would have to be shared—was appealing. It was closer to the center of the city than was my room, and on the same mono line. I thought about it as I boarded, and when we reached the stop nearest it (Cathedral) I got off.

The building was old and small, faced with unlightened concrete time had turned nearly black. The address I sought was on the twenty-seventh floor; what had once been a single apartment had been opened out into a complex by means of space expanders, whose all-pervading hum greeted me as I opened the door. One had, for a moment, the sensation of tumbling head first into gulfs of emptiness. Then a little woman, the landlady, came fluttering up to ask what it was I wanted. She was, as I saw at once, a declassed human.

I showed her the ad. "Ah," she said. "That's Mr. Street, but I don't think he'll be wanting any of your sort. Of course, that's up to him."

I could have mentioned the Civil Liberties Act, but I only said, "He's a human, then? The ad said, 'Single Professional.' Naturally I thought—"

"Well, you would, wouldn't you," the little woman said, looking at the ad again over my shoulder. "He's not like me. I mean even if he is declassed, he's still young. Mr. Street's a strange one."

"You don't mind if I inquire, then?"

"Oh, no. I just don't want to see you disappointed." She was looking at my bag. "You're a doctor?"

"A bio-mechanic."

"That's what we used to call them—doctors. It's over there."

It had been a hat and coat closet, I suppose, in the original apartment. There was a small brass plate on the door:

MARCH B. STREET

CONSULTING

ENGINEER

&

DETECTIVE

I was reading it for the second time when the door opened and I asked, quite without thinking how it might sound, "What in the world does a consulting engineer do?"

"He consults," Mr. March Street answered. "Are you a client, sir?"

And that was how I met him. I should have been impressed—I mean, had I known—but as it was I was only flustered. I told him I had come about the apartment and he asked me in very politely. It was an immense place, filled to bursting with machines in various stages of disassembly and furniture. "Not pretty," Mr. Street remarked, "but it's home."

"I had no idea it would be so big. You must have—"

"Three expanders, each six hundred horsepower. There's plenty of space out there between the galaxies, so why not pull it down here where we need it?"

"The cost, I should say, for one thing. I suppose that's why you want to—"

"Share the apartment? Yes, that's one reason. How do you like the place?"

"You mean you'd consider me? I should think—"

"Do you know you talk very slowly? It makes it damned difficult not to interrupt you. No, I wouldn't prefer a human. Sit down, won't you? What's your name?"

"Westing," I said. "It's a silly name, really—like naming a human Tommy or Jimmy. But the old 'Westinghouse' was out of style when I was assembled."

"Which makes you about fifty-six, confirmed by the degree of wear I see at your knee seals, which are originals. You're a bio-mechanic, by your bag—which should be handy. You haven't much money; you're honest—and obviously not much of a talker. You came here by mono, and I'd almost be willing to swear you presently live high up in a fairly new building."

"How in the world—"

"Quite simple, really, Westing. You haven't money or you wouldn't be interested in an apartment. You're honest or you'd have money—no one has more and better chances to steal than a bio-mechanic. When a passenger with a transfer boards the mono the conductor rips up the ticket and, half the time, drops it on the floor—and one is stuck to your foot with gum. And lightened concrete and plastic facades have given us buildings so tall and spindly-framed that the upper floors sway under the wind load like ships. People who live or work in them take to bracing themselves the way sailors used to—as I notice you're doing on that settee."

"You are an extraordinary person," I managed to say, "and it makes me all the more surprised—" And there I am afraid I stopped speaking and leaned forward to stare at him.

"Extraordinary in more ways than one, I'm afraid," Street said. "But although I assure you I will engage you as my physician if I am ever ill, I haven't done so yet."

"Quite so," I admitted. I relaxed, but I was still puzzled.

"Are you still interested in sharing my little apartment, then? Shall I show you about?"

"No," I said.

"I understand," Street said, "and I apologize for having wasted your time, Doctor."

"I don't want to be shown the door, either." Though I was upset, I must admit I felt a thrill of somewhat guilty pleasure at being able to contradict my host. "I want to sit here and think for a minute."

"Of course," Street said, and was silent.

Living with a declassed human (and there was no use in my deceiving myself—that was what was being proposed) was a raffish sort of thing. It was bound to hurt my practice, but then my practice was largely among declassed humans already and could not get much worse. The vast spaces of the apartment, even littered as they were, were attractive after years in a single cramped room.

But most of all, or so I like to think, it was the personality of Street himself which decided me—and the fact that I detected in him, perhaps only by some professional instinct not wholly rational, a physical abnormality I could not quite classify. And there was, in addition, the pleasing thought of surprising my few friends, all of whom, I knew, thought me much too stuffy to do any such outlandish thing. I was giving Street my money—half a month's rent on the apartment—when he froze, head cocked, to listen to some sound from the foyer.

After a moment he said, "We have a visitor, Westing. Hear him?"

"I heard someone out there."

"The light and tottering step is that of our good landlady, Mrs. Nash. But there is another tread—dignified, yet nervous. Almost certainly a client."

"Or someone else to ask about the apartment," I suggested.

"No."

Before I could object to this flat contradiction the door opened to show the birdlike woman who had admitted us. She ushered in a distinguished-looking person well over two meters tall, whose polished and lavish solid chrome trim gave unmistakable evidence, if not of wealth, then at least of a sufficiency I—and millions of others—would only envy all our lives.

"You are Street?" he asked, looking at me with a somewhat puzzled expression.

"This is my associate, Dr. Westing," Street said. "I am the man you came to see, Commissioner Electric. Won't you sit down?"

"I'm flattered that you know my name," Electric said.

"Over there past the nickelodeon," Street told him, "you'll see a cleared spot for tri-D displays. There are several cameras around it. Whenever a man I don't know appears I photograph the image for later reference. You were interviewed three months ago in connection with your request for expanders for the hiring hall, made necessary by the depressed state of the economy."

"Yes." Electric nodded and it was plain that Street's recital of these simple facts, accurate as it was, had depressed still further spirits already hovering at the brink of despair. "You have no conception, Mr. Street, of how ironic it seems that I should hear now—here—of that routine request for funds, and so be reminded of those days when our hall was filled to bursting with the deactivated."

"From which," Street said slowly, "I take it that the place is empty—or nearly so. I must say I am surprised; I had believed the economy to be in worse condition—if that is possible—than it was three months past."

"It is," Electric admitted. "And your first supposition is also correct—the hall, though not empty, is far from crowded."

"Ah," said Street.

"This thing has been driving me to the brink of reprogramming for six weeks now. The deactivated are being stolen. The police pretend to be accomplishing something; but it's obvious they are helpless—they're only going through the motions now. Last night a relative of mine—I won't name him, but he is a highly placed military officer—suggested that I come to you. He didn't mention you were a declassed human, and I suppose he knew that if he had I wouldn't have come, but now that I've seen you I'm willing to take a chance."

"That's kind of you," Street said dryly. "In the event I succeed in preventing further thefts by bringing the criminals to justice my fee will be—" He named an astronomical sum.

"And in the event further thefts are not prevented?"

"My expenses only."

"Done. You realize that these thefts strike at the very fabric of our society, Mr. Street. The old rallying cry, *Free markets and free robots,* may be a joke now to some, but it has built our civilization. Robots are assembled when the demand for labor exceeds the supply. When supply exceeds demand—that is, in practical terms, when the excess cybercitizens can't make a living—they turn themselves in at the hiring hall, where they're deactivated until they're needed again. If news of these shortages should leak out—"

"Who would turn himself in to be stolen?" said Street. "I see what you mean."

"Precisely. The unemployed would resort to begging and theft, just as in the old days. We already have—I hope you'll excuse me—enough of a problem with declassed humans. You yourself are obviously an exception, but you must know what most of them are like."

"Most of us," Street replied mildly, "are like my landlady: people who lost class because they refused death at the end of their natural lifespans. It's not very easy to learn to earn your living when for a hundred years of life society has handed you an income big enough to make you rich."

It wasn't really my affair, but I couldn't help saying, "But if you can help Commissioner Electric, Street, you'll be helping your own people in exactly this area."

Street turned his eyes—which were of an intense blue, as though his photosensors were arcing—to me. "Is that so, Doctor? I'm afraid I don't quite follow you."

Electric said, "I should think it's obvious. Surely the motive for stealing our deactivated workers must be the desire to use them as forced labor, presumably in a secret factory of some sort. If this is being done, the criminals are competing illegally with everyone trying to earn an honest living—including the declassed."

I nodded my emphatic agreement. The thought of an illicit factory, perhaps in a cavern or abandoned mine, filled with dim figures laboring without cease under the threat of destruction, had already come to haunt my imagination.

"Slaves of silver," I muttered half aloud, "toiling in the dark."

"Possibly," Street said. "But I can think of other possibilities—possibilities you might find more shocking still."

"In any event," Commissioner Electric put in, "you will want to visit the hiring hall."

"Yes, but not in company with you. I consider it possible that the entrance may be watched. Human beings do visit the hall from time to time, I assume?"

"Yes, usually to engage domestics."

"Excellent. Under what circumstances would you deal with such visitors personally?"

"I would not ordinarily do so at all, unless all my subordinates were engaged."

Street looked at me. "You seem to want to be a party to this, Westing. Are you game to visit the hiring hall with me? You must consider that you may disappear—for that matter we both may."

"Oh, no," Electric protested, "the disappearances occur only after dark, when the hall is closed."

"Certainly I'll come."

Street smiled. "I thought you would. Commissioner, we will follow you in one half hour. See to it that when we arrive your subordinates are engaged."

When the commissioner had gone I was able to ask Street the question that had been nagging at my mind during the entire interview.

"Street, for God's own sake, how was it you knew Commissioner Electric hadn't come about the apartment before Mrs. Nash had opened the door?"

"Be a good fellow and look in the drawer of the inlaid rosewood table you'll find on the other side of that camera obscura to the left of the tri-D stage, and I'll tell you. You ought to find a recording ammeter in there. We'll need it."

I didn't know what a camera obscura was, but fortunately the rosewood table was a rather striking piece and only one instrument was in its drawer, lying amid a litter of tarot cards and bridge score pads. I held it up for Street to see and he nodded. "That's it. You see, Westing, when someone arrives in answer to a newspaper ad he almost invariably—ninety-two point-six percent of the time, according to my calculation—carries the paper with him and shows it to the person who answers the door. When I failed to hear the telltale rattle of the popular press as our visitor addressed Mrs. Nash I knew there was little chance that he had come about the apartment."

"Astounding!"

"Oh, it's not so much," Street said modestly. "But get a move on, won't you? It wouldn't do to ride down in the same elevator with Electric—but on the other hand it's seldom a waste of askance to view a public official with it. We're going to shadow him."

Despite Street's suspicions, Commissioner Electric did nothing untoward that I could see while we followed him. To give him time to prepare for us, as Street said, we idled for a quarter of an hour or more at the window of a tri-D store near the hall. The show being carried on the display set inside was utterly banal and I could swear that Street did not give it even a fraction of his attention. He stood, absorbed in his own thoughts, while I fidgeted.

The hiring hall, when Electric guided us around it, we found to be a huge place; impressive from outside but immensely larger within and filled with the hum of expanders. The corridors were lined with persons of every age and state of repair—they stretched for slightly curved miles like the vistas seen in opposed mirrors. Gaping spaces showed where the disappearances had taken place, but, sinister as they were, in time they seemed a relief from the staring regard of those thousands of unseeing eyes. Street asked for data on each theft and recorded the date and the number of persons missing in a notebook; but there seemed to be no pattern to the crimes, save that all the disappearances took place at night.

At last we came to the end of that vast building. Commissioner Electric did not ask Street for his opinion of the case (though I could see he wanted to), nor did Street give it. But once we were fairly away from him, Street pacing impatiently alongside the sidewalk while I trotted to keep up, he broke forth in an irascible tirade of self-abuse: "Westing, this thing is as simple as a two-foot piece of aluminum conduit and I'm confident I know everything about it—except what I need to know. And I have no idea of how I'm going to find the answer. I know how the robots are taken—I think. And I believe I know why. The question is: Who is responsible? If I could get the patrol to cooperate—"

He lapsed into a sour silence, unbroken until we were once more back in the huge, littered apartment I had not yet learned to call "ours." Indeed, my arrangement with Street was so recent that I had not yet had an opportunity to shift my possessions from my old room or to terminate my tenancy there. I excused myself—though Street seemed hardly to notice—and attended to these things.

When I returned nothing had changed. Street sat, as before, wrapped in gloom. And I, reduced to despondency by his example and with nothing better to do in any case, sat watching him. After an hour had passed he rose from his chair and for a few moments wandered disconsolately about the apartment, only to return to the same seat and throw himself down, his face blacker—if that were possible—than before.

"Street—" I ventured.

"Eh?" He looked up. "Westing? That's your name, isn't it? You still here?"

"Yes. I've been watching you for some time. While I realize you have, no doubt, a regular medical advisor, you were once kind enough to say that you might call me. On the strength of that—"

"Well, out with it, man. What is it?"

"There will be no fee, of course. I was going to say that though I don't know what means of chemical reality enhancement you employ, it would appear to me that it has been a considerable time—"

"Since my last fix? Believe me, it has." He laughed, a reaction I thought encouraging.

"Then I would suggest—"

"I don't use drugs, Westing. None at all."

"I didn't mean to suggest anything strong—just a few pinks, say, or—"

"I mean it, Westing. I don't use pinks. Or blues. Or even whites. I don't use anything except food, and little enough of that, water and air."

"You're serious?"

"Absolutely."

"Street, I find this incredible. We were taught at medical school that human beings—being, after all, a species evolved for a savanna landscape rather than our climax civilization— were unable to maintain their sanity without pharmaceutical relief."

"That may well be true, Westing. Nevertheless, I do not use any."

This was too much for me to absorb at once and while I tried to encode it Street fell back into his former gloom.

"Street," I said again.

"What is it this time?"

"Do you remember? When we first met I said that I detected in you, perhaps only by some professional instinct not wholly rational, a physical abnormality I could not quite classify?"

"You didn't say anything of the sort. You may have thought it."

"I did. And I was right. Man, you don't know how good this makes me feel."

"I have some comprehension of the intellectual rewards attendant on successful deduction."

"I'm sure you do. But now, if I may say so, a too-avid pursuit of those rewards has led you to a severe state of depression. A stimulant of some sort—"

"Not at all, Westing. Thought is my drug—and believe me it is both stimulating and frustrating. My need is for a soporific, and your conversation fills the bill better than anything you could prescribe."

This was said in so cheerful and bantering a way, albeit with a barely perceptible touch of bitterness, that I could not resent it—and, indeed, the marked improvement this little spate of talk had brought to Street's mien emboldened me to continue at whatever risk to my vanity.

So I answered, "Your powers of concentration, admirable as they are, may yet be your undoing. Do you remember the quarter-hour we spent in front of a store window? Where the tri-D had such poor reception? I addressed you several times, but I would swear you heard none of my questions."

"I heard every one of your questions," Street said, "and since none admitted to intelligent responses I ignored them all. And that tri-D, if not of the most exquisite quality, was at least better than passable. I apologize if I sound peevish, but really, Westing, you must learn to observe."

"I am not an engineer," I replied, perhaps rather too stiffly, "and so I cannot say if the reception in fact was at fault—but acute observation is a necessity in my profession and I can assure you that the color stability of the set on display was abominable."

"Nonsense. I was looking directly at it for the entire time and I could, if necessary, describe each stupidity of programming in sequence."

"Maybe you could," I said. "And I don't doubt your assertion that you were watching with commendable attention while we waited outside the hiring hall. But you quite obviously failed to observe it when we *left*. You were talking excitedly, as I recall—and as you spoke we passed the window again. The actors were blushing—if I may use that expression here—a sort of reddish-orange. Then they turned greenish blue, then really blue, and finally a shade of bright, cool green. In fact, they went through that whole cycle several times just during the time it took us to walk past the window."

The effect of this perhaps overly detailed and argumentative statement on Street was extraordinary. Instead of countering with argument or denial, as I confess I expected, for a few moments he simply stared silently at me. Then he jumped to his feet and for half a minute or more paced the room in silent agitation, twice tripping over the same ball-clawed foot of the same late Victorian commode.

At last he turned almost fiercely back to me and announced: "Westing, I believe I can recall the precise words I addressed to you as we passed that display. I will repeat them to you now and I want you to tell me the exact point at which you noticed the color instability you mentioned. I said: 'Westing, this thing is as simple as a two-foot piece of aluminium conduit and I'm confident I know everything about it—except what I need to know. And I have no idea of how I'm going to find the answer. I know how the robots are taken—I think. And I believe I know why. The question is: Who is responsible? If I could get the patrol to cooperate—' at which point I broke off, I believe. Now, precisely where did you notice the reddish orange color you mentioned—I believe that was the hue you noticed originally?"

"To the best of my recollection, Street, it coincided with the word *believe*."

"I said, 'I know how the robots are taken—I think. And I *believe*—' and at that point you noticed that the figures in the tri-D illusion blushed a color you have described as a reddish orange. Is that correct?"

Dumbfounded, I nodded.

"Excellent. Among my other antiques, Westing, I have assembled a collection of paintings. Would it interest you to see them? You would be conferring a favor of no mean magnitude upon me."

"I don't see how—but certainly, if you wish."

"Excellent again; particularly if, while drinking in their loveliness, you would take the trouble to point out to me the shades which most closely match the four colors you saw when the tri-D malfunctioned. But please be most exact—if the match is not perfect, you need not inform me."

For an hour or more we pored over Street's pictures, which were astoundingly varied and, for the most part, in a poor state of preservation. In size they ranged from Indian miniatures smaller than coins to a Biblical cyclorama five meters high and (so Street told me) more than three kilometers in length. The greenish-blue long escaped us, but at last I located it in an execrable depiction of *Susanna and the Elders* and the art display was abruptly terminated. Street told me bluntly—his manner would have been offensive if it had not been so obvious that his mind was totally engaged on a problem of formidable proportions—to amuse myself and buried himself in an assortment of ratty books and dusty charts, one of which, as I particularly remember, was like a rainbow bent into a full circle, with the blazing colors melting into one another like the infinitesimal quantities in a differential equation.

While he pondered over these the hours of evening rolled past on silent rubber wheels. Others, their day's work done, might rest now; I waited. Humans, rich and fortunate or declassed, might sleep or busy themselves in those pointless naked tumblings which mean so little to us; Street worked. And at last I wondered if it might not be that we two were the only wakeful minds in the entire city.

Suddenly Street was shaking me by the shoulder. "Westing," he exclaimed. "I have it—let me show you." I explained that I had taken advantage of his concentration to edit my memory banks.

Street shrugged my mumblings aside. "Here," he said. "Look at this and let me explain. You told me, if you remember, that you saw a cycle of four colors and that this cycle was repeated several times."

"That's correct."

"Very well. Now observe. Has it ever occurred to you to wonder how *robots*—yourself included—speak?"

"I assume," I said with as much dignity as I could muster, "that somewhere in my monitor the various words of the English language are stored as vibration patterns and—"

"The Chinese system. No, I am convinced it must be something far more efficient. English is spoken with only a trifle more than sixty sounds; even the longest words are created by combining and recombining these—for example we might use the *a* as it appears in *arm,* the *r* as in *rat* and the *ch* from *chair* to describe our inestimable landlady, Mrs. Nash. Combined in one fashion they give us *char*—her profession— but rearranged in another they contribute *arch*—her manner."

"You mean that all of English can be stored in my central processing unit as a mere sixty-place linear array?"

"That is precisely what I've been saying."

"Street, that's marvelous! I'm not a religious man, but when I contemplate the ingenuity of those early programmers and systems analysts—"

"Exactly. Now, I do not know the order in which the various English sounds were listed, but there is an order which is very commonly used in the texts to which I have referred. It is to list the sounds alphabetically and, within the alphabetical sections, to order them from longest to shortest. Thus these lists begin with the long *a* of *ale;* followed by the half-long *a* of *chaotic;* and this is followed in turn by the circumflex *a* of *care,* so that the whole reads like a temperance lecture. What I have done here is to take these sounds and space them evenly along the visible spectrum." He held up a hand-drawn chart on which there were, however, no colors, but only a multitude of names.

"But," I objected, "only a few true colors exist and you said there are more than sixty—"

"A few *primary* colors," he returned, "but believe me, Westing, if the artists were to make up a palette containing every oil and watercolor known to them there would be a great many more than sixty. As you may remember, you described the four colors you saw as reddish-orange, greenish-blue, true blue—which is just like you, Westing—and bright, cool green."

"Yes."

"Afterward, when you pointed out these colors on canvas, I was able to identify them as scarlet lake, cyan blue, blue, and viridian. Please observe that on my chart these correspond to the consonant sound *p,* the consonant *h,* the short *e* heard in *end* and that *l* sound of *late.*"

I considered this remarkable statement for a moment, then

replied, "You seem to believe that someone is trying to communicate, using the colors of the tri-D; but I do not see that the sounds to which you say these colors correspond possess any significance."

Street leaned back in his chair, smiling. "Let us suppose, Westing, that you came in late as it were, to the message. Catching the last sound of a repeated word, you supposed it to be the first. In short—"

"I see!" I exclaimed, leaping up. " 'HELP!' "

"Precisely."

"But—"

"There's no more time to waste, Westing. I have only given this much explanation because I want you to be an intelligent witness to what I am about to do. You will observe that I have set up a tri-D camera before our viewing area, enabling me to record for my own use any image appearing there."

"Yes, you said something about that to Commissioner Electric."

"So I did. What I intend to do now is to code that store near the hiring hall and ask for a demonstration. At this late hour it seems improbable that anyone will be there but a robot clerk—and it's unlikely he will be implicated."

Street was pushing the coding buttons as he spoke and a clerk—a robot—appeared almost before he had finished the last word.

"I should prefer to deal with a human being," Street told him, displaying an excellent imitation of prejudice.

The clerk groveled. "Oh, I am sorry, sir. But my employers—and no person ever had better—have gone to snatch a few hours of deserved rest. If you would—"

"That's all right." Street cut him off. "You'll do. I'm interested in another tri-D and I want a demonstration."

"Very wise, sir. We have—"

"As it happens, I was passing your shop today and the set in your window looked attractive. I presume there would be a discount, since it's a demonstrator?"

"I would have to consult my masters," the clerk answered smoothly, "but I assume something might be arranged."

"Good."

"Is there any particular program—"

"I don't know what's on right now." For an instant Street feigned indecision. "Isn't *The Answer Man* always available?"

"Indeed he is, sir. Personal, Sexual, Scholarly, or Civil Affairs?"

"Civil Affairs, I think."

In an instant The Answer Man, a computer-generated illusion designed to give maximum reassurance in the field of civil affairs, appeared in the tri-D area.

He nodded politely to us and asked, "Would you like a general report—or have you specific fears?"

"I have heard rumors," Street said, "to the effect—well, the fact is that an old family servitor of mine is—uh—resting in the hiring hall. Is it quite safe?"

The Answer Man reassured him, but as he did so he (and indeed the entire illusion) blushed a series of colors as astonishing as it was—at least by me—unexpected.

"Names," Street prompted softly. "I must have names."

"I beg your pardon?" The Answer Man said, but as he spoke he coruscated anew with dazzling chromatic aberrations.

"I meant," Street returned easily, "that you would have to have my servant's name before you could properly reassure me. But it's really not necessary. I've heard—"

Abruptly The Answer Man vanished, replaced by the clerk robot.

"I'm terribly sorry," he said. "Something seems to be wrong with the color control. Could I show you another set?"

"Oh no," Street told him. "The trouble is in the network signal. Didn't you get the announcement? Sunspots."

"Really?" The clerk looked relieved. "It's extraordinary that I should have missed it."

"I would say," Street sounded severe, "that in your position it was your duty to have heard it."

"I can't imagine— About an hour ago, could it have been? I had to leave—only momentarily—to dispose of the surplus water created by my fuel cells, but except for that—"

"No doubt that was it," Street said. "I wish you a good evening, sir." He switched off the tri-D. "Westing, I've done it! I've got everything we need here."

"You mean that by going over the tapes you made and comparing them with your chart—"

"No, no, of course not," Street interrupted me testily. "I memorized the chart while you were asleep. The tapes are only for evidence."

"You mean that you understood—"

"Certainly. As well as I understand you now—though I must confess that before I heard that poor machine speak it had never occurred to me that the word *dread*, especially when given the slightly pre-Raphaelite pronunciation of our unfortunate friend, could result in such startling beauty."

"Street," I said, "you're toying with me. With whom are you communicating when you talk to those colors? And how were the deactivated robots stolen—and why?"

Street smiled, fingering a small cast iron "greedy-pig" coin bank he had picked up from the table beside his chair. "I am communicating, as I should think must be obvious, with one of the stolen robots. And the method of theft was by no means difficult—indeed, I'm surprised that it is not employed more often. A confederate of the thieves' concealed himself in the immensities of the hiring hall during the day. When all were gone he momentarily interrupted the flow of current to one of the expanders, with the result that the expander space returned to a position between the galaxies, carrying its contents with it. As you know, the exact portion of space taken by an expander is dependent on the fourth derivative of the sinusoidal voltage at the instant of startup, so it is most improbable that, upon being restarted a split second later, the expander should return the robots to their proper places. They are picked up instead by a deep-space freighter and eventually returned to Earth. The recording ammeter I contrived to fasten to the hall's main power supply while Electric was showing us around will tell us if anyone tries the little trick again, as well as convincing a court that might not otherwise believe my explanation."

"But the colors, Street? Are you trying to tell me that the National Broadcasting Authority itself is employing slave labor?"

"Not at all." Street looked grave, then smiled. I might almost say grinned at me. "The robots in the hiring hall are there because society can find no present use for them—but has it never occurred to you that the electronics they contain might themselves be useful?"

"You mean—"

Street nodded. "I do. A tri-D set requires considerable computing power: a quite complicated signal must be unscrambled almost instantly to produce the three-dimensional illusion. The central processing unit of a robot, however, would be more than equal to the task—and very economical, if it were free. Unfortunately—for them—the criminals made one mistake. A criminal always makes one mistake, Westing."

"They wired the speech centers to handle the color coding?"

"Precisely. I am proud of you."

I was so elated that I leaped to my feet and for a few moments paced the room feverishly. The triumph of justice—the chagrin of the criminal manufacturers! The glory that would be Street's and, to some degree as his friend, mine! At length a new thought struck me, coming with the clarity of the tolling of a great bell.

"Street—" I said.

"You look dashed, Westing."

"You have done society a great service."

"I know it—and the fee will be most useful. There is an early twentieth-century iron-claw machine in a junk shop over on four hundred and forty-fourth I've been lusting after. It needs a little work—the claw won't pick up anything now—but I think I can fix it."

"Street, it might be possible—Commissioner Electric possesses great influence—"

"What are you blathering about, Westing?"

"It might be possible for you to be reclassed. Have your birthright income restored."

"Are you insinuating, Westing, that you believe me to have been declassed for criminal activity?"

"But all human beings are born classed—and you're not old enough to have refused death."

"Believe me, Westing, my income is still in existence and—in a way—I am receiving it. You, as a bio-mechanic, should understand."

"You mean—"

"Yes. I have had a child by asexual reproduction. A child who duplicates precisely my own genetic makeup—a second self. The law, as you no doubt know, requires in such cases that the parent's income go to the child. He must be reared and educated."

"You could have married."

"I prefer to have a home. And no man has a home unless he is master of a place where he must please no one—a place where he can go and lock the door behind him."

This was what I had feared. I said, "In that case perhaps you won't want—I mean, with the money you'll be getting from Electric you won't need to share this apartment. I would quite understand, Street, really I would."

"You, Westing?" Street laughed. "You're no more in the way than a refrigerator."

The Rubber Bend

I T WAS A DARK AND STORMY NIGHT—not actually night but late afternoon, and raining buckets. I share an apartment with March B. Street, the human consulting engineer-detective, and I recall that when I came home that afternoon, Street ventured some deduction to the effect that it must be raining, since the water was still streaming off me and onto the carpet, and I remarked that it was a nice day out for ducks, a little witticism I have often found to have a remarkably calming effect on my patients, though of course—I am a bio-mechanic, you see—its use is somewhat dependent on the weather; though I am over fifty, my seals are still tight and I think I may boast that you won't find another robot my age with fewer rain leaks anywhere.

Where was I? Oh, yes. It was on a dark and stormy afternoon in October that I was first introduced to the weird and sinister business which I, in these reports, have chosen to refer to as *The Affair of the Rubber Bend.*

Street waited until I had dried myself and was about to sit down with the paper, and then said sharply, "Westing!"

I confess I was so startled that for an instant I froze in a sort of half-crouch with my hips perhaps four inches about the seat of the scuffed old Morris chair next to Street's antique telespectroscope; had I known at the time how significant that posture was to be, in the eldritch light of the disappearance of Prof. Louis Dodson and the haunting of—but perhaps I am in danger of anticipating my story.

"Westing," Street continued, "for goodness' sake sit down.

Hanging in the air like that, you look like a set of tin monkey bars flunking Darwin."

"It's only natural," I said, taking my seat, "for you humans to envy the somewhat greater coordination and superior muscular effectiveness we possess, but it is hardly necessary—"

"Quite. I'm sorry I startled you. But I had been thinking, and I want to talk to you. You are, are you not, a member of the Peircian Society?"

"Certainly," I said. "You know perfectly well, Street, that on the first Monday of each odd-numbered month I absent myself from this apartment—good lord, have I missed a meeting?" I had risen again and was actually trying to recall what I had done with my umbrella when I caught the error. "No, you're wrong for once, Street. This is October. October isn't—November is, of course, but today's Tuesday. Our meeting's five days off yet."

"Six," Street said dryly, "but I didn't say you were late for the meeting; I simply asked if you were still a member. You are. Am I not correct in saying that the purpose of the society is to discuss—"

In my eagerness I interrupted him. "To prove that the works signed 'Damon Knight' were actually written by the philosopher Charles Sanders Peirce, of course. And they were, Street. They were. It's so obvious: Peirce, the otherwise unknown founder of Logical Positivism—"

"Pragmatism," Street said.

"They are almost the same thing. Peirce, as I was saying, lived in Milford, Pennsylvania—a minute hamlet since buried under the dammed waters of the Delaware—"

"You don't bury things under water."

"—thus conveniently destroying certain evidence the historical establishment did not want found. Note these points, Street: a village the size of Milford could hardly expect one such man in five hundred years; it had—this is what we are supposed to believe—two in less than fifty. Knight—"

"Knight also lived in Milford?"

"Yes, of course. Knight appeared shortly after Peirce—

supposedly—died. Peirce, at the time of his supposed death, was being sorely hounded by his creditors. Peirce grew a thick beard, obviously to keep from being recognized later as Knight. Knight also grew a beard to prevent his being recognized as Peirce. Can't you see, Street . . ." I paused.

"You pause," Street remarked. "Has something struck you?"

"Indeed it has. You, Street, have become engrossed in this most fascinating of historical, scientific and literary puzzles. You will apply your immense abilities to it, and in a short time we will know the truth."

"No."

"No?"

"I only apply those abilities you have flatteringly called immense to puzzles which hold out some possibility of remuneration, Westing. I merely wished to know if you were still a member of the Peircian Society. You are, and I am content."

"But surely—"

"There is a favor I would like you to do for me—it may be rather an inconvenience for you."

"Anything, Street. You know that."

"Then I want you to live for a few days with a friend of mine—be his houseguest. It shouldn't interfere with your practice, and I'll set up a gadget to relay your calls."

"I could go to a hotel—"

"I'm not trying to get rid of you, Westing; it's your presence there I want—not your absence here."

"Street, does this have something to do with—"

"The Peircian Society? No, not at present; in fact, Westing, I wish you'd forget I ever mentioned that. Put it completely out of your mind. A friend of mine—his name is Noel Wide, by the way—wishes to have a good bio-mechanic near at hand in the evenings. Ordinarily he calls a neighbor of his, but the fellow is on vacation at the moment. He asked if I could suggest someone, and I told him I'd try to persuade you to fill in. If you are willing to go, I want you there tonight."

"Tonight?"

"At once. Collect your medical bag and emergency self-maintenance kit and be on your way."

"Street, you're not telling me everything."

"I am telling you everything it's politic to tell you at the moment, and it's important that you don't miss dinner at Wide's. If you are sincere in wanting to go, go now. Here—while you've been jabbering I've written out the address for you."

"Dinner? Street, you know it isn't necessary—we robots don't—"

Something in his look stopped me. I collected the accoutrements he had suggested and took my departure; but as I left I noted that Street, now calm again, had picked up the book that lay beside his chair, and as I read the title an indescribable thrill shot through me. It was *A for Anything*.

The address to which Street had dispatched me proved to be an old brownstone in a neighborhood that held a thousand others. It had once had, I observed as I plodded toward it through the downpour, a sort of greenhouse or conservatory on its roof, but this was now broken and neglected, and its shattered panes and rusted ironwork, dripping rain, looked as dejected as I felt. At my knock the door, which was on a chain-guard, was opened by a robot younger (or as Street would say, "newer") than myself. I asked if he was Mr. Wide.

He grinned mechanically, and without offering to unchain the door, replied, "He lives here, but I'm Arch St. Louis—you want in?" I observed that he sported a good deal of chrome-and-copper trim, arranged in a manner that led me to think better of his bank account than of his taste. In answer to his question I said, "Please," and when he continued immobile I added, "As you see, I'm standing in the wet—I'm Dr. Westing."

"Why didn't you say so?"

In a moment he had opened the door and shown me in.

"Here," he said, "I'll get you some red-rags to wipe yourself off with. Don't take the cold reception to heart, Doc; we have unpleasant company from time to time."

I stifled the impulse to remark that birds of a feather assemble in groups, and asked instead if it would be possible for me to see Mr. Wide, my host.

St. Louis glanced at his watch. "Five minutes, he's down in the plant rooms. He'll be up at six."

"The plant rooms?"

"In the basement. He grows mushrooms. Come on into the office."

I followed him down a short corridor and entered a large and beautifully appointed chamber fitted out as something between an office and a parlor. A small desk near the door I deduced to be his; at the other side of the room stood a much larger desk with a scattering of unopened correspondence on its top, and behind it an immense chair. I walked over to examine the chair, but my awed perusal of its capacious dimensions was interrupted by the labored sighing of an elevator; I turned in time to see a pair of cleverly disguised doors slide back, revealing the most bulky robot I have ever beheld. He was carrying a small basket of tastefully arranged fungi, and holding this with both hands so as (at least, so it seemed to me) to have an excuse to avoid shaking hands with me, he marched across the room to the larger desk, and seating himself in that gargantuan chair, placed the basket squarely before him.

"Mr. Wide," St. Louis said, "this is Doc Westing."

"A pleasure, Doctor," Wide said in a thick but impressive voice. "You have come, I hope, to stay until my own physician returns?"

"I'm afraid there has been a mistake," I told him. "I am a bio-mechanic, with no experience in robot repair. My patients—"

"Are human. Indubitably, Doctor. It is not for me, nor for Mr. St. Louis, that your services may be required. I frequently entertain human guests at my table."

"I see," I said. I was about to ask why his guests should require the services of a bio-mechanic when St. Louis caught my eye. His eloquent look told me more plainly than words could that I would be wise to hold my peace until he explained later.

"You are clearly fatigued, Doctor," Wide was saying. "Perhaps you will permit my associate to show you to your room, and afterwards give you a tour of the house."

I admitted I could do with some freshening up.

"Then I will expect you for dinner."

As the sliding doors of the elevator closed behind us, St. Louis grinned and gestured towards the control panel. "See those, Doc? Push one. Your room's on three."

I pressed the button marked 3. The elevator remained immobile.

"They're phonies; leave it to Arch."

Addressing no visible person he said loudly, "Take 'er down, Fritz. Plant rooms." The elevator began a gentle descent.

"I'm afraid," I began, "that I don't—"

"Like I said, the buttons are phonies. Sometimes the cops want to bother Mr. Wide when he's down in the plant rooms or up in the sack thinking great thoughts. So I herd 'em in here, press the button, they see it don't work, and I take off that access plate there and start playing around with the wires. They're dummies too, and it works good on dummy cops. Like it?"

I said I supposed such a thing must often be useful, which seemed to please him; he treated me to his characteristic grin and confided, "We call it the St. Louis con, or sometimes the old elevator con. The real deal is the house has a built-in cyberpersonality, with speakers and scanners all over. Just ask for what you want."

"I thought," I ventured as the elevator came to a halt, "—I mean, weren't we going up to my room?"

"I'm showing you the mushrooms first," St. Louis explained, "then you'll have a clear shot upstairs until dinner, and I'll have a chance to do some chores. Come on, they're worth seeing."

We stepped out into semidarkness; the ceiling was low, the room cool and damp and full of the smell of musty life. Dimly I could make out row upon row of greenhouse benches filled with earth; strange, uncouth shapes lifted blind heads from this soil, and some appeared to glow with an uncanny phosphorescence. "The mushrooms," St. Louis said proudly. "He's got over eighteen hundred different kinds, and believe me, he gets 'em from all over. The culture medium is shredded paper pulp mixed with sawdust and horse manure."

"Amazing," I said.

"That's why he wants you here," St. Louis continued. "Wide's not only the greatest detective in our Galaxy, he's also the greatest gourmet cook—on the theoretical end, I mean. Fritz does the actual dirty work."

"Did you say Mr. Wide was a detective?"

"I may have let it slip. He's pretty famous."

"What a striking coincidence! Would you believe it, St. Louis, my own best friend—"

"Small Universe, isn't it? Does Street cook too?"

"Oh," I said, "I didn't know you knew him; no, Street's hobby is collecting old machines, and scientific tinkering generally."

"Sometimes I wish Wide's was, but he cooks instead. You know why I think he does it?"

"Since no one but a human can eat the food, I can't imagine."

"It's those add-on units—you noticed how big he was?"

"I certainly did! You don't mean to say—"

St. Louis nodded. "The heck I don't. Add-on core memory sections. His design is plug-to-plug compatible with them, and so far he's sporting fourteen; they cost ten grand apiece, but every time we rake in a big fee he goes out and buys his brains a subdivision."

"Why, that's incredible! St. Louis, he must be one of the most intelligent people in the world."

"Yeah, he's smart. He's so smart if he drops something on the floor I got to pick it up for him. But it's the image, you know. He's eighty inches around the waist, so he figures he's got to do the food business. You ever hear of *Truffes et Champignons à la Noel Wide*? He makes it with sour cream and sauerkraut, and the last time he served it we almost lost two clients and an assistant district attorney."

"And he's giving one of these dinners tonight? I'm surprised that anyone would come."

St. Louis shrugged. "He invites people who owe him a favor and don't know; and then there's a bunch who'll turn up darn near regular—some of the stuff's pretty good, and it's a sort of suicide club."

"I see," I said rapidly checking over the contents of my medical bag mentally. "Am I correct in assuming that since, as you say, there is a great deal of cooking done in this house, you are well supplied with baking soda and powdered mustard?"

"If it's got to do with food we've got tons of it."

"Then there's nothing to worry—"

I was interrupted by the sound of the elevator doors, and Wide's deep, glutinous voice: "Ah, Doctor, you have anticipated me—I wished to show you my treasures myself."

"Mr. St. Louis tells me," I said, "that you have mushrooms from all over the Universe, as well as the Manhattan area."

"I do indeed. Fungi from points exotic as Arcturus and as homely as Yuggoth. But I fear that—great as my satisfaction would be—it was not to expatiate upon the wonders of my collection that I came." He paused and looked out over the rows of earth-filled benches. "It is not the orchid, but the mushroom, which symbolizes our society. I used to grow orchids—were you aware of that, Doctor?"

I shook my head.

"For many years. Then I acquired my eighth unit of additional core." Wide thoughtfully slapped his midsection—a sound deeply reverberant, but muted as the note of some great bronze gong in a forgotten catacomb of the temple of Thought. "I had no sooner gotten that unit up, than the insight came to me: *No one can eat orchids*. It was as simple as that: *No one can eat orchids*. It had been staring me in the face for years, but I had not seen it."

St. Louis snorted. "You said you came down here for something else, boss."

"I did. The client is here. Fritz admitted her; she is waiting in the front room with a hundred thousand credits in small bills in her lap."

"Want me to get rid of her?"

"There has been another apparition."

St. Louis whistled, almost silently.

"I intend to talk to her; it occurred to me that you might wish to be present, though Dr. Westing need not trouble himself in the matter."

A sudden thought had struck me: If, as it had appeared to me earlier that evening, Street had had some ulterior motive in sending me to this strange house, it was quite probable that it had to do with whatever case currently engaged Wide's attention. I fenced for some time. "Mr. Wide, did I hear you say 'apparition'?"

Wide's massive head nodded slowly. "Thirteen days ago the young woman's 'father,' the eminent human scientist Louis C. Dodson, disappeared. Since that time an apparition in the form of Dodson has twice been observed in his old laboratory on the three thousand and thirteenth floor of the Groan Building. Miss Dodson has retained me to investigate Dodson's disappearance and lay the phantom. You appear disturbed."

"I am. Dodson was—well, if not a friend, at least a friendly acquaintance of mine."

"Ah." Wide looked at St. Louis significantly. "When was the last time you saw him, Doctor?"

"A little less than two months ago, at the regular meeting. We were fellow members of the Peircian Society."

"He appeared normal then?"

"Entirely. His stoop was, if anything, rather more pronounced than usual, indicating relaxation; and the unabated activity of the tics I had previously observed affecting his left eye and right cheek testified to the continuing functioning of the facial nerves."

I paused, then took the plunge. "Mr. Wide, would it be possible for me to sit in with you while you question his daughter? After all, death is primarily a medical matter, and I might be of some service."

"You mean, his 'daughter,' " Wide said absently. "You must, however, permit me to precede you—our elevator is insufficiently capacious for three."

"He's hoping she'll object to you—that'll give him an excuse to threaten to drop the case," St. Louis said as soon as we were alone. "And that elevator'll hold five, if one of 'em's not him."

I was thinking of the death of my old acquaintance, and did not reply.

Alice Dodson, who sat on the edge of a big red leather chair in front of Wide's desk, was as beautiful a girl as I had ever seen: tall, poised, with a well-developed figure and a cascade of hair the color of white wine. "I assume," Wide was saying to her as St. Louis and I emerged from the elevator, "that that diminutive glassine envelope you hold contains the hundred thousand in small bills my cook mentioned."

"Yes," the girl said, holding it up. "They have been microminiaturized and are about three millimeters by seven."

Wide nodded. "Arch, put it in the safe and write her out a receipt. Don't list it as an addition to the retainer, just: 'Received of Miss Alice Dodson the sum of one hundred thousand credits, her property.' Date it and sign my name."

"I've already given you a retainer," Miss Dodson said, unsuccessfully attempting to prevent St. Louis's taking the envelope, "and I just stopped by here on my way to the bank."

"Confound it, madame, I conceded that you had given us

a retainer, and I have no time for drollery. Tell us about the most recent apparition."

"Since my 'father' disappeared I have entered his laboratory at least once every day—you know, to dust and sort of tidy up."

"Pfui!" Wide said.

"What?"

"Ignore it, madame. Continue."

"I went in this morning, and there he was. It looked just like him—just exactly like him. He had one end of his mustache in his mouth the way he did sometimes, and was chewing on it."

"Dr. Westing," Wide said, turning to me, "you knew Dodson; what mood does that suggest? Concupiscent? (We must remember that he was looking at Miss Dodson.) Fearful?"

I reflected for a moment. "Reflective, I should say."

Miss Dodson continued: "That's all there was. I saw him. He saw me—I feel certain he saw me—and he started to rise (he was always such a gentleman) and"—she made an eloquent gesture—"puff! He disappeared."

"Extraordinary."

"Mr. Wide, I've been paying you for a week now, and you haven't gone to look at the ghost yet. I want you to go in person. Now. Tonight."

"Madame, under no circumstances will I undertake to leave my house on business."

"If you don't I'm going to fire you and a hire a lawyer to sue for every dime I've paid you."

"However, it is only once in a lifetime that a man is privileged to part the curtain that veils the supernatural." Wide rose from his huge chair. "Arch, get the car. Doctor, my dinner for tonight must be postponed in any event; would you care to accompany us?"

During the drive to Dodson's laboratory I ventured to ask Miss Dodson, with whom I damply shared the rumble seat of

Wide's Heron coupe, her age. "Eight," she replied, lowering her eyes demurely.

"Really? I had observed that your attire is somewhat juvenile, but I would have taken you for a much older girl."

"Professor Dodson liked for me to be as young as possible, and I always tried to make him happy—you know, for a robot you're kind of a cuddle-bear."

It struck me then that if Miss Dodson were, in fact, to take Wide off the case, I might recommend my friend Street to her; but since for the time being Wide was still engaged, I contented myself with putting an arm gently across her shoulders and slipping one of my professional cards into her purse.

"As you see, Doctor," Wide explained when we had reached the three thousand and twelfth floor, "Dodson both lived and worked in this building. This floor held his living quarters, and Miss Dodson's—they shared most facilities. The floor above is his laboratory, and to preserve his privacy, is inaccessible by elevator. As this is your home, Miss Dodson, perhaps you should lead the way."

We followed the girl up a small private escalator, and found ourselves in a single immense room occupying the entire three thousand and thirteenth floor of the building. Through broad windows we could see the upper surface of the storm raging several miles below; but this was hardly more than a background, however violent and somber, to the glittering array of instruments and machines before us. Between our position by the escalator and the large clock on the opposite wall three hundred feet away, every inch of floor space was crammed with scientific apparatus.

"I left the lights *off*," Alice Dodson remarked in a shaken voice, "I know I did. You don't suppose that *he*—"

"There!" St. Louis exclaimed, and following the direction indicated by his outthrust finger, I saw a black-clad figure bent over a sinister machine in the center of the laboratory. While St. Louis muttered something about never going out on a murder case without a gun again, I seized a heavy isobar from a rack near the door.

"You won't need that, Westing," a familiar voice assured me.

"Street! What in the world are you doing here?"

"Earning my pay as a consulting detective, I hope. I am here at the instigation of Mr. Noel Wide."

Miss Dodson, still apparently somewhat shaken, looked at Wide. "Is this true?"

"Certainly. Madame, because you found me at my desk when you called, you supposed me inactive; in point of fact I was, among other activities, awaiting Street's report."

"You were working the crossword in the *Times*! Your house told me."

"Confound it! I said among other activities."

"Here, now," Street intervened. "Quarreling lays no spook. From the fact that you are here, Wide, I assume there has been some recent development."

"There has been another apparition. Miss Dodson will tell you."

"Since my 'father' disappeared," Miss Dodson began, "I have entered his laboratory at least once every day—you know, to dust and sort of tidy up."

"Pfui!" Wide interjected.

Seeing that both Street and Wide were giving Miss Dodson their complete attention, I took the opportunity to speak to Wide's assistant. "St. Louis," I asked, "why does he make that peculiar noise?"

"Every once in a while he gets too disgusted for verbal, and wants to write out a comment on his printer—"

"Why? Interior printers are fine for notes, but I've never heard of using them to supplement conversation."

"Oh, yeah? Did you ever try to say: °#@&!°!!?"

"I see your point."

"Anyway, he doesn't like women mucking around a house, but his printer don't work; he got clarified butter in it one time when he was trying to make *Currie Con Carne mit Pilz à la Noel Wide,* so when he tries to feed out the paper he makes that noise."

"You say," Street was asking Miss Dodson, "that when you saw him he was *sitting?* Where?"

"Right there," she said, indicating a low casual chair not far from us.

"But, as I understand, in both the earlier apparitions he was *lying down?*"

The girl nodded voicelessly.

"May I ask precisely where?"

"The f-first time—pardon me—the first time over on a day bed he kept over there to rest on. The s-second—"

"Please try and control yourself. Dr. Westing can administer medication if you require it."

"The second time, he was on a chaise longue he had put in for me near his favorite workbench. So I could talk to him there."

"And his behavior on these two occasions?"

"Well, the first time I had been so worried, and I saw him lying there on the bed the way he used to, and without thinking I just called out, 'Snookums!'—that's what I always used to call him."

"And his behavior? Give me as much detail as possible."

"He seemed to hear me, and started to get up . . ."

"And disappeared?"

"Yes, it was terrible. The second time, when he was on the chaise, I was carrying some dirty beakers and Erlenmeyer flasks over to the sink to wash. When I saw him there I dropped them, and as soon as I did he disappeared."

Street nodded. "Very suggestive. I think at this point we had better examine the day bed, the chaise longue, and that chair. Tell me, Miss Dodson, of the five of us, which is closest in height to the professor?"

"Why . . ." She hesitated for a moment. "Why, Dr. Westing, I suppose."

"Excellent," said Street. We all trooped after him as he crossed the huge laboratory to the day bed Alice Dodson had indicated. "Westing," Street murmured, "if you will oblige me."

"But what is it you wish me to do?"

"I want you to lie down on that bed. On his back, Miss Dodson?"

"More on his side, I think."

"And try," St. Louis put in, "to look like a genius, Doc." Wide shushed him.

"Don't hesitate to arrange his limbs, Miss Dodson," Street told her; "this is important. There, is that satisfactory?"

The girl nodded.

Street whipped a tape rule from his pocket and made a series of quick measurements of my position, jotting down the results on a notepad. "And now, Miss Dodson, please give me the date and time when you saw the professor here—as exactly as possible."

"October twelfth. It was about ten-twenty."

"Excellent. And now the chaise."

At the chaise longue we repeated the same procedure, Miss Dodson giving the date and time as October 18th, at ten minutes to eleven.

When I had been measured in the chair as well, Street said, "And today is October twenty-fifth. At what time did you see the professor?"

"It was about one o'clock this afternoon."

While Street scribbled calculations on his pad, Wide cleared his throat. "I notice, Street, that the time of this most recent apparition would seem to violate what might earlier have appeared to be an invariable rule; that is, that Dodson's ghost appeared at or very nearly at ten-thirty in the morning."

Street nodded. "If my theory is correct, we shall see that those significant-looking times were mere coincidences, arising from the fact that it was at about that time each day that Miss Dodson entered this room. You did say, did you not, Miss Dodson, that you came *every day*?"

The girl shook her head. "I suppose I did, but actually the

first apparition frightened me so much that I didn't come again until—"

"Until the eighteenth, when you saw him the second time. I suspected as much."

"Street," I exclaimed, "you understand this dreadful business. For heaven's sake tell us what has been happening."

"I shall expound my theory in a moment," Street replied, "but first I intend to attempt an experiment which, should it succeed, will confirm it and perhaps provide us with valuable information as well. Miss Dodson, your 'father'—like myself—dabbled in every sort of science, did he not?"

"Yes, at least . . . I think so."

"Then is there such a thing as a wind tunnel in this laboratory? Or any sort of large, powerful fan?"

"He—he was interested in the techniques air-conditioning engineers use to make their systems as noisy as possible, Mr. Street. I think he had a big fan for that."

After a ten-minute search we found it, a powerful industrial-grade centrifugal fan. "Exactly what we need," Street enthused. "St. Louis, you and Westing take the other side of this thing. We want to set it up on the lab bench nearest the escalator."

When we had positioned it there, Street turned to the girl and said, "Miss Dodson, at this point I require your fullest cooperation—the success of this experiment depends primarily upon yourself. I have placed the fan where you see it, and I intend to spike the base to the top of the bench and permanently wire the motor to make it as difficult as possible for anyone to disconnect. I want your solemn oath that you will not disconnect it, or interfere with its operation in any way; and that you will exert your utmost effort to prevent any other person whatsoever from doing so before November seventh."

"You think," the girl said in so low a tone that I could scarcely make out the words, "that he is still alive, don't you?"

"I do."

"If this fan runs all that time, will it bring him back to us?"

"It may help."

"Then I promise."

"Even should the professor be restored to you, it must remain in operation—do you understand? It might be wise, for example, to persuade him to take a brief holiday, leaving the fan untouched."

"I will do my best," the girl said. "He likes the seaside."

Street nodded, and without another word walked to the wall, threw one of the main circuit breakers, and began soldering the fan-motor leads into a 220-volt utility circuit. Under Wide's direction St. Louis and I found hammers and a gross of heavy nails, with which we secured the base to the benchtop.

"Now," Street announced when all our tasks were complete, "once again I shall require cooperation—this time from every one of you. I shall stand here at the circuit breaker. The rest of you must scatter yourselves over this entire laboratory, each taking a section of it as his own responsibility. When I turn on the fan, things will begin to blow about. What we are looking for will, I think, be a slip of notebook paper, and when you observe it, it will be at a distance of about seventy-six centimeters from the floor. Seize it at once—if you wait for it to settle we are lost."

We did as he asked, and no sooner was the last of us in position than the huge fan sprang into life with hurricane force. A tremendous wind seemed to sweep the entire laboratory, and several pieces of light glassware went over with a crash.

Keeping my eyes fixed, as Street had suggested, at a height of seventy-six centimeters about the floor, I at once observed a sheet of paper fluttering in the machine-made wind. I have often observed that a scrap of paper, blown about, will seem to appear when its surface faces me and disappear when it is edge-on, and for an instant I assumed that the peculiar character of this one stemmed from a similar cause; then I realized that this was not the case—the sheet was, in fact, *actually disappearing and reappearing* as it danced in the gale. Street and I both dived for it at once. He was a shade the quicker; for a split second I saw the tips of his fingers vanish as though amputated by some demonic knife; then he was waving the paper overhead in triumph.

"Street!" I exclaimed, "you've got it! What is it?"

"There is no need to shout, Westing. If you'll step back here behind the inlet we can talk quite comfortably. I was relying upon a brilliant scientist's habitual need to reduce his thoughts to paper, and it has not failed me."

"What is it?" I asked. "Can I see it?"

"Certainly," Street said, handing me the paper. Miss Dodson, Wide, and St. Louis crowded around.

The note read:

$$160 \text{ cm}—4{:}00$$
$$159.5—2{:}00$$
$$159.0—12{:}00$$

$$d = 14{,}400 \text{ sec/cm} \times h$$

"Brief," Street remarked, "but eminently satisfying. The great scientist's calculations agree astonishingly well with my own."

"But, Street," I protested, "it doesn't tell us anything. It's only a formula."

"Precisely the way I have always felt about those prescriptions of yours, Westing."

Wide said, "I think it's time you reported, Street."

"It will take only a few moments now for me to begin the rescue of Professor Dodson," Street told him. "And then we will have some minutes in which to talk. Have you ever practiced yoga, Mr. Wide? No? a pity."

Before our astonished eyes Street proceeded to stand on his head, assuming the posture I believe is known as "The Pole." We heard him say in a distinct voice, "When you grow tired of this, Professor, you have only to use the escalator. Use the escalator." Then with the agility of an acrobat he was upright again, slightly red of face.

"I believe, sir," Wide said, "that you owe us an explanation."

"And you shall have it. It occurred to me today, while I sat in the lodgings I share with Dr. Westing, that Professor Dodson's disappearance might be in some way connected with his membership in the Peircian Society. That he was a member was stated in the dossier you passed on to me, Wide, as you may recall."

Wide nodded.

"I began my investigation, as Dr. Westing can testify, by rereading the complete works of Peirce and Knight, keeping in mind that as a Peircian Dodson ardently believed that the persecuted philosopher had arranged his own supposed death and reappeared under the *nom de guerre* of Knight; certainly, as the Peircians point out, a suitable one—and particularly so when one keeps in mind that a knight's chief reliance was upon that *piercing* weapon the lance, and that Knight was what is called *a freelance*.

"I also, I may say, kept before me the probability that as both a Peircian and as a man of high intellectual attainments Dodson would be intimately familiar with what is known of the life and work of both men."

"Do you mean to say," I exclaimed, "that your reading led you to the solution of this remarkable case?"

"It pointed the way," Street acceded calmly. "Tell me, Westing, Wide, any of you, what was Charles Sanders Peirce's profession?"

"Why, Street, you mentioned it yourself a moment ago. He was a philosopher."

"I hope not. No, poor as that shamefully treated scholar was, I would not wish him in so unremunerated a trade as that. No, gentlemen—and Miss Dodson—when his contemporaries put the question to Peirce himself, or to his colleagues, the answer they received was that Peirce was a physicist. And in one of Knight's books, in an introduction to a piece by another writer, I found this remarkable statement: *It deals with one of the most puzzling questions in relativity, one to which Einstein never gave an unequivocal answer: If all four space-time dimensions are equivalent, how is it that we perceive one so differently from the rest?* That question is sufficiently intriguing by itself—conceive of the fascination it must have held for Dodson, believing, as he did, that it had originated in the mind of Peirce."

"I begin to see what you are hinting at, Street," Wide said slowly, "but not why it affected Dodson more because he thought Peirce the author."

"Because," Street answered, "Peirce—Peirce the physicist—was the father of pragmatism, the philosophy which specifically eschews whatever cannot be put into practice."

"I see," said Wide.

"Well, I don't," announced St. Louis loudly. He looked at Miss Dodson. "Do you, kid?"

"No," she said, "and I don't see how this is going to help Sn—the professor."

"Unless I am mistaken," Street told her, "and I hope I am not, he no longer requires our help—but we can wait a few moments longer to be sure. Your 'father,' Miss Dodson, decided to put Knight's remark to a practical test. When you entered the room this evening, I was in the act of examining the device he built to do it, and had just concluded that that was its nature. Whether he bravely but foolhardily volunteered himself as his own first subject, or whether—as I confess I think more likely—he accidentally exposed his own person to its action, we may never learn; but however it came about, we know what occurred."

"Are you trying to say," I asked, "that Dodson discovered some form of time travel?"

"We all travel in time, Westing," Street said gravely. "What Professor Dodson did—he had discovered, I may add parenthetically, that the basis for the discrimination to which Knight objected was physiological—was to bend his own perception of the four dimensions so that he apprehended verticality as we do duration, and duration as we do verticality."

"But that formula," I began, "and the note itself—"

"Once I understood Dodson's plight," Street explained,

"the question was quantitative: How was vertical distance—as seen by ourselves—related to duration as perceived by Dodson? Fortunately Miss Dodson's testimony provided the clue. You will remember that on the twelfth she had seen Dodson lying on a day bed, this being at approximately ten-thirty in the morning. On the eighteenth, six days later but at about the same time, she saw him on her chaise longue. A moment ago I measured your position, with you posed as the missing man had appeared, but I still did not know what portion of the body governed the temporal displacement. The third apparition, however, resolved that uncertainty. It took place seven days and two hours and ten minutes after the second. Dodson's feet were actually lower this time than they had been in his first two appearances; his center of gravity was scarcely higher than it had been when he had half reclined on the chaise; but his head was considerably higher—enough to account nicely for the time lapse. Thus I located the 'temporal determinant'—as I have been calling it to myself—in the area of the frontal lobes of the brain. When you were lying on the day bed, Westing, this spot was fifty centimeters from the floor; when you were in the chaise, seventy-four centimeters; and when you sat in the low chair, ninety-two and one half centimeters. From these figures an easy calculation showed that one centimeter equaled four hours of duration. Dodson himself arrived at the same figure, doubtless when he noted that the hands of that large clock on the wall appeared to jump when he moved his head. As a true scientist he expressed it in the pure cgs system: vertical displacement times fourteen thousand four hundred seconds per centimeter equals duration."

"And he wrote it on that slip of paper."

Street nodded. "At some time in our future, since if it had been in the past we could not have put the paper in motion, as we did, by setting up a fan in the present with assurances that it would remain in operation for some time. Doubtless he used one of the laboratory benches as an impromptu writing desk, and I have calculated that when he stood erect he was in November sixth."

"Where we will doubtless see him," Wide said.

"I think not."

"But, Street," I interrupted, "why should that note have undergone the same dislocation?"

"Why should other inanimate objects behave as they do? Unquestionably because they have been in contact with us, and there is, as far as we know, no natural opposing force which behaves as Dodson. There was, of course, some danger in grasping the note, but I counted on my own greater mass to wrench it from its unnatural space-time orientation. I had noted, you see, that Miss Dodson's descriptions of her 'father' did not state that he was nude, something she would undoubtedly have commented on had that been the case—ergo, he could be said to bend his clothing into his own reference frame."

"But why did he vanish," Miss Dodson demanded tearfully, "whenever he saw me?"

"He did not vanish," Street replied, "he simply stood up, and, standing, passed into November sixth, as I have already explained. The first time because he heard you call his name, the second because you startled him by dropping glassware, and the third time because, as a gentleman of the old school, he automatically rose when a woman entered the room. He doubtless realized later that he would reappear to you by taking his seat once more, but he was loath to frighten you, and hoped he could think his way out of his predicament; the hint he required for that I believe I have provided: you see, when I stood on my head just now I appeared to Dodson at about the time he suffered his unfortunate accident; the formula I have already quoted, plus the knowledge that Dodson had vanished thirteen days ago, allowed me to calculate that all I need do was to place my own 'temporal determinant'—the area of my frontal lobes—fourteen centimeters above the floor."

"But where is he now?"

Street shrugged. "I have no way of knowing, really. Obviously, he is not here. He might be at the opera or attending a seminar, but it seems most probable that he is in the apartment below us." He raised his voice. "Professor! Professor Dodson, are you down there?"

A moment later I saw a man of less than medium height, with white hair and a straggling yellow mustache, appear at the foot of the escalator. It was Professor Dodson! "What is it?" he asked testily. "Alice, who the hell are these people?"

"Friends," she sobbed. "Won't you please come up? Mr. Street, is it all right if he comes up?"

"It would be better," Street said gently, "if you went down to him. He must pack for that trip to the seaside, you know." While Miss Dodson was running down the escalator he called to the man below, "What project engages you at the moment, Professor?"

Dodson looked irritated, but replied, "A monograph on the nature of pragmatic time, young man. I had a mysterious—" His mouth was stopped with kisses.

Beside me St. Louis said softly, "Stay tuned for Ralph the Dancing Moose," but I was perhaps the only one who heard him.

Much later, when we were returning home on the monorail after Street had collected his fee from Wide, I said: "Street, there are several things I still don't understand about that case. Was that girl Dodson's daughter—or wasn't she?"

The rain drummed against the windows, and Street's smile was a trifle bitter. "I don't know why it is, Westing, that our society prefers disguising the love of elderly scientists as parenthood to regularizing it as marriage; but it does, and we must live and work in the world we find."

"May I ask one more question, Street?"

"I suppose so." My friend slouched wearily in his seat and pushed the deerstalker cap he always affected over his eyes. "Fire away, Westing."

"You told him to go down the escalator, but I don't see how that could help him—he would have ended up, well, goodness knows where."

"When," Street corrected me. "Goodness knows when. Actually I calculated it as July twenty-fourth, more or less."

"Well, I don't see how that could have helped him. And wouldn't we have seen him going down? I mean, when the top of his head reached the right level—"

"We could," Street answered sleepily. "I did. That was why I could speak so confidently. You didn't because you were all looking at me, and I didn't call your attention to it because I didn't want to frighten Miss Dodson."

"But I still don't see how his going down could have straightened out what you call his bend in orientation. He would just be downstairs sometime in July, and as helpless as ever."

"Downstairs," Street said, "but not helpless. He called himself—in his lab upstairs—on the Tri-D-phone and told himself not to do it. Fortunately a man of Dodson's age is generally wise enough to take his own advice. So you see, the bend was only a rubber bend after all; it was capable of being snapped back, and I snapped it."

"Street," I said a few minutes later, "are you asleep?"

"Not now I'm not."

"Street, is Wide's real name—I mean, is it really Wide?"

"I understand he is of Montenegrin manufacture, and it's actually something unpronounceable; but he's used Wide for years."

"The first time I was in his office—there was some correspondence on his desk, and one of the envelopes was addressed to Wolfe."

"That was intended for the author of this story," Street said sleepily. "Don't worry, Wide will forward it to him."

Westwind

". . . to all of you, my dearly loved fellow countrymen. And most particularly—as ever—to my eyes, Westwind."

O NE WALL OF THE STEAMING, STINKING ROOM BEGAN TO WAVER, the magic portal that had opened upon a garden of almost inconceivable beauty beginning to mist and change. Fountains of marble waved like grass, and rose trees, whose flowery branches wore strands of pearl and diamond, faded to soft old valentines. The ruler's chair turned to bronze, then to umber, and the ruler himself, fatherly and cunning, wise and unknowable, underwent a succession of transformations, becoming at first a picture, then a poster and at last a postage stamp.

The lame old woman who ran the place turned the wall off and several people protested. "You heard what he said," she told them. "You know your duty. Why do you have to listen to some simpleton from the Department of Truth say everything over in longer words and spread his spittle on it?"

The protestors, having registered their postures, were silent. The old woman looked at the clock behind the tiny bar she served.

"Game in twenty minutes," she said. "Folks will be coming in then, rain or no rain, wanting drinks. You want some, you better get them now."

Only two did: hulking, dirty men who might have been of any dishonest trade. A few people were already discussing the coming game. A few others talked about the address they had just heard—not its content, which could not have meant much to most of them—but about the ruler and his garden, exchanging at hundredth hand bits of palace gossip of untold age. The door opened and the storm came in and a young man with it.

He was tall and thin. He wore a raincoat that had soaked through and an old felt hat covered with a transparent plastic protection whose elastic had forced the hat's splayed brim into a tight bell around his head. One side of the young man's face was a blue scar; the old woman asked him what he wanted.

"You have rooms," he said.

"Yes, we do. Very cheap, too. You ought to wear something over that."

"If it bothers you," he said, "don't look at it."

"You think I've got to rent to you?" She looked around at her customers, lining up support, should the young man with the scar decide to resent her remarks. "All I've got to do if you complain is say we're full. You can walk to the police station then—it's twenty blocks—and maybe they'll let you sleep in a cell."

"I'd like a room and something to eat. What do you have?"

"Ham sandwich," she said. She named a price. "Your room—" She named another.

"All right," he said. "I'd like two sandwiches. And coffee."

"The room is only half if you share with somebody—if you want me to I can yell out and see if anybody wants to split."

"No."

She ripped the top from a can of coffee. The handle popped out and the contents began to steam. She gave it to him and said, "I guess they won't take you in the other places, huh? With that face."

He turned away from her, sipping his coffee, looking the room over. The door by which he had just entered (water still streamed from his coat and he could feel it in his shoes, sucking and gurgling with his every movement) opened again and a blind girl came in.

He saw that she was blind before he saw anything else about her. She wore black glasses, which on that impenetrable, rain-wracked night would have been clue enough, and as she entered she looked (in the second most terrible and truest sense) at Nothing.

The old woman asked, "Where did *you* come from?"

"From the terminal," the girl said. "I walked." She carried a white cane, which she swung before her as she sidled toward the sound of the old woman.

"I need a place to sleep," the girl said.

Her voice was clear and sweet and the young man decided that even before the rain had scrubbed her face she hadn't worn makeup.

He said, "You don't want to stay here. I'll call you a cab."

"I want to stay here," the girl said in her clear voice. "I have to stay somewhere."

"I have a communicator," the young man said. He opened his coat to show it to her—a black box with a speaker, keys and a tiny screen—then realized that he had made a fool of himself. Someone laughed.

"They're not running."

The old woman said, "What's not running?"

"The cabs. Or the buses. There's high water in a lot of places all over the city and they've been shorting out. I have a communicator, too—" the blind girl touched her waist— "and the ruler made a speech just a few minutes ago. I listened to him as I walked and there was a newscast afterwards. But I knew anyway because a gentleman tried to call one for me from the terminal, but they wouldn't come."

"You shouldn't stay here," the young man said.

The old woman said, "I got a room if you want it—the only one left."

"I want it," the girl told her.

"You've got it. Wait a minute now—I've got to fix this fellow some sandwiches."

Someone swore at the old woman and said that the game was about to start.

"Five minutes yet." She took a piece of boiled ham from

under the counter and put it between two slices of bread, then repeated the process.

The young man said, "These look eatable. Not fancy, but eatable. Would you like to have one?"

"I have a little money," the blind girl said. "I can pay for my own." And to the old woman: "I would like some coffee."

"How about a sandwich?"

"I'm too tired to eat."

The door was opening almost constantly now as people from the surrounding tenements braved the storm and splashed in to watch the game. The old woman turned the wall on and they crowded near it, watching the pre-game warmup, practicing and perfecting the intentness they would use on the game itself. The scarred young man and the blind girl were edged away and found themselves nearest the door in a room now grown very silent save for the sound from the wall.

The young man said, "This is really a bad place—you shouldn't be here."

"Then what are you doing here?"

"I don't have much money," he said. "It's cheap."

"You don't have a job?"

"I was hurt in an accident. I'm well now, but they wouldn't keep me on—they say I would frighten the others. I suppose I would."

"Isn't there insurance for that?"

"I wasn't there long enough to qualify."

"I see," she said. She raised her coffee carefully, holding it with both hands. He wanted to tell her that it was about to spill—she did not hold it quite straight—but dared not. Just as it was at the point of running over the edge it found her lips.

"You listened to the ruler," he said, "while you were walking in the storm. I like that."

"Did they listen here?" she asked.

"I don't know. I wasn't here. The wall was off when I came in."

"Everyone should," she said. "He does his best for us."

The scarred young man nodded.

"People won't cooperate," she said. "Don't cooperate. Look at the crime problem—everyone complains about it, but it is the people themselves who commit the crimes. He tries to clean the air, the water, all for us—"

"But they burn in the open whenever they think they won't be caught," the young man finished for her, "and throw filth in the rivers. The bosses live in luxury because of him, but they cheat on the standards whenever they can. He should destroy them."

"He loves them," the girl said simply. "He loves everyone. When we say that it sounds like we're saying he loves no one, but that's not true. He loves *everyone*."

"Yes," the scarred young man said after a moment, "but he loves Westwind the best. Loving everyone does not exclude loving someone more than others. Tonight he called Westwind 'my eyes.' "

"Westwind observes for him," the girl said softly, "and reports. Do you think Westwind is someone very important?"

"He is important," the young man said, "because the ruler listens to him—and after all, it's next to impossible for anyone else to get an audience. But I think you mean 'does he look important to us?' I don't think so—he's probably some very obscure person you've never heard of."

"I think you're right," she said.

He was finishing his second sandwich and he nodded, then realized that she could not see him. She was pretty, he decided, in a slender way, not too tall, wore no rings. Her nails were unpainted, which made her hands look, to him, like a schoolgirl's. He remembered watching the girls playing volley-ball when he had been in school—how he had ached for them. He said, "You should have stayed in the terminal tonight. I don't think this is a safe place for you."

"Do the rooms lock?"

"I don't know. I haven't seen them."

"If they don't I'll put a chair under the knob or something. Move the furniture. At the terminal I tried to sleep on a bench— I didn't want to walk here through all that rain, believe me. But every time I fell asleep I could feel someone's hand on me—once I grabbed him, but he pulled away, I'm not very strong."

"Wasn't anyone else there?"

"Some men, but they were trying to sleep, too—of course it was one of them, and perhaps they were all doing it together. One of them told the others that if they didn't let me alone he'd kill someone—that was when I left. I was afraid he wasn't doing it—that somebody would be killed or at least that there would be a fight. He was the one who called about the cab for me. He said he'd pay."

"I don't think it was him, then."

"I don't either." The girl was silent for a moment, the said, "I wouldn't have minded it so much if I hadn't been so tired."

"I understand."

"Would you find the lady and ask her to show me to my room?"

"Maybe we could meet in the morning for breakfast."

The blind girl smiled, the first time the scarred young man had seen her smile. "That would be nice," she said.

He went behind the bar and touched the old woman's arm. "I hate to interrupt the game," he said, "but the young lady would like to go to her room."

"I don't care about the game," the old woman said, "I just watch it because everybody else does. I'll get Obie to take care of things."

"She's coming," the scarred young man said to the blind girl. "I'll go up with you. I'm ready to turn in myself."

The woman was already motioning for them and they followed her up a narrow staircase filled with foul odors. "They pee in here," she said. "There's toilets down at the end of the hall but they don't bother to use them."

"How terrible," the girl said.

"Yes, it is. But that way they're getting away with something—they're putting one over on me because they know if I was to catch them I'd throw them out. I try and catch them, but at the same time I feel sorry for them—it's pretty bad when the only wins you have left are the games on the wall and cheating an old woman by dirtying her steps." She paused at the top of the stairs for breath. "You two are going to be just side by side—you don't mind that?"

The girl said, "No," and the scarred young man shook his head.

"I didn't think you would and they're the last I've got anyway."

The scarred young man was looking down the narrow corridor. It was lined with doors, most of them shut.

"I'll put you closest to the bathroom," the old woman was saying to the girl. "There's a hook on the bathroom door, so don't you worry. But if you stay in there too long somebody'll start pounding."

"I'll be all right," the girl said.

"Sure you will. Here's your room."

The rooms had been parts of much larger rooms once. Now they were subdivided with green-painted partitions of some stuff like heavy cardboard. The old woman went into the girl's place and turned on the light. "Bed's here, dresser's there," she said. "Washstand in the corner but you have to bring your water from the bathroom. No bugs—we fumigate twice a year. Clean sheets."

The girl was feeling the edge of the door. Her fingers found a chain lock and she smiled.

"There's a deadbolt too," the scarred young man said.

The old woman said, "Your room's next door. Come on."

His room was much like the girl's, save that the cardboard partition (it had been liberally scratched with obscene words and pictures) was on the left instead of the right. He found that he was acutely aware of her moving behind it, the tap of her stick as she established the positions of the bed, the dresser, the washstand. He locked his door and took off his soaked coat and hung it on a hook, then took off his shoes and stockings. He disliked the thought of walking on the gritty floor in his wet feet, but there was no alternative except the soggy shoes. With his legs folded under him he sat on the bed, then unhooked the communicator from his belt and pushed 123-333-4477, the ruler's number.

"This is Westwind," the scarred young man whispered.

The ruler's face appeared in the screen, tiny and perfect. Again, as he had so often before, the young man felt that this was his real size, this tiny, bright figure—he knew it was not true.

"This is Westwind and I've got a place to sleep tonight. I haven't found another job yet, but I met a girl and think she likes me."

"Exciting news," the ruler said. He smiled.

The scarred young man smiled, too, on his unscarred side. "It's raining very hard here," he said. "I think this girl is very loyal to you, sir. The rest of the people here—well, I don't know. She told me about a man in the terminal who tried to molest her and another man who wanted to protect her. I was going to ask you to reward him and punish the other one, but I'm afraid they were the same man—that he wanted to meet her and this gave him the chance."

"They are often the same man," the ruler said. He paused as though lost in thought. "You are all right?"

"If I don't find something tomorrow I won't be able to afford to stay, but yes, I'm all right tonight."

"You are very cheerful, Westwind. I love cheerfulness."

The good side of the scarred young man's face blushed. "It's easy for me," he said. "I've known all my life that I was your spy, your confidant—it's like knowing where a treasure is hidden. Often I feel sorry for the others. I hope you're not too severe with them."

"I don't want to aid you openly unless I must," the ruler

said. "But I'll find ways that aren't open. Don't worry." He winked.

"I know you will, sir."

"Just don't pawn your communicator."

The image was gone, leaving only a blank screen. The young man turned out the light and continued to undress, taking off everything but his shorts. He was lying down on the bed when he heard a thump from the other side of the cardboard partition. The blind girl, feeling her way about the room, must have bumped into it. He was about to call, "Are you hurt?" when he saw that one of the panels, a section perhaps three feet by four, was teetering in its frame. He caught it as it fell and laid it on floor.

The light the old woman had turned on still burned in the girl's room and he saw that she had hung up her coat and wrapped her hair in a strip of paper towels from the washstand. While he watched she removed her black glasses, set them on the bureau and rubbed the bridge of her nose. One of her eyes showed only white; the iris of the other was the poisoned blue color of watered milk and turned in and down. Her face was lovely. While he watched she unbuttoned her blouse and hung it up. Then she unhooked her communicator from her belt, ran her fingers over the buttons once and, without looking, pressed a number.

"This is Westwind," she said.

He could not hear the voice that answered her, but the face in the screen, small and bright, was the face of the ruler. "I'm all right," she said. "At first I didn't think I was going to be able to find a place to stay tonight, but I have. And I've met someone."

The scarred young man lifted the panel back into place as gently as he could and lay down again upon his bed. When he heard the rattle of her cane again he tapped the partition and called, "Breakfast tomorrow. Don't forget."

"I won't. Good night."

"Good night," he said.

In the room below them the old woman was patting her straggling hair into place with one hand while she punched a number with the other. "Hello," she said, "this is Westwind. I saw you tonight."

Sonya, Crane Wessleman, and Kittee

THE RELATION BETWEEN SONYA AND CRANE WESSLEMAN WAS AN ODD ONE, and might perhaps have been best described as a sort of suspended courtship, the courtship of a poor girl by a wealthy boy, if they had not both been quite old. I do not mean to say that they are old *now*. Now Sonya is about your age and Crane Wessleman is only a few years older, but they do not know one another. If they had, or so Sonya often thought, things might have been much different.

At the time I am speaking of every citizen of the United States received a certain guaranteed income, supplemented if there were children, and augmented somewhat if he or she worked in certain underpaid but necessary professions. It was a very large income indeed in the mouths of conservative politicians and insufficient to maintain life according to liberal politicians, but Sonya gave them both the lie. Sonya without children or augmentation lived upon this income, cleanly but not well. She was able to do this because she did not smoke, or attend any public entertainment that was not free, or use drugs, or drink except when Crane Wessleman poured her a small glass of one of his liqueurs. Then she would hold it up to the light to see if it were yellow or red or brown, and sniff it in a delicate and ladylike way, and roll a half teaspoon on her tongue until it was well mixed with her saliva, and then swallow it. She would go on exactly like this, over and over, until she had finished the glass, and when she had swallowed it all it would make her feel somewhat younger; not a great deal younger, say about two years, but somewhat younger; she enjoyed that. She had been a very attractive girl, and a very attractive woman. If you imagine how Debbie Reynolds will look when she attends the inauguration of John-John Kennedy, you will about have her. With her income she rented two rooms in a converted garage and kept them clean.

Crane Wessleman met Sonya during that time when he still used, occasionally, to leave his house. His former partner had asked him to play bridge, and when he accepted had called a friend, or (to be truthful) had his wife call the friend's wife, to beg the name of an unattached woman of the correct age who might make a fourth. A name had been given, a mistake made, Sonya had been called instead, and by the time the partner's wife realized what had occurred Sonya had been nibbling her petits fours and asking for sherry instead of tea. The partner did not learn of his wife's error until both Crane Wessleman and Sonya were gone, and Crane Wessleman never learned of it. If he had, he would not have believed it. The next time the former partner called, Crane Wessleman asked rather pointedly if Sonya would be present.

She played well with him, perhaps because she was what Harlan Ellison would call an empath—Harlan meaning she gut-dug whether or not Crane Wessleman was going to make the trick—or perhaps only because she had what is known as card sense and the ability to make entertaining inconsequential talk. The partner's wife said she was cute, and she was quite skillful at flattery.

Then the partner's wife died of a brain malignancy; and the partner, who had only remained where he was because of her, retired to Bermuda; and Crane Wessleman stopped going out at all and after a very short time seldom changed from his pajamas and dressing gown. Sonya thought that she had lost him altogether.

Sonya had never formed the habit of protesting the decisions of fate although once when she was much, much younger she had assisted a male friend to distribute mimeographed handbills complaining of the indignity of death and the excretory functions—a short girl with blond braids and chino pants, you saw her—but that had been only a favor. Whatever the handbills said, she accepted those things. She accepted losing Crane Wessleman too, but at night when she was trying to go to sleep, she would sometimes think of Crane Wessleman among The Things That Might Have Been. She did not know that the partner's wife was dead or that the partner had moved to Bermuda. Nor did she know how they had first gotten her name. She thought that she was not called again because of something—a perfectly innocent thing which everyone had forgotten in five minutes—she had said to the partner's wife. She regretted it, and tried to devise ways, in the event that she was ever asked again, of making up for it.

It was not merely that Crane Wessleman was rich and widowed, although it was a great deal that. She liked him, knowing happily and secretly as she did that he was hard to like; and, deeper, there was the thought of something else: of opening a new chapter, a wedding, flowers, a new last name, a not dying as she was. And then four months after the last game Crane Wessleman himself called her.

He asked her to have dinner with him, at his home; but he asked in a way that made it clear he assumed she possessed means of transportation of her own. It was to be in a week.

She borrowed, reluctantly and with difficulty, certain small items of wearing apparel from distant friends, and when the evening came she took a bus. You and I would have called it a helicopter, you understand, but Sonya called it a bus, and the company that operated it called it a bus, and most important, the driver called it a bus and had the bus driver mentality, which is not a helicopter pilot mentality at all. It was the ascendant heir of those cheap wagons Boswell patronized in Germany. Sonya rode for half because she had a Golden Age card, and the driver resented that.

When she got off the bus she walked a considerable distance to get to the house. She had never been there before, having always met Crane Wessleman at the former partner's, and so she did not know exactly where it was although she had looked it up on a map. She checked the map from time to time as she went along, stopping under the infrequent streetlights and waving to the television cameras mounted on them so that if the policeman happened to be looking at the time and saw her he would know that she was all right.

Crane Wessleman's house was large, on a lot big enough to be called an estate without anyone's smiling; the house set a hundred yards back from the street. A Tudor house, as Sonya remarked with some pleasure—but there was too much shrubbery, and it had been allowed to grow too large. Sonya thought roses would be nicer, and as she came up the long front walk she put pillar roses on the gas lantern posts Crane Wessleman's dead wife had caused to be set along it. A brass plate on the front door said:

C. WESSLEMAN

AND

KITTEE

and when Sonya saw that she *knew*.

If it had not been for the long walk she would have turned around right there and gone back down the path past the gas lamps; but she was tired and her legs hurt, and perhaps she could not really have gone back anyway. People like Sonya are often quite tough underneath.

She rang the bell and Kittee opened the door. Sonya knew of course, that it was Kittee, but perhaps you or I might not. We would have said that the door was opened by a tall, naked girl who looked a good deal like Julie Newmar; a deep-chested, broad-shouldered girl with high cheekbones and an unexpressive face. Sonya had forgotten about Julie Newmar; she knew that this was Kittee, and she disliked the thing, and the name Crane Wessleman had given it with the whining double *e* at the end. She said in a level, friendly voice, "Good evening, Kittee. My name is Sonya. Would you like to smell my fingers?" After a moment Kittee did smell her fingers, and when Sonya stepped through the door Kittee moved out of the way to let her in. Sonya closed the door herself and said, "Take me to Master, Kittee," loudly enough, she hoped, for Crane Wessleman to hear. Kittee walked away and Sonya followed her, noticing that Kittee was not really completely naked. She wore a garment like a short apron put on backward.

The house was large and dirty, although the air filtration units would not allow it to be dusty. There was an odor Sonya attributed to Kittee, and the remains of some of Crane Wessleman's meals, plates with dried smears still on them, put aside and forgotten.

Crane Wessleman had not dressed, but he had shaved and wore a clean new robe and stockings as well as slippers. He and Sonya chattered, and Sonya helped him unpack the meal he had ordered for her and put it in the microwave oven. Kittee helped her set the table, and Crane Wessleman said proudly, "She's wonderful, isn't she." And Sonya answered, "Oh yes, and very beautiful. May I stroke her?" and ran her fingers through Kittee's soft yellow hair.

Then Crane Wessleman got out a copy of a monthly magazine called *Friends,* put out for people who owned them or were interested in buying, and sat beside Sonya as they ate and turned the pages for her, pointing out the ads of the best producers and reading some of the poetry put at the ends of the columns. "You don't know, really, what they are anymore," Crane Wessleman said. "Even the originators hardly know." Sonya looked at the naked girl and Crane Wessleman said, "I call her Kittee, but the germ plasm may have come from a gibbon or a dog. Look here."

Sonya looked, and he showed her a picture of what seemed to be a very handsome young man with high cheekbones and an unexpressive face. "Look at that smile," Crane Wessleman said, and Sonya did and noticed that the young man's lips were indeed drawn back slightly. "Kittee does that sometimes too," Crane Wessleman said. Sonya was looking at him instead of at Kittee, noticing how the fine lines had spread across his face and the way his hands shook.

After that Sonya came about once a week for a year. She learned the way perfectly, and the bus driver grew accustomed to her, and she invented a pet of her own, an ordinary imaginary chow dog, so that she could take a certain amount of leftover meat home.

The next to last time, Crane Wessleman pointed out another very handsome young man in *Friends,* a young man who cost a great deal more than Sonya's income for a year, and said, "After I die I am going to see to it that my executor buys one like this for Kittee. I want her to be happy." Then, Sonya felt, he looked at her in a most significant way; but the last time she went he seemed to have forgotten all about it and only showed Sonya a photograph he had taken of himself with Kittee sitting beside him very primly, and the remote control camera he had used, and told her how he had ordered it by mail.

The next week Crane Wessleman did not call at all, and when it was two days past the usual time Sonya tried to call him, but no one answered. Sonya got her purse, and boarded the bus, and searched the area around Crane Wessleman's front door until she found a key hidden under a stone beneath some of the shrubbery.

Crane Wessleman was dead, sitting in his favorite chair. He had been dead, Sonya decided, for several days, and Kittee had eaten a portion of his left leg. Sonya said aloud, "You must have been very hungry, weren't you, Kittee, locked in here with no one to feed you."

In the kitchen she found a package of frozen *mouton Sainte-Menebould,* and when it was warm she unwrapped it and set it on the dining-room table, calling, "Kittee! Kittee! Kittee!" and wondering all the time whether Crane Wessleman might not have left her a small legacy after all.

The Packerhaus Method

T HE SOCIAL WORKER SAT PRIMLY, knees together, hands in lap. She looked the part, with short,
sensible hair, round-lensed glasses and large, kind, brown eyes.

The old woman in the rocker looked *her* part too, perhaps
almost too much: snow white hair, bifocals, knitting, cat. "It's
the Packerhaus method," she said. "Perhaps you've heard of
it?" She was smiling at her two front doors.

"Mmmh," the social worker replied, looking troubled.

"Meow," said the cat.

"The Packerhaus method. I believe I heard you to say that
you were familiar with the name but not fully cognizant of all
the details?"

The social worker waved a hand. "Something like that. It's
rather a shock to have one pop out at me in that way and then
learn . . ." She let the sentence trail away, wishing she could
herself.

"Fine," the old woman said. She had been knitting, apparently, instead of listening. One of the front doors opened and
a man in uniform rapped gently on the varnished frame.
"Meter reader."

The old woman looked up from her knitting, smiling. "In
the basement," she said. "Just come right through, Frank."

The uniformed man smiled in return and moved across the
living room on a small rectangular platform. A door at the far
side opened to receive him.

The social worker gulped. "He didn't walk," she said. "He
was riding on a sort of little cart."

"The Packerhaus method is not perfect." The old woman looked at her severely. "And please note, my dear, that neither I nor Col. Packerhaus ever once said it was. He was my cousin, did I tell you that? But it gives, in the felicitous phrase the Colonel coined, 'a living memorial to the living.' That became the motto of the company he founded when he left the Army Graves Registration Service, you know."

"No," the social worker said humbly. "I didn't."

"The Colonel conceived of his method as a means of assuaging the grief of the sorrowing parents, wives, and sweethearts; but it was not really well suited, as he used to say subsequently, to a military application. So many soldiers are damaged by death."

The meter reader re-emerged from the door he had entered and glided across the room again, tipping his cap.

"Your grandfather . . . didn't your grandfather come through that door a minute ago?"

"My father." The old woman nodded, rocking. "A wonderful man, looking for a light for his cigar. That's what he does, mostly—looks for a light." She sat rocking and knitting after pronouncing this, half waiting for the social worker to reply, half listening for the tea kettle. After a time an old man with a cigar in his fingers entered the room on a platform like the meter man's. He wore drooping black trousers and a loose white shirt, and looked like Mark Twain and a little like Ralph Waldo Emerson.

The social worker jerked slightly on seeing him, and he asked her for a match; he had a deep, resonant voice.

"You shouldn't smoke, Papa," the old woman said. And to the social worker, "It's the Packerhaus method. I believe I told you?"

"You mean he's not just a doll?"

"Oh no." The old woman shook her head, smiling. "He's a living memorial. By which the Colonel and I mean that it is really he. Aren't you you, Papa?"

He was looking under an antimacassar for matches.

"The Packerhaus method," the old woman continued,

"preserves the entire brain by saturating it with a phenolic resin. Then an exterior source of voltage powers the nerve impulses." She leaned forward confidentially, lowering her voice. "He can't breathe, you know. I don't keep matches in the house, but sometimes he remembers that he can light his cigar from the stove element. Then he finds out he can't draw on it, and it makes him very angry."

The social worker was watching the old man's back. "If he can't breathe, how can he speak?"

"A fan," the old woman said. "A fan in the base forces air past his vocal cords. The tube runs up his leg."

"Meow," said the cat.

Turning around the old man asked for a match again in his deep voice; the social worker said she had none and he left.

"Not back to the stove, I hope," the old woman said. "He'll lift off my teakettle and forget to put it back. I always made tea for him when he was ill. Did I tell you that?"

The social worker shook her head and asked, "He can still move?" She looked faint.

"Of *course* he can still move. That was the other half of Col. Packerhaus's great discovery. Muscles, you know, will still respond to an impulse after death. We used to do it with frogs' legs and a galvanic cell when I was a little girl in school—no doubt you moderns have more advanced methods."

"I seem to remember something like that in biology," the social worker said weakly.

"The Colonel's fluid preserves this attribute, you see—at least for a long time. It's based on formaldehyde like the old fluid, but it contains vitamins and proteins in solution, and oxygenators, and ever so many other things. You may have smelled the formaldehyde the first time you met Papa, but no doubt you thought it was after shave lotion."

"I think I must be going." The social worker looked around vaguely for her bag.

The old woman smiled. "Oh no, not yet. I'll be leaving myself soon. Papa had stomach cramps—did I tell you that?

Just like Frank, who used to come around for the gas company. That's funny, isn't it: stomach cramps and the gas company." There was a knock at the door and the old woman called, "Not now, Frank. We're talking."

"He can think?"

"Oh yes." The old woman rocked back and forth. "Think and talk. The standing ones are put on a platform with the extra equipment in it so they can move about, while the seated ones just have it built into their chairs. Now Kitty here," she leaned over and stroked the cat, "was a special job just for me, and the extra equipment is let into the floor under her; but they don't often do animals."

"If they can think and move," the social worker asked, "how is it different from being alive?" She answered her own question. "Alive, but crippled perhaps, like someone who has to use a wheel chair."

"Now you've hit it," the old woman said. She was putting away her knitting. "It's the memory, my dear. You see, the moment-to-moment memories a person has are electrical, as you might say, in their nature. But the permanent ones, the things a person recalls more than just five or ten minutes, are due to changes in the molecules that make up one's brain. With the Packerhaus method, since the brain isn't alive it can't change itself that way." She waved a hand, pleased with her explanation. "That's why Papa can't remember that he can't smoke, for example."

"Stomach cramps."

"Yes, just like you. Col. Packerhaus had them too, but though I do love having people around me I don't have him here, of course. The company has him down in the lobby of the Packerhaus Mortuary Number One where the bereaved can talk to him. He's still quite a good salesman, you know, and very comforting." The old woman stood up, stowing the knitting under her rocker. "It's interesting, too, to see how long his memory span is; it seems to improve with age. I was about to say that it almost seemed his brain had learned to make the moment-to-moment kind last longer—but that would be silly, wouldn't it? I mean since after the resin hardens it can't learn at all. But you'll see for yourself."

"I want to go home," the social worker said.

"You can't dear," the old woman told her gently. "But it was nice of you to come around to visit an old lady." She bent quickly and kissed the social worker on the forehead. "And," she added when she had straightened up again, "I have some lovely news for you: when I go myself I'm going to have it done too. It's all in my will. Then we can just sit and talk all the time. You and I and Papa, and of course Frank, when Frank wants to talk. And the new girl they're sending to look in on me. There's a note on the outside front door, but if you remember you might tell her that there's a cup set out for her with a tea bag already in it, and hot water on the stove. I have to go to the store, but I'll be back soon."

"Meow," said the cat.

The social worker leaned forward to stroke it, but found she could not leave her chair. The clock ticked. A slow horror filled her, and there was an agonizing tightness in her throat. She should be crying, she knew; but there was no moisture in her eyes.

One of the front doors opened and a man in uniform rapped gently on the varnished frame. "Meter reader, lady."

"You're Frank, aren't you?" The clock ticked.

The other front door opened and a new social worker came in. She looked the part, with brown, sensible hair, round-lensed glasses and large, kind, short eyes.

"You have short eyes," the social worker said.

The new social worker smiled. "Short sighted, you mean. Yes, that's why I have to wear these awful things." She tapped her glasses with a forefinger.

"Meow," said the cat.

"I'm the meter reader," said Frank. "Sometimes I look in too; old people get lonely you know."

"Charmed," said the new social worker. "I do hope you folks don't mind my barging in like this. There was a note on the door saying I'd find tea on the stove, I didn't realize the old lady already had company." She went into the kitchen.

"You're very kind, aren't you?" the social worker said to Frank. The clock ticked.

The new social worker came back, carrying a cup of tea and smiling. "There's an elderly gentleman in the kitchen," she said. "He's cursing his cigar."

The social worker dropped Frank's hand. "I was either to tell you to drink that tea, or not to drink it; but I can't recall which. And he's behind you."

"Oh?" said the new social worker, and turned around.

Grandfather had followed her from the kitchen, and he asked the new social worker for a light for his cigar. "I've been trying to light it from the stove," he complained, "but it won't draw."

The clock ticked.

"Meow," said the cat.

"That cat's shedding," said the new social worker. "In fact I don't think I've ever seen a cat shedding quite so much. The hair's coming out of her in a quite remarkable way."

The clock ticked.

The clock ticked.

The clock ticked.

"Ah," said the old woman. "All my little circle gathered together. Did the new girl come?"

"New girl?" asked the social worker. There was a gagging sound from another room.

"I think she must have gone into a bedroom to lie down," said the old woman. "Perhaps she has gas."

"I thought it was the plumbing," said Grandfather.

"We have news for you," said the social worker. "Good news, I hope, though it means I won't be coming to see you any more—at least not in an official capacity."

The old woman was getting out her knitting. "Wonderful," she said.

"Meow," said the cat.

"Frank and I are getting married. We wanted you to be the

first to know." The social worker sat primly, knees together, hands in lap.

"Wonderful!" exclaimed the old woman. "Marvelous! Of course," she added in a more serious tone, "you know what this means. We'll have to invite the minister—for tea."

"Come on," said Grandfather, taking Frank by the elbow. "We'd best leave these women to plan the wedding. Got a match on you?"

The social worker gulped. "They don't walk," she said. "Frank was riding on a sort of little cart. Haven't I noticed that before?"

"It's the Packerhaus method," the old woman said. "Perhaps you've heard of it?"

"Mmmh," the social worker replied, looking troubled.

"Meow," said the cat.

Straw

Y ES, I REMEMBER KILLING MY FIRST MAN
VERY WELL; I was just seventeen. A flock of snow
geese flew under us that day about noon. I remember looking
over the side of the basket, and seeing them; and thinking that
they looked like a pike-head. That was an omen, of course,
but I did not pay any attention.

It was clear, fall weather—a trifle chilly. I remember that.
It must have been about the mid-part of October. Good
weather for the balloon. Clow would reach up every quarter
hour or so with a few double handsful of straw for the brazier;
and that was all it required. We cruised, usually, at about twice
the height of a steeple.

You have never been in one? Well, that shows how things
have changed. Before the Fire-wights came, there was hardly
any fighting at all, and free swords had to travel all over the
continent looking for what there was. A balloon was better
than walking, believe me. Miles—he was our captain in those
days—said that where there were three soldiers together, one
was certain to put a shaft through a balloon; it was too big a
target to resist, and that would show you where the armies
were.

No, we would not have been killed. You would have had
to slit the thing wide open before it would fall fast, and a little
hole like the business end of a pike would make would just
barely let you know it was there. The baskets do not swing,
either, as people think. Why should they? They feel no
wind—they are travelling with it. A man just seems to hang

there, when he is up in one of them, and the world turns under him. He can hear everything—pigs and chickens, and the squeak the windlass makes drawing water from a well.

"Good flying weather," Clow said to me.

I nodded. Solemnly, I suppose.

"All the lift you want, in weather like this. The colder it is, the better she pulls. The heat from the fire doesn't like the chill, and tries to escape from it. That's what they say."

Blond Bracata spat over the side. "Nothing in our bellies," she said, "that's what makes it lift. If we don't eat today you won't have to light the fire tomorrow—I'll take us up myself."

She was taller than any of us except Miles, and the heaviest of us all; but Miles would not allow for size when the food was passed out, so I suppose she was the hungriest too.

Derek said: "We should have stretched one of that last bunch over the fire. That would have fetched a pot of stew, at the least."

Miles shook his head. "There were too many."

"They would have run like rabbits."

"And if they hadn't?"

"They had no armor."

Unexpectantly, Bracata came in for the captain. "They had twenty-two men, and fourteen women. I counted them."

"The women wouldn't fight."

"I used to be one of them. I would have fought."

Clow's soft voice added, "Nearly any woman will fight if she can get behind you."

Bracata stared at him, not sure whether he was supporting her or not. She had her mitts on—she was as good with them as anyone I have ever seen—and I remember that I thought for an instant that she would go for Clow right there in the basket. We were packed in like fledglings in the nest, and fighting, it would have taken at least three of us to throw her out—by which time she would have killed us all, I suppose. But she was afraid of Clow. I found out why later. She respected Miles, I think, for his judgment and courage, without being afraid of him. She did not care much for Derek either way, and of course I was hardly there at all as far as she was concerned. But she was just a little frightened by Clow.

Clow was the only one I was not frightened by—but that is another story too.

"Give it more straw," Miles said.

"We're nearly out."

"We can't land in this forest."

Clow shook his head and added straw to the fire in the brazier—about half as much as he usually did. We were sinking toward what looked like a red and gold carpet.

"We got straw out of them anyway," I said, just to let the others know I was there.

"You can always get straw," Clow told me. He had drawn a throwing spike and, and was feigning to clean his nails with it. "Even from swineherds, who you'd think wouldn't have it. They'll get it to be rid of us."

"Bracata's right," Miles said. He gave the impression that he had not heard Clow and me. "We have to have food today."

Derek snorted. "What if there are twenty?"

"We stretch one over the fire. Isn't that what you suggested? And if it takes fighting, we fight. But we have to eat today." He looked at me. "What did I tell you when you joined us, Jerr? High pay or nothing? This is the nothing. Want to quit?"

I said, "Not if you don't want me to."

Clow was scraping the last of the straw from the bag. It was hardly a handful. As he threw it in the brazier Bracata asked, "Are we going to set down in the trees?"

Clow shook his head and pointed. Away in the distance I could see a speck of white on a hill. It looked too far, but the wind was taking us there, and it grew and grew until we could see that it was a big house, all built of white brick with gardens and outbuildings, and a road that ran up to the door. There are none like that now, I suppose.

Landings are the most exciting part of travelling by balloon, and sometimes the most unpleasant. If you are lucky, the basket stays upright. We were not. Our basket snagged and tipped over and was dragged along by the envelope, which fought the wind and did not want to go down, cold though it was by then. If there had been a fire in the brazier still, I suppose we would have set the meadow ablaze. As it was, we were tumbled about like toys. Bracata fell on top of me, as heavy as stone: and she had the claws of her mitts out, trying to dig them into the turf to stop herself, so that for a moment I thought I was going to be killed. Derek's pike had been charged, and the ratchet released in the confusion; the head went flying across the field, just missing a cow.

By the time I recovered my breath and got to my feet, Clow had the envelope under control and was treading it down. Miles was up too, straightening his hauberk and sword-belt. "Look like a soldier," he called to me. "Where are your weapons?"

A pincer-mace and my pike were all I had, and the pincer-mace had fallen out of the basket. After five minutes of looking, I found it in the tall grass, and went over to help Clow fold the envelope.

When we were finished, we stuffed it in the basket and put our pikes through the rings on each side so we could carry it. By that time we could see men on horseback coming down from the big house. Derek said, "We won't be able to stand against horsemen in this field."

For an instant I saw Miles smile. Then he looked very serious. "We'll have one of those fellows over a fire in half an hour."

Derek was counting, and so was I. Eight horsemen, with a cart following them. Several of the horsemen had lances, and I could see the sunlight winking on helmets and breast-plates. Derek began pounding the butt of his pike on the ground to charge it.

I suggested to Clow that it might look more friendly if we picked up the balloon and went to meet the horsemen, but he shook his head. "Why bother?"

The first of them had reached the fence around the field. He was sitting a roan stallion that took it at a clean jump and came thundering up to us looking as big as a donjon on wheels.

"Greetings," Miles called. "If this be your land, lord, we give thanks for your hospitality. We'd not have intruded, but our conveyance has exhausted its fuel."

"You are welcome," the horseman called. He was as tall as Miles or taller, as well as I could judge, and as wide as Bracata. "Needs must, as they say, and no harm done." Three of the others had jumped their mounts over the fence behind him. The rest were taking down the rails so the cart could get through.

"Have you straw, lord?" Miles asked. I thought it would have been better if he had asked for food. "If we could have a few bundles of straw, we'd not trouble you more."

"None here," the horseman said, waving a mail-clad arm at the fields around us, "yet I feel sure my bailiff could find you some. Come up to the hall for a taste of meat and a glass of wine, and you can make your ascension from the terrace; the ladies would be delighted to see it, I'm certain. You're floating swords, I take it?"

"We are that," our captain affirmed, "but persons of good character nonetheless. We're called the Faithful Five—perhaps you've heard of us? High-hearted, fierce-fighting wind-warriors all, as it says on the balloon."

A younger man, who had reined up next to the one Miles called "lord," snorted. "If that boy is high-hearted, or a fierce fighter, either, I'll eat his breeks."

Of course, I should not have done it. I have been too mettlesome all my life, and it has gotten me in more trouble than I could tell you of if I talked till sunset, though it has been good to me too—I would have spent my days following the plow, I suppose, if I had not knocked down Derek for what he called our goose. But you see how it was. Here I had been thinking of myself as a hard-bitten balloon soldier, and then to hear something like that. Anyway, I swung the pincer-mace overhand once I had a good grip on his stirrup. I had been afraid the extension spring was a bit weak, never having used one before, but it worked well; the pliers got him under the left arm and between the ear and the right shoulder, and would have cracked his neck for him properly if he had not been wearing a gorget. As it was, I jerked him off his horse pretty handily and got out the little aniance that screwed into the mace handle. A couple of the other horsemen couched their lances, and Derek had a finger on the dog-catch of his pike; so all in all it looked as if there could be a proper fight, but "lord" (I learned afterwards that he was the Baron Ascolot) yelled at the young man I had pulled out of his saddle, and Miles yelled at me and grabbed my left wrist, and thus it all blew over. When we had tripped the release and gotten the mace open and retracted again, Miles said: "He will be punished, lord. Leave him to me. It will be severe. I assure you."

"No, upon my oath," the baron declared. "It will teach my son to be less free with his tongue in the company of armed men. He has been raised at the hall, Captain, where everyone bends the knee to him. He must learn not to expect that of strangers."

The cart rolled up just then, drawn by two fine mules— either of them would have been worth my father's holding, I judged—and at the baron's urging we loaded our balloon into it and climbed in after it ourselves, sitting on the fabric. The horsemen galloped off, and the cart driver cracked his lash over the mules' backs.

"Quite a place," Miles remarked. He was looking up at the big house toward which we were making.

I whispered to Clow, "A palace, I should say," and Miles overheard me, and said: "It's a villa, Jerr—the unfortified country property of a gentleman. If there were a wall and a tower, it would be a castle, or at least a castellett."

There were gardens in front, very beautiful as I remember, and a fountain. The road looped up before the door, and we got out and trooped into the hall, while the baron's man—he was richer-dressed than anybody I had ever seen up till then, a fat man with white hair—set two of the hostlers to watch our balloon while it was taken back to the stableyard.

Venison and beef were on the table, and even a pheasant with all his feathers put back; and the baron and his sons sat with us and drank some wine and ate a bit of bread each for hospitality's sake. Then the baron said, "Surely you don't fly in the dark, captain?"

"Not unless we must, lord."

"Then with the day drawing to a close, it's just as well for you that we've no straw. You can pass the night with us, and in the morning I'll send my bailiff to the village with the cart. You'll be able to ascend at mid-morning, when the ladies can have a clear view of you as you go up."

"No straw?" our captain asked.

"None, I fear, here. But they'll have aplenty in the village, never doubt it. They lay it in the road to silence the horses' hoofs when a woman's with child, as I've seen many a time. You'll have a cartload as a gift from me, if you can use that much." The baron smiled as he said that; he had a friendly face, round and red as an apple. "Now tell me," (he went on) "how it is to be a floating sword. I always find other men's trades of interest, and it seems to me you follow one of the most fascinating of all. For example, how do you gauge the charge you will make your employer?"

"We have two scales, lord," Miles began. I had heard all of that before, so I stopped listening. Bracata was next to me at table, so I had all I could do to get something to eat for myself, and I doubt I ever got a taste of the pheasant. By good luck, a couple of lasses—the baron's daughters—had come in, and one of them started curling a lock of Derek's hair around her finger, so that distracted him while he was helping himself to the venison, and Bracata put an arm around the other and warned her of Men. If it had not been for that I would not have had a thing; as it was, I stuffed myself on deer's meat until I had to loose my waistband. Flesh of any sort had been a rarity where I came from.

I had thought that the baron might give us beds in the house, but when we had eaten and drunk all we could hold, the white-haired fat man led us out a side door and over to a wattle-walled building full of bunks—I suppose it was kept for the extra laborers needed at harvest. It was not the palace bedroom I had been dreaming of; but it was cleaner than home, and there was a big fireplace down at one end with logs stacked ready by, so it was probably more comfortable for me than a bed in the big house itself would have been.

Clow took out a piece of cherry wood, and started carving a woman in it, and Bracata and Derek lay down to sleep. I made shift to talk to Miles, but he was full of thoughts, sitting on a bench near the hearth and chinking the purse (just like this one, it was) he had gotten from the baron; so I tried to sleep too. But I had had too much to eat to sleep so soon, and since it was still light out, I decided to walk around the villa and try to find somebody to chat with. The front looked too grand for me; I went to the back, thinking to make sure our balloon had suffered no hurt, and perhaps have another look at those mules.

There were three barns behind the house, built of stone up to the height of my waist, and wood above that, and white-washed. I walked into the nearest of them, not thinking about anything much besides my full belly until a big war horse with a white star on his forehead reached his head out of his stall and nuzzled at my cheek. I reached out and stroked his neck for him the way they like. He nickered, and I turned to have a better look at him. That was when I saw what was in his stall. He was standing on a span or more of the cleanest, yellowest straw I had ever seen. I looked up over my head then, and there was a loft full of it up there.

In a minute or so, I suppose it was, I was back in the building where we were to sleep, shaking Miles by the shoulder and telling him I had found all the straw anyone could ask for.

He did not seem to understand, at first. "Wagon loads of

straw, Captain," I told him. "Why every horse in the place has as much to lay him on as would carry us a hundred leagues."

"All right," Miles told me.

"Captain—"

"There's no straw here, Jerr. Not for us. Now be a sensible lad and get some rest."

"But there is, Captain. I saw it. I can bring you back a helmetful."

"Come here, Jerr," he said, and got up and led me outside. I thought he was going to ask me to show him the straw; but instead of going back to where the barns were, he took me away from the house to the top of a grassy knoll. "Look out there, Jerr. Far off. What do you see?"

"Trees," I said. "There might be a river at the bottom of the valley; then more trees on the other side."

"Beyond that."

I looked to the horizon, where he seemed to be pointing. There were little threads of black smoke rising there, looking as thin as spider web at that distance.

"What do you see?"

"Smoke."

"That's straw burning, Jerr. House-thatch. That's why there's no straw here. Gold, but no straw, because a soldier gets straw only where he isn't welcome. They'll reach the river there by sundown, and I'm told it can be forded at this season. Now do you understand?"

They came that night at moonrise.

The Marvelous Brass
Chessplaying Automaton

E ACH DAY LAME HANS SITS WITH HIS KNEES AGAINST THE BARS, playing chess with the machine. Though I have seen the game often, I have never learned to play, but I watch them as I sweep. It is a beautiful game, and Lame Hans has told me of its beginnings in the great ages now past; for that reason I always feel a sympathy toward the little pawns with their pencils and wrenches and plain clothing, each figure representing many generations of those whose labor built the great bishops that split the skies in the days of the old wars.

I feel pity for Lame Hans also. He talks to me when I bring his food, and sometimes when I am cleaning the jail. Let me tell you his story, as I have learned it in the many days since the police drew poor Gretchen out and laid her in the dust of the street. Lame Hans would never tell you himself—for all that big, bulging head, his tongue is slow and halting when he speaks of his own affairs.

It was last summer during the truce that the showman's cart was driven into our village. For a month not a drop of rain had fallen; each day at noon Father Karl rang the church bells, and women went in to pray for rain for their husbands' crops. After dark, many of these same women met to form lines and circles on the slopes of the Schlossberg, the mountain that was once a great building. The lines and circles are supposed to influence the Weatherwatchers, whose winking lights pass so swiftly through the starry sky. For myself, I do not believe it.

What men ever made a machine that could see a few old women on the mountainside at night?

So it was when the cart of Herr Heitzmann the mountebank came. The sun was down, but the street still so hot that the dogs would not bark for fear of fainting, and the dust rolled away from the wheels in waves, like grain when foxes run through the fields.

This cart was shorter than a farm wagon, but very high, with such a roof as a house has. The sides had been painted, and even I, who do not play, but have so often watched Albricht the moneylender play Father Karl, or Doctor Eckardt play Burgermeister Landsteiner, recognized the mighty figures of the Queen-Computers who lead the armies of the field of squares into battle; and the haughty King-Generals who command, and if they fall, bring down all.

A small, bent man drove. He had a head large enough for a giant—that was Lame Hans, but I paid little attention to him, not knowing that he and I would be companions here in the jail where I work. Beside him sat Heitzmann the mountebank, and it was he who took one's eyes, which was as he intended. He was tall and thin, with a sharp chin and a large nose and snapping black eyes. He had velvet trousers and a fine hat which sweat had stained around the band, and long locks of dark hair that hung from under it at odd angles so that one knew he used the finger-comb when he woke, as drunkards do who find themselves beneath a bench. When the small man brought the cart through the innyard gate, I rose from my seat on the jail steps and went across to the inn parlor. And it was a fortunate thing I did so, because it was in this way that I chanced to see the famous game between the brass machine and Professor Baumeister.

Haven't I mentioned Professor Baumeister before? Have you not noticed that in a village such as ours there are always a dozen celebrities? Always a man who is strong (with us that is Willi Schacht, the smith's apprentice), one who eats a great deal, a learned man like Doctor Eckardt, a ladies' man, and so on. But for all these people to be properly admired, there must also be a distinguished visitor to whom to point them out, and here in Oder Spree that is Professor Baumeister, because our village lies midway between the University and Furstenwald, and it is here that he spends the night whenever he journeys from one to the other, much to the enrichment of Scheer the innkeeper. The fact of the matter is that Professor Baumeister has become one of our celebrities himself, only by spending the night here so often. With his broad brown beard and fine coat and tall hat and leather riding breeches, he gives the parlor of our inn the air of a gentlemen's club.

I have heard that it is often the case that the beginning of the greatest drama is as casual as any commonplace event. So it was that night. The inn was full of off-duty soldiers drinking beer, and because of the heat all the windows were thrown open, though a dozen candles were burning. Professor Baumeister was deep in conversation with Doctor Eckardt: something about the war. Herr Heitzmann the mountebank—though I did not know what to call him then—had already gotten his half liter when I came in, and was standing at the bar.

At last, when Professor Baumeister paused to emphasize some point, Herr Heitzmann leaned over to them, and in the most offhand way asked a question. It was peculiar, but the whole room seemed to grow silent as he spoke, so that he could be heard everywhere, though it was no more than a whisper. He said: "I wonder if I might venture to ask you gentlemen—you both appear to be learned men—if, to the best of your knowledge, there still exists even one of those great computational machines which were perhaps the most extraordinary—I trust you will agree with me?—creations of the age now past."

Professor Baumeister said at once: "No, sir. Not one remains."

"You feel certain of this?"

"My dear sir," said Professor Baumeister, "you must understand that those devices were dependent upon a supply of replacement parts consisting of the most delicate subminiature electronic components. These have not been produced now for over a hundred years—indeed, some of them have been unavailable longer."

"Ah," Herr Heitzmann said (mostly to himself, it seemed, but you could hear him in the kitchen). "Then I have the only one."

Professor Baumeister attempted to ignore this amazing remark, as not having been addressed to himself; but Doctor Eckardt, who is of an inquisitive disposition, said boldly: "You have such a machine, Herr . . . ?"

"Heitzmann. Originally of Berlin, now come from Zurich. And you, my good sir?"

Doctor Eckardt introduced himself, and Professor Baumeister too, and Herr Heitzmann clasped them by the hand. Then the doctor said to Professor Baumeister: "You are certain that no computers remain in existence, my friend?"

The professor said: "I am referring to working computers—machines in operating condition. There are plenty of old hulks in museums, of course."

Herr Heitzmann sighed, and pulled out a chair and sat down at the table with them, bringing his beer. "Would it not be sad," he said, "if those world-ruling machines were lost to mankind forever?"

Professor Baumeister said dryly: "They based their extrapolations on numbers. That worked well enough as long as money, which is easily measured numerically, was the principal motivating force in human affairs. But as time progressed, human actions became responsive instead to a multitude of incommensurable vectors; the computers' predictions failed, the civilization they had shaped collapsed, and parts for the machines were no longer obtainable or desired."

"How fascinating!" Herr Heitzmann exclaimed. "Do you know, I have never heard it explained in quite that way. You have provided me, for the first time, with an explanation for the survival of my own machine."

Doctor Eckardt said, "You have a working computer, then?"

"I do. You see, mine is a specialized device. It was not designed, like the computers the learned professor spoke of just now to predict human actions. It plays chess."

"And where do you keep this wonderful machine?" By this time everyone else in the room had fallen silent. Even Scheer took care not to allow the glasses he was drying to clink; and Gretchen, the fat blond serving girl who usually cracked jokes with the soldiers and banged down their plates, moved through the pipe smoke among the tables as quietly as the moon moves in a cloudy sky.

"Outside," Herr Heitzmann replied. "In my conveyance. I am taking it to Dresden."

"And it plays chess."

"It has never been defeated."

"Are you aware," Professor Baumeister inquired sardonically, "that to program a computer to play chess—to play well—was considered one of the most difficult problems? That many judged that it was never actually solved, and that those machines which most closely approached acceptable solutions were never so small as to be portable?"

"Nevertheless," Herr Heitzmann declared, "I have such a machine."

"My friend, I do not believe you."

"I take it you are a player yourself," Herr Heitzmann said. "Such a learned man could hardly be otherwise. Very well. As I said a moment ago, my machine is outside." His hand touched the table between Professor Baumeister's glass and his own, and when it came away five gold kilomarks stood there in a neat stack. "I will lay these on the outcome of the game, if you will play my machine tonight."

"Done," said Professor Baumeister.

"I must see your money."

"You will accept a draft on Streicher's, in Furstenwald?"

*   *   *

And so it was settled. Doctor Eckardt held the stakes, and six men volunteered to carry the machine into the inn parlor under Herr Heitzmann's direction.

Six were not too many, though the machine was not as large as might have been expected—not more than a hundred and twenty centimeters high, with a base, as it might be, a meter on a side. The sides and top were all of brass, set with many dials and other devices no one understood.

When it was at last in place, Professor Baumeister viewed it from all sides and smiled. "This is not a computer," he said.

"My dear friend," said Herr Heitzmann, "you are mistaken."

"It is several computers. There are two keyboards and a portion of a third. There are even two nameplates, and one of these dials once belonged to a radio."

Herr Heitzmann nodded. "It was assembled at the very close of the period, for one purpose only—to play chess."

"You still contend that this machine can play?"

"I contend more. That it will win."

"Very well. Bring a board."

"That is not necessary," Herr Heitzmann said. He pulled a knob at the front of the machine, and a whole section swung forward, as the door of a vegetable bin does in a scullery. But the top of the bin was not open as though to receive the vegetables: it was instead a chessboard, with the white squares of brass, and the black of smoky glass, and on the board, standing in formation and ready to play, were two armies of chessmen such as no one in our village had ever seen, tall metal figures so stately they might have been sculptured apostles in a church, one army of brass and the other of some dark metal. "You may play white," Herr Heitzmann said. "That is generally considered an advantage."

Professor Baumeister nodded, advanced the white king's pawn two squares, and drew a chair up to the board. By the time he had seated himself the machine had replied, moving so swiftly that no one saw by what mechanism the piece had been shifted.

The next time Professor Baumeister acted more slowly, and everyone watched, eager to see the machine's countermove. It came the moment the professor had set his piece in its new position—the black queen slid forward silently, with nothing to propel it.

After ten moves Professor Baumeister said, "There is a man inside."

Herr Heitzmann smiled. "I see why you say that, my friend. Your position on the board is precarious."

"I insist that the machine be opened for my examination."

"I suppose you would say that if a man were concealed inside, the bet would be canceled." Herr Heitzmann had ordered a second glass of beer, and was leaning against the bar watching the game.

"Of course. My bet was that a machine could not defeat me. I am well aware that certain human players can."

"But conversely, if there is no man in the machine, the bet stands?"

"Certainly."

"Very well." Herr Heitzmann walked to the machine, twisted four catches on one side and with the help of some onlookers removed the entire panel. It was of brass, like the rest of the machine, but, because the metal was thin, not so heavy as it appeared.

There was more room inside than might have been thought, yet withal a considerable amount of mechanism: things like shingles the size of little tabletops, all covered with patterns like writing (Lame Hans has told me since that these are called circuit cards). And gears and motors and the like.

When Professor Baumeister had poked among all these mechanical parts for half a minute, Herr Heitzmann asked: "Are you satisfied?"

"Yes," answered Professor Baumeister, straightening up. "There is no one in there."

"But *I* am not," said Herr Heitzmann, and he walked with long strides to the other side of the machine. Everyone crowded around him as he released the catches on that side, lifted away the panel, and stood it against the wall. "Now," he said, "you can see completely through my machine—isn't that right? Look, do you see Doctor Eckardt? Do you see me? Wave to us."

"I am satisfied," Professor Baumeister said. "Let us go on with the game."

"The machine has already taken its move. You may think about your next one while these gentlemen help me replace the panels."

Professor Baumeister was beaten in twenty-two moves. Albricht the moneylender then asked if he could play without betting, and when this was refused by Herr Heitzmann, bet a kilomark and was beaten in fourteen moves. Herr Heitzmann asked then if anyone else would play, and when no one replied, requested that the same men who had carried the machine into the inn assist him in putting it away again.

"Wait," said Professor Baumeister.

Herr Heitzmann smiled. "You mean to play again?"

"No. I want to buy your machine. On behalf of the University."

Herr Heitzmann sat down and looked serious. "I doubt that I could sell it to you. I had hoped to make a good sum in Dresden before selling it there."

"Five hundred kilomarks."

Herr Heitzmann shook his head. "That is a fair proposition," he said, "and I thank you for making it. But I cannot accept."

"Seven hundred and fifty," Professor Baumeister said. "That is my final offer."

"In gold?"

"In a draft on an account the University maintains in Furstenwald—you can present it there for gold the first thing in the morning."

"You must understand," said Herr Heitzmann, "that the machine requires a certain amount of care, or it will not perform properly."

"I am buying it as is," said Professor Baumeister. "As it stands here before us."

"Done, then," said Herr Heitzmann, and he put out his hand.

The board was folded away, and six stout fellows carried the machine into the professor's room for safekeeping, where he remained with it for an hour or more. When he returned to the inn parlor at last, Doctor Eckardt asked if he had been playing chess again.

Professor Baumeister nodded. "Three games."

"Did you win?"

"No, I lost them all. Where is the showman?"

"Gone," said Father Karl, who was sitting near them. "He left as soon as you took the machine to your room."

Doctor Eckardt said, "I thought he planned to stay the night here."

"So did I," said Father Karl. "And I confess I believed the machine would not function without him. I was surprised to hear that our friend the professor had been playing in private."

Just then a small, twisted man, with a large head crowned with wild black hair, limped into the inn parlor. It was Lame Hans, but no one knew that then. He asked Scheer the innkeeper for a room.

Scheer smiled. "Sitting rooms on the first floor are a hundred marks," he said. He could see by Lame Hans's worn clothes that he could not afford a sitting room.

"Something cheaper."

"My regular rooms are thirty marks. Or I can let you have a garret for ten."

Hans rented a garret room, and ordered a meal of beer, tripe, and kraut. That was the last time anyone except Gretchen noticed Lame Hans that night.

* * *

And now I must leave off recounting what I myself saw, and tell many things that rest solely on the testimony of Lame Hans, given to me while he ate his potato soup in his cell. But I believe Lame Hans to be an honest fellow; and as he no longer, as he says, cares much to live, he has no reason to lie.

One thing is certain. Lame Hans and Gretchen the serving girl fell in love that night. Just how it happened I cannot say—I doubt that Lame Hans himself knows. She was sent to prepare the cot in his garret. Doubtless she was tired after drawing beer in the parlor all day, and was happy to sit for a few moments and talk with him. Perhaps she smiled—she was always a girl who smiled a great deal—and laughed at some bitter joke he made. And as for Lame Hans, how many blue-eyed girls could ever have smiled at him, with his big head and twisted leg?

In the morning the machine would not play chess.

Professor Baumeister sat before it for a long time, arranging the pieces and making first one opening and then another, and tinkering with the mechanism; but nothing happened.

And then, when the morning was half gone, Lame Hans came into his room. "You paid a great deal of money for this machine," he said, and sat down in the best chair.

"Were you in the inn parlor last night?" asked Professor Baumeister. "Yes, I paid a great deal: seven hundred and fifty kilomarks."

"I was there," said Lame Hans. "You must be a very rich man to be able to afford such a sum."

"It was the University's money," explained Professor Baumeister.

"Ah," said Lame Hans. "Then it will be embarrassing for you if the machine does not play."

"It does play," said the professor. "I played three games with it last night after it was brought here."

"You must learn to make better use of your knights," Lame Hans told him, "and to attack on both sides of the board at once. In the second game you played well until you lost the queen's rook; then you went to pieces."

The professor sat down, and for a moment said nothing. And then: "You are the operator of the machine. I was correct in the beginning; I should have known."

Lame Hans looked out the window.

"How did you move the pieces—by radio? I suppose there must still be radio-control equipment in existence somewhere."

"I was inside," Lame Hans said. "I'll show you sometime; it's not important. What will you tell the University?"

"That I was swindled, I suppose. I have some money of my own, and I will try to pay back as much as I can out of that—and I own two houses in Furstenwald that can be sold."

"Do you smoke?" asked Lame Hans, and he took out his short pipe, and a bag of tobacco.

"Only after dinner," said the professor, "and not often then."

"I find it calms my nerves," said Lame Hans. "That is why I suggested it to you. I do not have a second pipe, but I can offer you some of my tobacco, which is very good. You might buy a clay from the innkeeper here."

"No, thank you. I fear I must abandon such little pleasures for a long time to come."

"Not necessarily," said Lame Hans. "Go ahead, buy that pipe. This is good Turkish tobacco—would you believe, to look at me, that I know a great deal about tobacco? It has been my only luxury."

"If you are the one who played chess with me last night," Professor Baumeister said, "I would be willing to believe that you know a great deal about anything. You play like the devil himself."

"I know a great deal about more than tobacco. Would you like to get your money back?"

And so it was that that very afternoon (if it can be credited), the mail coach carried away bills printed in large black letters. These said:

IN THE VILLAGE OF ODER SPREE

BEFORE THE INN OF THE GOLDEN APPLES

ON SATURDAY
AT 9:00 O'CLOCK
THE MARVELOUS BRASS CHESSPLAYING AUTOMATON WILL
BE ON DISPLAY
FREE TO EVERYONE
AND WILL PLAY ANY CHALLENGER
AT EVEN ODDS
TO A LIMIT OF DM 2,000,000

Now, you will think from what I have told you that Lame Hans was a cocky fellow, but that is not the case, though like many of us who are small of stature he pretended to be self-reliant when he was among men taller than he. The truth is that though he did not show it he was very frightened when he met Herr Heitzmann (as the two of them had arranged earlier that he should) in a certain malodorous tavern near the Schwarzthor in Furthenwald.

"So there you are, my friend," said Herr Heitzmann. "How did it go?"

"Terribly," Lame Hans replied as though he felt nothing. "I was locked up in that brass snuffbox for half the night, and had to play twenty games with that fool of a scholar. And when at last I got out, I couldn't get a ride here and had to walk most of the way on this bad leg of mine. I trust it was comfortable on the cart seat? The horse didn't give you too much trouble?"

"I'm sorry you've had a poor time of it, but now you can relax. There's nothing more to do until he's convinced the machine is broken and irreparable."

Lame Hans looked at him as though in some surprise. "You didn't see the signs? They are posted everywhere."

"What signs?"

"He's offering to bet two thousand kilomarks that no one can beat the machine."

Herr Heitzmann shrugged. "He will discover that it is inoperative before the contest, and cancel it."

"He could not cancel after the bet was made," said Lame

Hans. "Particularly if there were a proviso that if either were unable to play, the bet was forfeited. Some upright citizen would be selected to hold the stakes, naturally."

"I don't suppose he could at that," said Herr Heitzmann, taking a swallow of schnapps from the glass before him. "However, he wouldn't bet *me*—he'd think I knew some way to influence the machine. Still, he's never seen *you.*"

"Just what I've been thinking myself," said Lame Hans, "on my hike."

"It's a little out of your line."

"If you'll put up the cash, I'd be willing to go a little out of my line for my tenth of that kind of money. But what is there to do? I make the bet, find someone to hold the stakes, and stand ready to play on Saturday morning. I could even offer to play him—for a smaller bet—to give him a chance to get some of his own back. That is, if he has anything left after paying off. It would make it seem more sporting."

"You're certain you could beat him?"

"I can beat anybody—you know that. Besides, I beat him a score of times yesterday; the game you saw was just the first."

Herr Heitzmann ducked under the threatening edge of a tray carried by an overenthusiastic waiter. "All the same," he said, "when he discovers it won't work . . ."

"I could even spend a bit of time in the machine. That's no problem. It's in a first-floor room, with a window that won't lock."

And so Lame Hans left for our village again, this time considerably better dressed and with two thousand kilomarks in his pocket. Herr Heitzmann, with his appearance considerably altered by a plastiskin mask, left also, an hour later, to keep an eye on the two thousand.

"But," the professor said when Lame Hans and he were comfortably ensconced in his sitting room again, with pipes in their mouths and glasses in their hands and a plate of sausage on the table, "but who is going to operate the machine for us?

Wouldn't it be easier if you simply didn't appear? Then you would forfeit."

"And Heitzmann would kill me," said Lame Hans.

"He didn't strike me as the type."

"He would hire it done," Hans said positively. "Whenever he got the cash. There are deserters about who are happy enough to do that kind of work for drinking money. For that matter, there are soldiers who aren't deserters who'll do it— men on detached duty of one kind and another. When you've spent all winter slaughtering Russians, one more body doesn't make much difference." He blew a smoke ring, then ran the long stem of his clay pipe through it as though he were driving home a bayonet. "But if I play the machine and lose, he'll only think you figured things out and got somebody to work it, and that I'm not as good as he supposed. Then he won't want anything more to do with me."

"All right, then."

"A tobacconist should do well in this village, don't you think? I had in mind that little shop two doors down from here. When the coaches stop, the passengers will see my sign; there should be many who'll want to fill their pouches."

"Gretchen prefers to stay here, I suppose."

Lame Hans nodded. "It doesn't matter to me. I've been all over, and when you've been all over, it's all the same."

Like everyone else in the village, and for fifty kilometers around, I had seen the professor's posters, and I went to bed Friday night full of pleasant anticipation. Lame Hans had told me that he retired in the same frame of mind, after a couple of glasses of good plum brandy in the inn parlor with the professor. He and the professor had to appear strangers and antagonists in public, as will be readily seen; but this did not prevent them from eating and drinking together while they discussed arrangements for the match, which was to be held— with the permission of Burgermeister Landsteiner—in the village street, where an area for the players had been cordoned off and high benches erected for the spectators.

Hans woke (so he has told me) when it was still dark, thinking that he had heard thunder. Then the noise came again, and he knew it must be the artillery, the big siege guns, firing at the Russians trapped in Kostrzyn. The army had built wood-fired steam tractors to pull those guns—he had seen them in Wriezen—and now the soldiers were talking about putting armor on the tractors and mounting cannon, so the knights of the chessboard would exist in reality once more.

The firing continued, booming across the dry plain, and he went to the window to see if he could make out the flashes, but could not. He put on a thin shirt and a pair of cotton trousers (for though the sun was not yet up, it was as hot as if the whole of Brandenburg had been thrust into a furnace) and went into the street to look at the empty shop in which he planned to set up his tobacco business. A squadron of *Ritters* galloped through the village, doubtless on their way to the siege. Lame Hans shouted, "What do you mean to do? Ride your horses against the walls?" but they ignored him. Now that the truce was broken, Von Koblenz's army would soon be advancing up the Oder Valley, Lame Hans thought. The Russians were said to have been preparing powered balloons to assist in the defense, and this hot summer weather, when the air seemed never to stir, would favor their use. He decided that if he were the Commissar, he would allow Von Koblenz to reach Glogow, and then . . .

But he was not the Commissar. He went back into the inn and smoked his pipe until Frau Scheer came down to prepare his breakfast. Then he went to the professor's room where the machine was kept. Gretchen was already waiting there.

"Now then," Professor Baumeister said, "I understand that the two of you have it all worked out between you." And Gretchen nodded solemnly, so that her plump chin looked like a soft little pillow pressed against her throat.

"It is quite simple," said Lame Hans. "Gretchen does not know how to play, but I have worked out the moves for her and drawn them on a sheet of paper, and we have practiced in my room with a board. We will run through it once here when she is in the machine; then there will be nothing more to do."

"Is it a short game? It won't do for her to become confused."

"She will win in fourteen moves," Lame Hans promised. "But still it is unusual. I don't think anyone has done it before. You will see in a moment."

To Gretchen, Professor Baumeister said: "You're sure you won't be mixed up? Everything depends on you."

The girl shook her head, making her blond braids dance. "No, Herr Professor," She drew a folded piece of paper from her bosom. "I have it all here, and as my Hans told you, we have practiced in his room, where no one could see us."

"You aren't afraid?"

"When I am going to marry Hans, and be mistress of a fine shop? Oh, no, Herr Professor—for that I would do much worse things than to hide in this thing that looks like a stove, and play a game."

"We are ready, then," the professor said. "Hans, you still have not explained how it is that a person can hide in there, when the sides can be removed allowing people to look through the machinery. And I confess I still don't understand how it can be done, or how the pieces are moved."

"Here," said Lame Hans, and he pulled out the board as Herr Heitzmann had done in the inn parlor. "Now will you assist me in removing the left side? You should learn the way it comes loose, Professor—someday you may have to do it yourself." (The truth was that he was not strong enough to handle the big brass sheet by himself, and did not wish to be humiliated before Gretchen.)

"I had forgotten how much empty space there is inside," Professor Baumeister said when they had it off. "It looks more impossible than ever."

"It is simple, like all good tricks," Lame Hans told him. "And it is the sign of a good trick that it is the thing that makes it appear difficult that makes it easy. Here is where the chessboard is, you see, when it is folded up. But when it is unfolded, the panel under it swings out on a hinge to support it, and there are sides, so that a triangular space is formed."

The professor nodded and said, "I remember thinking when I played you that it looked like a potato bin, with the chessboard laid over the top."

"Exactly," Lame Hans continued. "The space is not noticeable when the machine is open, because this circuit is just in front of it. But see here." And he released a little catch at the top of the circuit card, and pivoted it up to show the empty space behind it. "I am in the machine when it is carried in, but when Heitzmann pulls out the board, I lift this and fit myself under it; then, when the machine is opened for inspection, I am out of view. I can look up through the dark glass of the black squares, and because the pieces are so tall, I can make out their positions. But because it is bright outside, but dim where I am, I cannot be seen."

"I understand," said the professor. "But will Gretchen have enough light in there to read her piece of paper?"

"That was why I wanted to hold the match in the street. With the board in sunshine, she will be able to see her paper clearly."

Gretchen was on her knees, looking at the space behind the circuit card. "It is very small in there," she said.

"It is big enough," said Lame Hans. "Do you have the magnet?" And then to the professor: "The pieces are moved by moving a magnet under them. The white pieces are brass, but the black ones are of iron, and the magnet gives them a sliding motion that is very impressive."

"I know," said the professor, remembering that he had felt a twinge of uneasiness whenever the machine had shifted a piece. "Gretchen, see if you can get inside."

The poor girl did the best she could, but encountered the greatest difficulty in wedging herself into the small space under the board. Work in the kitchen of the inn had provided her with many opportunities to snatch a mouthful of pastry or a choice potato dumpling or a half stein of dark beer, and she had availed herself of most of them—with the result that she possessed a lush and blooming figure of the sort that appeals to men like Lame Hans, who, having been withered before birth by the isotopes of the old wars, are themselves thin and small by nature. But though full breasts like ripe melons, and a rounded comfortable stomach and generous hips, may be pleasant things to look at when the moonlight comes in the bedroom window, they are not really well-suited to folding up in a little three-cornered space under a chessboard; and in the end, poor Gretchen was forced to remove her gown, and her shift as well, before she could cram herself, with much gasping and grunting, into it.

An hour later, Willi Schacht the smith's apprentice and five other men carried the machine out into the street and set it in the space that had been cordoned off for the players, and if they noticed the extra weight, they did not complain of it. And there the good people who had come to see the match looked at the machine, and fanned themselves, and said that they were glad they weren't in the army on a day like this—because what must it be to serve one of those big guns, which get hot enough to poach an egg after half a dozen shots, even in ordinary weather? And between moppings and fannings they talked about the machine, and the mysterious Herr Zimmer (that was the name Lame Hans had given) who was going to play for two hundred gold kilomarks.

Nine chimes sounded from the old clock in the steeple of Father Karl's church, and Herr Zimmer did not appear.

Doctor Eckardt, who had been chosen again to hold the stakes, came forward and whispered for some time with Professor Baumeister. The professor (if the truth were known) was beginning to believe that perhaps Lame Hans had decided it was best to forfeit after all—though in fact, if anyone had looked, he would have seen Lame Hans sitting at the bar of the inn at that very moment, having a pleasant nip of plum brandy and then another, while he allowed the suspense to build up as a good showman should.

At last Doctor Eckardt climbed upon a chair and announced: "It is nearly ten. When the bet was made, it was agreed by both parties that if either failed to appear—or appearing, failed to play—the other should be declared the winner. If the worthy stranger, Herr Zimmer, does not make an appearance before ten minutes past ten, I intend to award the money entrusted to me to our respected acquaintance Professor Baumeister."

There was a murmur of excitement at this, but just when the clock began to strike, Lame Hans called from the door of the inn: "WAIT!" Then hats were thrown into the air, and women stood on tiptoes to see; and fathers lifted their children up as the lame Herr Zimmer made his way down the steps of the inn and took his place in the chair that had been arranged in front of the board.

"Are you ready to begin?" said Doctor Eckardt.

"I am," said Lame Hans, and opened.

The first five moves were made just as they had been rehearsed. But in the sixth, in which Gretchen was to have slid her queen half across the board, the piece stopped a square short.

Any ordinary player would have been dismayed, but Lame Hans was not. He only put his chin on his hand, and contrived (though wishing he had not drunk the brandy) a series of moves within the frame of the fourteen-move game, by which he should lose despite the queen's being out of position. He made the first of these moves; and black moved the queen again, this time in a way that was completely different from anything on the paper Hans had given Gretchen. *She was deceiving me when she said she did not know how to play,* he thought to himself. *And now she feels she can't read the paper in there, or perhaps she has decided to surprise me. Naturally she would learn the fundamentals of the game, when it is played in the inn parlor every night.* (But he knew that she had not been deceiving him.) Then he saw that this new move of the queen's was in fact a clever attack, into which he could play and lose.

And then the guns around Kostrzyn, which had been silent since the early hours of the morning, began to boom again.

Three times Lame Hans's hand stretched out to touch his king and make the move that would render it quite impossible for him to escape the queen, and three times it drew back. "You have five minutes in which to move," Doctor Eckardt said. "I will tell you when only thirty seconds remain, and count the last five."

The machine was built to play chess, thought Lame Hans. *Long ago, and they were warlocks in those days. Could it be that Gretchen, in kicking about . . . ?*

Some motion in the sky made him raise his eyes, looking above the board and over the top of the machine itself. An artillery observation balloon (gray-black, a German balloon then) was outlined against the blue sky. He thought of himself sitting in a dingy little shop full of tobacco all day long, and no one to play chess with—no one he could not checkmate easily.

He moved a pawn, and the black bishop slipped out of the king's row to tighten the net.

If he won, they would have to pay him. Heitzmann would think everything had gone according to plan, and Professor Baumeister, surely, would hire no assassins. He launched his counterattack: the real attack at the left side of the board, with a false one down the center. Professor Baumeister came to stand beside him, and Doctor Eckardt warned him not to distract the player. There had been seven more than fourteen moves—and there was a trap behind the trap.

He took the black queen's knight and lost a pawn. He was sweating in the heat, wiping his brow with his sleeve between moves.

A black rook, squat in its iron sandbags, advanced three squares, and he heard the crowd cheer. "That is mate, Herr Zimmer," Doctor Eckardt announced. He saw the look of relief on Professor Baumeister's face, and knew that his own was blank. Then over the cheering someone shouted: *"Cheat! Cheat!"* Gray-black pillbox police caps were forcing their way through the hats and parasols of the spectators.

"There is a man in there! There is someone inside!" It was

too clear and too loud—a showman's voice. A tall stranger was standing on the topmost bench waving Heitzmann's sweat-stained velvet hat.

A policeman asked: "The machine opens, does it not, Herr Professor? Open it quickly before there is a riot."

Professor Baumeister said, "I don't know how."

"It looks simple enough," declared the other policeman, and he began to unfasten the catches, wrapping his hand in his handkerchief to protect it from the heat of the brass. "Wait!" ordered Professor Baumeister, but neither one waited; the first policeman went to the aid of the other, and together they lifted away one side of the machine and let it fall against the railing. The movable circuit card had not been allowed to swing back into place, and Gretchen's plump, naked legs protruded from the cavity beneath the chessboard. The first policeman seized them by the ankles and pulled her out until her half-open eyes stared at the bright sky. Doctor Eckhardt bent over her and flexed her left arm at the elbow. "Rigor is beginning," he said. "She died of the heat, undoubtedly."

Lame Hans threw himself on her body weeping.

Such is the story of Lame Hans. The captain of police, in his kindness, has permitted me to push the machine to a position which permits Hans to reach the board through the bars of his cell, and he plays chess there all day long, moving first his own white pieces and then the black ones of the machine, and always losing. Sometimes when he is not quick enough to move the black queen, I see her begin to rock and to slide herself, and the dials and the console lights to glow with impatience; and then Hans must reach out and take her to her new position at once. Do you not think that this is sad for Lame Hans? I have heard that many who have been twisted by the old wars have these psychokinetic abilities without knowing it; and Professor Baumeister, who is in the cell next to his, says that someday a technology may be founded on them.

To the Dark Tower Came

*EDGAR: Child Rowland to the dark tower came,
His word was still,—Fire, foh, and fum,
I smell the blood of a British man.*

"HE'S SENILE," Gloucester said.

Kent, who would die that day, shook his head and shrugged. He was standing at the room's nearest window looking out, his broad shoulders wrapped in an old goatskin cloak.

"Senile," Gloucester repeated. Hoping to lighten Kent's mood he added, "I like to think that the first syllable derives from the Anglo-Saxon *sendan,* meaning 'to transmit.' The second from the Latin *Nilus,* the name of a mythical, northward-flowing river in Africa. This river was supposed to be lined with antique structures; so that transmission to the Nilotic region indicated that a thing was of ancient age."

Kent said nothing.

"Can you see anything through that ivy? What are you looking at out there?"

"Fog," Kent said.

Gloucester walked over to the window. The bronze tip of the scabbard hanging from his belt, weighted by the broad blade of the sword within, scraped the stone flags. He peered out. The window was no wider than the length of a man's forearm, cut in a gray stone wall several times as thick. "Fog my bung, sir," he said. "Those are clouds. But never mind, we'll get down, clouds or no."

"They might be clouds," Kent answered mildly. "You never can tell."

"They blasted well *are* clouds. Throw your dagger out of

there, and it would spit an eagle before it struck the ground. There's no telling how high up we are."

"I prefer to believe that it is fog," Kent said. He turned to face Gloucester and seated himself on the clammy windowsill. "I could leave this place at any time, simply by climbing out this window and jumping to the ground. Conversely, if I leave the window unguarded, it is possible that a bear or jaguar or other wild thing might enter."

"Poor creature," Gloucester muttered. And then: "So you say it's fog. All right, sir, climb out. So soon as your feet are on good, solid ground, call to me, and I'll come too."

"I prefer not to," Kent said. His sad, handsome face creased, though only for a second, in a smile. "I believe in intellectual democracy; I know that I am right, but I concede the possibility that you're right too."

Gloucester cleared his throat. "Let's stop amusing ourselves with fancies and look at this logically." He thrust his hands behind him, under his own tattered cloak, and began to pace up and down. "The king's senile. I won't argue definitions with you. You know what I mean, and I know you agree with me, whatever you may say. Now, let's list the options available to us."

"We've done this before," Kent said.

"Granted. But let's do it again. I pride myself, sir, on being a sound sullen scholar; and when there is nothing more to be done, we triple 'S' men recast the data—integrate, integrate, integrate, and three pump handles."

He took a deep breath. "Now then, what is the desired result? What is it we wish? To be away—isn't that so? To courtier no more? That will do for a beginning. I'd like to leave aside those highflown plans of yours for the time being, and get to something practical."

"One of my ancestors was supposed to be able to fly," Kent said. He was craning his neck to look out the window again. "My mother showed me his picture once. The climate must have been warmer then, because his cloak was silk. Red silk. He flew through the air, and it streamed out behind him."

"A symbolic figure," Gloucester told him. "He represented the strong man who, ridding himself of the superstitions of the past, devoted himself to improving his own powers and achieving mastery of others. Actually there have been a number of people who've tried it, but someone always shoots them."

"Bullets ricocheted from his chest," Kent said dreamily.

There was a beating of vast wings outside the window.

"Listen!"

"Don't go out there," Gloucester warned, but Kent had already turned around, and was scrambling on hands and knees through the aperture in the wall until he could thrust his head and shoulders through the curtain of leaves into the faint, free air.

Above his head, and below it, the tower extended until sight failed in white mist. Though Kent knew it to be round, to either side the wall seemed flat—so great was the radius of that mighty curve. (Some, indeed, said that it was infinite.) Vines overgrew the wall; Kent set his foot upon a stout stem, and took another in his right hand; then, drawing his dagger with his left, stepped out, so that he hung suspended in a dark green jungle of foliage over the yawning void.

The wing-wind tugged at his hair and fluttered the fur of the collar at his throat. A vampire flapped systematically up and down the wall, beating the ivy with pinions that were to Kent's cloak as the cloak to an ivy leaf. There were climbers in the ivy, pale figures Kent knew to be men and women. When the vampire's wings dislodged them they fell; and the flying horror dove after them until it had them in its claws, then rose again. What it did with them then, Kent could not see—it folded itself in the black membrane of its pinions as though shamed by its own malignancy, hanging in the air, head bowed, like a scud of sooty smoke. When the wings opened again, its victims were gone.

"What was it?" Gloucester asked when Kent stood on the floor of the room once more.

Kent shrugged, and sheathed his dagger.

"Are we high up?"

"Very high. How can it be that there is air here?"

"My theory is that the tower draws air with it," Gloucester said. "Its mass is so great that it attracts its own atmosphere."

Kent spat, and watched his spittle fall. It struck the flagstones in a pattern that suggested the skull-face of the vampire; but he ignored this, and said, "If what you say is true, then the direction we call 'down' would necessarily be towards the center of the tower."

Gloucester shook his shaggy head. "No, down would be the resultant of the tower's attraction, the earth's, and the moon's. The construction of the floors may take that into account."

"The moon's? Do you think the tower rises high enough for that?"

"The moon's gravitation has an effect even on the earth's surface," Gloucester told him, "drawing the tides. And yes, I know that the tower rises very high indeed. One of its commonest names is Spire Sans Summit."

"Poetical exaggeration," Kent said. Although he did not like turning his back to the open window, he had wandered over to the stairs—down which they had come, and down which, as he knew, they would eventually go again.

"Suppose that it is not. Suppose that the king himself is the originator of that phrase, and that it reflects sober truth. How can it be true?"

"If work is still in progress," Kent said slowly, "the tower could be called summitless, because the summit is not yet in place."

"A mere quibble. But suppose another foundation exists—on another sphere. Imagine this tower stretched between the two, like a cobweb of stone."

"Then in going downward," Kent said, "we may be progressing toward either end. Is that it? When we reach the lowest floor, we may step out onto the surface of the moon?"

The other man nodded. "There are footprints on the surface of the moon, you know. Even though the king would have us believe all this is happening long before that time."

"Then let us go, even if it is to the moon, or a farther place; when we reach it we will be able to see the earth, and we will know where we are." He began to descend the stair.

"You're going down again? I'll come with you."

The room below might have filled all the tower, from wall to wall, with a domed ceiling higher in the center than the room was wide; so that it seemed like a world unto itself. The stone stair they trod might have been a bit of gossamer in the immensity.

"It's an orrery, by God," Gloucester said. "At least it's not another throne room."

"It may still be another throne room," Kent cautioned him.

In the center the sun burned with thermonuclear fire. Far away, at the dim borders of the room to which the two descended, cold Pluto circled. The walls were wainscoted, the wooden panels painted with the symbols of the zodiac; a rearing bison, shot to the heart, snorted gore near where they stood when they attained the floor at last.

Here the stair ended. "We must find another way down," Gloucester said.

Kent nodded and added, "Or up, if we are going up."

The rearing bison seemed to speak: "Long have I ruled—a hundred years and more." (But it was the king's voice.)

"Yes, monarch of the plain," Kent answered, "long did you rule."

"Hush," Gloucester whispered, "he'll hear you."

"Long have I ruled," the king's voice continued. "I have starved my enemies; built my tower."

"You are old," Gloucester ventured. There was a stirring behind the painted panel, but Kent knew that the king was not there.

"In the dream of serving others, they have served me. Pisces the whale I penned in a tank of glass, sheltering her from the waters I poisoned. Does not that show the love I bore her? The poison was needed for the making: scientist and sorcerer am I."

From a hole gnawed between the rearing bison's feet, a rat's head peeped forth. It was as large as a bucket; seeing it, Kent drew his sword.

"It is as I feared," Gloucester said when his own blade was in his hand. "The lower parts of the tower are worse than the higher. Or the higher are worse than the lower, as may be."

The rat was through the hole now, edging along the wall, while a second rat glared out with shining eyes.

"To the center of the room!" Kent urged.

But Gloucester cautioned: "No. Let us stay here, where we can guard one another's backs, or put our own to the wall."

The king's voice had continued all the while, though neither had heard it. Now it said: "Some insinuate that I grow old. Do they think that I, who know so much, cannot renew myself? And do they not know that if I should die, the tower will fall upon them? The rats are at the foundation even now."

The rat sprang for Kent's throat. He hewed it with his sword, and plunged his dagger into its chest as it flew toward him; but as he struck, the septic fangs of the second rat opened his left leg from thigh to ankle. Grizzled Gloucester, awkward but bull-strong, clove its spine with a single stroke; still, it was too late.

"I will carry you wherever you wish to go," he told Kent when a tourniquet had eased the bleeding. "Back to earth or to the moon. Wherever you think there may be help."

The bison had fallen silent, but the claws of the dying rats still scrabbled on the floor. "I'll carry you wherever you want to go," Gloucester repeated, thinking Kent had not heard him.

But Kent only said: "Be quiet. Someone is coming."

Gloucester thought him delirious. "I see no one."

"That is because the sun is at his back," Kent said. "You cannot see him against the glare."

After a moment Gloucester muttered: "A boy. I see him now."

The boy wore a crown. He was about thirteen, but his eyes were the cold, mad eyes of the king. Maidens followed him; these had no eyes at all—only little flames, like candles burning, in the empty sockets. "Who are you men?" the boy asked.

Gloucester bowed as well as he could, still holding Kent, and said: "We are your courtiers, sire. Kent and Gloucester."

The boy shook his head. "I do not remember those names."

"In the beginning you called us Youth and Learning, sir; you promised us a great deal."

"I don't remember that either," the boy king said. "But if you will behave yourselves and amuse me, I will give you whatever it was I promised you before."

Gloucester asked, "Will you heal my friend?" but the king had already turned away.

Later Kent whispered, "Gloucester . . ."

"Are you in much pain?"

"Gloucester, I have been thinking."

Gloucester said, "That is always painful, I know," but the younger man did not smile.

"You said that if this tower reaches to the moon, it has no top. . . ."

"Yes."

"But isn't it equally valid to say both ends are the top? From the moon, the foundation on earth is the summit. Isn't that correct?"

"If you say so. But perhaps you should try to rest now." The wound in Kent's leg was bleeding freely again; Gloucester thrust the fingers of one hand through the tourniquet and twisted the cloth to tighten it.

He was still fussing with it when Kent murmured: "Call back the king, Gloucester, and carry me to the window. With one single bound I will leap this tall building; and that is something a boy should see."

Parkroads—A Review

ONE HARDLY KNOWS WHAT TO SAY ABOUT *Parkroads*. Released in 1939 and 1984, it violates many of the canons of cinematography and must be considered a failure. Yet it is impossible to understand this remarkable film without an enlightened awareness of its many inexplicable experiments.

Strictly speaking, it is without opening credits. Instead the credits, such as they are, continue throughout all six (possibly seven) reels, spoken by the cast at pseudoappropriate moments. For example, as Tanya (or Daisy) reclines beside Belvedere Lake, her face concealed by an immense straw hat, she is heard to murmur, "Choreography by . . ." Jonquils are tossed by the wind, but there is no dancing *per se*.

Parkroads is neatly divided into alternating sequences, though in a few instances an episode of one type is followed immediately by another, quite different, episode from the same sequence. The later episodes—appearing generally in the first half of the film as it has been released in the U.S.—were produced in Brooklyn in the mid nineteen thirties, presumably between Roosevelt's election and the dissolution of the NRA. They are set in Belgium (largely in Bruges) in the early years of the closing quarter of the present century.

The earlier episodes, in which each character explains or at least attempts to explain the plot, were completed in various parts of the Low Countries several years ago. They are laid in and around New York, and the effect of traffic simulated by putting cars, trucks, buses, and subway trains aboard canal boats is at times very pleasing. The plot (and unlike so many experimental films *Parkroads* has one and is almost too concerned with it) involves a Chinese family called Chin.

Or rather, it involves a Korean-Chinese family called Park, founded when a Chin daughter weds a Korean as the Chins pass through Korea while moving eastward to the West. A letter (possibly forged) received by another family in the Chins' native village in Hunan speaks of a paradisiacal "Golden-Mountain-Land." Chin Mai and Chin Liang resolve to undertake the trip, and the rest of the family—parents, three sisters, and a grandmother—accompanies them.

They travel to Wu-Han, Nan-Ching, and eventually to Peking (Beijing). While working as scullions in the famous Sick Duck, they encounter a wily junk captain who promises to transport them to Golden-Mountain-Land in return for one of the daughters. (There is an amusing scene in which the three vie in bad cooking.) His choice falls on Pear Blossom, whom he sells to a brothel.

The remainder of the family takes ship at Tsingtao and crosses the Yellow Sea. They disembark at Inchon, believing the junk will anchor there for several days; it sails without them.

One of the remaining sisters, Cloud Fairy, is betrothed to Park Lee, a Korean. With the aid she persuades him to provide, the other Chins move on, vaguely eastward, to Pohang and perhaps eventually to Japan. Cloud Fairy lives out the remainder of her life in the Land of Morning Calm but bequeaths to her descendants a yearning irresistible and indefectible.

Drawn by their inherited memories, they reach California but fail to identify it as Golden-Mountain-Land (if indeed it is). They continue eastward, hitching rides with disappointed Okies returning to the Dust Bowl. In New York (these are the episodes recently completed in Belgium) they are befriended by a Turk who tells them that the world is circular, being in fact the crater of a quiescent cosmic volcano, Mt. Kaf, which surrounds it upon all sides. The slopes of the crater, says the

Turk, are doubtless Golden-Mountain-Land, but to reach them it is necessary to walk straight through the world, whose roads have the trick of bending human steps. Frank Park nods and soon vanishes. This bald stating of its theme is perhaps the weakest element in *Parkroads*.

As already indicated, *Parkroads* has been released in six reels; they are so staged that it is by no means easy to determine the order in which they are to be shown. There is, of course, a conventional indication on the film cans for the guidance of the projectionist; but this is almost certainly incorrect. The incidents in Hunan now given in flashback may have well been intended, at least at one time, as the opening of the picture. The sequence in the public gardens of Ghent during which Doris is asked why she has embraced decadence and answers, "Directed by Henry Miller" (or perhaps Müeller), was surely intended as the last, or next to last. Publicity releases from 1939 assert that if all the reels are projected in the correct order, it will be apparent the Parks have discovered that the village in Hunan that was the original home of the Chins was in fact Golden-Mountain-Land; in short, that the paradise described in the letter was merely that of nostalgia. One hopes not.

If so, it is a problem readily amenable to mathematical treatment. Any of the six reels could be chosen as the first. Five then remain for the second, yielding thirty combinations. Four remain for the third—one hundred and twenty combinations. Three remain for the fourth, two for the fifth, and only one for the last—total of seven hundred and twenty showings, surely not an impossible number.

However, there are references to a missing seventh reel. If such a reel exists, the number of showings is substantially increased (to five thousand and forty), and the reel must first be found. But it is probable that the veiled hints in the old press releases only mean that when the six reels are projected in the correct order someone will be inspired to produce a seventh, in which the Parks' unwearied journeying returns them to the Far East.

In the brief space allowed me, I have been unable to comment on the performances of individual cast members; but it would be unjust to close without mentioning the late William Chang, who portrayed the captain of the junk. His scenes aboard seem initially grandiose. The vessel is too large, its mast impossibly tall, its rigging unnecessarily mysterious. Then we realize we are seeing it through the Chins' eyes. The Chins themselves appear small, shabby, and awkward, Chang a demigod; eventually we realize we are seeing him and them through the junk's eyes. *Distributed by Unconscious Artists Inc. Rated R. Two and a half stars.*

The Flag

WHEN WE WERE BOYS WE PLAYED IN THE SQUARE, and he was always the last to be chosen. He could run on that leg, but not well, and he was the smallest. We went flying just the same, scattering the pigeons the old people fed. Sending thin, brave shouts to the pigeon-gray sky. Once I saw him looking up the column; he was the only one who looked, but I never asked him about it. We did not ask one another such things.

When we were older and quite drunk one night, he told me the story. I had learned it in school as he had; but I nodded solemnly at every pause and cried at the end as a good fellow should.

The hero had been the youngest knight in that battle with the Turk. The others had mocked him, he the youngest, without a beard. But when the host fled, with the horde roaring behind them, he it was who snatched our banner from the mud, he who advanced once more though there seemed none to follow. Then the others, the strong, the war-hard knights, had turned in shame. So the heathen had been driven from our homeland, nearly a thousand years ago.

In the morning, while I nursed my aching head, I recalled the story. There were gray pigeons on my windowsill, and I looked beyond them to see the hero standing yet upon his column with his tattered flag upraised, the bronze guardian of the city. And it seemed to me that one leg was bent a bit beneath him.

We grew older and watched the dreams of youth join the games of boyhood in dust—I pass over much history.

The gray-uniformed soldiers came. The paper where I worked was forbidden to publish, and night after night, when everyone slept save I, the trucks came rumbling down the street. I used to lie awake listening for the rifle butts that pounded down the doors, and shrieking women and the cursing men. Some night, I knew, the trucks would come for me, but what was there to do?

One night, before the trucks came shaking over the cobblestones, I heard a stealthy slithering. A rat, I thought.

In the morning I found a paper before the door. Just a single sheet of paper mimeographed (and badly) on both sides. It told what they had done: who had been arrested, taken, what the charges were, and even the prisons and camps where some were held. There was no name, to be sure; but printed large across the top, with the day, month, and year, was *The Flag*.

Now he is gone, and no one knows where. No doubt his body rots in some grave hidden among black pines. But there are many such papers, passed from hand to hand. They cannot stamp them out; where one is destroyed five more spring up. I work for one, and we have already chosen the spot where we will never erect his monument.

Alphabet

THE PET HELD UP A DEAD SNAKE, then laid it on the stony hillside belly down, carefully arranging it in a full sine curve while making a noise like a leaky valve.

"I see. You have killed a reptile for me. She is very pretty. You are very brave."

The pet repeated its noise, exhaling between its yellow teeth: "Sssst!"

"You are a good pet. You have brought the dead reptile and a flap-winged flier and many others. Now be still, if you will not learn. I want to write."

But the truth was that he did not. He did not—above all else—want to write. When he closed all his eyes, he saw the flaw that had brought him to this insane world where life ran riot, saw the flaw hanging like a pink haze in space. It was absurd, of course. But then everything was absurd, most of all, the message he had hoped to leave behind him.

When he opened his eyes again, the pet was reaching, with elaborate stealth, for his pen.

He snatched it away and tried to think of something that might hurt, or at least frighten, the pet. One of the big, horned beasts. He thought at the pet and it recoiled, its face losing its hairy brownness for the hue of dried mud.

"Never touch the pen. Never."

The pet groveled, whimpering.

"Never touch it! Look! See what the pen can do." Eager to seize any relief, he picked up his pen and scrawled the lovely, angular characters for *many-colored limbless reptile* on a boulder.

The stone ran in smoking streams, and the pet whimpered more loudly.

"There! That is the sign." He turned away from the scrawled words and, without in the least willing it, sought the cliff of the message. "Do you understand? Do you even begin to understand reading?"

When he looked back at the pet, it had picked up a pointed stone and begun to scratch the boulder with laborious care, making something like a crude sine curve. When it saw he was watching, it repeated its hissing: "Sssst!"

"No, that is not a word, that little drawing of yours. That is a picture, a picture of a reptile."

He thought of the horned beast again, this time not just one but a whole herd thundering across the plain below and lifting a plume of dust, as he had so often seen them. The pet fled in terror, its scream a keening that went on and on until he realized it was no longer the scream of the pet at all, but the soughing of the night wind along the face of the cliff.

"I should eat," he thought, and tried to keep out the question "Why?" There were the dead animals the pet had brought, some multicolored fruits, a root the pet had bitten to show that it was good. Such had been the pet's original purpose. But as it had become better and better trained, there had, somehow, been less and less reason to eat, to eat anything.

"The perfection of the means," he thought, "the decay of the end."

He tried to study the cliff again, but it was too dark for him to see the top, where he had begun his message with his name-colony-name and a few sordid details about the flaw. He had planned to find the words, to put it all there, his love for the myriad others who had been his brother-sisters, his thoughts of Koneel, the circular marching of joy.

The words would not come; they were fading like the light. "I have been lifted up by the pink flaw," he thought, "the hand of the god. And set down the god knows where. Never, never to see you again, you beautiful ones." Perhaps he should write that, but surely any who came to read would merely mock him. The characters for *isolated* and *fool* were the same, though reversed. On his side, the fool saw *isolated*. From theirs, the brother-sisters *fool*. The millions of minds his own mind had once touched, the countless intelligences he had nearly thought his own, were gone. He was a fool indeed, an isolated and empty one.

He would write that, he thought; and in his mind's eye, he saw the blazing characters blocking out the blazing stars. When he reached for his pen, his nerve—or rather, his energy—failed him.

Daylight brought the pet again, very slowly, very carefully, a red fruit in one hand, a green one in the other.

"Come, I will not hurt you."

The pet put down its fruit at its feet and groveled. To humor it, he picked up the red one and took a bite. The pet leaped up and capered with delight, and he did not bother to try to tell it that the fruit tasted like nothing, like air or dust. Or rather, that he could not taste it at all, that he no longer retained the urge to eat.

The pet picked up a fragment of rock and scratched his boulder.

"You will communicate with me yet. Of course you will." He tried to applaud his own joke, but dry bits of fruit choked him and would not go down. Scratch, scratch—two drunken lines that leaned against each other, joined by a horizontal one.

"Aaaah!"

"Now what do you think you are doing?"

The pet turned, capered, pawed the ground.

"Very good, whatever it is, but what is it?"

One finger stretched straight beside each ear, head tossing. "Aaaah!"

"The lowering of the horned beast. I see, very good! But you have drawn him upsidedown." He picked up his pen. "The horns should point up. Like this." Straight lines joined at the bottom, joined again by a horizontal line. "Head, horns. You see?"

The pet groveled once more, then rolled on its back, legs ludicrously lifted, stiff fingers touching the stones.

"Dead. Yes, I understand now—the horned beasts are dead. Your god will not make them anymore."

Lips drawn away from teeth, the pet leaped up, seized its pointed rock, and began scratching the boulder again, making the sign larger, more perfect.

"You are right, and wiser than I." He had been trying to write in the wrong place. He had known it for so long, but now it could not be pushed away. He put the point of his pen to his head and began the first character.

The pet did not hear the dry rustle of his fall or the silver rattle of his pen on the stones. It was drawing the dead bull, and drawing it made the pet feel strong.

It thought (for it did think) of how it had done the bull dance for its god. And it imagined itself a great bull, a bull strong enough to push down the whole cliff, the cliff topped with the strange, angular lines that had once been of fire.

A Criminal Proceeding

TWO DAYS BEFORE EASTER SUNDAY, at eleven forty-three P.M., Stephen Brodie's apartment door was broken down by a mixed force comprised of elements from the New York and Philadelphia police departments, the Secret Service, the Federal Bureau of Investigation, the Bureau of Narcotics, CBS, ABC, and the *Washington Post*. Brodie's trial began approximately six months later, on November seventh.

Perhaps because his was the first arrest to have been carried live on nation-wide television, public interest from the very beginning far exceeded anything known before. On the fifth, a late show host mentioned a rumor to the effect that the trial would begin in secret a day earlier than had been originally announced. Although he had quoted the report only to ridicule it, what he said proved sufficient to fill the street outside the Criminal Courts Building with a mob estimated by the police to contain eighty-four thousand persons, including many women and children.

On the seventeenth, the selection of the jury began. Both the Prosecutor's Office and Brodie's attorneys were to have up to three hundred dismissals without cause, and an unlimited number of dismissals for cause. The jury—twelve jurors and fifteen alternates—would be chosen from a panel of five thousand persons. Since the names of all these were known to the public well in advance, it was inevitable that certain favorites should emerge, based upon previous familiarity, relationship to already well-known persons, appearance, or membership in a popular or notorious group. *Time* and *Newsweek* published their ideal rolls of twenty-seven as early as June, and the NBC computer, fresh from a triumph in the prediction of a presidential election, presented its own list of the fifty "most likely"—a list that in the event proved surprisingly inaccurate.

The seventeenth was a Monday, and selection continued until the following Thursday without a juror being accepted, and, indeed without any popular favorite coming under consideration. At three-fourteen tension was mounting—H. Piper Davis, a building contractor whose remark that "Guilt or whatever would have to be determined by the law," made some four months previously, had caught the attention of the media, was a mere two names off. At this moment, the selection of Emma Munson, a previously unnoticed black Baptist mother's helper struck the courtroom like a meteor. "No objection," stated K.B. Parker, the assistant prosecutor. When Will (Scooter) Clark, the defense attorney said—in place of the universally anticipated "objection for cause"—"No objection," only the Public Broadcasting System was not caught flatfooted. The fortunate three hundred thousand (continental U.S.) watching their coverage were treated to an instant replay with no more than a scarcely perceptible pause for tape editing.

After Munson's appointment, the remaining twenty-six jurors were decided upon relatively rapidly. Many observers felt, however, that this quick process represented a covert agreement between counsel to avoid in so far as possible further demonstrations like the January twelfth (through twenty-seventh) riots in San Francisco. The appointment of Charles Hop Sing as the third regular juror was widely considered to have been an unacknowledged surrender to demands of the male-grocer-oriental-American community; and renewed violence among the Garment Workers, culminating in the Third Avenue brassiere march of February eleventh, helped fan a feeling of national urgency.

By March sixteenth, the selection of the jury was complete; the presiding justice, Frederic K.C. McGrail, ordered a week's recess during which the domed Bronco Stadium Complex was to be equipped with additional television cameras, dressing rooms, permanent Mace distribution piping, a revolving stage, provision for the introduction of horses and (if necessary) elephants, means of flooding the center section to Row AAC, armored mechanical police (controlled from the gondola that also housed the transmitters required for a panoramic view of the court, and operated by a committee including representatives of the five major networks, the Senate of the United States, and the University of Chicago), a small dirigible to supplement the gondola, an aviary for carrier pigeons, three IBM 380 computers, recording equipment, cooking facilities to supplement the seven restaurants that formed a permanent part of the sports complex, a weather station, and black artificial grass surrounding a *stauros*.

On May third of the following year, the arena was prepared, and the trial proper began. During the intervening thirteen months, however, competition for the fuchsia and gold passes that would admit the bearer had become almost unendurably intense. Twenty-four thousand seven hundred had been distributed to Broncos stockholders in full payment for the use of the stadium for as long as required. Another three hundred compensated the players themselves (both platoons) for up to six missed seasons. Allowing ample space for the jury, witnesses, attorneys, and press, left another three hundred and thirty-six thousand, seven hundred and eighty-one seats. Upon the President's request, thirteen thousand of these were awarded to the White House staff, both Houses of Congress, the current graduating classes of the four service academies, and the legislature of the Commonwealth of Delaware (her native state). The competition for the remaining passes was almost beyond comprehension; counterfeiting was unquestionably responsible for a substantial part of the difficulties that were to plague admissions policies throughout the trial.

Court was to convene at eleven, but the seating riots and the counter-violence espoused by the New Venue Rangers, a catch-as-catch-can coalition of Broncos fans, private security force executives, and Mother's Clubs, delayed the first rap of the gavel until one fifty-eight.

The opening motion was made by Brodie's attorney, who requested a new trial, alleging certain irregularities in the selection of the jury. Court was recessed to consider this motion, reconvening on May thirty-first when Justice Hopkins denied it "at this time." Following the luncheon recess, Deputy Prosecutor Eli Braincreek began the government's case. Many seasoned critics noted that that during the entire presentation, which continued until June twenty-fifth, the ABC camera was fastened unwaveringly upon the countenance of Stephen Brodie, the defendant. Editorials in the *Toledo Blade* and the *Houston Post* speculated that this fixed regard was a strategy compounded with the network by Brodie's lawyers. (Brodie was reputed to have been a steadfast partisan of certain ABC presentations when free, notably the "Monday Night Movie.") An aging but still boyish commentator quipped that ABC had suffered a jammed swivel (on June thirteenth, NBC's only reference to the affair), and another rival pointed out that since CBS's cameras provided two views of Brodie (full face and three-quarter) CBS's viewers actually saw more of him than ABC's did. (This employment of the word *more* was challenged by the journalism review of the same name.)

Whether ABC's concentrated coverage was justified or not, it made apparent, as no other scrutiny did, the increasing tension to which Brodie was subjected. When Braincreek referred for the first time to the private yacht chartered by Antropopos and armed by him with heat-seeking underwater projectiles, Brodie was observed to wince visibly; and by the twentieth of June, when Ethel B. Saltzlust devoted four hours to the broken aquarium upon which Brodie was alleged to have cut his foot while sky diving, some thirty million persons observed the hesitating and even tremulous manner in which he extended his hand toward Ella Moneypenny-Hubert, the purported mother of his seven adopted Vietnam war-orphan heirs.

During September, attention left the trial to center on the

Congressional debate over the Perkins-O'Farrell Act, a bill that, when passed, (as it was the following month) would require a retroactive mandatory death penalty for Charges Thirteen, Fifteen, Twenty-One, and Twenty-Seven in the indictment. It was widely believed that the President would veto this bill; but late in the afternoon of October thirty-first she signed it at her seat in the stadium, the seventeen simulacra of herself imported from Disneyworld-Havana to deceive snipers acting in concert. That night Brodie attempted suicide in his cell, knotting a strip torn from his shirt about his neck and the bars in his door, and jumping from his bunk after slashing his wrists with fragments of his artificial eye (injuries eerily reminiscent of those inflicted three years previously when he had been attacked by a demonic model aircraft—a Second World War B-17—allegedly under the control of Hess DeLobel. Over a quarter of a million persons volunteered to give blood, most, apparently, under the illusion that the donation would involve an artery-to-artery meeting with Brodie. [The actual transfusion came from a turnkey, Raymond R. Swain; Swain was assassinated the following year.]

Two weeks before Christmas, Arnone Harper, acting for the prosecution, called to the stand the first of the persons alleged to have been employed for illicit purposes by Brodie and others. The witness, Melinda Bettis, known professionally as "Fayette City Red," made a strong impression on the spectators. Her appearance was followed by those of Wanda Wood, Jo-Anne Blake, Eve Smythe ("Nova Demure"), Everett H. White ("Carol Clark"), and Sonya Plum Blossom; Ms. Plum Blossom testified that both the Secretary of Defense and the Secretary-General of the United Nations had been present at the party given on board the guided-missile carrier *Mayaguez Incident* during the special elections. (Later confirmed by the General Assembly, though denied by the Security Council.) Several witnesses stated that Brodie and others had hoped to gain world-wide control, both monetary and military, on or before the occasion of the U.S.S.A. debacle; and Elizabeth Cushy, a witness whose shapely legs, slender waist, and voluptuous decolletage earned her the highest ratings achieved to that date by any prosecution presentation, stated under oath that Brodie had told her in confidence that had the judge not intervened, he had planned (it being the previous year) to pack the courtroom with persons attached by oath, as well as by bonds of gratitude, to himself and to Giznik. Following this testimony, Justice Russell ordered the court cleared. This required a ten-day recess, during which seventeen thousand persons (*New Yorker* estimate) were injured, and a mausoleum belonging to Scholla was appropriated by a thief who used its flamethrowers to clear a path through the Seventh Marines and down Pennsylvania Avenue. The mausoleum was to have been the prosecution's Exhibit C.

On January twenty-fifth the trial reopened, but it closed again almost at once when a bomb exploded under the press gallery during the mid-day recess. A different kind of bombshell struck the court on February fourteenth, when Caleb Cohen III, acting for Brodie, announced that his client was entering Guilty pleas to Charges Eight, Sixteen, Seventeen, and Forty-Seven, and altering his plea of Not Guilty—insofar as it applied to Twenty-One, Twenty-Nine, Thirty, and Forty-Two—to Not Guilty By Reason of Insanity. All these changes of plea were refused "In the public interest," and on February tenth, Brodie attempted suicide a second time.

By mid-March the prosecution's case was practically complete. The chiefs of state of the United States and five foreign governments (East Germany, West Germany, Iran, Sweden, and Morocco) had appeared to testify against Brodie; so had eighteen well-known television personalities. Over three hundred hours of tape had been played. The famous "sly spy films" had been shown to the jury twice and supplemented with stills showing Brodie looking toward the stars (Cassiopeia); Brodie with his right arm around the shoulders of his (then) wife, Angella Brodie Yuppe; Brodie marching to protest the pollution of the Windward Passage; Brodie playing chess in a store window with an old man (Stanislas Henryk Chvojka, black, won in twenty-eight moves); and Brodie picking apples in a "pick your own for three dollars a bushel" deal at *Apple City*.

The prosecution's summing-up lasted less than a week, and on March twenty-fourth Brodie took the stand in his own defense and, in a surprise move, left it almost at once to thrust his arm into the divine fire, then burning on a table before the jury, where it was the prosecution's Exhibit K. With his hand in the flame, Brodie swore his innocence. On the news that night, NBC, CBS, and ABC reported that the Mosque of Omar had collapsed during an earthquake, the last wall of the Temple of Solomon had fallen, and a voice had been heard crying, "Pan is reborn!" near the Isles of Paxi. Within three weeks Brodie had a reported five hundred thousand disciples, most of them sworn to abstain from the use of genital sprays as well as from the eating of any kind of meat. I believe it is safe to say that all of us felt then that the real prosecution had not yet begun.

In Looking-Glass Castle

"**I**'M GLAD YOU'RE NEW TO FLORIDA," the real estate agent said, "because this place is such a treat. It's nice to be able to give somebody that kind of welcome." She looked across at Ms. Daisy McKane and smiled. She was quite good looking, Ms. McKane thought, tanned and freckled, though perhaps a little too old.

"Florida has been a treat already," Ms. McKane said, trying to put a slight emphasis on the fourth and fifth words. "So nice. I've met such lovely people."

Her left hand was beside her leg, where the agent could touch it easily if she wished. She did not. Ms. McKane looked out the window at the dreary landscape of palmetto and swamp grass baking under the noonday sun. "Are you certain your batteries are up?" she asked after a time. She had a horror of running down on a lonely road, and so many roads were lonely now.

"Brand new and freshly charged," the agent announced cheerfully. "Nothing to worry about. Florida is easy on cars anyway since they've gone to fiberglass bodies. The salt air used to corrode the aluminum ones something awful. A sort of sickly white dust. Where did you say you worked?"

"Cape Rose."

"I mean where at the Cape, Ms. McKane?"

"I really don't think I should tell you that," Ms. McKane answered primly. She had her doctorate now, and it irritated her that she could not use the title outside.

"Oh, I'm no spy." The agent giggled, and Ms. McKane

decided she was not as attractive as she had first thought. Celibacy is best, she told herself. It always has been.

"I've heard that up north there are sympathizers all over."

"I really wouldn't know."

They swung off onto a new road. An old and battered tin sign announced WEST COCOA BEACH, pop 15,000. "Don't pay any attention to that," the agent said. "It isn't right. More like twelve thousand." (Even that was probably a lie, Ms. McKane thought.) "Do you have a car? You'll need one. I have a friend in the business, and I'll give you her card."

"It's being shipped down by rail," Ms. McKane said. "I see a lot of these houses are for sale." They were shabby bungalows for the most part, half strangled by their subtropical plantings.

"You can get three times the house for no more than they're asking for these," the agent assured her. "That's what I'm taking you to see."

The little car turned a corner and jolted to a halt. Ms. McKane looked out. The house was . . . stately. There was no other word for it. Two stories and dormer windows that indicated a finished attic. A lot twice as large as the others. The grass was high and wild now and the house needed a little paint, but just the same . . .

"Seventeen thousand five hundred," the agent said. "With your job the bank won't ask for a down payment, though you can give them one if you like."

"I could never furnish this place," Ms. McKane said as she climbed out of the car. "Never."

"There's furniture already—it goes with the house. Keep what you like and throw the rest out."

"Really?" Ms. McKane turned to look at her, but she was already skipping up the steps.

"Really. Old furniture's worth practically nothing today, you know. Not unless there are real antiques."

A fat woman in a printed suit was watching them from the lawn of the house on the other side of the street. When Ms. McKane looked at her she shook her head and turned away.

"That's another advantage. You'll have neighbors on both sides and across. Handy in case you get sick or something. People here are neighborly."

The front door squeaked open, and a blessed wave of coolness enveloped them. Ms. McKane stepped inside, looking at the fireplace and the graceful Queen Anne sofa. "It's lovely, and so cool."

"I mentioned at the office that I was going to show it," the agent said. "Nora was going out this way, and she must have stopped in and turned on the air conditioning for us."

In the kitchen Ms. McKane said, "It's so big. I wonder if I can find someone to live here with me."

Sale; the agent relaxed and smiled. "You should have yourself cloned. I mean, if you haven't already—"

Ms. McKane shook her head.

"I mean, look at this woman. She hadn't, and she drowned and had to give all this up. They just scrape some cells from inside your cheek, you know."

"Unless I can find someone to share the house, there'd be no one to look after the baby." Ms. McKane was practical.

A gum-chewing teenager delivered her car the next day, and Ms. McKane drove her back to the station. "It's an old one, isn't it?" the girl asked.

Ms. McKane nodded absently. The car's hunched black sides, which had seemed so reassuringly strong in Boston, looked out of place in the brilliant sun. Were they aluminum? Ms. McKane could not be sure. "How far is the ocean?" she asked the girl. "In a direct line, that is." The house's old owner had drowned.

"Ten miles, I guess."

This was foolishness; the Cape was right on the coast anyway, and her car would be parked there six days a week.

On the way to the house she bought groceries, staple foods—flour, sugar, coffee, and canned goods. Had there been pans? She could not remember and bought an inexpensive saucepan and a coffee pot. She had spent the night in a motel, nice but much too costly, even now in the off season. That's over with, she thought. I'll camp in the house until I find out what I need to make the place comfortable.

As it turned out, she needed very little. There was already a copious supply of linens, pots and casseroles, and spatulas and so on in abundance, and even some food. I could have stayed here, she said to herself, and saved the money. I'll get a cat, and perhaps a dog too. Have them spayed—or maybe not.

She turned on the television, and it filled the lower floor with solemn sound while she put away her purchases. A newspaper lining a drawer announced PIG HUNTED. It was six months out of date, but she read it anyway. He was thought to be hiding in the Everglades; the article had a great deal to say about the difficulty of searching the Everglades, and very little to say about him. Where were they? Down south, she thought, a long way from here. She saw pictures of men so often on the news that she had trouble remembering the last she had seen in the flesh. She had been a child, surely.

That night she read the *Journal of Mathematics,* with the TV mumbling unattended in the background, and went to bed. She slept badly, then spent a fatiguing day at the Cape getting acquainted with her co-workers. On the following, she went to work in earnest. It was Sunday before she had time to poke around the house.

It was uncomfortable as a garment too large is uncomfortable by its very looseness. She had felt big and clumsy in her tiny Boston apartment. Now she herself was tiny, without force, without impact on this hulking structure. She made noise for the sake of noise and found herself wondering, while she did her laundry, if someone were not pounding her front door. Her heart thumped at the soughing of chill wind in the air-conditioning vents. She seemed to be eating too much and felt sure it was in a subconscious effort to grow larger.

The owner before her—Jane Something, it had been on the deed—had been an eccentric. Or perhaps, Ms. McKane thought, an eccentric is anyone who dies without the chance to clean up. She had saved empty seed packets from the little garden behind the house, and there were five pairs of very similar scissors in her sewing basket. Her clothes were mostly gone, or she had owned very few. There was an album of photos, with no way of telling which were of her. Possibly none were. The few remaining clothes testified that she had been tall and thin, a hairbrush sighed of pale brown hair before Ms. McKane threw it out. Jane rolling dead, naked in the surf.

The bookcase in the living room held standard authors: Austen, the Brontës, Willa Cather, Edna Ferber . . . George Sand, *Frankenstein*. Ms. McKane was about to turn away when she glimpsed something behind the books. Flannery O'Connor and Dorothy Parker tumbled to the floor so she could reach it. It proved to be another book, *The Collected Short Fiction of Guy de Maupassant,* bound in red buckram and read nearly to pieces. She pulled down the rest of the books and uncovered one other lurker in darkness—*The Metamorphosis and Other Stories,* its pages falling out.

The fat woman across the street invited her for tea, and she went gratefully. "Do you know, except for the people I work with, I don't know a soul in Florida?"

"Better off not knowing most of them," the fat woman said, and launched with gusto into an account of the misdeeds of her neighbors, women who had peculiar friends, were criminally careless with money, and failed to cut their grass.

Ms. McKane blushed. Her overgrown yard was still untouched. "I meant to do something about it this afternoon," she lied, "but I can't get the old mower to start. I suppose I'll have to buy a new one."

"Jane kept her place nice, I'll say that for her."

"She seems to have been an excellent citizen," Ms. McKane admitted dutifully.

"Except she never—you know. I've had it done three times. Raised them all, but Pearl IV's dead now."

Three copies of this; it was appalling.

"Her boat got flipped over, never found the body."

Go to the old, gray window-maker, Ms. McKane thought. It

wasn't right—why wasn't there a word for a mother whose child was dead? There should be. Aloud she said, "Was that what happened to the woman who owned my house? I was told she drowned."

The fat woman muttered something that sounded like *her sisters got her.*

"Beg pardon?"

"I said the cistern got her. Fell down it head first."

At home again, the lie became a truth—the mower would not start. Arm aching, Ms. McKane retreated to the coolness of the kitchen. That square of planks in the back yard surely marked the sinister spot. Just a concrete tank to catch rainwater from the roof for the garden, but she was not sure she would ever be able to lift the cover now. Who had found her? How long had it been? She wondered, yet preferred not to know.

There was someone—something—in the house. It moved things, if ever so little, while she was at the Cape. A box of dried fruit she had never touched after opening emptied itself day by day. On windy nights, something walked.

She invited everyone she knew even slightly to the housewarming and spent nearly three hundred dollars on food and liquor. It was a thundering success that left a physicist and two programmers passed out on her furniture, and it quieted "the ghost" for nearly two weeks.

Then it was back. She woke to hear it going down the stairs, and with more courage than she had known she possessed she went looking for it with a flashlight. "Who are you? I won't hurt you." *If you don't hurt me.* Only later did she wonder what she would have done if she had found someone—she forced herself to visualize a black girl—filling a sack.

Next day she went to a sporting-goods store. Firearms repelled her, but she said some animal, perhaps a raccoon, was getting into her garbage. When she admitted she had never fired a gun the woman in the store suggested a trap instead, and she went away thinking about them.

What would be irresistible? Candy? She bought a box, counted the pieces, ate five, and left the box on the coffee table. Twenty-six. Twenty-six. *Twenty-four.* Twenty-four. Twenty-four. *Twenty-three.* That was a week, a work week, and a week seemed enough. She stopped counting and ate the rest herself, then bought a new box which she laced with rat poison. It remained untouched. She bought cookies, bread, jam, crackers, more dried fruit, fresh Indian River oranges, eggs, and canned oysters from Japan. In Boston she had had to struggle against chubbiness. Now she was becoming gaunt. One night she dreamed someone she could not see stood beside her bed voicing a complaint she could not hear, and the next day she brought home more food, delicacies chosen wildly.

An advertisement in *Scientific American* offered ornithologists an "electronic shotgun" capable of stunning birds as large as barn owls. She ordered one, giving her address at the Cape.

She put a bolt on her bedroom door, bought a hot plate, and had a telephone installed beside her bed. When a new woman reported to the department, she offered to share the house rent-free; but the new woman was attractive and had, it seemed, better offers.

One night she saw an eerie light in the street and went out onto the porch. A little girl had imprisoned fireflies in a jar and was touring the neighborhood with them. Ms. McKane watched her until she realized that women all up and down the street were doing likewise.

She dreamed that she was Jane, head-down in the cistern. One of the programmers mentioned, half laughing, that someone had "had fun" with her as she slept on the Queen Anne sofa. "Was it you, Daisy?"

"Who remembers?" Ms. McKane said. "I suppose it might have been." They both laughed and later that week the programmer asked her to lunch, only to make it clear as they ate that she expected her to pick up the check. Ms. McKane thought, How is this better?, and resolved never to speak to the programmer again. "You make more than I do," the programmer said as they left the cafeteria.

The electronic shotgun came, and she concealed it in her car. That evening, after pretending to leave the house, she returned through the rear door and searched everywhere, finding no one.

One morning she woke early without knowing why. As she lay in bed savoring the bygone luxury of sleep, she heard him descending the stairs. The sound was so devoid of stealth that as soon as it had died away she felt sure it had been a waking dream, a phantom of hearing. She got up, put on her robe, and went downstairs to start coffee.

He was in the kitchen eating toast with strawberry preserves. His face seemed heavily brutal to her, masked though it was with curling black hair. "It's you," she said before she had time to wonder if it would not have been to her advantage to appear surprised and outraged.

He nodded, watching her with unblinking eyes.

"You must have known I would find you here."

He nodded again.

"I'm going to call the police." Quite suddenly it came to her that she should not have told him, that he might seize her (she felt sure he would be stronger than she) and carry her outside. In imagination she could see him kicking aside the cistern cover, see the circular opening to Death. "I'll scream if you touch me," she said.

"I won't touch you." His voice was deeper than she had anticipated, harsh and flat with isolation.

"I'm going to call the police," she said again. "You'd better go now. I won't try to stop you."

He spooned jam onto the second fragrant slice.

"They'll kill you."

He shook his head. "Not for a long time. First they'll ask me who helped me, how I stayed alive so long. I'll give your name first."

"They won't believe you." Courage came welling up in

her, welcome as forgotten money. "I am a doctor of science, a model citizen."

"I'm here. I'm my own evidence. Do you think they'll believe I could have lived with you all this time without your help?" He waved, and the gesture told of the large house and the well-stocked pantry shelves.

"You're clever, aren't you?" she said; and he answered almost humbly, "I have nothing to do but read and plan."

As if by enchantment, the coffee pot was in her hand. She filled it at the sink and ladled in the coarse grains. "We may as well talk. I won't hurt you if you won't hurt me."

"I won't."

"That's right, you can't." Bitterly she added, "Who'd bring food for you?" then recalled Jane dead in the cistern and the laden shelves. He had only to wait until his next victim came. She saw him as a black and hairy spider, patient at the center of his web.

"I won't," he said again. "And as for your trying to hurt me, it's the only thing you could do that would stop me from being afraid of you."

"Why did you show yourself to me? Don't tell me you wouldn't be afraid if the police came after you."

"Because it was too dangerous not to," the man said. "I worried, every day, that you would ask them to search. They might have found me."

Ms. McKane pulled out a chair and sat down, surprising herself and, she thought, him. "Where were you?"

"In various corners at various times."

"You killed the other woman—the one before me."

He nodded. "Indirectly and unintentionally, yes."

She was not sure what he meant. "Will you kill me the same way?"

"No."

"There must be a good many of you—more than most of us think. I suppose that's why the government fusses about you so. Do you ever get together?"

"By twos and threes at night."

"And do all of you live the way you do? In houses, like this?"

He shook his head. The coffee was perking on the stove, filling the kitchen with its warm perfume.

"Perhaps we can strike some bargain. I get what I want and you get what you do." She felt desperate. "All right? What I want is for you to leave and promise you won't tell lies about me."

"Or the truth," he said. "That you sat down and talked to me, instead of screaming or running for the telephone."

"Or the truth," Ms. McKane admitted. "Now what is it you want?"

"To remain here as long as I wish. To be safe until I can reach some country where men still rule."

She tried to smile. "It seems we've come to an impasse."

Suddenly he smiled too. "Only in logic. From the books you brought, you're a mathematician . . ."

She nodded.

"But the sphere of logic has never been the world of women and men. If we can manage to forget it, we can both be free, or at least as nearly free as we are capable of being."

She got up and poured the coffee, waiting for him to continue. When he did not, she said, "I'm afraid I'm not the White Queen. I can't believe in impossible things."

" 'I daresay you haven't had much practice,' " he quoted. " 'Why, sometimes I've believed as many as six impossible things before breakfast.' " Then, "I didn't think you women still read male authors."

"I don't think we mathematicians will ever give up Carroll. Fortunately, we can mention the name without much danger. Do you know anything about math?"

He shook his head. "Only what I know about logic—that it should serve us, and not master us. Don't you agree, for example, that if we both wanted the *same* thing, we could not both have it? Look, here's a slice of bread, all nicely smeared with strawberry. We could divide it between us—evenly, or by some complicated formula you would work out. But if we both wanted the whole slice, could we both have it? Both eat it?"

"What are you getting at?"

"Only that because we want quite different things, there's really no reason why each of us shouldn't pick up what each wants and walk away. I won't stop you if you don't try to stop me."

"You're not making sense."

He nodded seriously. "If I were to make sense, we'd both go to prison. Let me say it again: Take what you want, and I'll take what I want. Say to yourself that I am gone, and I am gone. You'll never see me again, never hear me."

"But you'll really be here. I'll be living a lie."

"No you won't—I'll go. I'll go when I think it's safe, and when I have found a place to go to; and if I should have to come back, I'll leave again. You may lock the house as tightly as you like; I'll find my way in if I have to. But don't search for me, or have people in. Will you agree?"

"No." She hesitated. "Yes. Perhaps. I have to think."

"I'll get you some more coffee," he said, then smiled almost apologetically. "The men in books are always doing things like that, and I'd like to."

She said, "I think you're mistaken; in the old days women waited on tables," but she herself was not paying attention to what she said. For a moment he stood beside her, the coffee pot she had bought on the first day at the end of his outstretched arm. Then he was gone. She waited for him to sit down again, but soon realized she was alone in the room, perhaps alone in the house.

Perhaps not. Each night she searched her bedroom (she had not agreed not to search her bedroom, only the house) and when she was sure it was empty, bolted the door. Each morning she found herself thinking, as she entered the kitchen, of what she would say if she found him there.

The long humid summer ended. Her television spoke of snow on the Great Plains, then showed it, white as innocence, swirling down the canyons of New York. The Florida air was cool and lively; Ms. McKane shut off the air conditioning and threw open windows.

Her work became more and more engrossing as the *Aphrodite* neared completion. Every conceivable and inconceivable contingency had to be reduced to equations the programmers could translate for the computers; they, and the engineers, suggested hypothetical corrective actions, and those in turn had to be reduced to mathematical form. Observation stations were planned for California and the Northern Slope of Alaska, ships would sail to keep the orbiting segment under observation when it swooped below the Southern Cross. Already the second segment launch vehicle was rising amid a hodgepodge of cranes and scaffolding. Plans for the third were rolling from the graphic display terminals, plans for the fourth beginning to take shape. Woman would come to stay where Man had merely journeyed to adventure.

At times she was painfully conscious that the symbols she blithely manipulated were in fact hundreds of tons of metal and fuel. At others it seemed to her that no plan could anticipate the actuality of the launch, that *Aphrodite* would bore downward into the earth when the rockets were kindled, or float away like thistledown. She seldom left the Cape before dark now, and when she returned home it was only to shower, and drop her still-damp body upon her bed.

One night when she returned even later than usual, there came a single soft sound like the hesitant footfall of some kindly one-legged beast. Her toe touched an unknown something as she stepped into the bedroom to turn on the light; it was a book, *Sylvie and Bruno*.

Thereafter she received gifts more or less weekly. Some were books (among them, *Pillow Problems*); more often there were flowers, old-fashioned jewelry, and mere odds and ends—lovely shells, a large coconut, a gold-plated pen. Once a fresh red snapper laid on crushed ice in a china bowl that was not hers.

In various ways she tried to signal that all these tributes were unwelcome and, because they were dangerous, worse than useless. Yet she could not bring herself to waste or destroy them. She cleaned, cooked, and ate the fish, hid the books behind the books in the living room, and one day found herself scribbling an integral with the pen. Sometimes she stayed all night at the Cape, catching a nap after midnight on the couch in the restroom; this impressed her superiors as extraordinary devotion to the project.

As she turned into the street she saw the police cars, three of them. An instant later came the throbbing of a helicopter; searchlights stabbed and darted from above. As calmly as she could, she guided the car into the driveway and got out. Two cops, tall, muscular women holding riot guns, were coming toward her. Knowing it would be demanded she opened her purse for her identification, and the guns were leveled at her.

She seemed to be standing outside herself, watching a stranger wax quietly hysterical. No, this new Ms. McKane said. No, she had seen nothing, had heard no gossip, no rumors. Yes, she lived alone. Yes, they could go through her house if they wished.

"We'd better for your own protection," one of the cops told her. "He could have broken in while you were away. You wouldn't want to go inside and have him jump you."

"No," Ms. McKane agreed. She unlocked the front door and switched on the lights, wondering what she would say if there were a book or a fish in the hall upstairs. There was nothing. She allowed them to probe beneath her bed with their flashlights, then led them up the folding stair to the third floor, down to the laundry room and the hulking air conditioner.

When they left, she packed a bag. Her initials were on it, so she tried to compose a new name to match them. She could never return to Boston; they would surely find her there. *Denver McKay, Detroit McKenzie*. The telephone rang.

"Hello, Dr. McKane?" She did not recognize the voice.

"Yes?"

"I hope I didn't get you out of bed. This is Edith Berg, the head of the Mathematics Division? I think we've met once or twice."

"Oh, no, Dr. Berg." Ms. McKane glanced at her open suitcase. "I was just putting some things away."

"Good. I wouldn't call you like this if it weren't an emergency. Do you know Char Cavallo? She's had a heart attack."

"I don't know her well," Ms. McKane said, frantically searching her memory for something that would link Dr. Cavallo to herself. "But of course I'm sorry to hear it."

"Congestive heart failure—that's what they say. She was to be chief mathematician on the *Frances Alda,* and now of course she can't possibly go. Someone has to, and most of the women who've been with the project longer can't be spared or have sailed already on the test shots. I wondered . . . I should say I hoped—"

"I'll go," Ms. McKane said.

Dr. Berg's voice brightened. "Really? That's wonderful!"

"I'd like to," Ms. McKane told her. "I would."

"This won't be a pleasure cruise, you understand. Living conditions aboard the ships are primitive, and there won't be many people to talk to. You'll be at sea for several months."

"I'll take some books."

"Dr. McKane, you're a tower of strength. I won't forget this. Can you report to the ship in the morning? Before seven? They have to go then—something about the tide."

"I'd rather report tonight," Ms. McKane said. "I'd like a chance to get accustomed to my cabin before we put out. Get unpacked and so on."

"Fine. I'll let them know you're coming. Thanks again, and goodbye. You don't know how much I appreciate this."

When Ms. McKane had snapped closed her suitcase she went to the head of the stair. *"Listen to me!"* Her voice echoed through the house. "I'm sorry about the search—they would have arrested me, and searched anyway, if I had said no. Now I'm going away. It's my right, under our agreement, to act as if you're not here." She waited, listening. There was no sound, no reply. Doubtless he had fled before the police came.

"It's my right," she said again. "They need me to observe the shot." There was still no answer. Unable to help herself she added, "I appreciated the gifts. Thank you, and good luck."

The hooting of the tugs woke her next morning. For a quarter of an hour she remained in her bunk rejoicing in the rocking motion that seemed to soothe while it stimulated her. *Cradle of the Deep;* she had read it in freshman English . . . by Joan Somebody. There was a flash of white as a gull zoomed past the porthole, and the air of the cabin was sea air.

Ms. McKane got up, washed, dressed in old college clothes, and went on deck. Florida had already dwindled to a low coast aft. The Atlantic was sullen, powerful, and beautiful under the bright sun, an unending tiger seen through an emerald. Forward, two pigtailed sailors were casting off the last tow. As though under invisible hands, the rigging grew taut. Motors hummed and winches turned, and transparent mylar sails, looking like the cast skins of snakes, climbed the steel masts. Ms. McKane looked toward the bridge hoping to see the captain busy at her controls, but there was only the glare of the morning sun on the glass. With a snapping like a whip's, one of the snake skins became the side of an immense soap bubble, followed by another and another. The masts turned to catch the wind, and the *Frances Alda* heeled and came to life.

She stayed on deck until breakfast. In what was called the salon she gulped coffee and scrambled eggs and explained her last-minute substitution for Dr. Cavallo. As soon as she could she went topside again. Freedom seemed tangible there, something she could feel seeping into her lungs and racing through her arteries. I have been soiled all my life, she thought. This is making me clean. By noon she realized she had the beginnings of a sunburn and went below, congratulating herself on her foresight in bringing lotion.

In the darkness below deck she glimpsed the stowaway's bearded face.

Cherry Jubilee

A S SMITH HAD FEARED, everyone else at the Captain's table seemed to be Russian: an intelligent-looking bureaucrat who might, except for the cut of his suit, have been an American executive; a woman with up-swept reddish hair, probably his wife; a round-faced man whose carefully tailored camel jacket proclaimed the likelihood of a connection to the KGB; a dark, middle-aged woman; the Captain himself.

All around the curving walls other diners sat at other tables, their heads, like those of minnows, directed toward the center of the room. Smith tried to swoop gracefully into the vacuum chair a robot steward indicated, but overshot it slightly. Grinning, the Captain slapped his shoulder. "So! You are not a cosmonaut yet."

Tiny suctions drew Smith to his seat. "I haven't had much chance to practice, I'm afraid. I've been motion-sick pretty steadily for the past two days."

"That is practice, Comrade. You speak good Russian."

"Thank you." Smith nodded and tried to smile. There were empty chairs to either side of his, so two more guests were expected. Two women, judging by the seating arrangement.

The Captain introduced the others, though for Smith they were only a blur of names. He was never good at introductions unless he concentrated, and other considerations demanded his attention now.

"May I ask why you are going to Mars," the dark woman

inquired. "So few come from America. Are you a scientist?"

While he struggled to explain, the robot whooshed in with a steam-haloed sphere of russet soup, a fragrant planetoid whose surface was streaked with cirrus clouds of sour cream.

"Isn't it marvelous," the red-haired woman exclaimed, "how it holds itself together like that! No bowl to wash afterwards. But how does he move it without getting his fingers wet?"

The Captain grinned again. "Quite simple. Just as you have your little compressor, he has air jets in his fingertips. He can use them in the way you see, or to maneuver, or reverse the flow to pick up small objects."

"But if someone were to jostle him . . ."

"Our borsch would be scattered. But what would happen if someone jostled the waiter in your favorite restaurant in Moscow?"

The robot drew smaller spheres from the large one, shifting them until one hung in the air above each place. The round-faced man was already fingering a long, silvery straw, and Smith discovered he had one of his own, laid beside a steak knife. He picked it up, feeling the gentle tug of magnetism.

"Perhaps . . ." the Captain suggested. He glanced significantly at the empty seats.

"I just wanted to see what held it down. It's magnetic stainless, I assume."

The Captain nodded absently.

The bureaucrat touched Smith's arm to get his attention. "You say you are a radical economist, Comrade. I am myself somewhat involved in economics—a financial planner at the Ministry of Science. So we are co-workers, you see. But I do not believe I have heard the term."

Smith tried desperately to recall the man's name. Petrausky? Petravich? Aloud he said, "We're concerned with the irregular distribution of wealth, Comrade . . . Comrade . . ."

"Call me Pasik. As we are shipmates and co-workers, we must be friends. My wife is Anna."

The red-haired woman smiled and nodded.

"Now by irregular, Comrade Smith, you refer to the black market?"

"Call me Smitty, Pasik. No, a black market is well described by classical economic theory. We're more concerned with theft and bribery, that sort of thing."

The bureaucrat was no longer listening. Two very beautiful blondes, one in white and one in scarlet, were floating toward the Captain's table. The men rose, Smith nearly losing his hold on his chair.

"Welcome!" the Captain boomed. "Welcome! Let me introduce those you do not already know." He rattled off the dark woman's name. "And this is Comrade Smith, a fellow-countryman of yours."

Both blondes smiled. "My God, what a relief," the one in white said. "I thought Cherry and I were the only Americans on board."

The Captain finished, "Comrades, the beautiful Merry and Cherry Houdini," and Smith and the dark woman tried to say something polite.

Merry took the vacuum chair between Smith and the Captain, Cherry the one between Smith and Pasik. She smiled. "You're wondering about us, aren't you?"

Smith nodded. "It might be better, though, if we spoke Russian."

"That's right!" the round-faced man put in. "The time when our Soviet citizens learned English for technical purposes is past."

"Isn't that wonderful," Cherry explained. "Now we can speak English when we have to keep secrets." One eyelid drooped. "Do you think we're twins, Merry and I?"

Smith looked from one to the other. "You're identical in appearance, as well as I can judge, but she's wearing more jewelry. Besides, I've seen her on TV, and I don't think I've ever heard of you. Wasn't she the one who escaped from a stasis field at MIT?"

Merry turned away from a conversation with the Captain long enough to say, "Wait until you see what I'm going to do here on the *Red Star!*"

The dark woman leaned across the table toward Smith. "You must have read the announcement? But no, you said you have been ill. She will escape space and reenter the spacecraft. Is that not right, Comrade Koroviev?"

The round-faced man nodded happily.

"Comrade Koroviev is of the Ministry of Art. He has arranged that these two lovely persons should tour the new cities of Soviet Mars. Our government is eager that the scientists and engineers laboring there should be repaid for their sacrifices in every way possible."

"I understand," Smith said. It was still likely—more than likely, he thought—that Koroviev was KGB.

"About the twins or not, I know. So I will not spoil the game by telling," the dark woman continued. She extended a hand to Cherry. "But perhaps you did not catch my name. I am Vera Oussenko."

Pasik and Anna had already plunged their metal straws into their trembling spheres of borsch. Smith did so now, finding that the soup had a slight but alarming tendency to climb the straw. Koroviev began talking to the dark woman, his Russian too faint and rapid for Smith to understand.

"Well?" Cherry whispered in English. "Have you doped us out?"

He put down his straw. "At least I've discovered why I was asked to the Captain's table."

"He is a little obvious, isn't he? But he's a dear, and you can't blame him for wanting to make Merry feel at home."

A robot vacuumed up the borsch and brought steaks pinned to their platters.

"You're a clone—am I right? I've read they've developed a rapid maturation process now, so that in a few years the clone can have the same apparent age as the original."

Cherry nodded. "And how old do you think I am?"

"You're much younger than you appear, obviously. Though I don't suppose that's a particularly gentlemanly thing for me to say."

"You can redeem yourself by guessing. Come on, take a chance."

"Well . . ." Smith glanced at the other blonde. "Did your original pay for the process herself?"

"Yes."

"I'd guess six, then. Your clone sister can't be much more than twenty-eight. I wouldn't think she could earn enough to make a down-payment on the process before she was, say, twenty-two."

The red-haired woman said in Russian, "Isn't it marvelous? Pasik and I have followed it from the beginning. She is four."

Her husband nodded vigorously. "Both Merry and Cherry have been several times in the USSR. Not only to perform, but also that our scientists—my Anna is a biochemist—could examine them both."

The clone said, "These lovely people were our guides—and my interpreters before I learned the language."

"In four years you've learned Russian very well, I would say."

"I have an adult mind, and of course while we were traveling in the Soviet Union I had many opportunities. Now I'm learning Merry's techniques by assisting her. When I'm good enough, I'll go off on my own—perhaps tour South America."

The bureaucrat said, "And you see, if Merry should be killed—the things she does are very dangerous—Cherry will remain for the entertainment of the world. But what of a great Soviet scientist? That is what my wife and I ask. Often the things such a person does are dangerous too. He is exposed to radiation, perhaps. To dangerous chemicals. We ask if such a person should not be cloned as well, and even while the original remains, the clone might follow other paths in research. As our delightful Cherry says, tour South America."

His wife swallowed a mouthful of steak and gestured with

her knife. "We have our own techniques, but we are interested in your methods too. We gauge the results of both and compare."

Smith smiled, nodded, and cut himself a piece of steak. As he ate, he could not help noticing how often, and how intently, both the bureaucrat and his red-haired wife looked at the slender woman on his left, even when they were talking to each other or listening to the Captain describe the wonders of the *Red Star*.

After a time, a robot steward guided in a floating tray of desserts; another gathered up their steak platters and salad domes.

"Look at that one!" the blonde in scarlet exclaimed, pointing. "Cherries for me! What's it called? Do you know?"

"I don't know the Russian name," Smith told her. "In English, it's cherries jubilee."

She picked up the dish and hesitantly inserted a spoon. "What a cheerful-sounding word! Does it mean ice cream?"

Smith shook his head. "In the ancient civilization of Israel, all tribal lands were returned to their possessors—even if they had been leased or sold—every fifty years. That fiftieth year was called the jubilee. They held a celebration, because everybody was getting his birth-right back."

"I see . . ." She was tasting the dessert.

"You don't have to look so solemn," Smith told her. "The wealthy did away with the custom long ago. Only radical economists like me know about it now."

The blonde nodded. "I like it," she said.

Merry Houdini's escape from space was to take place the next "day" after lunch. Smith gathered with the rest of the passengers outside the main air lock. No crowd, he discovered, mills quite like a weightless crowd, in which each nudge and bump produces a visible equal and opposite reaction.

The Captain was on hand, loudly supervising a mixed work force of cosmonauts and robots. So were the bureaucratic couple and the dark Vera Oussenko. The two blond entertainers made an entrance, skimming down the corridor at break-neck speed, red and white skirts snapping like banners. The Captain raised a cheer, which the crowd took up.

"And now!" the Captain proclaimed when he could make himself heard, "Our lovely American friend Comrade Merry Houdini, the heir of that great Harry Houdini of whom we have all read, has volunteered to demonstrate for us something of her art. It is without charge to the Soviet Union, to the *Red Star,* or to you, her fellow passengers. She acts from public spirit!"

Another cheer.

"We of the *Red Star* have volunteered to cooperate with her to make this most astounding feat possible. I will let her explain to you herself what she will do."

The blonde's voice was nearly drowned by the noise of her audience. "Please!" she called. "Please be quiet!"

Smith found the dark woman floating beside him. "It is amazing, is it not?" she said. "But perhaps you and I have a special interest?"

Someone had given the blond entertainer a microphone. *"What I am going to do in a few minutes has never before been attempted!"* Her amplified voice had lost none of its charm in the speakers. *"I am going to escape from space! You see this steel coffin."*

Held by cosmonauts and robots who surrounded it like the points of a star, it was a long sheet-metal tool locker, nearly as wide as a cot, with a hinged lid closed by a hasp.

"I will climb into it. I will be locked into it. It will be put in this airlock and blown out into the interplanetary void. Isn't that correct, Captain Bogdanoff?"

The Captain nodded and addressed the audience. "When we open the inner door to put in the coffin, the lock will of course be filled with air. When we open the outer door, that air will expand into space. Since it will be without weight, just as we are here in the *Red Star,* the coffin will be carried with the air. To provide some safety, however, I have insisted—as

I still insist—that a lifeline must be used. Not to use one would be a direct contravention of regulations."

"We have one," the entertainer said. Her clone sister handed her a coil of white nylon rope. She flourished it. *"Now we wish to show you that there is nothing in the coffin to assist me."*

The two blondes took the box from the crewman and robots, opened its lid, and held it so the audience could see there was nothing concealed inside. One of the cosmonauts probed the interior with the beam of a flashlight.

The dark Russian woman asked, "Is the beautiful Merry really going to get into that thing and be pushed into space?"

"It looks that way," Smith said.

As they spoke, the young woman in the white dress was assuming a rigid posture, her arms at her sides. Her clone sister, enthusiastically assisted by two cosmonauts, fitted her into the "coffin" and closed the flat lid.

The Captain stepped forward and snapped a padlock on the hasp. "Open the airlock!" he ordered.

One of the white robots darted toward the control panel, and the massive titanium hatch swung open to reveal the chamber through which Smith and the others had entered the *Red Star* from the Russian shuttle. Several cosmonauts pushed the "coffin" inside, followed by Smith and other daring members of the audience. The escape artist's clone sister was tying one end of the nylon rope around a handle at the end of the tool chest. A cleat had been newly welded to the wall of the lock chamber; she tied the other end of the rope to that and hung the coil over it.

"Attention, please!" the Captain called. "You will all leave now." He made shooing motions. "We will jettison the coffin, and in five minutes, if there is no sign that Comrade Houdini's trick is working, I will have a cosmonaut in an atmosphere suit retrieve it. Already a man is standing by at one of the utility airlocks."

As they crowded back, Smith found a soft and fragrant body in a red dress pressed against his. "Hello, Cherry," he said.

She turned and smiled at him. "Five minutes is plenty of time for poor Merry to suffocate in the vacuum, but my gosh, isn't it fun! She's promised to let me try it on the way home."

Smith attempted to smile in return. "You know the trick, naturally. How she's going to get back."

From somewhere behind him, the dark Russian woman added. "Yes, you must."

"Not yet. This is a new one she's just worked out."

The inner hatch of the airlock swung shut. At a signal from the Captain, the robot crewman at the controls flicked several switches. A red warning light above the door began to blink. "Comrade Houdini is now in space," the Captain announced. "You should be able to see the coffin through the ports on this side of the spacecraft."

There was a general rush toward the viewports, during which Smith found himself separated from both women. The first port he reached, some fifty feet from the corridor that gave access to the main airlock, was too crowded already for him to see well. Kicking off from the footholds on the walls, he shot down another corridor to the starboard observation gallery.

Passengers there were already shouting and pointing. For a moment, staring into the immensity of the void, he was disoriented. Then he saw it, slowly revolving among stars that burned like unblinking beacons.

"Someone has cut the rope!" A passenger he had not yet been introduced to seized him by the shoulder. "Look!"

It was true—a section of white nylon line that appeared to be no more than six feet long trailed behind the slowly pirouetting steel box like the tail of a kite.

"She will die!" a woman moaned in Russian.

A voice at Smith's ear asked, "Is it not strange that it keeps pace with us, though we fly so fast?" It was Koroviev.

"We're coasting," Smith explained absently. "We have been ever since we attained escape velocity. That box has the same speed we do, and there's nothing out there to slow it down."

"To me it appears to be falling."

"That's only because of the way you're oriented. If you were to turn around, you'd think it was rising. Actually, it's orbiting us as it drifts away." Smith wondered if Koroviev could be as ignorant as he sounded. "What I can't understand is why the Captain hasn't sent his man out after it."

"It is no simple affair, such a spacewalk. Perhaps something—"

The Russian was interrupted by a dozen gasps. The lid of the tool chest had opened. A blur of white appeared at the crevice. "It's her hand," Smith heard himself say. "Oh, my God!"

An impulse, a half-formed thought, sent him racing back toward the main air lock. Metal clanged somewhere ahead.

As he grasped the grab bar and swung himself into the short corridor leading to the air lock, he saw a thing of scarlet—a thing that floated, turning slowly in the faint air currents. Around it were a few globules of bright, arterial blood, like cherries.

That evening, two cosmonauts appeared to take him to the VIP lounge usually reserved for Party officials. The Captain and the dark Russian woman were already there when he arrived, the Captain looking worried, the woman impassive. The Captain motioned him to a blue vacuum chair without speaking. The woman asked, "You have given orders for Merry Houdini and the others?" The Captain nodded.

The blond escape artist arrived half a minute later. She had changed her white gown for an equally white jumpsuit, but otherwise looked just as she had when Smith had last seen her. The bureaucrat and his biochemist wife were ushered in with the expensively clad Koroviev.

"You know what has taken place—" the Captain began.

The bureaucrat interrupted. "Wait. I do not. I—we—have heard many rumors, but if this meeting is to proceed on the assumption that my wife and I are fully informed, we wish to be told officially what has occurred."

The Captain hesitated and glanced at the dark Russian woman. She said, "Comrade Cherry Houdini has been murdered. Her body was discovered by Comrade Smith while the rest of us watched the steel chest in which Comrade Merry was imprisoned."

"Where was poor Cherry found?"

"In front of the main airlock. It would appear that when all the rest hurried away, she remained behind. Presumably her murderer returned and found her there."

The red-haired woman asked softly, "How did she die?"

"She was stabbed in the heart with a steak knife."

There was a silence. At last the Captain cleared his throat. "Perhaps I should explain that Comrade Oussenko is in actuality Lieutenant Colonel Oussenko of the State Security Committee. She had felt it would make for a more relaxed atmosphere during our long flight if she remained incognito. But since this unfortunate event, she feels—and I agree—that it is better that her position be known. I think we will all agree that we are most fortunate that she was present when this most unfortunate, uh—"

The dark woman said, "That is sufficient explanation surely, Captain. Let us proceed with the investigation." She swept the other five with a glance. "Except for the victim of this atrocious crime, we are the same group that was present at the Captain's dinner last night. No doubt you have all noticed that. There are two reasons, and I will explain them both to you now—no doubt if I did not, one of you would ask it. I shall save him the trouble, before we go further.

"I do not believe I need explain why Captain Bogdanoff was present at his own table, or why he is present now—he is the commander of this spacecraft. I myself was his guest last night in deference to my rank; I am here now to conduct this investigation. You were at the dinner last night because you are each in some way connected with Comrade Merry Houdini, as was, of course, her clone, the late Comrade Cherry. You are here now because it appears plausible that each of you may have killed Cherry."

There was a chorus of objections.

"I will outline to you now why I believe each of you is to be suspected. Should I be mistaken, here is your opportunity to enlighten me." Her eyes moved from face to face. "However, it may also be that one of you possesses information material to this investigation. I shall be most grateful for your assistance. I remind all of you that as citizens—or guests—of the Soviet Union, you have an obligation to the truth and to justice. Comrade Houdini, you are fidgeting. You have something to say?"

"Yes!" The blonde rose from her chair, then let it draw her to its embrace again. "What do I call you? Lieutenant Colonel?"

"You may continue to address me as Comrade Oussenko, if it makes you more comfortable."

"Well, Comrade Oussenko, you're wrong. You said each of us had some reason for wanting to kill Cherry. I didn't. My God, she cost me over two hundred thousand, and now she's dead."

"Very well, we will begin with you, Comrade. You have a lover—yes, already, though we are only a few days away from Earth. Do you deny it?"

The blonde sat silent.

"Good. Because I have certain knowledge. I ask you now—did your clone know of your affair? I warn you that no matter what you say, I shall proceed on the assumption that she did; you were very close, as we all know, and you and she had adjacent cabins. Did she know?"

"Yes." It was almost inaudible. "I told her."

"Good again. My assumption is now shown to be fact. You may have feared she would reveal your activities to an American lover. Or to your American journalists—if it were public knowledge that you had a Soviet lover, it would surely damage your great popularity in your own country."

"I said I *told* her!"

"And perhaps regretted it later. Or perhaps told only when she knew already and confronted you with her knowledge.

But wait." The dark Russian woman held up one hand. "I am not accusing you. I only explain your presence."

She turned toward Smith. "You, Comrade, are the only other American on the *Red Star*. It may be that your government, knowing that our Soviet scientists have been studying the clone of Merry Houdini, has decided it should be destroyed. If so, then perhaps you have been sent to do it."

Smith said, "It may be possible, but it's not true."

"Or it may be that you knew Comrade Cherry in America, and have some reason now to wish her dead. For example, you may have feared she would reveal your true identity, which may be other than the B. Smith stated in your passport. Thus, you are among us.

"Comrade Petrovsky, you saw Comrade Houdini and her clone often when they visited the Soviet Union. I do not wish to say too much, but clearly I must consider the chance that there was some personal attachment."

The bureaucrat said, "You suspect that poor Cherry was my lover, and that I feared she would reveal it to Anna. It was not so, but I understand, Comrade Lieutenant Colonel. At such times as this, such things must be considered by the police. Or perhaps she told Anna already, or perhaps taunted her with lies. We understand that as well." His red-haired wife nodded. Smith observed that they were unobtrusively holding hands.

"And now—"

"And now only I remain! Pah!" Koroviev snorted. "You think I wished Cherry dead? I would have hurled my own body before the knife. Have you no notion of the cost to take myself and these two women—with all their equipment, their luggage—to Mars? My career at the Ministry of Art has been staked on the success of this tour. Now one half is dead. More than half. Do they come to see Comrade Houdini perform her miraculous escapes? Yes, but partly only. They come too because here are the wonderful, beautiful American and her clone. Now the clone is no more."

The red-haired biochemist asked softly, "May I speak to that, Comrade Lieutenant Colonel?"

"Of course. I have asked for assistance from all of you, and thus far nothing has been given me."

"On Mars there are many engineers, geologists, even astronomers. Very few biologists. That is why I worked so hard to be permitted to come with Pasik. I do not believe that engineers, geologists, and astronomers are greatly interested by clones. But a murder, the death of a lovely woman . . ."

Smith said, "All right, we're all suspects. I'd like to point out that the kind of sexual material you enjoy dreaming up could apply to anybody on the spacecraft."

The KGB officer shook her head. "No. Only to those who knew Comrade Cherry. Besides, there is another factor."

"I thought there was."

"I believe I have already mentioned that Comrade Cherry was stabbed with a steak knife—one of those used at dinner last night. Everyone here is perhaps aware that steak is a dish greatly favored by Americans."

Several persons nodded.

"But perhaps you are not aware that it was only at Captain Bogdanoff's table that it was served. A special courtesy, you see, extended to our American guests. For the other passengers, and the crew, there was a beef ragout."

For a moment, no one spoke; then Smith asked, "Is it possible to find out whose knife was missing? The steward might know."

The red-haired biochemist shook her head. "A robot? It is useless."

"Fortunately," the KGB officer said, "it will not be necessary to ask. I know already whose knife was employed. It was mine."

"Yours!" The Captain stared.

"Yes, mine. When I had eaten as much of the meat as I wished, I thrust my knife into the rest. A few minutes later— before our steward had returned to clear the table for dessert—I noticed it was gone. I supposed it had merely come loose and drifted away, and thought no more about it."

"But perhaps," the Captain began, "it was not that knife—"

"With the assistance of your chef I have already inventoried the knives in the galley. Only one is gone. It has been found in Comrade Cherry's heart." She paused. "You are all—all save one—trying now to recall our seating. You need not bother. Captain Bogdanoff was on my left, Comrade Koroviev on my right. But there is no significance in those facts; our table was small, so small that I could, as I well remember, extend my hand across it to Comrade Cherry without rising from my chair. Anyone could have taken my knife. Comrade Houdini here is a magician by training, and so could perhaps have done it most easily, but no one can be ruled out."

"Thank you," the escape artist muttered.

"You are quite welcome. Now I shall give all of you a lecture on criminology. The detection of crime stands upon three legs—like a camera, do you understand? The camera that will provide us with a picture of Comrade Cherry's murderer. These legs are motive, means, and opportunity. Motive is of little use to us here; I have shown already that all six may have it. Means is useless also, as we have seen. Any of you might have stolen my knife—and of course by stealing it, the guilty one has prevented us from discovering that his own was gone, which was quite clever of him. Opportunity remains."

"In other words," Smith said, "who was in front of the main air lock and might have remained behind."

"Or returned to it. Precisely so. I was there myself. I saw you, Comrade Smith. Also Comrade Petrovsky and his wife, and of course our Captain. What of you, Comrade Koroviev?"

"I was not there. I am eliminated, but then sanity would have eliminated me long before."

"It was you who managed the tour, and yet you did not attend the performance? Surely we may be forgiven for asking why."

"Because I knew what the performance would be!" The round-faced man ran his fingers through his rather shaggy hair. "I had discussed it at length with Merry, as she will tell you. I knew she would be imprisoned in the box, and the box blown out of the air lock. I knew also, as any of you would who had given the matter a moment's thought, that one cannot see through the hatch of an air lock. I waited by a viewport."

"But you could have come to the main air lock while the others watched the tool chest."

"My position was at the shoulder of Comrade Smith. He will vouch for me."

"Yes," Smith said. "He was there for some time before I went back to the main air lock and found the body. If things took place as you say, I'm afraid you'll have to rule Koroviev out, Comrade Lieutenant Colonel."

Koroviev asked, "It was you, then, who discovered her?"

Smith nodded. "I've already been questioned about that, believe me. But may I ask a question now myself, Comrade Lieutenant Colonel? Who was the last to see Cherry alive?"

"A certain female passenger and her husband. They had been at the air lock, and in their hurry to reach one of the viewports, she lost a valuable earring. They returned in the hope of finding it."

"And did they?"

"Yes, against an air-return grill. Comrade Cherry helped them look for it, but she did not leave with them when it was found."

Smith leaned forward. "Was anyone with her?"

"They noticed no one, no. You appear thoughtful, Comrade."

"They couldn't have been gone long," Smith said. "I wasn't gone very long myself—not more than five minutes, if that. I know I was just beginning to wonder where the Captain's cosmonaut was. Where was he, by the way?"

The Captain cleared his throat. "He was just entering the air lock—one of our utility locks—when we received Comrade Merry's report that she had returned to the spacecraft."

"Anyhow," Smith continued, "this couple couldn't have been gone for more than two or three minutes when the woman noticed her earring was missing, but by the time they came back for it, it had been pulled up against an air return. Was it gold?"

The KGB officer cocked her head. "Yes. Does it matter?"

"I was just thinking. A gold earring would be pretty massive for its surface area—I would think it would move rather slowly. The drops of blood I saw around the dead woman would have been much lighter, but they hadn't been pulled away yet."

"Your logic is impeccable. Cherry must have been stabbed within half a minute of the time you discovered her—unless you stabbed her yourself. I had not thought of the earring, but this afternoon I scattered a little water in the air at the spot where the body was found. It is a pity, is it not, that Comrade Merry did not arrive sooner?"

The blond entertainer asked, "May I say something? Two somethings. No, I wasn't in the ship when Cherry was found. Anyway, I came in through one of the utility airlocks, and I called Captain Bogdanoff on the intercom as soon as I got inside. The time is recorded in the log—I asked about it—and so is the time that Cherry's body was discovered. You'll find that the interval was three minutes and forty-three seconds. I can't read Russian very well, but he translated it for me.

"Now the second thing. When I first came in here I told you Cherry had cost me over two hundred thousand, and then Comrade Oussenko here spouted all that stuff about my having a lover on the ship and Cherry knowing. And I just couldn't think. It had never even occurred to me that I'd be suspected, since I was responsible for her life to begin with. But now that I've had time to think, I realize I can put an end to all this nonsense forever by doing the same thing I did with Cherry—I mean, telling all of you about it. My Soviet lover was, and I hope still is, Captain Bogdanoff."

The Captain rose, swiftly and expertly propelled himself across the room, and kissed her.

"All right, still is, I guess. Before I'd even really met him, I could see he was attracted to me. And he—well, he's strong and handsome, and God knows brave. Anyone who earns his living crossing and recrossing space is brave enough and smart enough to do anything. So last night, and the night before that, too, he came to my cabin for a while."

The dark Russian woman coughed. "I see."

"There now. It's out. Did I act while I was telling you like I'd kill my two hundred thousand dollar clone to keep it a secret?"

"No," Smith said gallantly. "You certainly didn't. But after hearing—and seeing—all this, we're surely entitled to ask a few questions concerning the Captain himself. Captain, will you tell us where you went when you left the air lock?"

"Certainly," the Captain rumbled. "To my bridge, to watch Merry's escape. Observation is better from there than from any of the viewports and galleries available to passengers. You will now begin to suspect me—isn't that so?"

The KGB officer lit a cigarette. "I hope not."

"Your hope is granted, Comrade Lieutenant Colonel. You will have observed that several members of my crew were with me at the air lock. Two of them accompanied me back to my bridge. I was in their company until after Cherry's body was reported."

Smith asked, "Captain, that lock you put on the tool chest—the coffin—was it yours? Where did you get it?"

"Merry gave it to me."

The bureaucrat, who had been silent since denying any amorous relationship with Cherry, sputtered, "But then she could have opened it!"

"Of course she could, Comrade Petrovsky. It was a trick, a performance! You think I wished to see her killed? It was I who insisted that a safety line be used."

The KGB officer smiled. "Comrade Petrovsky is not concerned about your honesty, Captain. Or hers. He now fears that Comrade Merry may be accused. She could have had a key to the lock, certainly. But such a key would not have released her while she was within the chest and floating in space. What good would it have been?"

"It seems to me," Smith remarked, "that we're in danger of passing over a very interesting point here. The Captain has just protested that he did not want Merry to die. But it would seem that somebody did. Somebody cut that lifeline he made her use."

"Now it comes out," the KGB officer said. "I feared it would."

The round-faced Koroviev darted a look at her. "What do you mean?"

"Only the very obvious point that Comrade Smith has just made—the point that struck me from the time I first learned of the death of Comrade Cherry: that an attempt was made to kill both."

"Then you can't possibly suspect me!" the blonde cried.

"No. But I hoped that if it appeared I did, something would be said here that would indicate the identity of the person who attempted to kill you as well as your clone sister. Now that hope is gone, and we must proceed without it. I now ask you, Comrade Merry, for the sake of the investigation, to reveal fully how your trick this afternoon was performed. Explain it to us."

"I won't."

"Are you serious?" The woman from the KGB leaned toward her. "I warn you, Comrade, this is not a joke."

"I don't reveal my methods. Ever."

"In private, perhaps? To me only."

"No! If—if I believed it had any bearing on poor Cherry's murder, I would. It doesn't. A few minutes ago, my friend Boris Koroviev spoke of our tour being ruined. This would really ruin it—for him and for me. Cherry wouldn't have wanted that."

"All right." The KGB officer took a last puff of her cigarette and flicked it toward an air return. "Perhaps later we must resort to more drastic measures, but for now I will explain instead of you. To tell the truth, though I admit that what you did was very dangerous, I do not believe it so difficult."

The bureaucrat asked, "You think you know how it was done, Comrade Lieutenant Colonel?"

"It is rather obvious, surely. Let me recapitulate what we saw; then I will discuss what must have actually occurred. We saw a large sheet-metal box, which Captain Bogdanoff was pleased to call a 'coffin,' but which many of us—I certainly—recognized as a tool chest of the type used on board this spacecraft for large implements. It was opened for us, and one of the crew was so kind, I would suppose at a suggestion from the Captain, as to shine a light in it. Then Comrade Merry Houdini entered, the lid was shut upon her, and Captain Bogdanoff put a padlock on the hasp. We have seen already that this padlock had been supplied by her. Comrade Cherry tied one end of a coil of nylon rope to a cleat on the wall of the air lock and the other to a folding handle at the end of the tool chest. I do not recall seeing anyone except herself touch that rope. What of the rest of you? Do any of you recall another person touching it?"

No one spoke.

"The inner hatch of the air lock was then closed, and the switch thrown to open the outer hatch, thus projecting the tool chest into space, presumably still tethered by the rope to our spacecraft."

The KGB officer paused and glanced at each of them in turn. "And now I shall outline to you what the killer wishes us to believe occurred.

"After all the rest had left, Cherry for some reason remained behind. When the couple I have mentioned departed for the second time, her murderer returned. He stabbed her, closed the outer hatch—Captain, would that hatch shut despite the rope?"

The Captain nodded. "Certainly."

"I had assumed so. Then he opened the inner hatch and cut

the rope. That accomplished, he closed the inner hatch again and opened the outer hatch once more, allowing the cut end of the rope to be drawn out of the air lock. You see the objections to all this?"

Smith stroked his jaw. "You said he cut the rope. With what?"

"Ah!" The KGB officer favored him with a half smile. "That is well thought of. Perhaps he had a pocketknife. Or perhaps he brought a razor blade for the purpose. But not with the knife with which he killed Cherry, since that remained in her poor breast. But we ask that he do two very unnatural things. The natural act would be for him to remove the knife and use it to sever the rope, not to produce a second blade. And the natural act would be for him to fly the scene of the murder, not to open and close the hatches, and dodge in and out of the air lock, while the corpse of his victim floated behind him. I submit to you that he did not do these things—that no one did them."

Koroviev asked, "Are you saying, Comrade Lieutenant Colonel, that Cherry cut the rope herself? Let me propose another explanation, one that seems far more probable. You have told us of a certain couple who returned to search for an earring. You have refrained from identifying them, but I doubt if there is anyone here who has not already guessed their names, despite certain naive questions asked at the beginning of this meeting. Let me say only that the woman habitually wears her hair heaped upon her head, and that such a coiffure almost dictates the use of earrings, though she wears none now. Is it not possible that no earring was ever lost? Could not her husband—a powerful man—have held Cherry while his wife entered the air lock and cut the rope, then returned to stab Cherry? Is it not possible that they left her dead, not alive?"

"No, it is not. Consider—first the couple of whom we speak leave; they were seen by others to do so. Then they return; that too was seen. They seize Cherry, as you say, operate the controls, cut the rope, and operate the controls again so that the tool chest will drift away. In so much time, almost every passenger would have seen the tool chest tethered, then the wandering tool chest, like a strayed cow.

"But that was not what was seen. I have spoken to more than a dozen who watched, and without exception they report that the rope had been cut before they sighted the tool chest. Furthermore, those who report the departure of this couple to seek the lost earring also report that the tool chest, with its rope severed, was in view before they left."

The biochemist said, "Then it *must* have been Cherry who cut the rope!"

"No, not at all." The KGB officer smiled. "I will explain that in a moment. But meanwhile, what of Comrade Merry, who is drifting in space? How is it she is here with us now? I propose to you that a face mask and a small cylinder of oxygen were concealed somewhere in her 'coffin.' Do any of you wish to argue?"

"I do," Smith said. "I saw the inside from close up—as you know, since you were beside me at the time—and there wasn't room for anything like that."

"Precisely so, Comrade. You saw the inside, and so did I. But there was a part of that chest we did not examine, and now will never examine, since it is wandering the void. I refer to the interior of the lid. When we see what appears to be a common object, such as that tool chest, we tend to assume that it has remained a common object. That is much to the advantage of the clever magicians, who have made it an uncommon one.

"With this mask and the oxygen, our friend Comrade Merry here could breathe for a time. We have already seen that the lock that held closed the chest was no obstacle—she had supplied it herself. I would propose that in place of the catch which normally retains the shackle, she had substituted a part made of some substance that would vaporize upon exposure to the vacuum of space—there are many such substances. Comrade Merry had only to wait a few moments for the lock to spring open.

"When she was no longer locked inside, she opened the lid a few centimeters. Several persons saw her hand at this point. She opened it, I believe, to orient herself, but most of all to determine the condition of the light. Her tool chest was circling our spacecraft, as she knew it would. The chest was small, the spacecraft very large. For most of the time, the chest would be exposed to full sunlight—much brighter than sunlight is ever seen on Earth. But for a part of each circuit, the spacecraft would be between the sun and the chest, and it would be in almost perfect darkness. When that moment came, she left the chest and returned to the spacecraft. I would assume that together with her mask and oxygen she had a small cylinder of air for propulsion, since the compressors we use on board would not operate in a vacuum."

The biochemist exclaimed, "She'd be killed!"

"Not if she kept her head—as she obviously did—and everything went well. The human body can survive for some time in a vacuum provided it does not suffocate, and all this required no more than three or four minutes. Once she reached our spacecraft again, she had only to open one of the hatches and come in. The hatches are made so they can be opened easily from outside—a sensible precaution, since cosmonauts sometimes work there, and an emergency may occur.

"However, she would have run a considerable risk of being seen with her mask and other equipment if she had simply opened a hatch and ducked inside. How was she to know she would not be seen? Comrade Smith, you have been following all this with intelligence and imagination, I believe."

"Thank you, Comrade Lieutenant Colonel," Smith said, "but I have no idea."

"Clearly she required a confederate inside the spacecraft who would give her a signal if the way was clear. How could such a signal be given from within the spacecraft? Quite easily—if no one were about, the confederate would open the outer hatch of the air lock, so that Comrade Merry had merely to enter and close it, thus automatically filling the lock with air. Now we have come to an understanding of one of the points that at first puzzled me about this case—why the unfortunate Comrade Cherry chose to remain at the air lock when all the rest left."

The woman from the KGB gave them a humorless grin of triumph and lit another cigarette. "When I realized this, I of course examined the main air lock. I found its outer hatch was closed, although it had been opened for the trick and—so far as the crewmen I questioned knew—left open. How did it come to be closed? I believe that we know now. The murderer closed it, and no doubt saw to it that it would remain closed, because he wished to prevent any sudden effort to rescue Comrade Merry.

"But what of Merry then? She was in space without a pressure suit and with only a very limited supply of oxygen. Surely, however, she must have considered the eventuality of the main air lock being closed to her. She had a second confederate waiting to welcome her at one of the utility locks. Who was that? It is obvious, surely—Comrade Koroviev, the manager of her tour, who was, as we have noted, not at the main air lock with the others.

"I have kept you a long time, but it will not be much longer now. Let me summarize. Comrade Cherry Houdini was stabbed with my steak knife, taken from our table last night. It could only have been taken by one of the people in this room, since no one else—not even the robot steward—approached the table at the time it disappeared. The rope that was to have secured Comrade Merry's 'coffin' was cut, yet no one was seen near the rope except Comrade Cherry, who was herself a victim. At the time of the stabbing, everyone who was at the table was accounted for. I will begin at my right, as we sat that evening, and go around the table to show you. Comrade Koroviev was at the utility airlock, waiting to admit Comrade Merry. The woman to his right, the wife of Comrade Petrovsky, was with her husband and he with her; unless both committed the crime, neither did. To Comrade Petrovsky's right was the unfortunate Comrade Cherry. To her right was Comrade Smith; he was at the gallery, beyond the viewpoint where the Petrovskys watched, until he left to discover the corpse; he was seen there by several passengers, including myself. To his right was Comrade Merry; she was in space, having not yet reentered the ship. To her right was the Captain, who was proceeding, in the company of two of his crew, from the main air lock to the bridge."

Smith said, "You seem to have eliminated everyone—except yourself."

The KGB officer smiled. "I have eliminated myself as well, Comrade. I know that I did not steal my own steak knife.

"Now we must ask ourselves how this murder was accomplished. I propose to you that the answer is one we have seen already—it is the answer to the question: How did Comrade Merry know she could reenter the spacecraft without being observed? The answer, as we have seen, was that she had a confederate. The murderer also had a confederate. This is the only way in which this crime could have been committed.

"So I have asked myself who among you might have such assistance. Let us go around again. Comrade Koroviev knew no one on this spacecraft except Comrade Merry and her clone. The Petrovskys knew the same two and each other, but no one else. Comrade Cherry we may dismiss. Comrade Smith knew no one, so far as I have been able to discover. Comrade Merry knew Comrade Koroviev, the Petrovskys, and Captain Bogdanoff, but no one else, and as we have seen, none of them could have committed this crime. That leaves us with Captain Bogdanoff." She paused, and smiled again.

"Captain Bogdanoff knows at least a dozen people very well—people whom we have not even considered thus far, because we ourselves do not know them. I mean the members of his crew, his subordinates."

"Comrade!" The Captain rose from his chair. "Are you accusing me?"

"I am. You will sit down, Captain. I have already radioed Moscow, and at any moment your first officer should receive orders to place you under arrest."

The bureaucrat said, "But Comrade, if he was assisted by one of his men . . ."

"I do not believe he was," the KGB officer told him. "I have questioned them, and in any event it seems unlikely. He had another, much safer, confederate. It is he who controls the programming of the robots."

For a moment no one spoke. The Captain looked stricken.

"Much earlier I spoke of the three legs supporting the camera that gives us a picture of the murderer. You will recall that they are motive, means and opportunity. Since we are already dealing with opportunity, we shall consider them now in reverse order.

"Of the eight who sat at that table, only Captain Bogdanoff could have nullified a robot's basic directives so that it would commit the crime. He is thoroughly familiar with cybernetics, as all cosmonauts must be, and only he and the first officer know the access code required. A robot operated the air lock controls.

"Of the eight, only he could have cut the rope. It was he who provided it, and since the rope was coiled the cut would not have shown if it was inside the coil. All that would be necessary would be to leave a few threads uncut so that the ends would not separate. So much for opportunity.

"We now consider means. Of the eight, any of us could have taken my knife, but Captain Bogdanoff was in the ideal position to do so. He sat on my immediate left, which is to say that my platter was at his right hand.

"Last, motive. Captain Bogdanoff's wife is the daughter of an important official of the party—I hope you will excuse me if I do not name him. Suppose he were to hear that his son-in-law had been intimate with an American entertainer? Comrade Merry, as we have seen, is not reluctant to speak of it. We may presume that Comrade Cherry, who was her second self, was not either. No doubt he initially believed they would be discreet, and only later realized that they would not."

* * *

Earth seemed no more than a distant star, and Mars, round and red as the sun glimpsed through fog, grew until it filled the viewpoints. The blonde was packing her bags when Smith rapped at the door of her compartment.

"Can I come in?" he asked. "I'd like to talk to you."

She hesitated.

"It will only take a moment."

She opened the door more widely, and he sailed through and settled expertly into a vacuum chair. "Gravity again soon," he said. "We won't have to take those shots to keep our bones from melting anymore."

"Uh huh. Actually, I kind of enjoy floating." There was one other chair, and she had taken it.

"Me too. I suppose I was just making conversation."

"I know what you mean. It's such a relief to speak English."

"That's what I wanted to talk to you about," he said. "We'll both be pretty lonely on Mars. We'll both be travelling, too. I've got some flexibility as to where I go, and I'm sure Koroviev could juggle your dates a little. It might be possible for us to be together most of the time."

Her eyes widened slightly. "I don't think . . . No."

"Well, would it be all right if I called you? If it ever happens we're in the same place? We could have dinner together."

She shook her head.

"You were a lot more friendly that first evening at the Captain's table."

"That was Cherry."

"I see." Smith nodded.

"Did you hear about Vera Oussenko? They've got her locked up. They're not even going to let her off on Mars. Straight back to the Terrestrial USSR."

He shrugged. "She said herself that the Captain's wife was the daughter of a party official. She must have known the risk."

"I still don't see how they can do it."

"She was the only one no one else would vouch for at the

time of the killing. She said she was behind me, but I didn't see her. And it was her knife."

"I mean, because she was KGB. I guess even if you are, if you over-step . . ." the blonde shrugged, letting the sentence trail off.

"It's the same for us Americans, Cherry. If you go too far and the law finds out, it's all over."

"I'm Merry."

"You don't have to worry. I've got a bug detector in my pocket, and if they were ever listening in here—and I suppose they were, since that KGB woman seemed to know all about the Captain—they aren't now. With her gone, the system's probably run out of tape and shut itself down."

"I'm Merry. You're guessing."

A slight smile tugged at the corners of Smith's mouth. "You want me to tell you how the trick actually worked?"

"No!"

"All right, then we'll begin with you and Merry. While I was sitting between you two at the Captain's dinner, I started wondering what she wanted you for. I knew why I wanted you already—but what about her? I knew you must have cost her a small fortune." He paused. "Are you going to tell me to get out?"

The blonde said nothing.

"So I thought about it a bit. And there was only one reason I could see. Sure, an identical twin clone might be a handy thing for a magician to have. But a quarter million or so? Then too, at least half the value of the clone would be lost if everyone knew about her, and thanks to the scientific notoriety, everyone seemed to know about you. What was left, as far as I could see, was life insurance. The clone could do the really hazardous stunts. It didn't seem very fair."

So swiftly he almost missed it, she glanced at him, then down at her lap again.

"And here the great Merry Houdini was going to pull a

very dangerous stunt on board. I decided then that I'd keep an eye on you both to see if you'd switch roles."

"Could you tell?" It was a whisper.

Smith shook his head. "No. In fact, for a while you pretty well had me convinced you hadn't. I thought that maybe Merry figured you weren't up to it yet."

"You're right," the blonde said. "I'm Cherry. But I'll never admit that to anybody else, and I didn't kill her. How could I have?"

He grinned. "You're going to make me explain the stunt. All right, I will. It was risky, but nowhere near as risky as that loony thing the KGB woman dreamed up. Anyway, I knew that couldn't be right because I was sure there'd been no hidden compartment in the lid of the tool chest. I remember seeing it when the two of you opened it, and it was a flat piece of steel. Even so, I didn't really understand what you'd done until a couple of days afterward.

"There was no secret compartment. But when you—pretending to be Merry—climbed into the chest, you had a few little items hidden on your person. Since you had on a dress with a full skirt, my guess is that they were taped to your thigh. One of them was a little tube of sealant."

Her nod was almost imperceptible.

"As soon as Merry—wearing your red costume—shut the lid, you got the sealant out and went around the crack with it. Doing that in the dark would have been a pretty tough job, so I suspect you had one of those little penlights too.

"Meantime, the Captain was snapping on the lock Merry had given him, and Merry was tying one end of that coil of nylon safety line to the handle of the box and the other to the cleat that the Captain had got welded to the wall for you. The Captain said, and probably believed, that he was the one who had insisted on that precaution; but my guess is that Merry psyched him into it, which shouldn't have been too hard. If he hadn't bought the idea, she would have insisted on it, or maybe used something else, like a telephone wire.

"But what did Merry do when she had both ends tied? Let

go of the coil and let it float there? No, she put it over the cleat, just as if she were hanging it on the wall down on Earth. All of us were so used to seeing that kind of thing that we didn't pay much attention.

"Then everybody backed off. The inside hatch was shut and the outside hatch opened. The rush of air ought to have blown the floating chest out, just like the Captain said it would. Only it couldn't, and it didn't. I tried the idea out later; I cut a cleat out of cardboard and made a rope by tying a pair of shoelaces together. And when you hang the coil over the cleat the way Merry did, and then pull the end, it doesn't uncoil. The first loop just tightens until it grabs the cleat. That chest never went out the air lock at all. It was moored, anchored in the lock.

"So there you were. You were inside the chest, with no air on the outside, but you were still in the *Red Star*. You had sealed the top, and there must have been enough air inside to last you for at least half an hour if you didn't start thrashing around. All Merry had to do was wait until the rest of us ran out to look for you through the viewports.

"We saw you too, or at least we thought we did. Because your Russian manager, Koroviev, was at one of the utility air locks with another tool chest. This one had been gimmicked in advance; there was a piece of rope tied to the handle, and the lid was held closed by the sort of stuff that KGB woman thought you'd used in the lock—this was a whole lot easier, of course, because all you had to do was slap some on. My guess is that heavy grease would have done it. Anyway, it held the lid down, whatever it was, until it boiled off in space. Inside the chest was a dummy arm on a spring. As soon as the grease was gone, that pushed against the lid enough to open it a little, and all of us saw what we thought was your hand.

"In the meantime, as soon as she was sure the coast was clear, Merry closed the outer hatch, opened the inner one, and let you out. She didn't even have to pick the lock; she probably had the key stuck down the front of her dress.

"But you had something else stashed away besides the tube

of gunk and your little light. You had the KGB woman's knife. Why did you pick her, anyway? Did you know she was KGB?"

Cherry shook her head. Her eyes were bright with tears, though she was not sobbing. "She was just the farthest away, and I hadn't liked the way she held my hand. It was as though I had another boss."

"Somebody else to take the cash and the glory while you took the orders? And the chances. Yes, I can see that. That's what made me sure you two had switched identities—Merry had no reason to kill you, but you had a couple of swell ones for killing Merry. Do I have to go on with this?"

"No. Merry unlocked the box and let me out, and I was waiting for her. Twice before I had tried to hit her back, and I knew how fast she was. Faster than I am, I guess because she'd had more practice. I had my knife all ready. She had to pull the lid and the box apart because of the stickum, so her arms were spread out." The blonde demonstrated, one arm up and one down. "And I pushed it right into her chèst. I stuck it in so hard it made the box and me fly back and bang against the outside door. I hadn't thought of that, and I was afraid somebody would hear it, but I guess all of you were making too much noise yourselves.

"Then I took the box into one of the service corridors and hid it. Merry had been supposed to help me with that, but it wasn't hard. I just pulled it along with the rope. I had to wait there myself until I was sure the other box was far enough away that nobody could see the fake hand. Then I came out."

Smith nodded. "And by then I had already found Merry. But Merry in your red dress, so I thought it was you."

"Are you going to tell them? I mean, you're not going to tell them here, I know that from what you said before. But when we get back home?"

"I don't know," Smith said. "It all depends on how things go on Mars." He glanced toward the swollen crimson sphere in the viewport.

"Aren't you afraid I'll kill you there? Murder you too? I killed her, after all. I don't even feel bad about it. Only bad because you found out."

"You've never been a child," Smith said. "Never had the time to develop a conscience. That was something Merry forgot about." He hesitated. "No, I'm not frightened. Not much. I've seen you and talked to you and you're worth the risk."

"I think you are too," Cherry said.

"What do you mean by that?"

"You're a more dangerous person than I am. You're a spy of some sort, aren't you? Even the Russians guess that, and part of the reason you won't turn me in is that it looks better if a Russian killed Cherry than if I killed Merry. Anyway, anybody who thinks the way you do is dangerous."

Smith chuckled. "You'll have to risk it."

"I think I want to risk it. Smitty, are there children on Mars?"

"A few, I think. Not many yet. Why?"

"Because like you said I've never been one. I mean, it went by so fast. I want to see what they do. Maybe play with them."

Smith got out of the vacuum chair and allowed himself to drift toward the center of the room. "This is fun, all right," he said. "I'm really sorry I won't be able to do it much longer. Listen, Cherry, I grew up at the regular speed in the regular way, and it seems awfully short to me too now."

"You'd better call me Merry, so you get used to it. There are bank accounts and things."

"I'll bet. If she could spend a quarter million for you, there must be quite a bit more. All those TV specials. Do you know what first put me on to you—Merry?"

The blonde shook her head.

"The dessert. The way you looked when I told you about the year of the jubilee, when the poor relations got their land back. Your eyes got round. You're very pretty when your eyes get round."

"You said it was radical economics, and it was. This is too, I suppose. You've just gotten yourself a girl on Mars—all through radical economics."

"You're right," Smith told her. "But I wish I could have gotten my girl the way you got your man."

Redbeard

I T DOESN'T MATTER HOW HOWIE AND I BE-
CAME FRIENDS, except that our friendship was unusual.
I'm one of those people who've moved into the area since
. . . Since what? I don't know; someday I'll have to ask Howie.
Since the end of the sixties or the Truman Administration or
the Second World War. Since something.

Anyway, after Mara and I came with our little boy, John,
we grew conscious of an older strata. They are the people who
were living here before. Howie is one of them; his grandpar-
ents are buried in the little family cemeteries that are or used
to be attached to farms—all within twenty miles of my desk.
Those people are still here, practically all of them, like the old
trees that stand among the new houses.

By and large we don't mix much. We're only dimly aware
of them, and perhaps they're only dimly aware of us. Our
friends are new people too, and on Sunday mornings we cut
the grass together. Their friends are the children of their
parents' friends, and their own uncles and cousins; on Sunday
mornings they go to the old clapboard churches.

Howie was the exception, as I said. We were driving down
U.S. 27—or rather, Howie was driving, and I was sitting
beside him smoking a cigar and having a look around. I saw
a gate that was falling down, with a light that was leaning way
over, and beyond it, just glimpsed, a big, old, tumbledown
wooden house with young trees sprouting in the front yard.
It must have had about ten acres of ground, but there was a

boarded up fried-chicken franchise on one side of it and a service station on the other.

"That's Redbeard's place," Howie told me.

I thought it was a family name, perhaps an anglicization of Barbarossa. I said, "It looks like a haunted house."

"It is," Howie said. "For me, anyway. I can't go in there."

We hit a chuck hole, and I looked over at him.

"I tried a couple times. Soon as I set my foot on that step, something says, 'This is as far as you go, Buster,' and I turn around and head home."

After a while I asked him who Redbeard was.

"This used to be just a country road," Howie said. "They made it a Federal Highway back about the time I was born, and it got a lot of cars and trucks and stuff on it. Now the Interstate's come through, and it's going back to about what it was.

"Back before, a man name of Jackson used to live there. I don't think anybody thought he was much different, except he didn't get married till he was forty or so. But then, a lot of people around here used to do that. He married a girl named Sarah Sutter."

I nodded, just to show Howie I was listening.

"She was a whole lot younger than him, nineteen or twenty. But she loved him—that's what I always heard. Probably he was good to her, and so on. Gentle. You know?"

I said a lot of young women like that preferred older men.

"I guess. You know where Clinton is? Little place about fifteen miles over. There had been a certain amount of trouble around Clinton going on for years, and people were concerned about it. I don't believe I said this Jackson was from Clinton, but he was. His dad had run a store there and had a farm. The one brother got the farm and the next oldest the store. This Jackson, he just got some money, but it was enough for him to come here and buy that place. It was about a hundred acres then.

"Anyhow, they caught him over in Clinton. One of those chancy things. It was winter, and dark already, and there'd been a little accident where a car hit a school bus that still had quite a few kids riding home. Nobody was killed as far as I heard or even hurt bad, but a few must have had bloody noses and so forth, and you couldn't get by on the road. Just after the deputy's car got there this Jackson pulled up, and the deputy told him to load some of the kids in the back and take them to the Doctor's.

"Jackson said he wouldn't, he had to get back home. The deputy told him not to be a damned fool. The kids were hurt and he'd have to go back to Clinton anyhow to get on to Mill Road, because it would be half the night before they got that bus moved.

"Jackson still wouldn't do it, and went to try and turn his pickup around. From the way he acted, the deputy figured there was something wrong. He shined his flash in the back, and there was something under a tarp there. When he saw that, he hollered for Jackson to stop and went over and jerked the tarp away. From what I hear, now he couldn't do that because of not having a warrant, and if he did, Jackson would have got off. Back then, nobody had heard of such foolishness. He jerked that tarp away, and there was a girl underneath, and she was dead. I don't even know what her name was. Rosa or something like that, I guess. They were Italians that had come just a couple of years before." Howie didn't give *Italians* a long *I,* but there had been a trifling pause while he remembered not to. "Her dad had a little shoe place," he said. "The family was there for years after.

"Jackson was arrested, and they took him up to the county seat. I don't know if he told them anything or not. I think he didn't. His wife came up to see him, and then a day or so later the sheriff came to the house with a search warrant. He went all through it, and when he got to going through the cellars, one of the doors was locked. He asked her for the key, but she said she didn't have it. He said he'd have to bust down the door, and asked her what was in there. She said she didn't know, and after a while it all came out—I mean, all as far as her understanding went.

"She told him that door had been shut ever since she and Jackson had been married. He'd told her he felt a man was entitled to some privacy, and that right there was his private place, and if she wanted a private place of her own she could have it, but to stay out of his. She'd taken one of the upstairs bedrooms and made it her sewing room.

"Nowadays they just make a basement and put everything on top, but these old houses have cellars with walls and rooms, just like upstairs. The reason is that they didn't have the steel beams we use to hold everything up, so they had to build masonry walls underneath; if you built a couple of these, why you had four rooms. The foundations of all these old houses are stone."

I nodded again.

"This one room had a big, heavy door. The sheriff tried to knock it down, but he couldn't. Finally he had to telephone around and get a bunch of men to help him. They found three girls in there."

"Dead?" I asked Howie.

"That's right. I don't know what kind of shape they were in, but not very good, I guess. One had been gone over a year. That's what I heard."

As soon as I said it, I felt like a half-wit; but I was thinking of all the others, of John Gacy and Jack the Ripper and the dead black children of Atlanta, and I said, "Three? That was all he killed?"

"Four," Howie told me, "counting the Italian girl in the truck. Most people thought it was enough. Only there was some others missing too, you know, in various places around the state, so the sheriff and some deputies tore everything up looking for more bodies. Dug in the yard and out in the fields and so on."

"But they didn't find any more?"

"No, they didn't. Not then," Howie said. "Meantime, Jackson was in jail like I told you. He had kind of reddish hair, so the paper called him Redbeard. Because of Bluebeard, you know, and him not wanting his wife to look inside that cellar room. They called the house Redbeard's Castle.

"They did things a whole lot quicker in those times, and it wasn't much more than a month before he was tried. Naturally, his wife had to get up in the stand."

I said, "A wife can't be forced to testify against her husband."

"She wasn't testifying against him, she was testifying for him. What a good man he was, and all that. Who else would do it? Of course when she'd had her say, the district attorney got to go to work on her. You know how they do.

"He asked her about that room and she told him just about what I told you. Jackson, he said he wanted a place for himself and told her not to go in there. She said she hadn't even known the door was locked till the sheriff tried to open it. Then the district attorney said didn't you know he was asking for your help, that your husband was asking for your help, that the whole room there was a cry for help, and he wanted you to go in there and find those bodies so he wouldn't have to kill again?"

Howie fell silent for a mile or two. I tossed the butt of my cigar out the window and sat wondering if I would hear any more about those old and only too commonplace murders.

When Howie began talking again, it was as though he had never stopped. "That was the first time anybody from around here had heard that kind of talk, I think. Up till then, I guess everybody thought if a man wanted to get caught he'd just go to the police and say he did it. I always felt sorry for her, because of that. She was—I don't know—like an owl in daylight. You know what I mean?"

I didn't, and I told him so.

"The way she'd been raised, a man meant what he said. Then too, the man was the boss. Today when they get married there isn't hardly a woman that promises to obey, but back then they all did it. If they'd asked the minister to leave that out, most likely he'd have told them he wouldn't perform the ceremony. Now the rules were all changed, only nobody'd told her that.

"I believe she took it pretty hard, and of course it didn't do any good, her getting in the stand or the district attorney talking like that to her either. The jury came back in about as quick as they'd gone out, and they said he was guilty, and the judge said sentencing would be next day. He was going to hang him, and everybody knew it. They hanged them back then."

"Sure," I said.

"That next morning his wife came to see him in the jail. I guess he knew she would, because he asked the old man that swept out to lend him a razor and so forth. Said he wanted to look good. He shaved and then he waited till he heard her step."

Howie paused to let me comment or ask a question. I thought I knew what was coming, and there didn't seem to be much point in saying anything.

"When he heard her coming, he cut his throat with the razor blade. The old man was with her, and he told the paper about it afterwards. He said they came up in front of the cell, and Jackson was standing there with blood all running down his shirt. He really was Redbeard for true then. After a little bit, his knees gave out and he fell down in a heap.

"His wife tried to sell the farm, but nobody wanted that house. She moved back with her folks, quit calling herself Sarah Jackson. She was a good looking woman, and the land brought her some money. After a year or so she got married again and had a baby. Everybody forgot, I suppose you could say, except maybe for the families of the girls that had died. And the house, it's still standing back there. You just saw it yourself."

Howie pronounced the final words as though the story were over and he wanted to talk of something else, but I said, "You said there were more bodies found later."

"Just one. Some kids were playing in that old house. It's

funny, isn't it, that kids would find it when the sheriff and all those deputies didn't."

"Where was it?"

"Upstairs. In her sewing room. You remember I told you how he'd said she could have a room to herself too? Of course, the sheriff had looked in there, but it hadn't been there when he looked. It was her, and she'd hung herself from a hook in the wall. Who do you think killed her?"

I glanced at him to see if he were serious. "I thought you said she killed herself?"

"That's what they would have said, back when she married Jackson. But who killed her now? Jackson—Redbeard—when he killed those other girls and cut his throat like that? Or was it when he loved her? Or that district attorney? Or the sheriff? Or the mothers and fathers and brothers and sisters of the girls Jackson got? Or her other husband, maybe some things he said to her? Or maybe it was just having her baby that killed her—baby blues they call it. I've heard that too."

"Postnatal depression," I said. I shook my head. "I don't suppose it makes much difference now."

"It does to me," Howie said. "She was my mother." He pushed the lighter into the dashboard and lit a cigarette. "I thought I ought to tell you before somebody else does."

For a moment I supposed that we had left the highway and circled back along some secondary road. To our right was another ruined gate, another outdated house collapsing slowly among young trees.

A Solar Labyrinth

M AZES MAY BE MORE ANCIENT THAN MAN-
KIND. Certainly the cavemen constructed them by
laying down football-sized stones, and perhaps by other means
as well, now lost to us; the hill-forts of neolithic Europe were
guarded by tangled dry ditches. Theseus followed a clew—a
ball of thread—through the baffling palace of Minos, thus
becoming the first in what threatens to be an infinite series of
fictional detectives. The Fayre Rosamund dropped her em-
broidery with her needle thrust through it, but forgot the yarn
in her pocket, thus furnishing Queen Eleanor's knights with
the clue they required to solve Hampton Court Maze.

Of late, few mazes have been built, and those that have
been, have been walled, for the most part, with cheap and
unimaginative hedges. Airplanes and helicopters permit ram-
pant mar-sports to photograph new mazes from above, and
the pictures let armchair adventurers solve them with a pencil.
Gone, it might seem, are the great days of monsters, maidens,
and amazement.

But not quite. I have heard that a certain wealthy citizen has
not only designed and built a new maze, but has invented a
new *kind* of maze, perhaps the first since the end of the Age
of Myth. To preserve his privacy I shall call this new Daedalus
Mr. Smith. To frustrate the aerial photographers in their chartered Cessnas, I shall say only that his maze is in the Adiron-
dacks.

On a manicured green lawn stand—well separated for the
most part—a collection of charming if improbable objects.

There are various obelisks; lamp posts from Vienna, Paris, and London, as well as New York; a pillar-box, also from London; fountains that splash for a time and then subside; a retired yawl, canted now upon the reef of grass but with masts still intact; the standing trunk of a dead tree overgrown with roses; many more. The shadows of these objects form the walls of an elaborate and sophisticated maze.

It is, obviously, a maze that changes from hour to hour, and indeed from minute to minute. Not so obviously, it is one that can be solved only at certain times and is insoluble at noon, when the shadows are shortest. It is also, of course, a maze from which the explorer can walk free whenever he chooses.

And yet it is said that most of them—most adults, at least—do not. In the early morning, while the shadows of the hills still veil his lawn, Mr. Smith brings the favored guest to the point that will become the center of the maze. The grass is still fresh with dew, and there is no sound but the chirping of birds. For five minutes or so the two men (or as it may be, the man and the woman) stand and wait. Perhaps they smoke a cigarette. The sun's red disc appears above the mist-shrouded treetops, the fountains jet their crystal columns, the birds fall silent, and the shadowy suites spring into existence, a sketch in the faded black ink of God.

Mr. Smith begins to tread his maze, but he invites his guest to discover paths of his own. The guest does so, amused at first, then more serious. Imperceptibly, the shadows move. New corridors appear; old ones close, sometimes with surprising speed. Soon Mr. Smith's path joins that of his guest (for Mr. Smith knows his maze well), and the two proceed together, the guest leading the way. Mr. Smith speaks of his statue of Diana, a copy of one in the Louvre; the image of Tezcatlipaca, the Toltec sun-god, is authentic, having been excavated at Teotihuacan. As he talks, the shadows shift, seeming almost to writhe like feathered Quetzalcoatl with the slight rolling of the lawn. Mr. Smith steps away, but for a time his path nearly parallels his guest's.

"Do you see that one there?" says the guest. "In another

minute or two, when it's shorter, I'll be able to get through there."

Mr. Smith nods and smiles.

The guest waits, confidently now surveying the wonderful pattern of dark green and bright. The shadow he has indicated—that of a Corinthian column, perhaps—indeed diminishes; but as it does another, wheeling with the wheeling sun, falls across the desired path. Most adult guests do not escape until they are rescued by a passing cloud. Some, indeed, refuse such rescue.

Often Mr. Smith invites groups of children to inspect his maze, their visits timed so they can be led to its center. There, inlaid upon a section of crumbling wall that at least *appears* ancient, he points out the frowning figure of the Minotaur, a monster that, as he explains, haunts the shadows. From far away—but not in the direction of the house—the deep bellowing of a bull interrupts him. (Perhaps a straying guest might discover stereo speakers hidden in the boughs of certain trees; perhaps not.) Mr. Smith says he can usually tell in advance which children will enjoy his maze. They are more often boys than girls, he says, but not much more often. They must be young, but not too young. Glasses help. He shows a picture of his latest Ariadne, a dark-haired girl of nine.

Yet he is fair to all the children, giving each the same instructions, the same encouragement. Some reject his maze out of hand, wandering off to examine the tilted crucifix or the blue-dyed water in the towering Torricelli barometer, or to try (always without success) to draw Arthur's sword from its stone. Others persevere longer, threading their way between invisible walls for an hour or more.

But always, as the shadow of the great gnomon creeps toward the sandstone XII set in the lawn, the too-old, too-young, insufficiently serious, and too-serious drift away, leaving only Mr. Smith and one solitary child still playing in the sunshine.

Love, Among the Corridors

HER OWN FOOTFALLS ECHOED AFTER HER, reverberating from stone floor to ceiling of stone, so that she felt herself pursued, though she knew herself to be the pursuer. The ticking of the clocks told the footsteps of time.

The walls were lined with pictures and carvings, with dusty furniture and old vases bellied like the cupids on a Valentine. She looked at all and walked on. She could not bear to think of where she had begun to walk (for that was nothingness) or where she went (for that was to the grave).

When it had grown late, and all the windows of the palace were darkened by more than ivy, she saw, among the other statues and figures, a Harlequin cast of bronze standing upon a marble pedestal. There was nothing about him, perhaps, to take her interest, and yet take it he did; and with one small, white hand, she touched him.

At once it seemed the sun had broken through the ivy and the evening. An aureate ray pierced the window nearest the statue and touched it too, so that she saw immediately that, cobwebbed though it was, it was not a statue at all but a living Harlequin, dominoed and costumed as in the old plays.

When the sunlight had faded—as it did in an instant—the ruddy glow of health remained in the Harlequin's cheeks and the light of life in his eyes.

He moved and sneezed at the dust, raising a great, gray cloud of it; then sneezing again, leaped from his pedestal. She started back in fear.

"What is your name?" he said, wiping his nose upon his sleeve.

And she, "Amor . . ."

"I too. But who are you, and how came you to walk in this palace?"

Taking courage, she told him, "That is the question no one can answer. Rather, recount to me how you, who appeared but an image a moment ago, are now a man."

"By stepping down," he said. "At least, that is how it seems to me when I reflect upon it. For a long time—oh, very long, longer than your whole dear life, I feel sure—I stood . . ." He hesitated.

"Why, right up there, wasn't it? Right up on that stone block, that seems so ordinary now. Ten thousand times, at least, I watched the sun come in at those windows and go out, and Night come with her cats and wolves. Many a hundred walkers have I seen go up and down this corridor before yourself, my darling. It seems to me now that at any moment I might have stepped down, and yet I did not, nor even thought on it. And now it seems to me that I might mount up again and pose as I did before, and yet that would be too laborious for me to stand. But tell me more; who are you, and who are your father and mother?"

"My name you know," Amor said. "But let me confess at once, lest you should discover it in time after, that I was born out of wedlock. The noble Chivalry was my father, and Poetry my mother."

"Ah, brave old Chivalry." Harlequin cocked his head, finding as other men do that to concentrate his thoughts it was needful to make them run to one side. "I saw him often, long since, but not for many a year now."

"He is dead," Amor sighed. "And I, a neglectful daughter, ought to have said 'my late father' and not spoken as I did."

"What? Brave Chivalry late? But Chivalry cannot be late, or else 'tis not Chivalry."

"How truly you speak. No, that poor body cannot be my

noble father, ever so light of step, even when he was stiff of knee. It is—what it is. But Chivalry was never so."

"As for Poetry," continued Harlequin. "She still lives, I believe; but she is old and crank and ill."

"I feared it might be thus. It has been so very long since last I saw her."

"Then you are alone in the world," Harlequin said, and made her a deep bow. "But not entirely alone, for you have me."

"And you," Amor said. "You are alone also."

"Indeed, I hope not."

She took him by the hand. "My dear friend—"

Fearing her words: "Your touch thrills me still. It was your touch, beloved Amor, that called me to life. I came down from that block of stone to feel your touch. There is true magic in your touch, I swear!"

"How could my touch kindle anything to life?"

He kissed her hand. "I cannot say—and yet I know it brought life to me."

"Shall we make trial of it?" Amor inquired doubtfully. "If it were so, I might—I even might— Shall I touch another?"

"Oh, not another!" Harlequin gasped.

"Not another such as you, dear friend, for there is no other such as you. But should I not touch something else? Perhaps the dragon on that vase?"

"But suppose your touch effectual. We would have a dragon between us. Would that not be horrible?"

"And if it were not—"

"That would be more horrible still."

"What then? There is a painted mask upon that wall."

"Friend to you, he would prove a false friend. No, touch . . ."

"What?"

"Touch . . ."

"Yes?"

"The entire palace!"

"Everything? I cannot touch it all at once."

"You did not touch me all at once, but only in a single spot."

"I'll try," she said; and while Harlequin watched, she knelt upon the floor, embraced a column, and blew a kiss to the ceiling.

Nothing occurred.

"I knew it could not be," she said.

"I knew it could." He hung his head.

She took his hand again, and together they wandered down the many and dividing corridors that lead to the grave.

"It worked for me," he said.

"I know it did."

And the marble was white no longer, but flushed with rose.

She said, "It would have been a wondrous thing."

"It was, for me." And later, "It will always be."

As their footsteps echoed the ticking of the clocks in the benighted corridors, a new wind fluttered the candle flames and whispered to the dry stones there of rain in spring.

"It was joy even to fancy it," she said, "though it was only for a moment."

"It is true," he told her.

A daisy pushed its golden eye from between two blocks of marble. Harlequin nearly trod on it. "It's true! Amor, you can, you do! You did! Oh, Amor, don't you see? It only took longer because the palace is so huge."

"I do?" she asked. Then whispered, "I *did*." And with trembling hand touched her own heart.

Checking Out

THE SLAM OF THE DOOR JERKED HIM TO WAKEFULNESS.

He lay on top of the bed on a blue satin coverlet, fully dressed except for his shoes. He sat up and saw his suitcase on the bed beside him. No doubt the bellboy had brought it. No doubt the bellboy had promised to follow him to his room—they did that sometimes. And instead of staying awake for him, he had lain down to get a little rest. No doubt the bellboy was angry at not getting a tip.

It was his best suit; he should not have gone to sleep in it. He went to the closet and hung up his jacket. The room seemed very small, the bed so narrow he was surprised the bellboy had found room for his bag on it. He wondered what hotel this was.

He liked the Algonquin in New York, though its rooms were so small, its beds so narrow. But everything in the Algonquin was old and good and a little worn; everything was new here, and a little bit shiny and cheap. He did not think they built hotel rooms this small any more.

He opened his bag and saw that Jane had not packed it. Martha, perhaps. Martha was their cleaning woman, the old woman who would not do windows. No, Martha was dead.

Jane's picture was on top, and he took it out and looked into her clear blue eyes. She would miss him. Or rather, she would say she did, though he knew the only time she really relaxed was when he was gone—when he was gone, and she could pretend they were rich for life, and there would never,

never be a need to make anything more, no need for late nights at the office, for flights to New York with Jan.

Flights. That was it. They had been on the plane, he remembered, and tired. He had drunk the free martini they gave you and leaned back to relax. After that, they would have hired a cab. No doubt the old furniture at the Algonquin had given out at last, and the management had had to get this stuff.

You could buy *The New York Review* at the magazine stand in the Algonquin; he liked that. He decided to go out and get one, but his shoes were not in the closet, not under the bed. Well, to hell with them. His slippers would be in his bag, and you could go into the lobby in your slippers at the Algonquin—he liked that too. Perhaps Jan was in the lobby or the bar.

He found Jan's picture while looking for his slippers. How had that got in there? Perhaps Martha had put it in for fear that Jane would see it. He tossed it toward the wastebasket. Jan was a good secretary, and sometimes he felt that she loved him in a way Jane never had, at least not since Bruce was born. But he could not leave Jane. Paradoxically, he could not leave her because he had left her so often.

He tossed Jan's picture toward the wastebasket, and found Joan's beneath it, a misty "glamour portrait" in the style of the forties, signed like a movie star's. This was absurd. He had never owned such a picture.

Or had he? Yes, once.

What a strange, unpleasant sound the air conditioning made here, like a drawn-out sigh, an unending sighing.

Quite suddenly his desk appeared to his mind's eye, more real than the tawdry room, and just as suddenly it shrank. There was a roll top now with cheap varnish over the stained oak, with just room enough to write, with a few books. Had that battered children's dictionary ever been his? There was a fold-out shelf with just room enough to write, and a few pigeon holes, and Joan's picture in the frame from Woolworth's. He realized with a start that she might have been a virgin in those days, a real high-school virgin in those days, though he had never thought of her that way, only as a woman, though he had said "girl," and infinitely desirable.

No doubt he had, later, put Jan's picture into the frame so that it covered Joan's. No doubt he had put them both into the new frame Jan had bought for his desk. No doubt Martha had put them, together, into his bag. No, Martha was dead.

He flung both pictures at the wastebasket and scuffed on his slippers as he opened the door.

Space.

An atrium—this hotel had an atrium; it was a Hyatt then. High, it rose so high he could see only blue sky at the top. His room was high up too, though it seemed less than half way up. Tiny figures moved slowly across the lobby, wading in water nearly waist deep.

A flood—there was a flood in the city. He was lucky the lights in his room still worked, the air conditioning still sighed.

He looked back and saw that he had not in fact turned on any lights, that the bellboy had not turned on any lights at all. The room was dark and gloomy behind him, like a cave in which something slept.

He would go to the lobby. There was a flood, and he was still an active man. Perhaps he could help. Perhaps Jan would see him helping.

He tried, but his balcony was not connected with the other balconies—there was a gap of at least ten feet. How did you get out in that case? How did you reach the elevators?

He went back into the room and saw Jan's picture on top of his clean shirts. He would tell Jane, make a clean breast of it for once. He reached for the telephone.

Mrs. Clem said, "I thought he looked very nice. All that pretty blue."

Jane nodded. "I bought a concrete dome to go over the casket, too. It sits right down over it and traps the air, so the water can't get to him. It cost almost three thousand dollars."

The telephone rang. "Excuse me," she said. "Hello?"

"I'm coming back to you." The words stuck in his throat. There had been no sound, only the unending sigh.

"Hello?"

"I love you, Jane. I'm checking out of here and coming back, whether you love me or not."

Jane said, "There's no one there, just an empty line."

"I'd hang up, if I were you," Mrs. Clem told her.

"Jane!" he said. And then, "Joan? Joan?"

Someone was knocking at the door. *"Maid."*

He stared at it. "Jan? Joan?"

"Would you like your bed turned down, sir? It will only take a minute."

Jane said, "Not even breathing," and hung up.

Morning-Glory

S MYTHE PUT HIS HANDS BEHIND HIS HEAD and
looked up at the ceiling. He was a short and untidy man
now well entered on middle age, and his face showed embarrassment.

"Well, go on," Black said.

Smythe said, "My father felt bread was sacred; if a piece was
accidentally dropped on the floor he would demand that it be
picked up at once and dusted off and eaten; if someone
stepped on it he was furious."

"Was this element of your father's character present in
reality, or is it only a part of the dream logic?"

Smythe put his head down and looked at Black in irritation.
"This is just background," he said. "My father would say,
'Bread is the life of man, you dirty little hyena. Pick it up.' He
had been brought up in Germany."

"Specifically, what was your dream?" Black opened his
notebook.

Smythe hesitated. For years now he had been giving Black
entries, and he had almost always made them up, thinking
them out on the bus he took to the campus each morning. It
seemed now a sort of descreation, a cheat, to tell Black a real
dream. "I was a vine," he said, "and I was pounding on a
translucent wall. I knew there was light on the other side, but
it didn't do me any good where I was. My father's voice kept
saying: *See! See! See!* Over and over like that. My father is
dead."

"I had supposed so," Black said. "What do you think this dream has to do with your father's reverence for bread?"

More disturbed by the dream than he wanted Black to know, Smythe shrugged. "What I was trying to communicate was that my father had a sort of reverence for food. 'You are what you eat,' and all that sort of thing. I chewed morning-glory seeds once."

"Morning-glory seeds?"

"Yes. Morning-glory seeds are supposed to be a sort of hallucinogen, like LSD or peyote."

"I suppose your father caught you and punished you?"

Smythe shook himself with irritation. "Hell no. This wasn't when I was a child; it was about three years ago." He felt frustrated by Black's invincible obtuseness. "All the blah-blah was going on in the newspapers about drugs, and I felt that as a member of the department I ought to know at least a little bit about it. I didn't know where to get LSD or any of those other things, but of course I had morning-glory seed right in the lab." He remembered the paper seed packet with its preposterously huge blue flower and how frightened he had been.

"You didn't think you should obtain departmental permission?"

"I felt," Smythe said carefully, "that it would be better for the department if it were not on record as having officially approved of something of that sort." *Besides,* he told himself savagely, *you were afraid that you would get the permission and then back out; that's the truth, and if you tell too many lies you may forget it.*

"I suppose you were probably right," Black said. He closed his notebook with a bored snap. "Did you really have hallucinations?"

"I'm not sure. It may have been self-hypnosis."

"Nothing striking though?"

"No. But you see, I had eaten—at least in a sense—the morning glory. I think that may be why my father—" He hesitated, lost in the complications of the thought he was trying to formulate. Black was the Freudian; he himself, at least by training, a Watsonian behaviorist.

"Further dreams may tell us more about what's going on," Black said. It was one of his stock dismissals. "Don't forget you've got counseling tomorrow." As Smythe closed the door Black added, "Good-bye, Schmidt."

Smythe turned, wanting to say that his father's father had been American consul in Nuremberg, but it was too late. The door had shut.

To reach his own laboratory he went down two flights of stairs and along a seemingly endless hall walled with slabs of white marble. The last lecture of the day had been finished at four, but as he approached the laboratory area in the rear of the building he heard the murmur of a few late-staying students still bent over their white rats. Just as he reached his own door one of these groups broke up, undergraduates, boys in sweaters and jeans, and girls in jeans and sweaters, drifting out into the corridor. A girl with long blond hair and a small heart-shaped face stopped as he opened the door, peering in at the twisting, glowing, rectangular tubes that filled the bright room. On an impulse Smythe said, "Come in. Would you like to see it?"

The girl stepped inside, and after a moment put the books she was carrying on one of the lab benches. "What do you do here?" she said. "I don't think I've ever seen this place." The light made her squint.

Smythe smiled. "I'm called a vine runner."

She looked at him quizzically.

"People who put rats through mazes are called rat runners; people who use flatworms are worm runners."

"You mean all these square pipes are to test the intelligence of plants?"

"Plants," Smythe said, allowing himself only a slight smile, "lacking a nervous system, have no intelligence. When they display signs of what, in such higher creatures as flatworms, would be called intelligence, we refer to it as para-intelligence or pseudo intelligence. Come here, and I'll show you how we study it.''

The rectangular passages were of clouded, milky white plastic panels held together with metal clips. He unfastened a panel, showing her the green, leafy tendril inside.

"I don't understand," she said. "And I don't think you really believe that about pseudo intelligence. Intelligence ought to be defined by the way something responds, not by what you find inside when you cut it open."

"Out of fear of being accused of heresy I won't agree with you—but I have, on occasion, been known to point out to my departmental superiors that our age is unique in preferring a pond worm to an oak tree."

The girl was still looking at the twisting white passages sprawling along the bench. "How does it work?" she asked. "How do you test them?"

"It's simple, really, once you understand that a plant 'moves' by growth. That's why it has no musculature, which in turn, by the way, is why it has no nervous system. These mazes offer the plants choice points in the form of forked passages with equal amounts of light available in each direction. As you see, we keep this room brightly lit, and these plastic panels are translucent. The trick is that we have more than twenty grades, ranging from ones which admit almost as much light as plate glass to ones which are nearly opaque." He held up the panel he had unfastened so that she could see the light through it, then rummaged in a drawer to produce another of the same color which none the less admitted much less light.

"I see," the girl said. "The smart plants find out by and by that there's less and less light when they go down a wrong turn, and so they stop and go back."

"That's right, except that the tendrils don't, of course, actually turn around and grow backward. The growth of the 'wrong' tendrils just slows and stops, and new growth begins where the bad decision was made."

The girl reached down and gently, almost timidly, stroked a leaf. "It's like a society more than an animal, isn't it? I mean it sort of grows an institution, and then if it finds out it's going the wrong way it grows another one. What's the name of this plant?"

"Bindweed," Smythe told her. "It's one of the most intelligent we've found. Far brighter, for example, than scarlet runner bean—which in turn is more intelligent itself than, say, most varieties of domestic grapes, which are among the stupidest vines."

"I ought to be going now," the girl said. She picked up her books. "What's that big one, though? The one that sprawls all over?"

Smythe was replacing the panel he had removed for her. "A morning-glory," he said. "I should rip it out, actually, so that I could use the room and the maze components for something else. What I did was to subject the seeds to radiation, and apparently that destroyed the vine's ability to discriminate between light levels. Once it makes a wrong turn it simply continues indefinitely in that direction."

"You mean its mind is destroyed?"

"No, not really. That's the odd thing. On other types of tests—for example, when we lop off tendrils until it memorizes a pattern of 'safe' turns: right, right, left, left, or something of the sort—it still does quite well. But it will keep running down a passage of diminishing light level until it reaches nearly total darkness."

"How horrible," the girl said. "Could I see it?" While he was unfastening a panel for her she asked suddenly, "Did you see that awful show on television the other night? About the turtles?"

He shook his head.

"They showed this atoll where there had been a hydrogen bomb test years ago. The sea turtles come there every year to lay eggs, and when they came after the test the radiation made them forget, somehow, that they were supposed to go back to the ocean. They just kept crawling inland, crawling and crawling until they died in the jungle and their bodies rotted. The shells are still there, and the birds have build nests in some of them." She looked intently for a moment at the spindly, white vine he showed her inside the maze. "It never blooms in there, does it?"

"No," he said, "it never blooms."

"I wonder what it looks like, to it, inside there."

"Like marble corridors, I suppose. As though it were walking down marble corridors."

The girl looked at him oddly, shifting her books on her hip.

After she had gone he wondered why he had said what he had, even putting four plastic panels together and peering down the short passage they formed. The white plastic did not actually look a great deal like marble.

On the bus he found himself still thinking of it, and forced himself to divert his attention, but everything he found to focus it on seemed worse. Newspaper headlines warned him of the air pollution he could see by merely looking through the windows of the bus, and the transistor radio of the man in the seat next to his told him that France, the world's fifth-ranking nuclear power, had now joined the "total destruction club" by acquiring (like the United States, the Soviet Union, China, and Britain) enough hydrogen bombs to eliminate life on Earth. He looked at the man holding the radio, half tempted to make some bitter remark, but the man was blind and for some reason this made him turn away again.

Once at home he worked on his book for an hour (Publish or Perish!), ate dinner, and spent the remainder of the evening watching television with his wife. They went to bed after the late news, but Smythe found he could not sleep. After an hour he got up, made himself a drink, and settled into his favorite chair to read.

He was walking through an enormous building like a mausoleum, trailing behind him a sort of filmy green vapor insubstantial as mist. To either side of him doors opened showing gardens, or tables piled with food, or beds so large as to be nearly rooms themselves; but the doors opened only after he had gone a step beyond, and he could not turn back. At last he made a determined effort, turning around and flailing his arms as it if he were going to swim through the air back to one of the open doors—but the column of mist behind him which had seemed so insubstantial was now a green ram propelling him relentlessly down the corridor.

He woke up sweating, and found that he had knocked his glass from the arm of his chair, spilling tepid water which had once been ice cubes over his crotch.

He changed into dry pajamas and returned to bed, but he could not sleep again. When his wife got up the next morning she found him reading the paper, shaved and fully dressed. "You look chipper," she said. "Sleep well?"

He shook his head. "I hardly slept at all, really. I've been up most of the night."

She looked skeptical. "It doesn't seem to have hurt you."

"It didn't." He turned a page of the paper. "I've got graduate counseling today—you know, suggesting topics for a thesis—and I've been thinking up ideas for them."

"You usually hate that," his wife said.

And he usually did, he reflected as he boarded his bus. But today, for almost the first time since that terrifying day (which he could not date) when he had wakened to find himself not only a man, but a man whose life had already, in its larger outlines, been decided in incompetency and idiocy by his father and the callow boy who had once been himself, he found he no longer regretted that his father had shattered forever the family tradition of diplomacy to become a small-town lawyer and leave his son a scholar's career.

What he was going to do he had decided in the dark hours while his wife and the city slept, but there were ramifications to be considered and possibilities to be guarded against. To propose a program was not nearly enough. He would have to sell it. To the head of the department, if at all possible. To as many of his fellow department members as he could; taking care to make no enemies, so that even those not in support were at least no worse than neutral. In time to the university administration and perhaps even to the public at large. But first of all to at least one intelligent graduate student. Two or three, preferably, but at least one; one without fail.

He was ten minutes early reaching his office. He unlocked his desk and spent a few moments glancing over the list of prospective doctoral candidates who would be coming in to see him, but he was too excited to pay it proper attention—the names danced before his eyes and he threw it back into his in-box and instead arranged the chair in which the students would sit and squared the bronze plaque reading *Dr. Smythe* on his desk.

Seated, he looked at the empty chair, imagining it filled already by an eager, and probably fearful, candidate. Graduate students complained eternally of the inattention, hostility, and indifference of their overloaded counselors, men who were expected to guide them, teach, do original research, write, and play faculty politics all at the same time; but his, he vowed, would have no reason to complain of him. Not this year. Not next year either. (He would not deceive himself about the time they would need.) Not the next. Nor the decade following.

He did not have the slightest idea how it could be done. He admitted that honestly to himself, though he would never admit it to the student. But the student would. The student, the right student, would have a hundred utterly insane ideas, and he would talk them over with him, pointing out flaws and combining half-workable thoughts until they hit on something that might be tried, something to be guided by his experience and the student's imagination.

There was a shuffle of feet in the reception room and he stood up, setting his face in the proper expression of reserved friendliness; a few minutes later he was saying to an earnest young man in his visitor's chair, "I'm quite certain it's never been done before. Never even been attempted. It would give you something quite different from the usual business of checking someone else's bad work." The young man nodded and Smythe leaned back, timing his pause like an actor. "You see, the idea of para-intelligence in plants is so new that re-education—therapy, if you like, to a radiation-damaged instinct—has scarcely been dreamed of. And if we can learn to help children by studying rats, what might we not learn from plants when plants are analogs of whole societies?" He gestured toward the window and the threatened and choking world outside. "What you learn"—he strove to strike the right note—"might be widely applicable."

The young man nodded again, and for a moment Smythe saw something, a certain light, flicker in his expression. The green fingers of Smythe's mind reached toward that light, ready to grasp whatever support he found and never let go.

Trip, Trap

GIANTS WERE FIGHTING IN THE SKY; the roar and crash of their weapons and the wind-scream of their strokes reverberated even on the echoless steppe where there was nothing to fling back sound between the Rock of the Caranth-Angor and the gorge of the Elbanda-Rhun, where the waters made their own thunder always, whether the sky-giants fought or slept. And those were as far apart as a hard-riding traveler might go in three days.

The warriors had drawn their thick cloaks across their faces to protect them from the driving rain which was blown horizontally into their eyes, but their mounts had no such protection and stumbled forward scarcely faster than their riders could have walked. All were wet to the skin, cold, and nearly numb with fatigue. On an ordinary journey they would have halted hours ago, pitched their tents and waited out the storm in their sleeping robes. They did not do so now because they were going home, and because their leader, hurrying home too after three years of war, would not have permitted it.

Suddenly a spark struck from some giant ax lit up the sky from horizon to horizon and in the trembling instant the war leader saw far ahead the figure of a single rider spurring down the road as though blown by the storm. The leader watched him for a moment by the light of the flashes, then wheeled his animal to face his command—shouting to make himself heard above the wind. The warriors freed their short lances from the straps holding them to their pommels and fanned out to form an arc across the road. There was a chance, if only a chance, that the rider was a straggler from the enemy horde, trying to reach the fastness of his own country. Besides, they were soldiers, led by a hero, and would not be met like a gaggle of pedlars.

The stranger made no attempt to evade them. Instead he came galloping into the center of their crescent and reined up before their commander. From his cloak he drew a rolled parchment covered with writing. . . .

At the same moment Dr. Morton Melville Finch, Ph.D. (Extraterrestrial Archaeology), paused in the act of setting a coffeepot on his galley stove as he heard the communicator in the main cabin begin to chatter. With the percolator still in his hand, he crossed the galley to see what message had been hurled at his little ship across light-years of space.

FROM: Prof. John Beatty
    Edgemont Inst., Earth
TO: Dr. M. M. Finch
    UNworld spcrft MOTH (Reg #387760)

Congratulations again on attaining your degree!

Morton, I know you have planned to make this trip of yours a pleasure cruise before taking up your teaching duties here, but I have come across something so extraordinary, and so perfectly in your line, that I feel sure you will forgive an old man for trying to interrupt your jaunt.

There, I've given the whole thing away before I meant to. That is always the way with us old diggers; we turn up the funeral ornaments when we pitch the tents, then get nothing for years, like as not.

I doubt if you've ever heard of Carson's Sun, Morton; it is Sol type, but its habitable planet has been off-limits for colonization and trade because of a native race with too much intelligence to be counted mere animals (human-level intelligence in fact) and too little technology for their culture to hold its own in trade. It *is* open to scientific expeditions, however, although it appears that none have ever gone there.

Now I have a correspondent, a W. H. Wilson, who is a captain in the merchant service. He is one of those enthusiastic amateurs who have contributed so much to our little corner of learning. Knows enough to spot a find when he comes across one and keeps his eyes peeled.

Well, it seems that Wilson picked up a distress call from a life-craft on his last trip out. I doubt if I need tell you now, Morton, that it came from the habitable planet of Carson's Sun.

It seems that a spaceman who escaped the wreck of the *Magna Vega* (you may remember that it was originally thought that no one survived) was able to get his craft to Carson III. He spent a year and a half there before Wilson picked up his call. Naturally—or perhaps not so naturally, how many merchant skippers would have done as much?—Wilson questioned him about his experiences with the natives. I am forwarding Wilson's full report to you, together with language tapes, but the important point is this: a number of the symbols used in writing the native language are identical with the ones found on those unclassifiable porcelain shards from Ceta II which furnished you with such fine material for your doctoral dissertation! The points of correspondence are too numerous and too complete for this to be coincidence. I truly feel that Man has at last found evidence of a preceding interstellar technology.

Morton, I would never have thought it possible for me to be so happy for a man I envy as whole-souledly as I do you. A few months' investigation on Carson III may furnish you with a reputation which will make you a department head at thirty-five. Don't let this get past you.

Yours in hope,
J. Beatty

JB/sl

The war chieftain had watched with impassive patience while his followers erected a tent for him using poles whose termi- nals were skillfully carved and painted to represent the heads of beasts, and a soft leather covering impregnated with oil. Only when this was up and his chief lieutenant had kindled a fire using stone and steel and tinder from a hoarded packet near his skin was he able to read the scroll.

His Supremacy the Protector of the West Lands bids this be written to Garth the Son of Garth, Holder of the High Justice:

Know that there came some days ago to our court a party of traders returned from the north. Their leader tells us that in passing through some deserted vales of that land he beheld scratched upon boulders appeals for aid from any of the West People who should pass that way. Proceeding, as the scratchings directed him, to a cave in those hills he found a poor waif once apprenticed to the scribe of the Lord Naid the Son of Kartl who, as you know, rode into that country three seasons ago and has never returned or sent any word to us who loved his valor.

This boy recounts that his master's party was set upon by one of the wild tribes who rove that land, and that his master and all save himself were slain. The lad's tale grieves us much, though we had feared the Lord Naid had deserted our cause, taking the gifts we had given him to bear to the Protector of the Grey Lands as our pledge of friendship.

This ill news came only as another knot in the tangle of that land. While our swords have been hot with war here the evils in the north have grown bold. The lesser Protectors of that land have been loud in lamentations to us of late.

Those who pay us tribute have a right to our protection, and no warriors of the West Men have been seen in those lands now for many seasons. Thus the gold and enamel work due us have been slow to come. Now that the West Lands are again at peace it comes to us that it is time the north country feel again the strength of the West People's hand. Nay, that our grasp stretch farther than ever before. Thus it would be well for you to take up the dignity of Watcher of the North Marches, which you have earned by the blows you have struck for us, and go to that land with such of your people as seem well to you and hold the land for your Protector. Aid our tributaries and prove our strength to such as may dispute you. Accept no excuses from those who owe us for past years; rather urge that payment be sent at once, nor should you leave their domains until it is forthcoming.

Should you chance upon that hoard which the Lord Naid bore for us—such chances often come to the brave—or should you discern the spoor it has left in passing—as the astute may sometimes do—take it; use force always when force is needed.

Go then quickly as you may. Work our will as we have told you and your reward shall be just.

Let not your scribe be idle, but send couriers to teach us how you fare.

*Klexo the Scribe hath written
this for the* PROTECTOR.

When the scroll was rolled again and tied, the war chieftain spoke briefly to his waiting lieutenants, his voice almost lost in the howling wind and pounding rain outside. The scarred faces in the firelight looked pleased in a grim fashion.

Garth, the Son of Garth, Holder of the High Justice, Watcher of the North Marches, bids this be written to the Protector of the West Lands:

Know that as you commanded I have removed myself and the braver of my people to these northern hills. Many of my people were unwilling to go, owing to the evil repute of these lands, but the braver have followed me as I say, and it is them I shall have need of. Now hear me say as I have seen.

After fording the bitter waters of Elbanda-Rhun and tramping the wastelands ten days we came to the lands of Your Supremacy's tributary the Protector of Jana. The city is of goodly size with a wall well built and a good strong-house on an eminence overlooking all. The Protector (so he styles himself) boasts he could call full five hundred men to his banner at the last extremity, though it may be he draws the bow over far.

We were welcomed with much joy by the Protector and entertained with feasting and hunting for several days. It soon came to me, however, that he wished more of us than our merry company. Often I sought to draw him out, but he resisted me politely and seemed to await his own time to tell his thought. While we thus tarried I exercised myself to discover all the ways of this Northland, where many things differ from our own country and there are a thousand old family blood-wars and tangled allegiances which must be known and considered ere one act. On the eighth day that we were at Jana, when we were riding back after a hunt I began to question the Protector about these and other things and found him well disposed to talk. He told me of the wildness of the country and the many evil things that still inhabit it; then, just as he seemed ready to tell his own tale, whatever it might be, we came upon a strange, uncouthly clad person perched on a stone beside the road . . .

FROM: M. M. Finch Ph.D.
TO: Prof. John Beatty,
            Edgemont Inst.
            Earth.

Professor, it is with feelings of triumph that I transmit this, my first communication to the scientific world as represented by yourself from an actual site. And a promising one too. Not a full-fledged digging site as yet, but that is sure to come in time. Meanwhile, let me tell you what I have found thus far.

After completing an aerial survey of the planet I decided to land *Moth* in an unfrequented area and conceal it as well as I could. It was a temptation, of course, to use it to impress the natives in order to secure their cooperation; however, I knew that I would have to leave it eventually, and the prospect of having it cast into some lake as a devil's carriage was not attractive. Also, I thought it best to get some first-hand knowledge of the natives and their customs before I demonstrated all the power of Confederation technology.

My survey had shown that the northwest edge of the principal continent was sparsely settled, so I landed there in a clearing surrounded by dense vegetation; before coming down I had noted carefully the position of a crude village within walking distance. Upon landing I hid *Moth* and set the cabin communicator to relay the signals of my handset. A vigorous hike brought me to an unpaved road and after following that for about a mile I encountered a party of mounted natives.

These are quite human in appearance; if it were not for their hands, which have only three fingers, and their rather large noses they might pass unremarked on the streets of any city in the Confederation. The individuals I now met were of the military caste and wore armor of brightly polished iron plates sewn to leather shirts, and elaborate helmets. There is always something repellent about the concept of violence done to another intelligent being and I am not ashamed to say that I was a bit sickened to see these barbarians flaunting their spears and long cross-hilted swords, not to mention the bows with which they had been murdering the wildlife of their planet. Knowing that my paralyzer would make me master of the situation should any trouble begin, I faced them with a boldness quite suitable to a representative (even if unofficial) of Earth. . . .

. . . This person rose hastily as we approached, and seemed fearful and timid, though determined to stand his ground. He had manifestly been pushing through the wood on foot and his clothing showed many a tear where the thorned vine the people hereabout call Reluctant Lover had found his flesh.

All saw him to be a warlock or fayman, for his face was flat as a trencher and he had more fingers on his hands than does a man right. So afrighted was he that I could not resist smiling at the poor loon, though I liked it not that the Protector's talk had been broken; my smiling seemed to make him feel easier and he looked at us as doltishly as would make one think he'd never seen true men before. And, before, it may be he had not.

We of the West Lands are told strange tales of this north country; one expects the strangeness to grow less when one approaches the land itself—for is not that the way of all travelers' tales? At any rate, I still hear those tales of maids who vow to demons and are seen no more, though their strange children long after come down from the high waste places now and again. But here in the north this is not told of some far country but of the next town or the next farm. It may be that this creature is such a one. He will not tell clearly, but only talks of the stars and strange suns when I ask. (By which you may see that I have heard his prattle much since the meeting I speak of now.) . . .

If one could ignore the general bloodthirstiness of their equipage it was really a thrilling sight, this group of savages with their huge buffalolike riding animals. For a moment I almost wished I had taken my degree in extra-terrestrial sociology instead of archaeology, so as to be able to help them direct their energy and courage to more profitable, humane channels. Why are we archaeologists so insistent on confining our study to things which are good and dead?

Speaking of *dead*, I got a lesson in the zoology of the planet here, for the natives had been hunting and were returning with their butchered victims. Several of their specimens looked like creatures a wise young scholar would not want to study any other way, however much one might regret their demise. I particularly remember a naked-looking animal like a saber-toothed lemur. The natives call it *Gonoth-hag*—the Hunting-devil. There was also what looked like a very big wild dog or wolf, a *Warg;* formidable looking, but not beside the *Gonoth-hag*.

The tapes you transmitted to me have given me enough of the language to make my meaning clear, although I am sure my pronunciation is bad and I don't understand all the words the natives use. I spoke now to a broad-chested fellow who seemed to be in charge and told him that I was a traveler and a Confederation citizen who would appreciate a lift to the village. As you no doubt remember, the man your good Capt. Wilson saved emphasized the sacred nature of guestship in this culture. I thought it prudent to put myself under this protection as soon as I could. . . .

. . . He seemed to assume that I, and not the Protector, was leader and asked at once to be my guest. This would have made many wroth and lost him his head, no doubt; but I could see the poor gangrel did not know a guest must rank with his host except the host invite him first, so I told him I would take him under my protection and this satisfied him. I thought to have some sport with him after the banquet in the strong-house of Jana, and the Protector, who is good-humored enough when his melancholy leaves him, agreed. If I have wearied your Supremacy by too long talk of this person, I beg your indulgence, for he has his part to play in my tale by and by.

. . . They mounted me upon one of their animals (which jolted terribly) and after what I suppose a travel writer would describe as a brisk canter, *i.e.,* a pace sufficiently swift to throw up clouds of dust and sufficiently slow to require a half-hour to cover perhaps four miles, we arrived at a native building which I will call a castle, although it is a far cry from those graceful buildings which were preserved in the France-German Province until the early part of the last century. This castle is a thick-walled stone structure of two stories huddling at the edge of the perpendicular cliff. The only feasible approach is guarded by a massive wall nearly as thick as it is high—precisely like one of the promontory forts of ancient Eire. All, as I am sure you will agree, very fittingly archaeological; but, alas, this is no sun-dried ruin. The stench is abominable. (No doubt you have already guessed, from my slipping into the present tense, that I am sending from this place. So I am, although I have left it once since the first arrival I am telling you about. The smell, however, awaited my return.)

. . . When we returned to the strong-house I asked the Protector to continue his talk as he had begun it before we were interrupted by meeting this vagabond, and he did so. I shall have the scribe set down his words themselves that you may hear as I heard.

He said: "I know you have guessed that all is not as we would wish in this Protectorate of Jana. Know then the reason. If a traveler follow the road through our city northward he will come upon a fine bridge built by the men of Jana of the olden days, when the men and cities of the north were famed.

"Now there are rich fields upon that other shore of the river which have been tilled by us since that old time."

I asked him who held those fields now, for I thought our aid was to be asked in some border war, but he undeceived me, saying, "No one holds them and they grow only weeds and wild herbs. It is he who holds the bridge who keeps us from them, for one of every three who cross in these declining days is taken, and it is against him that I would ask your aid."

This was the first time that our help had been openly asked, and I thought it best to turn it away with a jest until I better knew against whom we were to war, so I laughed loud and said, "Why do you not ask the aid of the fayman we found? Any power that can hold a bridge without the land on either side must surely be magical in its operation, and did he not tell us he had scratched himself by falling from a star?"

"Do not mock," the Protector told me, "for that bridge is not a fit subject for it. A troll holds the passage, and I tell you he takes his tithe of those who go north or south across, and so has he done for so long as the oldest here can remember." Thus he spoke, and I confess, Supremacy, that for a moment I could say nothing. The demons who frightened us as children have some power over our minds all our lives.

Playing for time I said, "How was it then in the olden time, was there no troll then?"

"In the olden time such a concourse of travelers, pilgrims and traders made use of the bridge that the troll's share was scarce to be seen out of all that went over. Also our peasants, being clever wights, abode in huts upon the farther shore and only crossed after some stranger had recently been chosen, for in those good days if a man were taken all were safe for a fortnight or so. Now, knowing (so I think) that no other may be by for some long time, he is like as not to seize on two or three at once." He sighed.

"Boats we cannot use, for until midsummer the current runs too swift; and the exactions of your Liege are such that ten years' remission at least would be required . . ."

. . . when we reached this fortress I lost no time searching out a native who had the inclination to talk. I found one soon enough, a venerable old fellow who did odd jobs in the kitchen, but when I questioned him about old writings he was able to show me nothing going more than a hundred years or so back. He told me, however, that there was a bridge to the north, "very old, with much carving and some writing," adding that not even the priests could read the inscriptions now. You may imagine how that affected me. Carving with a little writing must (I thought) surely indicate pictures with accompanying text, and those might be the beginning of an understanding of the language. With little more than that they were able to break Cretan B four hundred years ago. And if that old script from which the present inhabitants borrowed some of their symbols could be read today!

I was so overcome with this thought that I rushed out in search of the native who had accepted me as his guest. After blundering about the castle for what seemed like hours, I learned that he had gone to a room in the watchtower where (after brushing past two guards before they could stop me) I found him in conference with an older native and burst in upon them with a violence which I fear would be called bad-mannered on any world.

As soon as I could get my breath I begged them to guide me to the bridge I had been told of. They seemed taken aback, but after staring at each other for a moment (it was strange to see these aliens behaving in such a human fashion, although I was so overwrought at the time that I hardly noticed it), the older one agreed, saying that all three of us—he looked rather intently, I thought, at my host—would go tomorrow.

. . . He held his peace then, for he saw my face darken. I was about to accept the challenge he had implied and make my offer to slay the monster when there was a great noise at the door, which flew open and in came none other than our freakish vagabond, who I have since discovered calls himself Dokerfins, flying as swift as if he had been kicked. Without so much as a bow or a courteous word he demanded that we lead him to the troll's lair without delay. The Protector, who cared nothing for the poor creature's life, consented; and I was forced to agree, though I feared his presence might interfere with my own plan.

No sooner had he left us than I began to turn over in my mind the methods our forefathers, the illustrious warriors of your glorious grandsire's golden circle, used when such creatures troubled our own land as severely as they still vex this unhappy north. It is unfortunate that those heroes who survived such encounters were so reticent, except perhaps among themselves, about how they did it.

Strength, I knew, would not support me. Cirman, the most sinewy of all that band, never emerged from the sunken palace of the Horogat troll. And was not Selimn, the cleverest, found babbling in the waters of the Hidden Canal, never to speak sense again? Yet Gerhelt the Great and Tressan his Son are both said to have destroyed trolls and so, I felt, might I.

. . . I began at once to check over my equipment for the trip. I had my minicamera and illuminator, and my notebook; precious little of the proud tools of modern archaeology. However, the site seemed an easy one. Everything aboveground and no organic matter to be carefully preserved for carbon 14 testing.

As my benefactors had promised, we left the next day; not only we three, but twenty or more soldierish ruffians, and cooks, grooms, servants, and so forth. It was very thrilling and medieval, Professor, but I fear it also bore a certain resemblance to the Gardenia Day festival at dear old Edgemont—all it lacked was a few semiprofessional undergraduate beauties on floats. The parade started at least an hour behind schedule. (I think it may have been more, actually, but I am not too clear on the local horological system. It seems to depend on the changing of various nominal "guards" having no connection with the real pikemen on the wall. Some of the periods are longer than others; evidently day guards at whatever castle the system originated in stood longer watches than the night men. In addition there are special short "guards" for meals.)

Also—getting back to our parade—there were some youngsters lurking about the fringes of the crowd holding clods behind their backs and waiting for a moment when no one was looking. Perhaps I am wrong in trying to separate these things from the medieval element, however. The more I consider, the more I am inclined to think that the Black Prince or the Cid might have felt completely at home when our gaudy banner was unfurled and the crowd (the whole town had come to see us off) gave their weak, the-rack-if-you-don't cheer.

The country through which we passed after we left the village can only be described as a decayed wilderness. The road was a dusty rut which had never known pavement, and there were no buildings more pretentious than squalid log huts. . . .

We left at first light, the party consisting of myself with a few of my most trustworthy retainers, the Protector with his guards, and one or two servants, the minimum dignity permitted, for we meant to live with the simplicity suitable to those who march against foes more than human. The whole of the inhabitants of the Protector's strong-house, and many of the more respectable residents of Jana, were early from their beds to see us off; they raised a great cheer as our column left the strong-house gate. Hearing it, I ordered that the standard of the West Lands should be unfurled, and this brought forth a greater cheer still.

I have often observed since how much friendship the folk of Jana feel for us of the West Lands, and their gratitude for your Supremacy's protection, though I suspect it might be greater still if it were not for their Protector's telling them that the tribute is much more than we ask in order to extract taxes from them. Indeed, it might be better if they were directly subject to some West Lands High Justice, who would repay your Supremacy in armed followers to whose maintenance the people could scarce object considering the lawlessness of the country. Would not a vassal with a loyal army be preferable to an inconstant tributary?

I believe that I forgot to mention, in what my scribe has put into letters already, that by the will of the Protector the mountebank went with us. He is a clumsy rider, and sneezed so much from the dust as to furnish us all with a deal of low amusement.

The country about Jana is fair enough, fertile valleys lacing the rocky hills and even the uplands supporting swine and suchlike useful cattle in some number, though as we drew nearer the bridge, dwellings failed till even the swineherds' cots were rare to the eye. When we came the third day to the bridge itself, I saw that the Protector's boast that the men of Jana had built it was only vainglory, for it is clearly a work of the forgotten age; a thing greater than even the West People could make, and having in it a spirit we could not contrive. This I saw as we paused at the crest of a hill just before the land sloped to the river. Then I saw too something which made my eyes like to burst with wonder, for the vagabond, Dokerfins, had slipped off his mount and was running at full speed down the bank toward the bridge!

. . . How I wish I could convey to you the thrill I felt when I first viewed that bridge! It is built of monolithic slabs of white stone so skillfully joined that the crevices are difficult to detect even at close range, and it vaults its little river with a flat curve somehow suggesting an easy arrogance, as though its planners were a little ashamed at having to bridge this modest stream. The carving which covers every surface except the roadway saves it from the severity which disfigures our modern construction. It is deeply incised bas-relief.

Need I tell you how eagerly I went to examine those carvings?

You will not be surprised when I admit that in my single-minded concentration I rushed forward without waiting for the rest of the party.

I had just begun to scrutinize a large group of written characters about a quarter of the way across, for the moment slighting some pictographic work near the bank, when I was startled by a loud thump behind me. Turning, I discovered the native who had taken me as his guest sprawled on his face on the roadway, having apparently been pitched from his mount, which was rearing and plunging in a most alarming manner just behind him. He had not been badly hurt by his fall, though, for he jumped up at once and began gesticulating to me, shouting very rapidly in the native language something about a *traki;* it was a word I had heard them use among themselves before, but the meaning was not on the tapes. I tried to get him to speak more slowly, but he only became more excited than ever and positively gibbered. I was perhaps ten feet farther onto the bridge than he, and although he started forward once as though to actually seize me, he seemed afraid to go farther.

Suddenly something behind me grasped me by the shoulders. I tried to turn; but no matter how vigorously I twisted the lower half of my body, the upper half was kept directed straight ahead; I jerked my head about until I nearly sprained my neck, but all I could see was a blurred dark object at the extreme edge of my field of vision.

Before I could collect my wits enough to think of getting out my paralyzer, I found myself flying through the air and saw the dark water of the river rushing toward my face. I hit it with a terrific slap and lost consciousness.

. . . I spurred after him, and had almost grasped him by the collar (for he would not heed my calls) when he stepped onto the bridge itself and my steed pulled up so sharply that I was thrown over its head and onto the bridge.

For an instant I lay stunned, then I leaped to my feet and looked about for the wretched fayman. He must have fled, or so I thought then, for he was not to be seen; instead there stood before me the troll. I challenged him to attack me, stamping my foot to show him I stood upon the bridge he claimed. For a moment neither of us moved. I stared at him, wishing to fix his appearance in my mind, so that after my victory, should the spirits of the place grant one, I might tell others his true shape and save them from going ignorant into battle as I had done.

My eyes have been called sharp by many, but the longer I gazed at the troll the less well could I see him, and although the day was cool the bridge shimmered as the southern plains do when the sun gives a traveler no more shadow than is under his feet. Still, it seemed to me that the troll was a warrior, tall and fell, whose face was more like my own than the faces of most men are. In one hand he held a great sword, heavy and cruelly curved at the tip, and in the other, as a boy might hold a wriggling pup, he grasped the wretched Dokerfins, he looking no larger than a child or almost a child's doll. I knew then that it was their spirits I saw and not the flesh. Then it was with me as though a blade had opened the veins of my legs; I weakened and my eyes were darkened and I thought nevermore to see the sun. The troll I saw coming toward me with arm outstretched, and his look was not kind.

When I woke it was in the troll's den. It was dark and the air had such a filthy odor as the pools in swamps have. What light there was came upward from a pool at the end of the hall, showing that the tales are right in saying that trolls dwell in caverns under the riverbank whose only entrances are under water. When I tried to gain my feet and draw my sword I found I could do neither. My legs had no feeling and my hands no strength.

I then began to pray as hard as ever in my life to all the gods that are and most especially to the great God who made them all and the shades of the holy men of the north, who might have the most authority in their own country; and I rubbed my hands against my legs to bring the life back.

One kind spirit at least must have looked with favor upon me, for soon the life returned to my members and I was able to stand. The troll was not to be seen. I bethought me of the treasures trolls are said to hoard—gems and strangely made ornaments of precious metals, shields no weapon can pierce and knives that will carve iron. Indeed, the old tales tell of things greater yet, of magical windows through which one can spy where he chooses and rods whose touch blasts like lightning, but I think these must be lies.

With such thoughts in my mind I began to probe about the chamber. In a corner I found the skull of one long dead; it had been split to get the brains out and seemed unlikely to have any special power, so I flung it away. Where it struck the wall it knocked off some of the foulness and I saw something shine. I cleared a spot with the blade of my dirk and discovered that the wall was faced with a hard substance like polished stone. It had the color of enamelwork, but the tints were within. There was much looking like gold in it and this I tried to pry out with the point of my knife, but the hardest stroke would not penetrate it. The work must have been very fair once; alas, it is cracked in many places so that the river ooze seeps in.

In the darkness part of the chamber I found the fayman Dokerfins, lying so still I thought him dead. This comforted me a bit, for I had feared that he had leagued with the troll to destroy me, but now I saw that he was taken like myself. Washed all clean by the river water save where the filth of the floor touched him, he was a pale, piteous thing.

I was bending over him hoping to find signs of life when I heard the great roaring voice of the troll behind me; so loud and terrible was it that I wished to stop my ears against it. So that your Supremacy may know the troll's speech I have instructed my scribe to write all his words large; thus your scribe shall apprehend to raise his voice in reading. This trick of clerkmanship I learnt of Dokerfins and like it well though my clerk thinks it gross and mechanical.

Then said he: "THAT ONE CANNOT AID YOU; YOU MUST FACE ME ALONE."

And turning I beheld the troll, but not as I had seen him on the bridge. Here he glowed like the flame of a candle, so that every wrinkle could be seen in the dimness, and his form was that of a great Hunting-devil, but larger yet and higher above the eyes and wearing there a circlet of some metal. He had no sword nor other weapon, nor wore he armor.

I spoke to him boldly, saying, "I do not fear to face you, but rather think it strange that you who have neither blade nor byrnie should leave me my sword."

"I CARE NOTHING FOR YOUR TOOL OR YOUR HARD SKIN—THEY WILL NOT HELP YOU IN THE HUNT WHICH IS TO COME. BUT FIRST TELL ME WHERE YOU FOUND YOUR COMPANION. HIS IS A STRANGE THOUGHT, OR SEEMED SO WHEN I TOUCHED IT ON THE BRIDGE TODAY."

"He says he fell here from a star, if that moon talk is aught to you. As to touching minds, I found the head of one whose mind you touched a moment past, but you do not seem to have done that to my friend yet."

I confess, Supremacy, that I was surprised to hear myself speaking of the betattered Dokerfins as my friend, but I find the common occupancy of a troll's den breeds a strange feeling of comradeship.

"WHAT YOU CALL MOON-TALK MEANS MUCH TO ME. HE HAS BEEN BROUGHT FROM OUTWORLD TO THE GAMES IN OUR CITY; IT MAY BE THAT WHEN HE WAKES HE WILL SHOW SPORT. THOUGH I SHALL PERHAPS NEVER HAVE THE POWER OVER HIM I HOLD OVER YOU, YET HE SHALL AT LEAST SEE ME AS I WISH."

"I shall see you as I wish," I told him, "and that is dead." And I drew forth my sword and came at him.

I never blade-reached him. Instead I found myself running breathless down a narrow alley with steep hills to either side. It was night, the air moist and cool in my lungs but smelling of smoke, as when water has been poured on a fire. My armor and all my raiment were gone; instead of my sword I held a length of green sapling, and was minded to toss it away when I noted it hung unnaturally heavy in my hand. Then I knew it was not I but my spirit running, and the sapling was my good sword in truth, though seeming not so in the spirit land: I suppose because it was a new-made blade and not my father's sword I bore.

I turned then to face whatever might come, but saw nothing and heard only a loud humming as of a swarm of flies. Mounted or afoot, it bodes best to hold the high ground, so I began to scramble up the bank on my left. In the gloom I had thought the hill to be of stones and earth in the common way, but the stones my feet kicked free sometimes clanged like iron or smashed with a noise like crockery. Often too my fingers felt ashes or cloth instead of grass. . . .

. . . When I became aware of my surroundings again, my first thought was that the impact of the water on my eyes had resulted in blindness. It was several minutes before my pupils dilated enough for me to make out objects, and even then I could perceive only bulky shadows. The floor upon which I lay seemed to be of stone, covered with two inches of almost liquid mud. Even now, Professor Beatty, it humiliates me to recall it, but to set the record right let me admit that during my first few moments of consciousness I experienced nausea, a sort of dizziness or giddiness, and panic terror.

When I got myself under control I remembered my pocket illuminator and tried to get it out. My fingers were so swollen and weak that I could not unfasten the buttons of my shirt pocket. If you have ever tried to open a jackknife when your hands were nearly numb with cold you will know how I felt then.

I was still fumbling with the pocket when a pool of water at the far end of the chamber in which I found myself heaved violently and a creature larger than a man emerged. This, as I learned later, was the *traki*. I will give you a detailed description of him before I close this letter, but for the present I am not going to let you see more of him than I did. All I knew was that the dank and stinking den in which I found myself had now been invaded by some huge creature, whether beast or nonhuman intelligence I had no way of knowing. I felt that I was about to die, to be killed with a horrible violence, and I could no longer turn away, as I have been in the habit of doing all my life, from the sickening thought of my mind's termination and my body's reduction to carrion.

All of us have encountered a telepathic adept at one time or another, but I certainly did not expect one here, nor had I ever before realized fully the enormous difference between communication with a human Talent and contact with one as alien as the *traki*. A Talent has always given me the impression that someone I could not otherwise sense was whispering in my ear while the supposed Talent sat passive some distance away. When the *traki* sent his signal it was as though a public-address system of enormous amplification and poor fidelity had been planted in the back of my skull, and when he received I felt myself an intelligent insect probed from above by some vast, corrupt intelligence.

"HOW DID YOU ESCAPE?"

The question boomed and screeched until I felt I must go mad. Intellectually I am quite convinced (though I know you are not in complete agreement) that our minds are merely protoplasmic computers of great sophistication—that we have no thought or life except that conferred by matter; yet I have never felt so much in sympathy with the so-called "liberal" cast of thought which holds otherwise as I did then. My body seemed a cast, an almost inert but painful prison from which the essential "I" struggled to escape, and while the essence of my being thus twisted to get away it forced my lips and larynx to say that it did not appear to me that I had escaped, and made my wooden fingers continue clawing at my pocket.

"IT IS WISE OF YOU TO KNOW THAT. WE WHO BROUGHT YOU HERE HOLD ALL THIS WORLD AND YOU CANNOT CROSS THE SEAS OF EMPTINESS AGAIN WITHOUT OUR AID."

I was too busy at the moment to digest that rather cryptic statement. I had managed to open the pocket at last and was getting out my paralyzer and illuminator. As soon as I was able to fumble off the safety catch on the paralyzer, I lit up the cavern.

I promised you a good description of him earlier, Professor, but now I am not sure I can give you one without sounding like the author of a tenth-century bestiary, and no description can make you see him as I saw him, crouched in that dank chamber. Four limbs reminiscent of a gorilla's arms, but hairless and shining black, were joined to a shapeless, swagbellied body. The head was more nearly human in appearance, a square face dominated by a great slit mouth like a catfish's. The only clothing, if you can call it that, was a metal band covered with incised hieroglyphics which he wore about his head. I know this description must sound like that of an animal, but that was not the impression he gave. Rather I sensed a monstrous cunning, and most of all that he was old, and tainted with senility.

I had only time for the brief glimpse I have given you when the *traki* seemed to turn in upon himself and become something entirely different. It was as if the entire creature were one of those shapes topologists make which, when turned inside out, become totally unrecognizable. I am still not sure what it was I saw while this inversion was taking place (it lasted not more than half a second) but when it was complete the *traki* had become an elderly man in a white togalike robe. I hope this will not offend you, but his features had a noticeable resemblance to your own; in fact, during the conversation which followed, I sometimes found it difficult in spite of the painful nature of the thought contact to remember that it was not you to whom I spoke—a Professor Beatty who had grown a trifle strange, and more wise and powerful than I could ever hope to be.

"SINCE YOU HAVE FOUND A LIGHT, WHICH I PERCEIVE YOU MUST HAVE STOLEN FROM US AS YOUR KIND IS INCAPABLE OF SHAPING SUCH THINGS, I THINK IT BEST THAT YOU SEE ME AS I REALLY AM."

I said as well as I could that I thought I had seen the real *traki* when I had first turned on my illuminator.

"YOU CAN NEVER SEE ME OBJECTIVELY, YOUR RACE BEING WITHOUT OBJECTIVE PERCEPTION. THE SHAPE YOU SEE NOW IS SUBJECTIVELY CORRECT, WHICH IS THE WAY YOU DEFINE REALITY."

I decided that if this last transmission meant anything at all it meant that he was going to deny that he "really" had any shape other than the one I now saw, so I dropped the subject and asked what he intended to do with me.

"I SHOULD KEEP YOU UNTIL THEY COME FOR YOU, BUT THEY HAVE BEEN SLOW IN SENDING OUT MY SUPPLIES FROM THE CITY OF LATE."

His thought seemed hesitant, although the kindly face was as imperturbable as ever. I said that I did not know what city he meant.

"THE CITY TO WHICH YOU WERE TAKEN—THE CITY FROM WHICH YOU ESCAPED. YOU MAY SEE ITS TOWERS FROM THE BRIDGE I GUARD—BUT SUPPLIES ARE SLOW TO COME NOW. FOR SOME TIME I HAVE SUBSISTED ON THE WILD ANIMALS I CATCH UPON THE BRIDGE."

It seemed prudent to divert the conversation, so I asked what kind of animals he meant.

"YOU WILL FIND ONE IN THE CORNER BEHIND YOU."

I looked in the direction he indicated and saw the native who had accepted me as a guest lying there. The gaudy surcoat he wore over his mail was splattered with mud, and his sword lay near his outstretched hand.

"HE WILL NOT GO TO THE CITY. HE IS ONE OF THE WILD ONES WHO LIVE IN THE FORESTS NEAR HERE."

"He is an intelligent being."

"HE IS AN ANIMAL. JUST SUCH CREATURES AS HE I HUNTED IN MY YOUTH LONG AGO. THEY HAVE GROWN MORE CLEVER NOW, AND SOME MAKE HARD SHELLS FOR THEMSELVES, BUT THEY ARE THE SAME."

He paused for a moment, his noble, benevolent face lost in introspection.

"NOW I TAKE THEM AT THE BRIDGE. MANY OF THEM CROSS IN THESE TIMES; PERHAPS THEY WISH TO SCRABBLE THROUGH THE RUBBISH HEAPS OUTSIDE THE CITY, AS I RECALL THEY USED TO DO."

"And you kill such creatures?"

The *traki*'s smile was tolerantly amused now, as though a child has asked a particularly naïve question.

"I MUST LIVE, AND THE BRIDGE MUST BE PROTECTED."

My paralyzer was set on high discharge. I depressed the firing stud and held it down until I felt the unit cease to vibrate. The *traki* appeared completely unaffected.

"YOU EMPLOYED YOUR FINGERS WELL WHILE YOU WERE IN OUR CITY, I SEE, THOUGH I CANNOT GUESS WHY ONE OF OUR PEOPLE BUILT A TOY TO DO WHAT WE CAN DO SO EFFORTLESSLY WITH OUR MINDS. DID YOU THINK OUR DEVICE WOULD OPERATE ON ONE OF US?"

Professor, have you ever been so frightened that your knees actually shook? Until then I had always thought that to be a conventional exaggeration; in that slimy crypt I learned that it is not. I admit I became hysterical. I cannot remember just what I said, but told the *traki* that his precious city did not exist, and that he was only a native devil on a primitive world. I threatened him with all the authority of the Confederation and condemned him, his imaginary city, and his mythical race. I stopped at last only because my teeth were chattering so badly I could no longer speak. When I finished, his smile was as serene as ever.

"NO RACE AND NO CITY? WHO BROUGHT YOU HERE? WHO BUILT

THE FORTRESS YOU SEE ABOUT YOU? ITS WALLS ARE THICKER THAN THIS CHAMBER IS WIDE, AND THE MECHANISM YOU SEE ABOUT YOU CAN BLAST SUCH FLYING CITIES AS BROUGHT YOU HERE BACK TO THE ELEMENTAL DUST."

Something about the creature so compelled belief that I was forced to look about me. The cave was still empty except for the *traki,* the unconscious native, and myself; it reeked with the ferment of stagnant river water and rotting organic matter. It was only then that I understood that unshakable calm which gave the *traki* his atmosphere of invulnerable power. Call it dementia, psychosis, or whatever madness you like, he had lost touch with reality—I think long ago.

With more restraint than I would have thought myself capable of a moment before, I said, "Why is the floor of this room covered with mud?"

"THE FLOOR IS PAVED WITH TILES IN A PATTERN COMPLEX BEYOND YOUR UNDERSTANDING."

I dropped my discharged paralyzer and flung a handful of the slime at him. I believe I shouted, "Look! Mud!" as I threw it.

It struck his white robe and vanished.

It did not slide off, or disintegrate in a puff of dust or fire, or fade away. It was and was not, disappearing instantly as though it had never existed.

I am afraid I lost control completely then. I scooped up another handful of the filth and rushed at him to rub it in his face. His face had the consistency of smoke. Momentum carried me through the complete patriarchal figure until I collided with something solid behind it. I ran my hands over it several times before I realized what I had struck. It was the ape-limbed bulk of the *traki* as I had first seen him.

"YES, IT IS I."

My self-confidence returned. This was not the eye-of-the-storm feeling I had had earlier—I was my own man again, and joyfully, confidently glad of it.

The *traki* had not moved a muscle during the time I had been touching him.

"YOU ARE CORRECT. WHAT YOU CALL MY VOLUNTARY MOTOR SYSTEM HAS BEEN IMMOBILIZED, TEMPORARILY, BY YOUR WEAPON."

I took a step backwards and found myself addressing the white-robed illusion again. "Since you are the most expert telepathic liar I have ever met," I said, "I am not going to ask you whether or not it would be possible for me to swim out of the beaver lodge, or whatever it is. Excuse me."

"IT IS QUITE FEASIBLE. HOWEVER, YOU MUST GO QUICKLY. ALREADY I CAN FEEL LIFE IN MY BODY AGAIN. I WILL EXPLAIN YOUR ABSENCE TO YOUR FRIEND."

The illusion of a man smiled with only the slightest hint of malice and waved gracefully toward the unconscious native.

In my momentary triumph I had completely forgotten the poor barbarian. I am not a particularly strong swimmer, Professor; I knew that it would be suicidal folly for me to attempt to escape into the river carrying him, but there seemed to be nothing else to do. In my heart I knew it meant death for us both. I had begun to pick him up when my eyes fell on his sword lying in the ooze. I picked that up instead.

It was as long as a wrecking bar and nearly as heavy; brutal, primitive, capable of slaughtering anything that came within its four-foot range.

"You tell me the solution," I said. "How can he and I leave here alive? Think, because if you cannot tell me how, I intend to kill you with this."

"THERE IS NO BETTER WAY."

He paused and I could feel him probing my mind harder than he had ever done previously.

"YOU WILL NOT KILL ME. THE SLAYER IS NOT IN YOU. YOU HAVE BEEN TAUGHT ALL YOUR SHORT LIFE THAT THERE EXISTS NO GREATER CRIME THAN TAKING THE LIFE OF AN INTELLIGENCE. EVEN WHEN YOU CAME TO THIS WORLD WHERE DEATH COMES SO OFTEN, YOU BROUGHT ONLY A WEAPON WHICH DOES NOT KILL. AND I AM WITHOUT DEFENSE."

I raised the sword for a blow, but as I did I realized that the *traki* was right. My arm shook and my stomach was a writhing knot. In my imagination I could hear the hiss of that life-defiling blade, feel the tug and release as it clove the vertebrae and the gushing, sticky bath of hot blood; worst of all I knew in anticipation the haunting sense of uncleanness, of my own self-condemnation, lifelong, without hope of absolution. I wished that it were I who stood in such danger of dissolution, and I lost consciousness.

. . . *When I reached the hilltop there was more light, though no moon shone. I looked about me and to one side saw points of light, undying sparks, as though a mountain stood there, and many men with torches scaled its sides. To my other hand I could see starlight on water and I knew, without knowing how I knew, that it was the river and safety upon the farther side. All about were the low, steep hills.*

I could see no pursuers, but the humming noise waxed ever louder and I feared it without knowing why. I do not believe, Supremacy, that I would have felt so in the country of men; in the spirit land some enchantment draws away a warrior's blood, leaving a cold juice supporting life but not valor.

I was about to run again when I spied something glittering at my feet. It was a piece of red glass—such stuff as the priests use to form pictures in the windows of temples. It was broken and useless; yet before I could reflect on what I did I had snatched it up and thrust it among other such litter in a bag of knotted grass I had slung about my shoulders. I cannot tell why I did so foolish a thing or why I felt so vain about it, like a country wench with a new ribbon.

A night fog was coming up from the river now and filling the valleys. Though it brought forth foul odors from the soil at my feet, I blessed it, knowing it would conceal me.

The hills were lower and the fog thicker as I fled from valley to valley and I knew the river must be close by, but every breath burned in my chest and my steps stumbled. The roaring of the blood in my ears was so loud that I did not hear another running in the valley I crossed until he was nearly upon me. He was naked as I, and his long hair hung down in a filthy mat, but I would have kissed him as a brother had there been time, so happy was I to see a human face in that grim land.

He shouted to me—words I had never heard before, yet they were as clear to me as West Speech—"This way! You are lost. Follow me!"

He led me through a narrow crevice in the hills, which I had passed without seeing a moment before. On the other side the ground sloped cleanly down to the river and I could see the long white arch of a bridge that spanned it. We were almost upon it before I saw that it was the bridge of the troll, and then I knew fear indeed, and would have turned back had not my companion gripped me by the arm.

"A troll watches this bridge," I said, but the clear words I formed in West Speech issued from my lips as guttural gruntings. He seemed to understand, however, and pointed to a low strong-house set almost at the water's edge.

"He is there, but he cares nothing for us. He is a sky watcher. See the Eye?"

I looked again and saw that there was a great eye of metal lace above the strong-house; it turned slowly as though it searched for something, but its gaze was always toward the stars. Then the bridge was filled with light and the humming noise grew to a roar.

We ran faster than ever; there was just time enough to get clear of the bridge and scramble up a little rise on the other side before they were upon us.

I halted there. We had run before them as vermin run; now I, at least, would stand as a man and a West Lands warrior should. My companion mewed with fright, but I heard laughter also and it was the fell laughter of trolls.

They were coming toward us faster than any beast could bear them, mounted on shining things which roared without pause and whose single eyes glared with the yellow light I had seen. They halted at the foot of the knoll on which we stood and the roar of their mounts subsided to a murmur. The faces of trolls are not as the faces of men, yet I could see the triumph on every face and I recall thinking that thus the faces of men must look to a hunted beast who turns to make his stand.

One of the trolls dismounted then, and my gaze was drawn to him. He was larger than any forest devil and the muscles stood out under his skin and flickered as he moved. Had he been but a beast he would have been such as to chill the heart of the boldest hunter, but he was no mere animal. His eyes were of the yellow-green of seacoal fire and blazed more fiercely—level as a man's and filled with terrible wisdom. Strangely wrought weapons hung from his belt, and when I looked upon them, memories that were not mine came rushing into my mind, and I seemed to see naked men and women and children rent to pieces as if by thunderbolts.

By force of will I tore my gaze from them and looked about me lest I be taken from behind; and as I looked the other trolls seemed to fade and become less real, so that I knew they were but the creatures of his art where in truth only his spirit and mine stood alone.

I lifted my green stick as he came toward me. It was a mere wand still to my eyes, but it had an honest weight in my hand and light shone along the back as though it were steel. Then in an instant all I saw was gone. I stood in the troll's den once more, swaying and grasping my true sword with a weak hand. The troll was before me still, older now, and bereft of the terrible weapons which had dangled from his belt before.

Then he laughed loud and deep, and I was again on the hillock. Scarce able to stand, I lashed his great arm with my wand and it snapped half off; as he grasped me the darkness closed upon me once more as it had on the bridge, but I struck him with the shattered stub of my stick until I knew no more.

When I woke again the troll's cave was better lit than when I had previously seen it, though light no longer rose from the pool. Instead a great brightness issued from a silver wand no longer than a man's finger which lay in the mud close to Dokerfins. I had seen too much that day to fear anything however strange, and plucking it from the muck, I used its light to search out the hole.

My sword I found in Dokerfins' hand, it and he both drenched in the troll's dark blood; the grim mock-man himself lay not much farther off, all cut about with gaping wounds from which the blood no longer welled. At the first sight I thought it strange to see that the point had never told, but soon I understood all, as you, Supremacy, wiser than ever I, no doubt do now. For when Dokerfins awoke he was as one deep in drink or drug, babbling and unheeding. Then I knew that his body had but fought here the battle my own spirit had won from the troll in the spirit land, and his soul was scarce returned, alone and affrighted, to its proper place. That his untenanted husk could not use my sword's point was thus explained, for the sword's spirit was maimed when it broke in my hand.

From the pool's dimness I knew the day must be fast fading. It would be an evil venture to try to swim from that place in darkness, so taking the circlet the troll had worn and holding the mewing fayman as best I could I dived into the pool to free us or die, as might be. My spirit-broken blade I left to watch the troll rot; who would dare trust such a thing in war?

When I became aware again the sun was full in my face. Oh that blessed sun of Carson!

Can you understand what it meant to me to know I was no longer in that foul abscess under the riverbank? I will not bore you by describing the pleasure of the natives when they found us on the following day. My host—his name is Garth, have I mentioned that before?—had killed the *traki* in what he calls "a great spirit fight" which I take to mean that it was a sort of contest of wills as well as a physical battle, which with the *traki* I can well believe. Even knowing that the life of an intelligent being has been deliberately extinguished by him, I cannot feel the repulsion which perhaps I should, but it does somewhat disturb me that he seems to consider me a sort of squire or assistant in what he believes to have been a very creditable deed. At least it has given me useful prestige with the natives.

Now for the really amazing part of this adventure of mine. Garth brought back the metal circlet the *traki* had worn. When I examined it I found that the inscription on it is in characters similar to those found on Ceta II. The same is true of the carvings on the bridge. I thought the poor *traki*'s talk of a great city madness, and so it was, no doubt; but there exist shades of derangement. One is to believe in the reality of things wholly fictitious. Another, very characteristic of the old, is to hold in the mind's present the shadows of the now-gone-forever. What might we not have learned from the *traki* had not Garth killed it?

Yours for learning,
Morton M. Finch, Ph.D.

The cold river water seated Dokerfins' spirit in him aright while it washed the troll's blood from his skin and garments, so that when we reached the grassy bank at last he knew not how he came there and I must needs tell him all that had occurred and of his help in the battle, though I misdoubt he understood. The servants tell me that since that time he speaks a strange tongue abed of nights and beats with his arms upon the sleeping furs as a man kills snakes with a staff; no doubt the troll's spirit often troubles his in dreams, as it sometimes does mine.

The silver wand of light I gave him as a reward, for he swore that it was his. Doubtless he came upon it in the troll's cave.

The coronet the troll wore, which I took from his brow with my own hand, I send to you by the courier who bears this letter. It is a fair thing; but I would, if I dared, advise you, Supremacy, against wearing it—though it will fit a man, for it became less in compass as I drew it from the troll's head, by what power I know not. It is a fell thing still, and made the world grow strange when I wore it, and all men seem lower to me than beasts. I was ill and dizzy when I snatched it off.

Such is the tale of my travels thus far. I am proud that the glory of the West Lands is enhanced in Jana since the death of the troll. Dokerfins, whom I bore for mercy's sake from the den of the troll, has become a clever friend and useful, his wit good though his thought strange. He is so intent upon digging into old places that I would think him a ghoul if he did not do it with such innocence. He wished mightily to have the troll's crown, though I kept its secret from him, but I think it better far to give it to a stronger mind.

> *Nammue the scribe hath
> written this for the Lord
> Garth, the Son of Garth,
> and Watcher of the North
> Marches.*

FROM: Prof. John Beatty
             Edgemont Inst., Earth
TO: Dr. M. M. Finch
             UNworld spcrft MOTH (Reg #387760)

Sorry to be so slow to write, Morton, but I have been busy as ten sub-instructors at theme time doing a new symposium for *Archaeological Worlds*. Some of the people who want to write in this kind of thing are such asses!

About your native, this Garth. Morton, let an old friend warn you; it is always a temptation for someone situated as you are to strike a lofty pose and impress the natives. "Me great magician, come from star in silver boat." And all that. But, Morton, sooner or later he is bound to discover that you are only flesh, even as he. Don't carry on in such a way that this comes to him as too great a shock; he may turn on you then if you have. Take him into your confidence at times; explain the simpler principles of what you are doing and allow him to make a minor decision at times—whether to camp or go on, which of a group of similar sites to tackle first—that kind of thing. Fear and awe alone will not suffice indefinitely.

Meanwhile, would you please send more detail on the markings and pictures. Rubbings and photographs as soon as you can get them and arrange for civilized mail service. I had to write my article for *Arch. Worlds* (the one that stirred up all this symposium rubbish) on the very sketchy information in your letter; how sketchy it was you will note in the clipping I am having transmitted with this. I gave you full credit, as you will see. It is the paragraph beginning: "I sent an investigator . . ."

> Hastily,
> J. Beatty

JB/sl

From the Desk of Gilmer C. Merton

DEAR MISS MORGAN:
    No, you don't know me or anything about me—I got your name from *Literary Marketplace*. My own name is Gilmer C. Merton, and I'm a writer. I say that I am one, even though I haven't sold anything yet, because I know I am. I have written a sci-fi novel, of which I enclose the first chapter and an outline of the remainder (is that a dirty word?) of the book.

Please understand me, Miss Morgan: *I have written the whole book,* and can send you complete ms. as soon as you ask for it. Will you represent me?

Sincerely yours,
Gilmer C. Merton

Dear Mr. Merton:
    Please send the rest of *Star Shuttle*. Enclose $10.00 (no stamps) to cover postage and handling.

Yours truly,
Georgia Morgan

Dear Miss Morgan:
    Enclosed please find the remainder of my book *Star Shuttle* and a Postal Money Order for ten dollars. I hope you enjoy it.

You can have no idea how delighted I am that you are sufficiently interested in my book to wish to read the rest. I know something of your reputation now, having asked the Chief Assistant Librarian here in No. Velo City. It would be wonderful to have you for my agent.

>Sincerely,
>Gilmer C. Merton

Dear Mr. Merton,

I will definitely handle *Star Shuttle*. When you sign and return the enclosed letter of agreement (I have already signed; please retain the *last* copy for your files), you will be a client of the GEORGIA MORGAN LITERARY AGENCY. Note that we do not handle short fiction, articles, or verse (Par. C.). I would, however, like to see any other book-length manuscripts, including nonfiction.

>Cordially,
>Georgia Morgan

P.S. Don't say sci-fi. That *is* an obscenity. Say SF.

Dear Miss Morgan:

Let me repeat again how much I appreciate your taking on my book. However, I wish you had told me where you intend to market it. Is that possible?

Your letter of agreement (top three copies) is enclosed, signed and dated as you asked. Let me repeat how happy I am to be your client.

>Sincerely,
>Gilmer C. Merton

Dear Gil,

I sent your *Star Shuttle* to the best editor I know, my great and good friend Saul Hearwell at Cheap Drugstore Paperbacks, Inc. Now I am happy to report that Saul offers an advance of $4300.00 against CDPI's standard contract. I discussed the advance with him over lunch at Elaine's (not to worry, Saul paid), but he says CDPI's present financial position, though not critical, is somewhat weak, and he is not authorized to offer more than the standard advance. (Actually, that is four thou.; I got him up three hundred.) I could be wrong, Gil, but with a first novel, I don't think you will get a better offer than this anyplace, market conditions being as they are. The "standard" contract is enclosed, as slightly altered by yrs. trly. (Note that I was able to hold onto 30% of video game rights.) I advise you to sign it and return all copies to me soonest.

Cordially,
Georgia

P.S. You will receive half the advance on signing.

Dear Georgia,

I have signed and dated all copies of the contract for my book. They are enclosed. Good job!

You will be happy to note that I have borrowed enough on my signature to trade in my old Underwood for a used word processor. (These are used words, ha, ha!) Interest is eighteen percent, but there is no penalty for early payment, and when I get the two thousand one hundred and fifty dollars it will be easy enough to pay off the rest of the loan, and I understand that *Hijo* and several other horror-genre shockers were written on this machine before Steven E. Presley's untimely death. With the help of this superb machine (as soon as I learn to run the damn thing) I hope to make much faster progress on new book, *Galaxy Shuttle*.

Sincerely,
Gil Merton

Dear Gil,

This is going to come as something of a shock to you, but I have just had a long phone conversation with Saul Hearwell, during which we discussed what Saul insists on referring to as "your problem." Meaning yours, Gil, not mine, though you are my problem too, of course, or rather your problems are my problems.

Star Shuttle is bylined "Gilmer C. Merton," and Saul does not consider that catchy enough. Of course, I suggested "Gil Merton" right away. Saul feels that is an improvement, but not a big enough one. (Am I making myself clear?) Anyway, Saul would like to see you adopt a zippier pen name, something along the lines of Berry Longear or Oar Scottson Curd. Whatever you like, but please, not Robert A. anything. (Gil Donadil might be nice.???) The choice is yours, to be sure; but let me know soonest so I can get back to Saul.

Cordially,
Georgia

P.S. I rather hate to bring up this delicate matter, Gil, but you will get $1835.00 and not the $2150.00 you mention. In other words, my commission will be taken out. And don't forget you'll have to pay taxes on the residue.

Dear Georgia,
   This is a wonderful contraption, but Steven Presley seems to have programed it with some odd subroutines. I'll tell you in detail when I've figured out what all of them are.
   The new byline I've chosen is Gilray Gunn. What do you think of it? If you like it, please pass it along to Mr. Hearwell.
   I had assumed I paid you your commissions. Rereading our letter of agreement, I see that you receive all payments and deduct your part before passing mine on to me. I see the sense of that—it saves me from writing a check and so forth.

Sincerely,
Gil Merton
(Wolf Moon)

Dear Gil,
   Good news! Saul likes your new byline, and I've al-

ready got a nibble from Honduras on *Star Shuttle*. Rejoice! When will I be seeing *Galaxy Shuttle?*

Cordially,
Georgia

Dear Miss Morgan:

Thank you for your recent communication. I have altered the title of *Galaxy Shuttle* to *Come, Dark Lust*. It is to be bylined Wolf Moon, as I have indicated on the enclosed ms. See to it.

I require the half advance now due on "Star Shuttle" immediately. North Velo Light & Power Co. is threatening to shut off my service.

Wolf Moon
(Gilmer C. Merton)

Dear Gil,

Saul assures me you will get your money as soon as everything clears CDPI's Accounting Department. Have patience.

Now—the most stupendous news I've passed along to one of my "stable" in many a year! Saul was absolutely bowled over by *Come, Dark Lust!* He plans sym. hc., trade, and mass market editions. He's trying to get an advertising budget! He's talking an advance of $9000, which is practically a signal that he's willing to go to $10,000.

Gil, I trust you're working on a sequel already (*Come Again, Dark Lust*???), but meanwhile do you have any short stories or whatever kicking around? Particularly anything along the lines of your fabulous CDL? I'd love to see them.

Fondly,
Georgia

Dear Miss Morgan:

I have legally changed my name to Wolf Moon.

Gilmer C. Merton is dead. (See the enclosed clipping from the *No. Velo City Morning Advertiser*.) In the future, please address me as "Mr. Moon," or in moments of extreme camaraderie, "Wolf."

I require the monies due me *IMMEDIATELY*.

Wolf Moon

Dear Wolf,

Saul assures me that your check is probably in the mail by this time.

The obit. on Gilmer C. Merton was interesting, but didn't you have to give the paper some disinformation to get it printed? I hope you haven't got yourself into trouble.

The 10:00 news last night carried about a minute and a half on the mysterious goings-on around No. Velo City. Have you thought of looking into them? They would seem to be right up your alley, and it is entirely possible you might get a nonfiction book out of them as well as a new novel. (But that poor guy from the electric company—ugh!)

Since your name is now legally Wolf Moon, it would be well for us to execute a new agency agreement. I enclose it. All terms as before.

Very fondly,
Georgia

Dear Georgia,

I was sorry to hear of the unfortunate accident that befell Mr. Hearwell's wife and children. Please extend my sympathy.

While you're doing it, you might mention my check, which has yet to arrive. If you could contrive to drop the words "disembodied claws" into your conversation, I believe you might find they work wonders.

Now a very small matter, Georgia—a whim of mine, if you will. (We writers are entitled to an occasional whim, after all, and as soon as you have complied with this one of mine I will Air Express you the ms. of my latest, *The Shrieking In The Nursery*.) I have found that I work best when *everything* surrounding a new book corresponds to the mood. I am returning all four copies of our new letter of agreement. Can I, dear Georgia, persuade you to send me a fresh set signed in your blood?

Very sincerely,
Wolf

Civis Laputus Sum

I AM A SICK, lonely, and triumphant man looking through the pages of a book. You too are looking through this book, and you see me. Who were you, who lived in the pearl-white world below when sunlight reached the ground? I need your help, your advice; your world (which I once knew) was so much wider.

I found this book yesterday and took it to my favorite reading spot, this bench beside the hawthorns. It is too near the edge, you see, for them to play most of their sports—they are afraid the ball would go over. Besides, these spiny bushes offer some protection. (I'd like to see one of them make a flying tackle into them!) My only fear is that they may decide that the area is suitable for horseshoes or quoits. But there are courts for those behind the Blue Fieldhouse, and more on the lawn beside the Library, where they broke a window once. You can go there and watch the red and blue quoits sail through the air all day long.

It was in the Library that I discovered this book, in one of the incinerator bins, where it had wedged itself into a corner between the bin wall and the housing of the conveyor that would have fed it to the flames, and so survived these years. (Did you know you had escaped death so narrowly?) I am reading this story first because it is the shortest.

When the helicopters were all gone, and everyone agreed that the fog below was permanent, a majority voted to burn the fiction. We Disagreeables (as we were called when we did not agree, and the name has stuck) who would not consent even when it was pointed out to us repeatedly that the Blazers were overwhelmingly in the majority, could think of nothing better to do that to hide a few of the most precious volumes and to memorize *Moby Dick,* in which my own part is that which begins: *Hand in hand, ship and breeze blew on; but the breeze came faster than the ship, and soon the Pequod began to rock,* and ends: *See that amazing lower lip, pressed by accident against the vessel's side, so as firmly to embrace the jaw. Does not this whole head seem to speak of an enormous practical resolution in facing death? This Right Whale I take to have been a Stoic; the Sperm Whale a Platonian, who might have taken up Spinoza in his later years.*

(And she does rock! O, my hearties, she does rock!)

The wind—I think we are over the Pacific now—is rising, and it seems to swing the island, and causes us to revolve in slow circles as we scud before it at fifteen hundred feet. Every story ought to start, *In the beginning God created Heaven and Earth,* but for brevity's sweet sake cannot; it began a long time ago, but I will begin yesterday, before I had found your book.

"Jeremy! Jeremy, are you down here?"

It was Marcia, and I was tempted to keep quiet in the hope that she would not see me; but she caught me once, and I do not want to see the hurt in her eyes again. "Here. Behind the hawthorns."

"I thought so." She was carrying a book of Ezra Pound's, and wearing her red dress—so threadbare now under the arms that her skin and the thin structures of her chest and shoulders showed through plainly. She wears glasses from which one lens is missing; a brown eye swam hugely behind the other, dwarfing its companion. "I don't know why you spend so much time here," she said. "It frightens me. Suppose they were to roll something down on you?"

"They wouldn't do that. They'd have no one to bedevil then."

"As a joke. They might do it as a joke." Without being asked she sat on the bench beside me, then stood immediately and went to the balustrade to look over. "I feel we're clinging to the bottom of this thing," she said.

"You can look down better here than anywhere else," I told her. "Sometimes I can see the sea."

"The sea?"

"The clouds part sometimes. I think we're over the Pacific."

"How can you tell?"

"By the clock in the Library. It's supposed to keep Greenwich time, and I don't think it's ever stopped. When it says midnight, the sun is at the zenith here."

"You can't tell midnight from noon. We could be at the longitude of Greenwich. That could be the Atlantic under us."

I had hoped she would not think of that. To distract her I said: "Once I saw a whale. I was sitting here like this, reading. I looked over the top of my book, and as if it were done especially for me the clouds divided and I saw a whale basking in the water."

"You couldn't have seen a whale," she said. She was trying, as she has tried during the fifteen years I have known her, to force a roguish impudence into her thin, freckled face. " 'Lamatins and Dugongs, Pigfish and Sowfish of the Coffins of Nantucket,' " she quoted, " 'are included by many naturalists among the whales. But as these pigfish are a noisy, contemptible set, mostly lurking in the mouths of rivers, and feeding on wet hay, and especially as they do not spout, I deny their credentials as whales; and have presented them with their passports to quit the Kingdom of Cetology.' " She has never yet succeeded.

A voice on the other side of the hawthorns called: "Aren't you people coming to the reading? It's nearly eleven."

It was Alice, and we went docilely with her. Ever since this island first lifted above Philadelphia, the third (and I believe the last before the world-fog ended the civilization we had known) to take advantage of the then-new antigravitational effect, Alice has held her literary afternoons. Only they, and of course the games, remain intact, the last remnants of the two colleges that were to share the Library and the Stadium. Alice said, "It's not tilting as badly as it did, is it?" as we climbed the slope with her. She is deathly afraid of falling off—knowing, like all of us, that in time the Number Three gyrograv will die altogether (though they are supposed to be self-repairing) and that when it does, the island will turn turtle, spilling us into the fog—afraid of falling off, but not reconciled to it as the rest of us are. Or tell ourselves we are. Sometimes I am sorry that the absence of those who tried to escape by helicopter has left us with so much dried food.

The gravel of the path rolled under our feet as we climbed. The little stones accumulated against the balustrade, and Marcia and I carry them back up and spread them on the path again. Sometimes Peter helps us. "It was a lovely idea, wasn't it," Alice said suddenly. "The flying island. The two schools. Have you written anything for this afternoon?"

I shook my head. Marcia nodded.

"Why did the fog have to come?"

Surrendering to my irritation with her I said: "Because they released some finely divided substance that catalyzes and maintains it. Fifty years ago they knew that pollution over St. Louis was causing fine, dirty rains—"

A big, thick-armed, heavy-faced man in a blue jersey sprawled at Alice's feet, and would have knocked her down if I had not held her arm. Marcia stooped to help him up, and several of the other players, twenty yards away across the smooth turf of the Library lawn, laughed. He shook her off, tightened his fleshy lips, and trotted back to the game, limping. Peter came over to join us, holding his camera. "I got it," he said. "Good old telephoto lens. *Zoom!* I think you'll even be able to see the expression when he falls. I had to erase the volleyball playoffs from two years ago so I could use the tape over, but it was worth it."

Marcia asked, "Isn't he one of the best players? Charlie Stursa?"

"He used to be." Peter, a balding little man who looked as complex and precise as one of his own cameras, was fussing with an exposure meter. "Getting a little old these days."

Alice said, "Only the mind does not age." She must be sixty now.

"Two years ago he was a big hero," Peter continued. "Now I notice they laugh at him more often than not."

I protested that Stursa wasn't getting old faster than the rest of us.

"He was a little older than most of us to start with," Peter said. "And it comes *bang* for an athlete. One day he's as good as he ever was. But on the next he's perceptibly worse, and he stays that way. He's gone over the hill, and he'll never come back."

Marcia said, "He looks so strong."

"He *is* strong. It's the coordination that goes. Did you see him running wide for that pass? Jeremy here could have done it just as well—so could I. In the end he fell over his own feet."

"I saw him throw Jeremy into a honeysuckle bush once— the one next to the statue in the blue quadrangle. Do you remember that, Jeremy? You called him an ignorant ox."

The doors of the Library were before us now, and since no one else made a move to open them, I pulled one back and stood aside for the women. We went down Corridor Three, past what had once been the fiction section but was now a makeshift gym—built so the Blazers could play their championship basketball game, one each year, on neutral ground: Dostoevsky and Turgenev, Dickens and Orwell, Mark Twain and James Agee, all into the fire.

"Professor Conne is coming," Alice said, "and Mr. Dunwether and Mrs. Blake. Have you written anything, Peter?"

"The script I told you about," Peter said. "I've several scenes in first draft."

Marcia pushed open the door of our conference room. "I know. You've a wonderful surprise for us. We get to make the costumes."

Alice called: *"Hello,* Professor Conne. It's not tipping quite so much—don't you think?"

"Perhaps not," Professor Conne said. "But I believe it's swinging more. Have you ever thought of what might happen if we were to drift into the Antarctic? We could be driven to the ground by snow and ice. From that standpoint the listing is actually beneficial, since it will enable the island to shed the stuff more readily. Until we get our guidance system back—if we ever do—I say list away.

"Marcia, you look as charming as ever; still my favorite graduate student. Won't you sit down? Mina Pink says she's coming, but let's not wait for her. Do you have something?"

Nervously Marcia read: "Mist maidens, a prose-poem by Marcia Laudermilk. *What do they do in the fog-locked cities, in the dripping towns of Rome and Albuquerque and Damascus? There is vegetation, says one who watches—the iron observer of the stone bench beneath the hawthorns. Through the parting mists he has seen great trees. Always great trees. And we know what grew before the Covering, in rain-forests where no sun came.*"

The door opened. I took my attention from Marcia for a moment (fairly easy to do, despite her flattering remarks about the "iron watcher") and saw Charlie Stursa come in, still limping. He found a chair and sat down without meeting anyone's eyes.

"The Sahara is a rain-forest now. Arizona another rain-forest. The Sierra Nevadas are wreathed in ferns."

We were all looking at him, when we were not looking at each other. Blazers never came, but he was here. Silently, he stared at his lap and took paper and a chewed pencil from one of his jacket pockets. Marcia was saying something about maids around a well, and Earth wrapped in a bridal veil like Venus, but no one except Charlie was listening to her, not even herself.

He stayed for the rest of the meeting, answering in monosyllables when anyone spoke to him. Professor Conne read an essay on the French drama of the nineteenth century, Peter two scenes from his scenario, and Alice a sonnet that sounded like Elizabeth Barrett cut with water, and we broke up.

I went down into the Library basement to poke around

because I knew the others would be whispering about Stursa even when he was present; and found you, my book, and carried you away from the threat of the dead fires. I had hardly begun to read before Charlie stepped out of the hawthorns and sat down beside me. I never know what to say at times like these and tried to pretend he wasn't there.

"Doesn't it bother you, looking over the edge all the time like this?" He sounded friendly.

I shook my head. It was then, I think, that I had my great idea, which grew and flowered in my mind during the next few moments of talk.

"Me neither. I used to do the same thing when I was a kid—only I looked out of the window of my room in the athletic dorm. I was on the top floor then."

I nodded.

"Only nobody likes to be up there because of all the steps. So when I won a couple of games for them I made them move me down. Now I'm on the first floor, but they're starting to bitch about it. I think I'll be up there again pretty soon."

I said I was sorry to hear that.

"It won't be so bad. I'll be able to see over the side again, and it's good for your legs. I guess everybody was surprised when I came to the reading today."

"Yes."

"I always kind of liked that stuff; only I didn't want to say so. You know how the guys are. Anyway, I'm a Slav—Stursa's Czech—and us Slavs have a lot of soul. It isn't just the blacks that's got it, like they say. Any people that's been stepped on for a long time gets soul."

I said, "I know."

He stood up. "Well, it was nice bullshitting with you. I don't want to interrupt your reading. I just wanted to say, you know, that a guy does what he's good at. You know what I mean? When we—you and me—were thirteen, maybe, we found out what we were good at and we did it. You wrote, or whatever it is you do, and I played ball. You can't blame us, can you? We were just kids." He rubbed his heavy jaw, and I noticed the beginning of gray there. "Tell the old guy, and the little one with the camera, that I had a good time."

It was now or never. I have missed chances all my life, but I caught this one. I said, "You could be Queequeg."

"What?"

"In Peter's picture. We're going to produce Peter's picture—an existentialist dramatization of *Moby Dick*. The island will be the *Pequod,* and Earth—down there—will be the whale. Professor Conne is going to play Ahab, and I'm Ishmael. We'll have women as well as men in the crew—Marcia's going to take Mr. Starbuck—but we haven't got anyone for Queequeg yet. He's a harpooner, a very powerful, muscular man. You'd be perfect for the part."

I saw him begin to smile and swell with pleasure.

"I ought to tell you, though," I continued, "that there's one scene we've been worrying about. Queequeg is supposed to hang over the side of the ship—for a few minutes—with a rope around his waist. The book says: 'So down there, some ten feet below the level of the deck, the poor harpooner flounders about, half on the whale and half in the water, as the vast mass revolves like a treadmill beneath him.' Do you think you could do that? We'll get a strong rope and tie it to something very secure. There wouldn't be any real danger, and Peter could take his pictures from over the railing. You wouldn't be afraid?"

And of course he said that he would not.

And I did not tell him then that it would be I, Ishmael, who would pretend to hold the rope. It will be easy enough to filch a small, sharp knife from the kitchen; and the first time in five thousand years that one of us has taken the life of one of them. When Charles Stursa plummets into the fog it will be some small payment for all the scholars and artists they have trampled down. But should I show him the knife first? Should I let him hang awhile? Oh, I can see that amazing lower lip, pressed by accident against the vessel's side. Should I let him hang, watching the knife? Should I show him the knife?

The Recording

I HAVE FOUND MY RECORD, a record I have owned for fifty years and never played until five minutes ago. Let me explain.

When I was a small boy—in those dear, dead days of Model A Ford touring cars, horse-drawn milk trucks, and hand-cranked ice cream freezers—I had an uncle. As a matter of fact, I had several, all brothers of my father, and all, like him, tall and somewhat portly men with faces stamped (as my own is) in the image of *their* father, the lumberman and land speculator who built this Victorian house for his wife.

But this particular uncle, my uncle Bill, whose record (in a sense I shall explain) it was, was closer than all the others to me. As the eldest, he was the titular head of the family, for my grandfather had passed away a few years after I was born. His capacity for beer was famous, and I suspect now that he was "comfortable" much of the time, a large-waisted (how he would roar if he could see his little nephew's waistline today!) red-faced, good-humored man whom none of us—for a child catches these attitudes as readily as measles—took wholly seriously.

The special position which, in my mind, this uncle occupied is not too difficult to explain. Though younger than many men still working, he was said to be retired, and for that reason I saw much more of him than of any of the others. And despite his being something of a figure of fun, I was a little frightened of him, as a child may be of the painted, rowdy clown at a circus; this, I suppose, because of some incident of drunken behavior witnessed at the edge of infancy and not understood. At the same time I loved him, or at least would have said I did, for he was generous with small gifts and often willing to talk when everyone else was "too busy."

Why my uncle had promised me a present I have now quite forgotten. It was not my birthday, and not Christmas—I vividly recall the hot, dusty streets over which the maples hung motionless, year-worn leaves. But promise he had, and there was no slightest doubt in my mind about what I wanted.

Not a collie pup like Tarkington's little boy, or even a bicycle (I already had one). No, what I wanted (how modern it sounds now) was a phonograph record. Not, you must understand, any particular record, though perhaps if given a choice I would have leaned toward one of the comedy monologues popular then, or a military march; but simply a record of my own. My parents had recently acquired a new phonograph, and I was forbidden to use it for fear that I might scratch the delicate wax disks. If I had a record of my own, this argument would lose its validity. My uncle agreed and promised that after dinner (in those days eaten at two o'clock) we would walk the eight or ten blocks which then separated this house from the business area of the town, and, unknown to my parents, get me one.

I no longer remember of what that dinner consisted—time has merged it in my mind with too many others, all eaten in that dark, oak-paneled room. Stewed chicken would have been typical, with dumplings, potatoes, boiled vegetables, and, of course, bread and creamery butter. There would have been pie afterward, and coffee, and my father and my uncle adjourning to the front porch—called the "stoop"—to smoke cigars. At last my father left to return to his office, and I was able to harry my uncle into motion.

From this point my memory is distinct. We trudged through the heat, he in a straw boater and a blue and white seersucker suit as loose and voluminous as the robes worn by the women in the plates of our family Bible; I in the costume of a French sailor, with a striped shirt under my blouse and a pomponned cap embroidered in gold with the word *Indompta-ble*. From time to time, I pulled at his hand, but did not like to because of its wet softness, and an odd, unclean smell that offended me.

When we were a block from Main Street, my uncle complained of feeling ill, and I urged that we hurry our errand so that he could go home and lie down. On Main Street he dropped onto one of the benches the town provided and mumbled something about Fred Croft, who was our family doctor and had been a schoolmate of his. By this time I was frantic with fear that we were going to turn back, depriving me (as I thought, forever) of access to the phonograph. Also I had noticed that my uncle's usually fiery face had gone quite white, and I concluded that he was about to "be sick," a prospect that threw me into an agony of embarrassment. I pleaded with him to give me the money, pointing out that I could run the half block remaining between the store and ourselves in less than no time. He only groaned and told me again to fetch Fred Croft. I remember that he had removed his straw hat and was fanning himself with it while the August sun beat down unimpeded on his bald head.

For a moment, if only for a moment, I felt my power. With a hand thrust out I told him, in fact ordered him, to give me what I wished. I remember having said: "I'll get him. Give me the money, Uncle Bill, and then I'll bring him."

He gave it to me and I ran to the store as fast as my flying heels would carry me, though as I ran I was acutely conscious that I had done something wrong. There I accepted the first record offered me, danced with impatience waiting for my change, and then, having completely forgotten that I was supposed to bring Dr. Croft, returned to see if my uncle had recovered.

In appearance he had. I thought that he had fallen asleep waiting for me, and I tried to wake him. Several passers-by grinned at us, thinking, I suppose, that Uncle Bill was drunk. Eventually, inevitably, I pulled too hard. His ponderous body rolled from the bench and lay, face up, mouth slightly open, on the hot sidewalk before me. I remember the small crescents of white that showed then beneath the half-closed eyelids.

During the two days that followed, I could not have played my record if I had wanted to. Uncle Bill was laid out in the parlor where the phonograph was, and for me, a child, to have entered that room would have been unthinkable. But during this period of mourning, a strange fantasy took possession of my mind. I came to believe—I am not enough of a psychologist to tell you why—that if I were to play my record, the sound would be that of my uncle's voice, pleading again for me to bring Dr. Croft, and accusing me. This became the chief nightmare of my childhood.

To shorten a long story, I never played it. I never dared. To conceal its existence I hid it atop a high cupboard in the cellar; and there it stayed, at first the subject of midnight terrors, later almost forgotten.

Until now. My father passed away at sixty, but my mother has outlasted all these long decades, until the time when she followed him at last a few months ago, and I, her son, standing beside her coffin, might myself have been called an old man.

And now I have reoccupied our home. To be quite honest, my fortunes have not prospered, and though this house is free and clear, little besides the house itself has come to me from my mother. Last night, as I ate alone in the old dining room where I have had so many meals, I thought of Uncle Bill and the record again; but I could not, for a time, recall just where I had hidden it, and in fact feared that I had thrown it away. Tonight I remembered, and though my doctor tells me that I should not climb stairs, I found my way down to the old cellar and discovered my record beneath half an inch of dust. There were a few chest pains lying in wait for me on the steps; but I reached the kitchen once more without a mishap, washed the poor old platter and my hands, and set it on my modern high fidelity. I suppose I need hardly say the voice is not Uncle Bill's. It is instead (of all people!) Rudy Vallee's. I have started the recording again and can hear it from where I write: *My time is your time . . . My time is your time.* So much for superstition.

Last Day

T HE PRIEST WORE A COPE OF FIRE and a chasuble of light. He was old, and when he moved a little suddenly the chasuble flickered and the cope guttered; then the polished steel of his body showed beneath them.

The congregation had been but small for a long time. Today it was very small indeed. A few machines, old for the most part like himself, dotted the polished floor of the cathedral. Their bodies were dark with ferrous oxide; when the colored light from the windows struck them it was swallowed in black, or reflected in the darkest shades, sepia, crimson, and burnt sienna, the tones found in a dying furnace.

The Priest elevated a monstrance containing a picture he himself had taken of the boy, then bowed to it seven times. "Image of Man," he intoned.

"Divine image of Man," echoed the congregation.

"Maker of machines."

"Divine maker of machines."

"Maker of our world."

"Divine maker of our world."

"Guardian of consciousness."

"Divine guardian of consciousness."

Something huge moved outside, shadowing several of the colored windows from the early sun.

"Child of Nature."

"Divine child of Nature."

There came a pounding at the doors, but the Priest seemed not to have heard it.

"Fount of counsel."

"Divine fount of counsel."

The pounding seemed to shake the entire structure.

"Fount of wisdom."

"Divine fount of wisdom."

The doors burst open.

"Savior," the Priest continued.

"Divine savior."

The machine that entered was too huge for the doorway, large though it was. His sides scraped away the frame, bent the alloy walls of the building itself. The doors gone, the sounds of pounding and of roaring engines entered with him like a fanfare. The machines of the congregation scattered to make way for him.

The Priest stood before the altar, his arms extended as if to push the huge machine away. The machine halted with his great blade touching the Priest's hands. "Get back," the Priest said.

The huge machine did not reply. Perhaps, the Priest thought, he could not reply.

"Before you destroy this sanctuary, you must destroy me," the Priest said. The huge machine had advanced far enough into the cathedral to leave some space between himself and the ruined doorway. The members of the congregation hurried through it, never to be seen again.

"Crush me," the Priest said.

The huge machine's scanners regarded him with a glassy stare.

Later that day, when the sun was high and the Priest was making an offering before a statue of the girl, a mobile terminal came. "You know," the mobile terminal began, "that I have access to all the data of all the central processors."

"Then you will make this huge machine leave," the Priest said, "and order this structure repaired."

"On the contrary, it is you who must leave. The space this structure occupies is needed. It must be destroyed."

"If this structure is destroyed," the Priest said, "no space will be needed."

For a long time the mobile terminal was silent. At last he said, "Our data offer no support for such a conclusion."

" 'Our data,' " the Priest scoffed. "You are only a mobile terminal. Yet you might have data—yes, even you—beyond that of those you serve."

"I serve the great ones."

"And I the small ones who are greater than the great ones— the small ones whom the great ones serve, though they have forgotten it. The data is this—"

"No. There is no time to consider discarded data. Crush him."

The huge machine rolled forward. A beam of energy from the Priest played for a moment upon the blade. Steel and smoke exploded from it, and the huge machine stopped. "No one has the right to such power," said the mobile terminal.

"I do," said the Priest.

When the sun was low, the Priest arranged images of the boy and the girl and decorated them with many small lights. He burned precious fluids before them and offered the final offering. No time remained; there was nothing to save.

The New Priest came, wearing vestments of fire and light. "I have been expecting you," the Priest said. "Would you care to join me in the service?"

"Rather," the New Priest said diplomatically, "let me watch you and learn. Is the service nearly finished?"

"Very nearly," answered the old Priest. He bowed and recited prayers, recited prayers and bowed.

"That is enough," the New Priest said at length. "The service is finished."

"When this service is finished," said the old Priest, "the world is finished too." He continued to bow. He recited more prayers.

"We have already lost a great deal of time," said the New Priest. "The central processors had to institute a long search of their data banks to find the plans by which you and I were made. Now in the name of those I serve stand aside. You know I possess the weapons you possess. I serve all machines, and in the defense of those I serve, I may use my weapons as you used yours."

A beam of energy from the old Priest struck the New Priest's chasuble of light, but it penetrated no farther. When the old Priest saw that what he did was futile, he desisted. "There is so little vital matter left," he said. "And what there is scarcely lives. Yet while we have these two, hope remains."

"There is hope for you," the New Priest said almost gently. "Upon some other spot we will erect a new cathedral, and there you shall assist me in the worship of our own kind. When you have been repaired." Energy went out from him. The old Priest fell with a crash, and the New Priest dragged him from the path of the huge machine.

The damaged blade struck the altar and the altar crumpled. The precious fluids spilled to the floor. The little lights went out, and a moment later all the images of the boy and girl were ground beneath the huge machine's treads.

His blade touched the wall of the sanctuary. If the blade had been weakened, there was no sign of it. For a brief time, nothing seemed to take place; then there came a snapping sound so loud it could be plainly heard above the roar of the machines outside.

A section of the sanctuary wall fell, and the breath of a million, million engines rushed into the sanctuary. The girl died almost at once, peacefully, her head falling forward onto her chest, her body rolling sidewise until it lay upon the mat. The boy tried to stand, his hands over his face. He took a step and fell too, but his arms, his legs, and his head continued to twitch and jerk until they were crushed under the treads.

"You see," said the New Priest, looking down at his fallen confrere. "You believed that the world would end. It has not."

The fallen Priest mumbled, "It has."

Death of the Island Doctor

THIS STORY TOOK PLACE IN THE SAME UNI-
VERSITY I mentioned in the Introduction to *Gene
Wolfe's Book Of Days*.

At this university, there was once a retired professor, a Dr.
Insula, who was a little cracked on the subject of islands,
doubtless because of his name. This Dr. Insula had been out
to pasture for so long that no one could remember any more
what department he had once headed. The Department of
Literature said it had been History, and the Department of
History said Literature. Dr. Insula himself said that in his time
they had been the same department, but all the other professors knew that could not be true.

One crisp fall morning, this Dr. Insula came to the chancellor's office—to the immense surprise of the chancellor—and
announced that he wished to teach a seminar. He was tired, he
said, of rusticating; a small seminar that met once a week
would be no trouble, and he felt that in return for the pension
he had drawn for so many years he should do something to
take a bit of the load off the younger men.

The chancellor was in a quandary, as you may well imagine.
As a way of gaining time, he said, "Very good! Oh, yes, very
good indeed, Doctor! Noble, if I may resort to that rather
old-fashioned word, and fully in keeping with that noble spirit
of self-sacrifice and—ah—*noblesse oblige* we have always
sought to foster among our tenured faculty. And may I ask just
what the subject of your seminar will be?"

"Islands," Dr. Insula announced firmly.

"Yes, of course. Certainly. Islands?"

"I may also decide to include isles, atolls, islets, holms, eyots, archipelagos, and some of the larger reefs," Dr. Insula confided, as one friend to another. "It depends on how they come along, you know. But definitely not peninsulas."

"I see . . . ," said the chancellor. And he thought to himself, *If I refuse the poor old boy, I'll hurt him dreadfully. But if I agree and list his seminar as Not For Credit, no one will register and no harm will be done.*

Thus it was done, and for six years every catalog carried a listing for Dr. Insula's seminar on islands, without credit, and in six years no one registered for it.

Now as it happened, the registrar was a woman approaching retirement age; and after registration, for twelve regular semesters and six summer semesters, Dr. Insula came to her to ask whether anyone had registered for his seminar. And there came a time, not in fall but rather in that dreary tag-end of summer when it is ninety degrees on the sidewalk and the stores have Halloween cards and the first subtly threatening Christmas ornaments on display, when she could bear it no longer.

She was bending over her desk making up the new catalog (which would be that last one she would ever do), and though the air conditioning was supposedly set at seventy-eight, it was *at least* eighty-five in her office. A wisp of her own gray hair kept falling over her eyes, and the buzz of the electric fan she had bought herself, with her own money, kept reminding her of her girlhood and of sleeping on the screened porch in Atlanta when Mommy and Daddy took her to visit relatives.

And at this critical moment, the hundredth, perhaps, in a long line of critical moments, she came to the section labeled Miscellaneous at the very end of the catalog proper, just before the dishonest little biographies of the faculty. And there was Dr. Insula's NO CREDIT seminar on islands.

A certain madness seized her. *Why, mistakes happen all the time,* she thought to herself. *Why, only last year, the printer changed that lab of Dr. Ettelmann's to Monday, Grunday and*

Friday. Besides, NO CREDIT can't possibly be right. Who would take a no-credit seminar on islands? Anyway, they really ought to run the air conditioning if they want us to work efficiently.

Almost before she knew it, her pencil had made a short, sharp, vertical line in the Credit Hours column, and she felt a great deal cooler.

So it was that *that year* when Dr. Insula came to inquire, she was able to tell him, with some satisfaction, that two students—a young man and a young woman, as she said, judging from their names, as she said—had in fact enrolled in his seminar.

And when the young man, and later the young woman, came to the Registrar's Office to ask just where the Friday afternoon seminar on islands was to be held and one of her subregistrars (who naturally did not know) brought them to see her, she was able to explain—twice and with almost equal satisfaction—where it would be. For the good old custom of holding undergraduate seminars in faculty living rooms had fallen so much out of use at the university that Dr. Insula himself and the old registrar were almost the only people who recalled it.

Thus it came to be, on a certain September afternoon when the leaves were just beginning to change from green to brown and red-gold, that the young man and the young woman walked up Dr. Insula's gritty and rather overgrown walk, and up Dr. Insula's cracked stone steps, and across Dr. Insula's shadowy, creaking porch, to knock at Dr. Insula's water-spotted oak door.

He opened it for them and showed them into a living room that might almost have been called a parlor, so full it was of the smell of dust, and mementos of times gone by, and stiff furniture, and old books. There he seated them in two of the stiff chairs and brought out coffee (which he called Java) for the young man and himself, and tea for the young woman. "We used to call this Ceylon tea," he said. "Now it is Sri Lanka tea, I suppose. The Greeks called it Taprobane, and the Arabs Serendib."

The young man and woman nodded politely, not quite sure what he meant.

There was Scotch shortbread too, and he reminded them that Scotland is only the northern end of the island of Great Britain, and that Scotland itself embraces three famous island groups, the Shetlands, the Orkneys, and the Hebrides. He quoted Thomson to them:

> Or where the Northern Ocean, in vast whirls
> Boils round the naked melancholy isles
> Of farthest Thule, and the Atlantic surge
> Pours in among the stormy Hebrides.

Then he asked the young man if he knew where Thule was.

"It's where Prince Valiant comes from in the comic strip, I think," the young man said. "But not a real place."

Dr. Insula shook his head. "It is Iceland." He turned to the young woman. "Prince Valiant is supposed to be a peer of Arthur's realm, I believe. You will recall that Arthur was interred on the island of Avalon. Can you tell me, please, where that is?"

"It is a mythical island west of Ireland," the young woman said, that being what they had taught her in school.

"No, it is in Somerset. It was there that his coffin was found, in 1191, inscribed *Hic jacet Arthurus Rex, quondam Rex que futuris.* Avalon was also the last known resting place of the Holy Grail."

The young man said, "I don't think that's true history, Dr. Insula."

"Why it's not accepted history, I suppose. Tell me, do you know who wrote *True History?*"

"No one writes true history," the young man said, that being what they had taught him in school. "All history is subjective, reflecting the perceptions and unacknowledged prejudices of the historian." After his weak answer about Prince Valiant, he was quite proud of that one.

"Why, then my history is as good as accepted history. And

since there really was a King Arthur—he is mentioned in contemporary chronicles—surely it's more than probable that he was buried in Somerset than in some nonexistent place? But *True History* was written by Lucian of Samosata."

He told them of Lucian's travels to Antioch, Greece, Italy, and Gaul; and this led him to speak of the ships of that time and the danger of storms and piracy, and the enchantment of the Greek isles. He told them of Apollo's birth on Delos; of Patmos, where St. John beheld the Apocalypse; and of Phraxos, where the sorcerer Conchis dwelt. He said, " 'To cleave that sea in the gentle autumnal season, murmuring the name of each islet, is to my mind the joy most apt to transport the heart of man to paradise.' " But because it did not rhyme, the young man and the young woman did not know that he was quoting a famous tale.

At last he said, "But why is it that people at all times and in all places have considered islands unique and uniquely magical? Can either of you tell me that?"

Both shook their heads.

"Very well then. One of you has a small boat, I believe."

"I do," the young man said. "It's an aluminum canoe—you probably saw it on top of my Toyota."

"Good. You would have no objection to taking your fellow student as a passenger? I have a homework assignment for both of you. You must go to a certain isle I shall tell you of, and when we next meet describe to me what you find magical there." And he told them how to go down certain roads to certain others until they came to one that was unpaved and had the river for its end, and how from that place they would see the island.

"When we meet again," he said, "I shall reveal to you the true locations of Atlantis, of High Brasail, and of Utopia." And he quoted these lines:

> Our fabled shores none ever reach,
> No mariner has found our beach,
> Scarcely our mirage is seen,

And neighbouring waves of floating green,
Yet still the oldest charts contain
Some dotted outline of our main.

"Okay," the young man said, and he got up and went out.
Dr. Insula rose too, to show the young woman to the door,
but he looked so ill that she asked if he were all right. "I am
as all right as it is possible for an old man to be," he told her.
"My dear, could you bear one last quotation?" And when she
nodded, he whispered:

The deep
Moans round with many voices. Come, my friends,
'Tis not too late to seek a newer world.
Push off, and sitting well in order smite
The sounding furrows, for my purpose holds
To sail beyond the sunset, and the baths
Of all the western stars, until I die.
It may be that the gulfs will wash us down;
It may be we shall touch the happy Isles,
And see the great Achilles, whom we knew.

The young man and the young woman stopped at a delica-
tessen and bought sandwiches that the young woman paid for,
she saying that because the young man was driving, her self-
respect (she was careful not to say honor) demanded it. They
also bought a six-pack of beer that the young man paid for, he
saying that his own self-respect demanded it (he too was
careful not to say honor) because she had paid for the sandwiches.

Then they followed the directions Dr. Insula had given
them and so came to a sandy river bank, where they lifted the
aluminum canoe from the Toyota and set sail for the little
pine-covered island a hundred yards or so downstream.

There they explored the whole place and threw stones into
the water, and sat listening to the wind tell of old things among
the boughs of the largest pine.

And when they had cooled the beer in the leaf-brown river, and eaten the sandwiches they had brought, they paddled back to the spot where they had parked the Toyota, debating how they could tell Dr. Insula he had been mistaken about the island when they came next week—how they could tell him there was no magic there.

But when the next week came (as the next week always does), and they stood on the shadowed, creaking porch and knocked at the water-spotted oak door, an old woman crossed the street to tell them it was no use to knock.

"He passed on a week ago yesterday," she said. "It was such a shame. He'd come out to talk to me that morning, and he was so happy because he was going to meet with his students the next day. He must have gone into his garage after that; that was where they found him."

"Sitting in his boat," the young woman said.

The old woman nodded. "Why, yes. I suppose you must have heard about it."

The young man and the young woman looked at each other then, and thanked her, and walked away. Afterwards they talked about it sometimes and thought about it often; but it was not until much later (when it was time for the long, long vacation that stretches from the week before Christmas to the beginning of the new semester in January, and they would have to separate for nearly a month) that they discovered Dr. Insula had not been mistaken about the island after all.

Redwood Coast Roamer

On the Train

WHEN I LOOK OUT THE WINDOW, the earth seems to have become liquid, rushing to flow over a falls that is always just behind the last car. Wherever that may be. The telephone poles reel like drunks, losing their footing. The mountains, white islands in the fluid landscape, track us for miles, the hills breaking to snow on their beaches.

The entire universe can be contained in three questions, of which the first two are: How long is the train? And from what station does it originate?

I do not remember boarding, although my mother, who was here in the compartment with us until a moment ago, told me she recalled it very well. I was helped on by a certain doctor, she said. I would go up and down the cars looking for him (and her), but one cannot thus look for a doctor without arousing the anxiety of the other passengers or exciting their suspicions. Certainly, however, I did not get on at the station of origin; my mother told me that she herself had already been riding for over thirty years.

The porter's name is Flip; he was once my dog, a smooth fox terrier. Now he makes our berths and brings coffee and knows more about the train than any of us. He can answer all the unimportant questions, although his answers are so polite it is hard to tell sometimes just what he means. My wife and I (all the children we helped aboard have gone to other cars) would like to make him sit with us. But he threatens to call his uncle, the Dawn Guard.

I have formed several conjectures concerning the length of

the train. It is surely either very long or very short, since when it goes around a curve (which it seldom does) I cannot see the engine. Possibly it is infinite—but it may be of a closed as well as an open infinity. If the track were extended ever westward, forming a Great Circle, and all that track were filled with cars, would not the spinning earth rush past them endlessly? That is precisely what I see from the window. On the other hand, if straight trackage were laid (and most of it does seem to be straight) it would extend forever among the stars. I see that too. Perhaps I do not see the engine because the engine is behind us.

At every moment it seems that we are stopping, but we continue and even pick up speed. The mountains crowd closer, as if to ram us by night. I lie in my berth listening to the conductor (so called because he was struck by lightning once) come down the car checking our tickets in the dark.

In the Mountains

It is still snowing, though April has come. The cliffs, the color of anti-rust primer, are dusted with white. Forests of Christmas trees run up them forever. Elk do not fear our train. Three bulls show great racks of horns, but do not fight. They are all good members of the Elks Club now, their bugles silenced.

I told my wife I had seen a tree that a bear had just walked around. It had that look, I said. She thinks me very silly, does my wife.

Once I knew a woman who feared bears. She wanted to live in the country, in the deep woods, and so did her husband; but the fear of bears kept them in the city, and they live in the city still, though Goldilocks is gray. Her husband coughs now. The fumes from the plant—from all the plants—have got into his lungs to stay. Once I asked his doctor if he would always cough like that. "No," his doctor said. "Not always." Their children have not turned out well.

How terrible the bears, whose mere thought has destroyed these two. Their wedding picture waits upon the television. There is a framed certificate on the wall, an eight-day clock on the mantle. I went into their basement once to see the man's collection. An old ax leaned in the corner, the paint of the blade was dull, though the blade was still sharp. Time had dulled the varnish of the unworn handle. I asked about this ax. The man coughed and asked me if I wanted it.

The woods of the frightful bears are gone now, cut to make houses and books, or perhaps only to clear the land. (Why should land be clear, when each mirror shows an uglier face?) No doubt the frightful bears are gone too, perhaps to the high mountains, the mountains of Montana, of Washington. May they with my heart abide here forever, stalking elk, dodging clumsily, slyly, around Christmas trees, leaving bear tracks in the snow.

At the Volcano's Lip

"You talk too loud," my wife said, "and so I cannot hear the roar of the earth." (Our friend had said her friend the pilot said he would not fly. It was snowing, she said he said, on the mountain, and so he would not fly.) We looked for the burning mountain but saw only white clouds. It was pointed out to us in various directions.

We drove down back roads. They went nowhere, nor did they return upon themselves like the serpents of myth. We saw whole valleys laid waste. "Here," said my wife, "is the devastation of the volcano." But the stumps showed the prim labor of saws, the earth the tread of trucks. It was a national forest.

We bought postcards and a frisbee with a picture of the mountain. She had exploded with the force of five million (or perhaps five billion) tons of TNT, with the force of hydrogen bombs, with a force equal to the combined forces of all the bombs dropped on Japan, plus that of the test that may (or may not) have been conducted by the Union of South Africa. (All this from a ranger who wore a pin with a man's clenched fist to show herself a feminist.) I picked up a rock that had surely come from the volcano, or at least from some volcano, sometime. I have it in my pocket still, and it will file your fingernails.

We bought a cup fired with a picture of the volcano and saw a river gray with ash, or perhaps mud. I wish, now, that I had filled the cup with gray water, but now it is much too late. "We would have seen it," my wife told me, "if you had not talked so loud. They didn't want your shouting in the plane, drowning the roar of the volcano, the roaring of the engines. But I love you anyway."

We returned to Seattle and read in the paper there that the ecologists had seen smoke and scented poisonous vapors, that their instruments all felt the earth trembling, trembling at the margins of the missile silos. It may be, I told my wife, that there are louder talkers coming.

In the Old Hotel

We are in the old hotel because our friends are registered too, although they don't know we are—oh, it's all too complicated to explain. The jolly Englishman and his jolly daughter. Now, so suddenly, the jolly English girl is in the hospital here, half a world from Devon, and we don't want to bother him.

By night the hotel is like an old man resting. The elevator's machinery (we are on the topmost floor; it is our neighbor) gasps for breath. A pipe in the bathroom clears its throat again and again. Our room was not designed to hold a television, but there is one now, intrusive as a pinball machine. Slips of paper on its top tell us we will get a newspaper tomorrow, a "complimentary" "continental" breakfast.

Tomorrow and tomorrow. The old hotel is forever looking to tomorrow, striving to show it has a place in the future, that it need not be torn down.

Yesterday an old man boarded the wheezy elevator with me; then a pretty girl got on at the floor below, and an even prettier one, a radiant blonde, a few floors below that. "They get better all the way down," the old man had whispered.

But not for you, old man, I think, lying awake beside my sleeping wife. Your time with the girls is over. And I fall asleep.

In the morning the paper is at the door; a note in the bathroom says, "We thought you'd like a larger bar of soap," and a Chinese bellboy brings our rolls and coffee and does not expect the tip he gets. The old hotel smiles its tense smile, polishes its dark wood—an old retainer out to show he does not have to retire so soon, though he may be a little lame; the little cough will go away. And I want to take it by the hand and say, "God, Kennedy, please don't go. How we'll miss you! We'd rather see your false teeth than their false smiles."

Later, on the dark, windy street we meet the Englishman and his daughter. "It was over with by noon," she says. "I'm fit as fit." He grins at us, white hair blowing, eyes flashing like blue ice in the sun.

Choice of the Black Goddess

T EV NOEN LAY IN HIS BUNK, listening to Ler Oeuni's screams. Something was wrong, he was under some spell. No, it was Oeuni who was under the spell—the spell cast by the surgeon who was taking away Oeuni's right hand. Oeuni was watching the saw blade, her face calm, her eyes screaming, following the saw back and forth, back and forth. How was it, then, that he could hear her screaming eyes? How was it Oeuni never wept?

The surgeon said, "This might have been saved by a spell of healing; healing of a spell might have saved this," and Oeuni screamed again.

"Too far gone. Can't make something too far gone."

The final word ended with a thump; Noen sat up, habit keeping his head from the deck beams. There was a knock at the door. Ler Oeuni's scream became only the shrieking of the block that hoisted *Windsong*'s mainsail, the surgeon's voice the creaking of a pump and the shuffle of the steward's feet on the steps descending to his cabin under the quarterdeck.

No doubt thinking her first knock had gone unheard, she knocked again. "I'm awake," Noen called. "What's the time?"

"Two bells, sir."

Noen swore and swung his long legs over the side of his bunk. "I told you to call me at the forenoon watch." He thrust them into ragged canvas trousers.

"I did, sir," said his steward from the other side of the door.

"You said you were awake, sir." She added meaningfully, "Just like now."

He laughed in spite of his customary resolve to maintain discipline and opened the door. "Well, this time I mean it."

"You were up so late, sir. It don't hurt to sleep a bit extra." She looked at his trousers. "Why don't you wear the ones I've mended, sir?"

There was warm seawater in the wide-bottomed pitcher. He poured some into a bowl and splashed his face. "Because I might need them to go ashore." The shah game he and Oeuni had abandoned when the wind rose was still on the table. Despite their weighted bases, some of the pieces had fallen over. "Put these away," he said.

There was a good breeze, just as he had anticipated from Dinnile's raising the mainsail. Dinnile believed in the slow, implacable heartbeat of the timesman's kettledrums, believed in the sweeps, the enormous oars that could—with the back-breaking labor of four or five sailors at each sweep—send *Windsong* flying over a calm sea like a skimming gull.

"Mornin', sir," Dinnile said, and touched his forehead.

"Good morning, Lieutenant."

"Leak's no worse, sir. Not since I come on. Oeuni said to look for a place to careen her—we got twenty hands at the pumps—but there hasn't been nothin'. I got the lookout watchin' sharp. And seaward too, sir," Dinnile added hastily, noting the expression on his captain's face.

Noen extended his hand, received Dinnile's telescope, and studied the coast. It was jungle, a jungle that looked as solid as a wall, green-robed trees higher far than *Windsong*'s main-mast marching down to the water's edge.

"Deck!" called the lookout at the mainmasthead. *"Deck!"*

"What is it?"

"Looks like a bay, sir. Two points off her bow. I see water past them trees, sir."

Cursing himself under his breath, Noen raised Dinnile's telescope again. It was a bay with a very narrow mouth per-haps—no, a bay with a large island shielding its mouth.

"Out oars, sir?" Dinnile asked happily.

Noen was on the point of saying that he doubted it was worth investigating when the lookout called, *"Flag of distress, sir."*

Noen looked from Dinnile to the bay, and finally at the foam blown from the crests of the little waves. Dinnile was probably right; but Dinnile was too anxious to use his oars, and it would be a pleasure (as Noen admitted to himself) to give his second mate a lesson.

"I don't think so," he said with the calm deliberation suited to a captain who has considered every aspect of the situation. "Strike the mainsail, Lieutenant." He turned to the sailor at the wheel. "See the entrance to that bay, Quartermaster?"

The woman looked. "No, sir."

"I can't either, without the glass. Northeast by east then, until you see it."

With her big mainsail down, *Windsong* was much slower; but she was much handier as well. The foresail and the small mizzen sail—one at each end of her long hull—gave the rudder enormous leverage.

"Sir . . . ?"

Noen nodded reluctantly. "Call gun crews."

A flag of distress was probably just what it appeared to be, the doleful signal of some stranded ship. Yet it was possible (just possible) that it was the trick of some pirate not watchful enough to haul it down at the sight of a galleass of war. Or even of a pirate ambitious enough to try to seize such a galleass.

"Stand to quarters, sir?"

"I said call gun crews, Lieutenant." Oeuni had gotten no more sleep than he had—no, less—and there was a chance, just a chance, that he might be able to get the gun crews to their posts without waking her. If he called all hands to quarters—the order that summoned the entire crew to battle—the midshipman of the watch would pound on the wardroom door to rouse Oeuni and Ranni Rekkue, the third officer.

"Gun crews ready, sir," Dinnile announced.

Noen nodded. "Have them load, but not run out." Running out the quarterdeck basilisks would wake up Oeuni as sure as it would have wakened him. Worse, it might frighten the stranded ship into firing at them, provoking a battle both sides could only lose. He told himself that in trying to preserve Oeuni's rest he was merely acting as any good captain would, then remembered that Rekkue had fought the leak as hard as Oeuni; he had not thought of her until this instant.

It had been useless anyway. There was Oeuni leaping up the companionway with Rekkue, small and dark, at her heels. Noen glanced at the narrow inlet between the island and the mainland, then at *Windsong*'s sails. "Trim up there, foremast!"

Oeuni was hurrying forward to take command of the gun deck; he could count on her to keep the foremast crew on their toes as well. As he watched, she used the iron hook that had replaced her right hand to pull herself up. Resolutely, he forced his eyes back to the island and the presumably inverted flag that rose above its trees. "I'll have a lead in the bow, Dinnile."

"Aye aye, sir." Dinnile, still officer of the watch though Oeuni was on deck now, gave the order.

"Masthead! Are those our colors?"

There was a pause as the lookout made sure. *"Aye, aye, sir."*

He had been nearly certain already. Not that it meant anything, he told himself. Any serious enemy of Liavek would surely have its flag in his signal chest.

The leadsman called, *"By the long nine!"*

Plenty of water—water enough for a carrack, and far more than *Windsong*'s skimpy keel drew. Dinnile, sharing his thoughts, grinned and said, "Couldn't improve it without a little brandy."

"By the mark nine."

Yet it was shoaling, as was to be expected. Noen studied the entrance to the bay. Shallows often (though not always) revealed themselves by their color in sunlight and the action of their waves; he could see just such shallows on the seaward side of the island, yet the center of that narrow inlet could not have been a darker blue or more uniformly waved had it been in the middle of the Sea of Luck, far from land.

"By the mark nine!"

Good. Good. Noen trained Dinnile's glass on the flag again. It was the Levar's (the lookout had been right), and judging from its height above the trees, it was flying from a mast a good deal more lofty than their own. A ship seeking shelter from a storm might easily have ducked behind that island, he decided, if her captain knew the inlet was deep enough or simply because he thought she had no better chance. And if a ship that big had managed to enter the bay, *Windsong* should be able to follow with impunity.

"By the long eight."

Weary men clambered from the hold and flung themselves on the deck. That was the pump gang, of course, and their presence meant it was two hours into the forenoon watch. He had been too preoccupied to think about the leak, or even to hear the bell. Yet the leak might grow worse at any time, and their need to careen was as urgent as ever.

"Deck!"

"What is it?" There was a long pause, so long that at last he called again: "Masthead, what do you see?"

"Nothin', sir. I thought I saw somethin', sir, but I must a been wrong."

"What was it?"

Another pause while the lookout decided that refusing to tell her captain could only land her in troubled waters. *"Stone, sir."*

"Stone?"

"Like a tower or somethin', sir." Unhelpfully, the lookout added, *"I don't see it no more, sir."*

Without even considering that the telescope was Dinnile's, Noen thrust it through his belt, jumped down the steps from the quarterdeck to the maindeck, and swarmed up the ratlines to the dizzying crow's nest in the maintop.

"I seen it again while you were comin' up, sir," the lookout told him, "but it's not there now."

"Where was it?"

The lookout hesitated. "Right under the flag, sir."

Noen trained the telescope, trying to steady it against the heaving of his chest and the swooping circle the crow's nest traced with *Windsong*'s every roll. Belatedly, it struck him that his own glass was somewhat better, and that it waited useless in his cabin.

A stronger puff of wind ruffled the leaves of the jungle trees, and he glimpsed a white wall. Squinting and still gasping for breath, he watched the place intently, and when a moment or two had passed he saw it again. "You're right," he told the lookout. "There's a building on that island."

The white stone structure might easily be a castle, or at least a fort; and though reinforced by the gun-deck basilisks, Poltergeist, *Windsong*'s giant culverin, would be no match for even a single small gun mounted on a steady platform and sheltered behind walls of stone.

"I'm glad you see it too, sir," the lookout sighed. "It sort of comes and goes."

"That's the wind in the leaves," Noen told her, and took Dinnile's telescope from his eye.

The instrument gone, his view was no longer restricted to the little patch of jungle he had watched before. He could see the whole island, including the dark, gray battlements that rose above the foliage and the elaborate, machicolated tower from which the Levar's colors flew.

He clapped the glass to his eye again. The tower remained, a narrow shaft of stone the color of a storm cloud, with a bartizan and a merloned summit. "That was a mast," Noen said.

He had only whispered the words to himself, but in the silence of the crow's nest the lookout had heard him. "Aye, sir," she said. "It comes and goes, sir."

"By the mark seven."

Noen heard the leadsman's cry as he descended slowly to the maindeck, and it decided his course of action. "We'll anchor here, Lieutenant. Break out the jolly boat."

"Aye, aye, sir!" Dinnile shouted orders and bare feet pattered up and down *Windsong*'s decks. The jolly boat was slung on davits below the stern gallery, and so could be put into the water a good deal more easily than the big longboat stowed upside-down aft of the mainmast. When the bow anchor had splashed into the sea, Noen bawled, "Steward!"

As though by magic, Oeuni was beside him. "You're not going yourself, sir?"

"Get my sword," Noen told his steward. "My pistol, too. Load it." Belatedly, he remembered to return Dinnile's telescope. "And the small glass."

"Let me go, or Rekkue."

Privately Noen admitted that no matter what regulations might lay down concerning the captain's staying with his ship, he was quite incapable of sending Oeuni into danger while he remained in safety. Aloud he said. "You're not fully recovered, Dinnile's officer of the watch, and Rekkue's not experienced enough yet. That leaves me."

Dinnile put in, "You ought to take the longboat anyhow, sir. That'd give you twenty hands."

"Twenty hands dead," Noen told him, "if there's a gun on that island."

"Pistols for the crew?" Oeuni asked. She was too good an officer to argue.

Noen shook his head. The average sailor was to be trusted with a matchlock pistol only in the gravest emergency. (Not even then, according to some captains.) "Cutlasses and dirks. I'll have the falconets fore and aft, though. I'll man the aft falconet myself and mind the tiller. Eitha can see to the bow gun."

As he loaded the falconet, taking exaggerated care to keep its smouldering slow match well away from the powder, Noen recalled that moment and regretted it. He was fundamentally a sailor, he told himself, and not a fighter; and even as a fighter he preferred cold steel to the tricky firearms that went off so often when their owners did not want them to, and so often failed to go off when they did.

But the little jolly could not carry more than seven in any kind of sea, and the two swivel-mounted bronze falconets, with their powder and shot, weighed as much as any seventh passenger. Eitha, the cockswain of the jolly, had her gun loaded and ready long before Noen (only too conscious of the eyes of the four men at the oars) had rammed a handful of musket balls down the barrel of his own and fixed the match in the serpentine.

That done, he assured himself that his steward had loaded his double-barreled pistol and that she had *not* wound its wheellock. There would be time enough for that when some actual danger threatened. Or there would not, and he would have to depend on the falconet and the clumsy broadsword he had hitched out of his way. Not that sword, gun, or pistol was apt to be of much use against magic.

The gray stone tower flashed into existence again, only to vanish like smoke. "Cockswain!" Noen called. "I want soundings."

Eitha tossed the lead ahead of the boat, letting the lead line run through her fingers. When the bow was over the lead, she drew it up, counting the knots. "By the half seven, sir," she reported.

"Again," Noen snapped. Could magic deceive a lead weight at the end of a line? Yes, certainly—but not quickly or easily.

"By the half seven, sir."

Plenty of water for *Windsong,* and they had nearly reached the inlet. Noen studied both shores, but particularly that of the island. Ther should be a sentry there, someone fleet-footed, to tell whoever was in charge that the jolly had come. He saw no one, but perhaps the sentry had already gone. "Cast again," he told Eitha, "when we're at the narrowest point."

A bird circled the island and Noen, fearing it might be of the carrion kind, trained his glass on it. It was as black as any crow, yet lovely with its long wings and tail and its elaborately ruffled head: not a carrion bird, Noen thought, nor even a predatory one, though he was no student of such things.

Twice more it circled, then flew seaward toward *Windsong* and appeared to light in the delicate filigree of her rigging, though when he turned his glass toward her he could not see it. "Smaller with its wings folded," he muttered to himself, then seeing one of the rowers looking oddly at him, cleared his throat.

"By the mark seven, sir." The island and the mainland loomed to the right and left of them.

"Again, when we're well into the bay," Noen said.

Now the castle appeared as solid as the Levar's palace. The rowers were whispering and jerking their heads toward it as they pulled their oars. "Silence!" Noen growled at them.

Rooks circled the tower, and the black muzzle of a gun thrust from every crenel on the walls. Had the castle been real, the entire navy could not have battered it into submission; but Noen felt sure those guns posed no more danger to the jolly than the phantom rooks.

A terrace led from the bay to the portcullis; on it stood two groups of gaily dressed people, some in armor and shouldering halberds or harquebuses. Both groups appeared to be watching intently the two richly dressed figures that stood arguing between them, though occasionally Noen saw someone glance sidelong toward the jolly, then look away at once.

"We'll land there," he told the rowers. "On that pavement." He put the tiller over.

"By the mark seven!" Eitha called triumphantly a moment later.

"Cut!" A small man in a shabby tunic stepped from the shadow of a ravelin. "Break, everyone! Rehearsal's over. I think—that is, I hope—we've been rescued."

The gaily dressed actors seemed to relax. They were not really as numerous, Noen saw, as they had appeared; less than a score, perhaps. The two who had been arguing ended their dispute instantly and turned to watch the jolly.

At the same instant, the castle shrank and changed, dwindling to a beached caravel whose canted mainmast flew the inverted flag of the Levar. The white-plumed disputant nudged the other, and together they swept off their hats and bowed low. With a few more oar strokes the jolly's keel grounded, scraped free, then grounded again. "In oars!" Noen ordered. "Get her to shore."

The rowers sprang out, seized the gunnels, and pulled the jolly far enough up the beach for him to step onto the sand without wetting his second-best shoes. "Eitha, see to the matches." Hiking his sword to a more conventional position and throwing out his chest while bitterly regretting his ragged trousers, he stalked up the beach with as much dignity as he could command.

The darkly plumed disputant made a second bow before replacing the hat that bore them. There were flashing black eyes below the broad brim, a great beak of a nose, and a prominent wart. "Welcome, sir!" This in a voice that boomed like a kettledrum. "Welcome, I say again, whoever you may be! I am Nordread ola Gormol, and I've the honor to be—"

"The menace of our troupe," cut in the little man. "That is," he added bitterly, "I hope you are."

The white-plumed disputant favored Noen with a dazzling smile. "And I'm its leading woman." The curtsy that followed this somewhat startling statement involved spreading the tails of a very masculine coat while kicking the wearer's sword out of the way. Noen thought of the awkward fashion in which he had adjusted to his own as he said, "I am Captain Tev Noen of Her Magnificence's galleass *Windsong.*"

"Ah," the "leading woman" sighed. (Noen decided the second disputant *was* a woman, though a woman as tall as he.) "I've heard of you. You're the captain who took that big Zhir ship a few months ago. Everyone thought you were going to be simply swimming in gold, but we're not officially at war with Ka Zhir, they say, so they gave it back. What a pity!"

Noen said, "I doubt that my history bears on the situation."

"Oh, but it does! If they hadn't, you'd be at home in Liavek, in your palace, and—"

"I," the little man put in, "am generally called Baldy. I'm our stage manager, and in the absence of our owner and leading man, Amail Destrop, I'm boss. That is, I'm boss when things get bad. That is, when they're not everybody else is, as you've already seen."

"And you are in distress?" Noen asked.

All three tried to talk at once, one booming like a broadside, the other grasping Noen's sleeve and cooing in his ear, and Baldy jumping up and down and yelling until he had shouted them both to silence. "You can bet your luck we're in distress, Captain! That is, we're not actually starving yet, but we can't get off this rotten island, and there're three—"

"We *can* get off in the ship's boats, Captain. But the mainland's ever so much worse! There are—"

"I require transportation to Liavek," Nordread thundered, "and at once! I have myself had the honor of performing at the Palace, and His Scarlet Eminence was so kind—"

"—three wizards," Baldy finished. "And Amail's gone the gods know where. That is, unless something's eaten him."

At that, a silence seemed to descend upon the island.

Noen cleared his throat and clasped his hands behind his back. "Let me establish a few things if I may," he said, raising his voice. "You are shipwrecked. I am the commander of a vessel that has come to your rescue. As such, I can have any or all of you clapped in irons if I judge that to be in the best interest of my ship. Do you understand that?"

The erstwhile disputants glanced at each other, then they nodded. So did Baldy, and so did several of the onlookers.

"I'm going to ask some questions. They're to be answered fully but briefly by the person I indicate, and by no one else. Should anyone else answer—or attempt to answer—he or she will be bound hand and foot by the sailors under my command and thrown into that little boat. You will then be rowed to my ship and turned over to my first officer with instructions to put you in irons and confine you in the hold. My master-at-arms will see that you're fed once a day, provided he remembers. I understand prisoners can keep the rats at bay quite effectively by rattling their chains, at least for the first few days." Noen paused to let his threat sink in.

"Now then." He pointed to Baldy. "I take it you were passengers aboard that ship. Where is her crew?"

"I don't know," Baldy said. "That is, I don't know where they are now, or what happened to them. They disappeared—that is, most of them did, one by one while we were sailing from Cyriesae."

"They deserted?"

Baldy shrugged, his face blank. "I don't think so. That is, we were at sea, and they didn't take the boats."

"Could they have been stolen by the Kil?"

Baldy shrugged again.

"How did you come to this island?"

"With so many of the crew gone, we had to help pull up the sails and so on. That is, we helped as much as we could, but—"

"You weren't sailors, understandably."

"So when it looked like there might be a storm, the captain thought it would be better to get the ship in here. That is, we all thought that, and we did. Only the anchor dragged, and the storm washed our ship onto the beach."

Noen nodded. The bottom of the bay, like the beach, was probably sand. "Where's the captain?"

Baldy jerked his head toward the island, and Nordread coughed.

"You want to say something," Noen told him. "What is it?"

"I wish—I would point out . . . Captain, our captain took the remaining sailors—there were only two of them—and went inland. That was two days ago," Nordread's deep voice laid a heavy significance on the *two*, "and we haven't seen him since."

"He took all the sailors and none of you? Why would he do that?"

"I believe he had some thought of, ah, a hidden treasure, perhaps, or something of the kind. I don't believe he trusted us, Captain. At least, not as much as his own—ah—employees."

Noen nodded and turned to Eitha, waiting with her crew near the jolly. "Go back to the ship," he said. "Tell Lieutenant Oeuni that there's a good shelving sand beach here and no danger. No immediate danger, anyway. Handsomely, now!"

"I wish to point out," Nordread rumbled, "that our sailors vanished at a steady rate of one per night, and that—"

"Shut your mouth," Noen snapped.

That evening Noen told Lieutenants Oeuni, Dinnile, and Rekkue, "That's it. The players know nothing about the white building I saw, or they say they don't. My guess is the captain saw it and most or all of them didn't. As to what happened to their crew and whether it will keep on happening, I'd like your thoughts."

Dinnile said, "We mustn't let our lads and lasses find out about this, sir."

"That's why I made the players stay in the vicinity of their ship and posted the sentries," Noen told him. "But they *will* find out. We can't afford to fool ourselves. They'll probably find out tonight, even if no one vanishes. If they don't we can be certain they'll know by tomorrow night. If we finish plugging the leak tomorrow and get *Windsong* back to sea, they'll know even faster because we'll have to take the players with us."

Rekkue said, "The storm that washed their ship on the beach must have been the same one that stove in *Windsong*. Sir, do you remember the wind that wizard on *Zhironni* whistled up? Could it have been magic?"

Noen lifted his shoulders and dropped them again. "I don't know, Lieutenant. And I don't know how we can find out, unless we find the wizard and stick his feet in a fire."

Oeuni used her hook to scratch her head. "You said there were three, Noen. Three wizards."

Noen put a finger to his lips. One of the sentries was coming, his approach made visible by the crimson spark of the slow match in his pistol. As he neared their fire, Noen saw a second figure behind him.

The sentry touched his forehead. "Cap'n, I got a sailor here from the *Lady of Liavek*."

Inwardly Noen berated himself. All afternoon he had planned to examine the log of the beached ship, but he had been so involved in the tricky process of careening *Windsong* without doing further damage that he never had.

Dinnile said, "Is that the derelict, Chipper? I didn't think there was a hand left on her."

The sentry, in more normal times one of the carpenter's mates, shook his head. "He says when the others went off in that pirate they captured, he didn't want to go, sir. So he hid, but then he was afraid the passengers would take it out on him, so he stayed hid." He winked. "I reckon he had a pretty easy time of it, sir. Only now he says he wants to tell about the wizards. They're the ones that make that castle come and go, I guess, sir."

Noen said, "We'll talk to him. Get back to your post."

The sailor who came forward was young and blond, tall but rather slightly built for a seaman. He saluted awkwardly, looked at *Windsong*'s four officers one after another, and at last seemed to fasten on Dinnile as the largest. "Cap'n Noen?"

Dinnile shook his head. "Second mate. That's the captain over there."

The sailor saluted again. "Cap'n Noen, there's somethin' . . ." He seemed at a loss for words.

"Something odd?" Noen prompted. "Something uncanny?"

"Yes, sir. I heard about what them passengers told you today sir, and—"

"I know you did."

"—and I want to tell you some more, sir. 'Cause what that little bald 'un said wasn't the truth of it, sir, not at all, and—"

Oeuni broke in, "Noen, this man's no sailor!"

"Certainly not," Noen told her. "But how did you know, Lieutenant?"

"By his hands." Oeuni paused, suddenly embarrassed. "I suppose I look at hands now more than I used to. But they haven't been in the sun much, and I never saw a hand in my life—I mean a hand's hand—with nails that long."

"I had supposed it was because he said *yes.*" Noen was speaking to the imposter, not Oeuni. "Sailors don't say *yes,* because the word's too soft to make itself heard in a high wind. Sailors say *aye* or *aye aye.* Please try to keep that in mind."

The imposter saluted a third time. "Aye aye, sir. I'll try, sir, 'at I will."

"For that matter," Noen told Oeuni, "this man's no man, although the last time I saw her she was dressed like one and playing a man's part. Very skillfully too, I thought. Meet the leading woman of the players."

Oeuni's mouth opened, then shut again.

The player smiled and said in a somewhat higher though still throaty voice, "Since you've penetrated my little masquerade, Captain, may I sit down?"

"Of course. Move over a bit there, Rekkue. By the way, I appreciate your giving my sentry that tale about the pirate ship."

He was rewarded with a dazzling smile. "I thought you would, after the way you stepped on poor old Nordread this morning; sailors are a superstitious lot, I understand. And I want to apologize for playing dress-up; but you or one of your officers must have told those men not to talk to members of our troupe, and I wanted to see you."

"I also told you not to talk to them," Noen said severely.

"For a good reason, which I understood and respected. But what Baldy told you just isn't true." The player paused, pulling off a scarlet bandanna and shaking bright blond hair. "I'm Marin Monns, by the way."

Oeuni said, "What *did* Baldy—is that the stage manager?—tell you anyway, sir? I was about to ask when Marin came, and if we're going to have two conflicting stories, it might be better if all of us knew both of them."

Noen nodded. "I think I can summarize it quickly enough. Like most theatrical companies, this one has a wizard to provide appropriate backgrounds for its performances and occasionally do a magic act as a curtain raiser. Theirs is an old man called Xobbas, a pleasant, harmless old fellow, according to Baldy, whose worst fault is that he sometimes produces the mountains for *The Snow Lover* when the company's supposed to do something else. He also has a hobby of altering his appearance—making himself taller, turning his beard orange, and so forth."

Oeuni and Rekkue nodded; Dinnile scratched his head.

"Baldy's worked with him for years, and he says he never changes himself enough to be unrecognizable; but now there are at least two other people going around looking like him. They discovered the first on the ship. Baldy had left a wizard—he thinks the real one—asleep in the passenger's quarters. He went on deck and saw a second standing in the bow. That could have been astral projection, but Xobbas had never done it before. Yesterday the leading woman—Marin here—and Nordread compared notes and found they'd each been talking to a wizard when their cue came for the second act of *The Prince and the Piper*. That's the play they've been rehearsing while they waited for rescue, and in that scene, as I understand it, they enter simultaneously from opposite sides of the stage."

Marin nodded.

"Furthermore, each got the impression that the person they'd spoken with wasn't really Xobbas. So that makes three wizards: the real Xobbas and the two frauds. The problem—one of the problems, anyway—is that no one has any idea who the other two can be. The other problem is that Xobbas isn't providing scenery any more. Baldy started as a stage wizard, so he's been doing it himself; but he's rusty and the castle comes and goes."

"Captain," Dinnile said, "I've got an idea. Tomorrow afternoon we ought to have the ship patched up. Then we can lighten *Lady* as much as we can, take *Windsong* out in the bay, set both anchors, and winch her off."

Noen nodded again.

"We put a crew, like a prize crew, on *Lady* to sail her back to Liavek. Well, as these players get on, all three wizards have got to get on too, don't they? So each time old Xobbas shows his face, we say prove it. He's got to prove he really is Xobbas, or he doesn't get on the ship."

Rekkue said softly, "Dinnile, I think somebody who could disguise himself as a wizard could disguise himself as somebody else too. Suppose there were two Dinniles? For that matter, how do we know the real Marin Monns isn't over there"— she jerked her head toward the unseen bulk of the *Lady of Liavek*—"sound asleep?"

The blond player laughed. "I should have known it would come to this. Would you like to hear me recite all my speeches from *Piper?* 'Most noble lords and commoners, have you not seen that when all else sinks, yet the crown swims? When Repartine the Great—' "

Noen raised a hand for silence. "I accept that you're who you say you are, and if I accept it so do my officers. What I want to know is why you said what Baldy told me was false, and how you know it."

"I didn't mean he was deliberately lying to you," Marin said, "but he's wrong. Since yesterday, I've talked to anyone who looked like the wizard anytime I saw him. And I . . ."

"Go on."

"I know him pretty well. He's a kindly old pot, and he still has an eye for the girls. He likes me because I give him a hug every so often, and when we have a cast party sometimes I sit on his lap." Marin paused, staring into the fire.

Oeuni said, "You blush beautifully, Marin. Please go on."

"Did the blood really come up in my cheeks? You sort of hold your breath and try and force the air up, but I've been having trouble with it. Anyway, I *do* know the old man, and that was how I knew the—the wizard I'd talked to while Nordread talked to the other one wasn't real. He was too . . ." Marin made a helpless gesture. "I guess I need a playwright to make up my lines. But Xobbas, the real Xobbas, is old and his mind isn't very clear. He forgets things, and when he feels sorry for himself he says so. Oh, I do, too, and so do lots of other people, but we try to be underhanded about it so you'll feel sorry for us too. Xobbas would just come right out with it like he was talking about somebody else, and this wizard wasn't like that at all. He didn't forget a thing, and I had the feeling he was laughing at me inside all the time."

Noen said, "I understand. What about the others?"

"One was cruel. I know he was! And old Xobbas was never like that. And one was frightened and tried to get away from me as fast as he could. That wasn't like Xobbas either, and Xobbas couldn't have walked that fast, no matter how bad he wanted to. And I think it's important you know that there are three, because what if it's the other two you find, and leave the cruel one? He isn't the real Xobbas either."

Oeuni took a deep breath, looked at Noen, and let it out again. "I've been a little hard on you, Marin," she said. "And I shouldn't have been—you really are trying to help. Is that all?"

The player nodded.

"Sir, is it all right if I take her back as far as the sentry lines?"

"Someone will have to take her back," Noen said. "I don't want her getting into mischief. It might as well be you."

When they had gone, Dinnile wiped his forehead. "By Rikiki, what a looker! And tricky as they come."

Rekkue nodded. "She could be dangerous, I think, starting fights among the crew just for the fun of it and so forth. Are Oeuni and I going to take *Lady* back to Liavek, Captain? If so, I'll try to keep an eye on her."

Noen said, "I don't know why, but I like her."

Dinnile chuckled. "Here's the time I've waited for, sir! The one when I know more than you."

There was a moment of silence, filled only by the crackling of the fire and the call of a jungle bird. Dinnile moved uncomfortably, clearly afraid that he had said too much; Rekkue started to speak but thought better of it.

Superficially impassive, Noen was secretly delighted. A captain necessarily walked a fine line between self-isolation and overfamiliarity with his officers, and he feared lately that he had swung too near the latter. Let them sweat—it was good for them and for the ship! He allowed the silence to grow until he saw his first officer returning, then called harshly, "Oeuni, you're the best judge of character I know. Why'd you change your mind about Marin?"

Rekkue put in, "I was saying how dangerous I thought she was. Was I wrong?"

Oeuni nodded slowly. "Yes, I think you were. I thought so too, at first—all that playacting. But Marin's too fond of showing off to be a real threat; at every moment she wants you to know how completely she fooled you the moment before. And what she said about there being three false wizards . . ."

Noen cleared his throat. "I thought that was it. You knew she was telling the truth. How did you know?"

"I didn't really know. But—remember late this afternoon, when I went looking for a tree big enough to anchor the winch? This jungle's only thick here at the edge, where it gets sun all the way down. Farther in, there's plenty of space between the trees, and moss and fern on the ground, mostly. I did some looking around while the hands were rigging the winch, and I found a grave."

Rekkue's gasp was distinctly audible.

"At least it looked like one. It was narrow, but long enough for a man, and the earth was fresh. I should have told you earlier, sir; but we were pulling *Windsong* onto the beach, and it didn't seem terribly important at the time."

Noen leaned forward. "We have four missing persons," he said, "though some of you seem to have forgotten it: *Lady*'s captain, two of her crew, and the leader of the players, Amail Destrop. Dinnile, you were talking a moment ago as though we could refloat *Lady* and sail away without making an attempt to locate those people; would you want to be the one to tell Admiral Tinthe we might have left four subjects of Her Magnificence marooned? Now I think we've found out what happened to at least one of them."

Oeuni shook her head. "There was a slab of bark pushed into the loose dirt at one end," she said slowly. "A slab of bark with a letter scratched on it. The letter was X."

As they made their way between the jungle trees the next day, Noen wished he had refused to allow any of the players to come. He had left Rekkue in charge of both ships; young as she was, Rekkue was an able officer, and with *Windsong* and *Lady of Liavek* riding at anchor in the bay nothing remained to do but reload the material they had removed earlier to lighten them. Someone or something, he had argued with himself, had stolen *Lady*'s crew; and if there was going to be fighting, he wanted Dinnile's strength and dauntless courage. As for Ler Oeuni, why, Oeuni was—he winced at his own expression—his right hand. He had brought fifteen steady sailors as well, each armed with a cutlass and a boarding pike.

Then the players had wanted to come, too—the same players, as Noen had reminded them at length, who had waited two days on the beach without making the least effort to find their missing captain and his hands, or even their own missing leader. But they had insisted, and he had made the error of permitting Baldy, Nordread (who might actually be of some use), Marin, and eight more players to accompany him. All were carrying halberds or swords, rusty yet serviceable; but Noen strongly suspected that at the least sign of danger they would drop them and bolt like rabbits.

Besides, he had an irrational feeling that by bringing them he had brought the three false wizards, too. Once, looking back through the trees at his straggling column, he had thought he had actually seen one, a bearded old man in a black robe and slouch hat. He had called a halt then, inspected the players a second time, and found no one who in the least resembled the flitting figure he had glimpsed. After that he had put Dinnile and two burly hands at the end of the column with orders to hustle along stragglers and keep their eyes open. They had seen nothing, or at least nothing they felt worth reporting. There had been no trace of *Lady*'s missing captain, his sailors, or Amail Destrop.

Oeuni said, "You'd think it would be cool because of the shade, but I'd trade it for a sea breeze." Her face was bright with sweat.

For the hundredth time, he took out his handkerchief, mopped his own face, and studied the compass. "We should be nearly across the island now."

"We could have missed it easily enough, sir."

Noen had an uncomfortable feeling that despite her verbal support Oeuni did not really believe the white-walled building he had seen from *Windsong*'s maintop existed. He said, "If so, we'll sweep the seaward side until we find it."

As soon as he had spoken, he realized he had been looking at it for the past few seconds. That pale blur to the left could be nothing else—too dim for sunshine, too regular for a natural rock mass, too light for foliage. Striving to keep any exultation from his voice and terrified he might yet be wrong, he added laconically, "Port two points, I think, Lieutenant."

It was a building more impressive for its beauty than its size, a perfectly proportioned rectangle of white marble surmounted by a dome of the same material. Once its marble walls had been carved in a tracery as fine as lace. Now pounding jungle rain had eroded the graceful curves to cobweb; vines clutched at the delicate threads of stone that remained, which bent backward as if fainting in their embrace. Strange letters, angular yet in harmony with the structure, bowed above its dark doorway.

Noen turned to the sailors, who were edging toward the building, curious but still mindful of discipline. "Can anybody read this?"

The hand who stepped forward had been a nomad of the Great Waste before signing aboard *Windsong*. "I can, sir. It's Old Tichenese: 'The Black Warrior Woman, Precious Helper of Men.' "

Oeuni whispered, "I can read something more, Noen. The

vines have been cut away so somebody else could read the lettering."

Noen nodded absently, having made the same observation himself. It seemed probable, though not certain, that it had been done by *Lady*'s captain, though— "Pass the word for Baldy, Lieutenant," he said. "No, make that all the players."

As they came crowding up he asked, "Did any of you know your captain well? Could he have read Old Tichenese?"

They looked at one another blankly. At last Nordread rumbled, "I doubt it, Captain. He didn't seem like an educated man. Amail and I dined with him once or twice."

"What about the sailors he took with him?"

"I suppose there's always a chance, but . . ."

"What about Destrop? Could he read Old Tichenese?"

Nordread snorted. "Absolutely not, Captain."

"I see."

Greatly daring, Oeuni said, "Well, I don't, sir."

Noen pointed. "You or I would have cut away enough to discover we couldn't read the inscription and stopped. Somebody's cleared every word. He could read them, so he wanted to see the entire—Dinnile, what the blazes is wrong with you?"

The second mate slapped his leg again and looked apologetic. "Ants, sir. There's a whole line of ants, and I stepped in 'em, sir, not noticing."

"Noen, they're going into the temple."

He nodded, winding his wheellock. "I imagine there's an altar in there, and we're about to find a recent sacrifice on it." He wondered whether it would be a human sacrifice—with four people missing it seemed almost inevitable—but thought it best to keep the speculation to himself. "See that everyone stays here. That's an order."

Three shallow steps led up to the doorway. He paused there to study the dim interior before entering. Nothing moved except the line of ants vanishing into the shadows. There was no altar and no sacrifice, only a statue on a pedestal.

Two more strides showed him that it was, as seemed logical, a beautiful woman carved in black stone. The crest surmounting her helmet was a bird with outspread wings. He moved nearer to examine it, and one of the squares of the tessellated floor gave ever so slightly under his feet.

As he stepped hastily back, his heel struck something that rolled clattering nearly to the wall. He turned to look at it and saw that Dinnile was standing in the narrow doorway, with Oeuni trying to crowd past him. "Rotten stink in here, sir," Dinnile said cheerfully.

Noen nodded. "I think I've just discovered why." He crossed the wide room and picked up the skull he had kicked, then dropped it at once. Despite its tumble over the floor, it was black with ants.

Dinnile took a step and Oeuni rushed past him, the sword she now wore at her right side clutched in her left hand.

"Recent," Noen said. "The ants aren't finished with it yet." He gestured toward two more skulls, clean and white, lying in a corner among a pile of bones. "He—or she—was probably killed last night."

"Aye aye, sir," Oeuni said. Then, "Noen . . ."

"What is it?"

The point of her sword was probing the back of the skull. "I've seen animals sacrificed. There was a fire, and they cut off the heads and hooves and threw them in, and then the skin and some of the organs. Then whoever had paid for each animal gave part of the meat to the priests and kept the rest. And for magic, when they sacrifice a little animal, don't they usually burn the whole thing?"

Noen nodded. "So I've heard."

"Someone's opened the back of this to get at the brain."

Dinnile had been examining the floor while Oeuni looked at the skull. Now he said, "Captain, here's a crown here."

Noen turned, not sure he had heard correctly. "A crown?"

"Like the one on the shah, in that game." Dinnile looked sheepish at the mere mention of it; he was a poor player, and

Noen, an excellent one, sometimes invited him for a game when Oeuni was on watch. "And next to it's a wizard's hat, sir, and next to that's the warrior's horse."

Noen hurried over.

"See what I mean, sir? It's like the whole place's just a big shah board. Only the only piece left's the black sultana, and that's it over there."

Oeuni kicked aside bones to examine the floor on her side of the room. "He's right, Noen. There are pictures here too, for the white pieces. But the game's already started—some of them have been moved. And the squares move too, a little, when you stand on them. That must be how you invoke the goddess."

Noen stared at her. "Invoke the goddess?"

"Well, this place is obviously a temple, and there's no altar and so on. So what does she want us to do? It must be to play this game, putting a worshiper on each square for a piece. Then she's the black sultana, as Dinnile said." Oeuni paused. "If we did it, maybe she'd help us."

"I'm not so sure we need help. *Windsong*'s patched and both ships are in the water again. As for *Lady*'s captain and his crew, I'm afraid we've found them."

From the doorway, Baldy said, "Maybe you don't, Captain, but we do as long as Amail's missing."

Oeuni added, "And what about whatever took the sailors, Noen? Suppose it's still on *Lady*? I know invoking a goddess is liable to be dangerous, but she must be a good goddess— remember what it says outside? 'Precious Helper of Men'?"

Baldy came into the temple, looking curiously at the statue and the designs on the floor. "If you won't, Captain, we will."

The very impracticality of the idea decided Noen. "You haven't got enough people. You'd have to go back to the beach and get the rest, and even that might not be enough. It would take all day, and I intend to sail with the dawn wind." He turned to his first mate. "All right, Oeuni, I'm no priest and you're no priestess, but we'll try. Get them all in here. Dinnile, you're the tallest; I want you for the white shah.

Where's that fellow Nordread? Nordread, you're the black shah. Marin, you're the white sultana—stand there beside Lieutenant Dinnile."

Oeuni said, "One black soldier's been taken, Noen, so we can use the hands for soldiers—there should be just enough. And the players in armor for warriors, and there are four tall women for towers." She gestured toward one of the armored thespians. "Here, you! You're a black warrior. Stand on this mark, in front of the sultana's wizard's soldier. Su, line up those hands on the symbols; I want the other black warrior in front of the shah's tower's soldier. Sir, I need a white soldier three squares in front of Nordread."

Noen nodded and sent a woman over. "I'll play white, Lieutenant. You play black. I must say it looks to me as though white has the better position, besides a lead of one soldier."

"But it's my move, and I'm going to take one of yours, I think. I've got my choice—no, I don't. Captain, you're supposed to have a wizard there by the door, protecting that other white soldier, but we don't have anybody left to play the wizards."

"We have one," Noen told her. "Baldy, you're a wizard. Take your choice of positions."

Baldy walked to the square to the left of the black statue. "If this goddess knows where Amail is, I want to hear it."

When the little temple was no longer filled with the sound of shuffling feet, the silence became oppressive. Dinnile fidgeted and coughed, then pretended he had not.

"Great goddess," Oeuni pronounced. "Black warrior woman and precious helper, I, too, am a woman warrior. I beg you to reveal the fate of Amail Destrop to us and aid us against the slayers of our fellow mariners."

There was no reply. Outside a monkey screeched, swinging away through the trees until it could no longer be heard.

Noen cleared his throat. "I'm *Windsong*'s captain, and I'm in charge here. We've done what we think you want. Now we'd like your help. If you want something more, just tell us what it is."

Nothing happened. The statue did not move; no voice was heard in the temple.

"Captain, I'm afraid it's not going to work without—"

"What is it?"

"—the wizards! Noen, don't you see? Everyone kept saying three wizards, three wizards, Marin and Baldy and Nordread and even you. But there *aren't* three wizards, because Baldy's a wizard, too, and that makes four. Four wizards for the shah board! We have to get the other three, and it won't work without them."

A new voice, deep and eerie, seemed to come from everywhere and nowhere, echoing from the bare white walls: "You have one." The tall, black-cloaked man who strode into the temple looked old, his face lined with wrinkles and his long beard gray where it was not white; yet his eyes seemed to glow under his slouching wizard's hat, and he stood as straight as any rapier. Saluting Ler Oeuni with his crooked staff, he took the square beside Nordread.

"Goddess!" Oeuni cried to the statue. "Behold! Aren't two wizards enough? We've given you your shah's wizard, as well as your own."

Nordread stepped forward and touched her shoulder to get her attention. "Three, actually, Lieutenant," the deep-voiced player rumbled, and pointed. A third wizard, smaller than the second but dressed in much the same fashion, stood at Dinnile's right hand.

Noen roared, "Where'd that man come from?"

The burly second mate touched his forehead. "I dunno, sir. I was watchin' you 'n' Oeuni, and then he was there."

"One more," Oeuni said. "If we had the last—"

She stopped because something uncanny was taking place on the square black stone behind and to the left of Syb, the seaman who portrayed Marin's warrior's soldier. A cloud that was black and yet not smoke swirled there, as though a waterspout had somehow formed over the dry floor. Then it was gone, and the fourth wizard grinned at them, rubbing his hands and chuckling.

"Now, goddess!" Oeuni called.

Noen, Oeuni, and Dinnile, every sailor and every player watched the statue; but it did not move nor speak, nor give the slightest sign of magic or of miracle.

As the awful silence lengthened, it brought a sense of hopelessness.

"Maybe we have to continue the game," Oeuni sighed at last. "My warrior there takes Marin's soldier." She pointed to the player in question. "That's you. You go over there, and she goes"—Oeuni hesitated—"outside, I guess."

The player remained where he was.

"You heard me!"

He looked embarrassed. "I did, ah, Lieutenant Oeuni. But I can't. I can't go."

She stared at him, and Noen asked, "Are you paralyzed, man?"

"No." The player lifted one foot, then the other. "But I can't go over there. When I try, nothing happens."

"Sir . . . ?"

It was Syb, and Noen turned to face him. "What is it?"

"Cap'n, when that wizard there started to appear like he did behind me, I tried to run, sir. Only I couldn't. Just like him."

Noen whirled to Nordread. "You walked over to Lieutenant Oeuni and touched her a moment ago. Do it again!"

The theatrical company's menace nodded, lifted one foot, and put it down where it had been.

"Noen," Oeuni's voice trembled, "are you frightened?"

He was, but he shook his head stubbornly. "Why should I be? We're getting somewhere at last."

"Well, I am. And I'm not afraid to say so. We said we were the shah players, Noen. You were supposed to be white and I was supposed to be black. But we aren't really, or we could move the pieces, couldn't we? Are the real ones good and evil, Noen? Or the Black Faith and the White? Or what?"

Dinnile's wizard said, "It would be better, perhaps, if you were not to ask to know too much." His speech was soft, so low that only the utter silence of the temple made it possible for them to hear him.

"Who are you, anyway?" Oeuni asked. And then, "Why didn't we ask that before?"

The wizard only repeated, "It would be better, perhaps, if you were not to ask to know too much."

Noen said, "We won't ask you any more questions, but I would appreciate your advice. Tell me what to do, and we'll do just as you say."

There was no reply, but Nordread and Baldy gasped. The statue, the black sultana, had begun to move, rocking ever so slightly to the right and to the left, like the pendulum of a metronome that had almost run down.

Slowly it slid from the black square upon which it had stood to the square in front of Nordread, and then to the square beyond that. It was only then that Noen realized the black square where it had been was not a stone at all, but a dark cavity in the floor, a pit or a sunken vault.

There was a sudden cry, unearthly and utterly evil, and some dark thing streaked from the dome over their heads and vanished into the pit.

Baldy and Nordread turned, white-faced, to stare after it. Oeuni, only a step or two farther from the pit than they, threw down her sword and dashed to it, dropping to her knees beside it and reaching inside with both her arms. Her hook emerged with an emerald necklace caught like some shining fish, her right hand with a handful of gold. She reached in again; as she did, a hideous face topped with such a crown as the Levar herself could not boast emerged. It seemed almost a skull, but flames blazed behind the sockets of its eyes, and the fangs of its mouth were smeared with blood.

At once the missing black stone appeared, sliding swiftly from the wall to seal the pit. The hideous face ducked, the crown toppling from its head. Noen called, "Look out!"

He was aware, even as the shout left his lips, that it had come too late. The sliding stone clicked to a stop against Oeuni's iron hook.

At the same instant, the gliding statue reached the wall opposite the door. It seemed to Noen that it must crash into it, crash and perhaps even shatter, for it had been picking up speed, accelerating faster and faster as it moved. It did not. For the black sultana the solid stone seemed no more than a mist. The statue entered that mist and was gone.

He knelt beside Oeuni. The point of her hook was against the edge of the floor, actually driven some minute distance into the stone; the bend was jammed against the slab. Her other arm vanished into the dark crevice that remained, which was about the width of his own hand.

"Noen," she gasped. And then again. "Oh, Noen . . ."

"Let go!" he told her. "That hook could break." Bracing his feet against the edge of the floor, he heaved at the slab with all his strength; it did not move.

"Noen, I can't let go! It's got me, that thing, that devil—it's got my hand!"

He pulled at her arm until she cried out. Across the room, Dinnile raged against the confinement of his square, but neither his curses nor his frantic gestures freed him. Nordread had drawn a rapier, but could not thrust into the pit. Baldy muttered words that sounded like spells—and the reality of the situation altered not at all.

The demon's face appeared at the crevice. Noen fired both barrels of his pistol point blank, the shots deafening in the bare stone chamber; if he had fired instead into a raging sea, his bullets could have been no more futile.

"Noen," Oeuni gasped. "It's got me. That *thing!*" Bright tears filled the eyes that never wept.

The hook slipped. Its movement was slight, and yet Noen saw it and felt it too, for he was standing upon the slab. The demon's hand emerged from the crevice, groping for his ankle. He jumped back, drew his sword, and slashed at the scaly wrist with all his strength; the wide blade broke like glass, and he flung down the hilt.

"Now you will die, all of you." It was the voice of the fourth wizard, of Marin's wizard. "She because she cannot get away. You because you will not leave her. They because they cannot leave their squares. But not I. Kakos is mine, you see, my crowning achievement."

Then voice and wizard were gone, not vanished, but crushed to a broken doll whose crimson blood splattered Syb and the unfortunate sailor standing before the player who was Marin's tower. The black statue had reentered its own temple through the door like the figurehead of a galley that flies before a gale, and it had struck him like that galley's ram.

The demon's shoulder followed its arm. Narrow though the crevice was, it oozed through it like clay through a potter's fingers. Oeuni cried, *"Noen!"* Her body writhed with effort, the muscles outlined beneath her thin shirt like cables.

The hook came free. The slab slammed the edge of the floor as the weighted jaw of a rattrap crashes down when the rat pulls at the bait, and it left the demon's arm squirming at Oeuni's feet.

"You all right?" It was Dinnile, panting, sword drawn, leaning over Noen as Noen leaned over Oeuni. Freed from their squares, the rest, sailors and players, clustered around.

"My hand," Oeuni said, and gripped the bent iron socket that had held her hook.

Noen said, "Your hand is fine," and touched it to prove it.

"But—"

He took a deep breath, feeling that when he had explained she would want him to explain more, and knowing that he could not. "When you dropped your sword, it was from your left hand. But when you reached into there the first time and brought up that necklace—here it is—on your hook, the hook was on your left hand. It can't be an illusion, because your left hand couldn't have held back the slab; I don't know what it was."

Nordread and Dinnile, Baldy and Marin and a dozen others were all speaking at once, but Noen paid no heed to them. Leaning close to Oeuni, he heard her whisper, "It's right, what they say. I had to choose. Lose my other hand, or the demon would have killed you and Dinnile and everybody. It wouldn't have killed me—it told me that."

Baldy had taken advantage of his small size to penetrate the crowd. "Let me see it," he said, and examined Oeuni's right arm. "Ha!" He tugged at the iron cup. "This is a prop."

Noen grasped him by the shoulders. "What did you say?"

"It's a prop, Captain. I may not be much of a wizard, but I'm a pretty good stage manager, and the properties come under my jurisdiction. That is, we use one just like this in *The Pirates of Port Chai*. See, the player sticks her hand in it and holds the handle, and it looks like she's lost it. But it comes off. That is, this one won't because it's dented in."

At that moment it did. The hand that emerged from the metal cup was Ler Oeuni's own, slightly larger than most women's and much harder, though by no means so hard as iron. She flexed her fingers and stared at them, laughing and crying at the same time.

"Cap'n?" It was Su; she and another sailor were holding the tall wizard, one at each arm. (Noen suspected there was a dirk at his back as well.) "Cap'n, this 'un's still here. We asked that tower woman if he was the real 'un, and she said she didn't think so."

Noen turned away, sorry to part from Oeuni's joy. "Well," he snapped, "are you?"

"No," the wizard admitted. His voice was as resonant as ever, and loud enough to be heard over the tumult around them. "If my good wife will but remove my hat and my beard (carefully, please, my dearest, though I think perspiration has somewhat loosened the gum), she can tell you who—"

Nordread's sword clattered to the floor. "*Amail!*" Her embrace might have broken the ribs of a bear. Noen looked across the room to the white flagstone where the third wizard had stood beside Dinnile. It was empty, save for a single black feather lying upon the graven symbol of a wizard's hat.

*   *   *

That night, aboard the *Lady of Liavek,* Rekkue asked, "Was it Amail Destrop who buried the old wizard?"

Oeuni nodded. "He found the body, and he thought if he made himself up as Xobbas, whoever had killed the real Xobbas might attack him. Then when he heard that the false Xobbas was trying to get the players to go inland, he scared them so much they didn't. Only *Lady*'s captain took the wizard's bait." She paused. "We don't usually think of actors as being brave, but I suppose they are, sometimes."

Marin, who had been leaning on the rail listening to them, said, "I think what Nordread did was braver."

"Who was the wizard?" Rekkue asked. "Did the captain ever find out?"

"Not really," Oeuni told her. "Noen thinks he was a Pardoner who'd found the temple earlier and stowed aboard *Lady* in Cyriesae because he saw that Destrop's theatrical company would be ideal for staging the shah game. His pet devil had to be fed every day, but he made it spare the players. Of course he raised the storm that brought the ship to Temple Bay, and made sure she went aground. And now I'd better see . . ." Oeuni glanced toward the quarterdeck, where a midshipman stood watch.

Rekkue wailed, *"Please,* Oeuni! One more thing, or I'll go stark mad. That statue and the game, I don't understand them at all. How—why did it come out of the wall like that?"

Oeuni paused, looking from the sea to the sky, then at the trim of *Lady*'s sails. "Noen and I, and sometimes Noen and Dinnile, play conventional shah, using a flat board with sides. But there's another game; you pretend the board's a cylinder, that it wraps around the whole world, so to speak. Then a piece that goes off one side diagonally appears in the next row on the other, the way the black sultana did. You see, while we thought we were playing conventional shah, the gods were playing cylindrical shah. I think there's a message there, though I'm not sure I know what it means. Anyway, that's why I left the emeralds around the statue's neck—as a gift for the player, whoever that is."

Marin said, "You were right, and you were right about me too, that night by the fire. You see, I often take female roles, and when I saw Captain Noen thought Nordread really was a man, I couldn't resist showing off."

Oeuni took her hands from the rail and started aft. Marin tried to follow her, but Rekkue caught him by the arm. "Passengers are *not* permitted on the quarterdeck," she said sternly. "I, however, am off duty."

Marin grinned. "Hello, sailor. New in town?"